The Hypno-Talkers Of Zlar
FOUR-IN-ONE

by
Doctor MC, Mad Scientist
doctor_m_c@hotmail.com

Ὑπό Τῷ
Ἡλιῷ

HYPO TO HELIO BOOKS
Houston

Paperback ISBN: 978-1-938293-20-7
Ebook ISBN: 978-1-938293-21-4

Book 2, Book 3, and Book 4 each contain a parody and/or other extended pop-culture reference. I won't say what the referred-to works are, but I'm sure you'll figure them out. My intention is homage and humor, not infringement.

In Book 4, the villain's name is based on a real person; the author wishes to thank his good friend Perrin Rynning for the use of his name.

This is a work of fiction. Names (with one exception), characters, places, and incidents are the product of the author's imagination, and any resemblance to actual persons, living or dead, business establishments, events, or locales is entirely coincidental.

All sexually active characters are eighteen or older.

All cover render art done by: Doug Sturk a.k.a. Sturkwurk

Fonts used in the front cover (and four front-cover reproductions): Antigrav BB, Mainframe BB, PanicButton BB, CatholicSchoolGirls BB, and LowRider BB, which are licensed from Blambot Comic Fonts & Lettering.

Contact Doctor MC at: doctor_m_c AT hotmail DOT com

BISAC Subject Headings:
Fic005000—Fiction > Erotica
Fic016000—Fiction > Humorous
Fic028030—Fiction > Science Fiction > Space Opera
Fic029000—Fiction > Short Stories (single author)
Fic032000—Fiction > War & Military
Fic036000—Fiction > Thrillers > Technological
Hum007000—Humor > Form > Parodies

HYPO TO HELIO BOOKS, 2427 Clearbrook Dr., Missouri City, TX, 77489-6061

BOOK 1

THE HYPNO-TALKER OF ZLAR

DOCTOR MC, MAD SCIENTIST

Author of
Three More Wishes

HYPO TO HELIO BOOKS

BOOK

Chapter 1
Aliens Invade

Tuesday, April 2
In a suburb of Wheat City, Kansas

Five minutes before the flying saucer landed in the street, Kevin MacDonald was mowing his front yard.

The day was warm for April, so Kevin was wearing tan shorts and a "Creedence Clearwater Revival Forever!" t-shirt.

As Kevin was pushing his mower, he caught movement out of the corner of his eye. Turning to look, he saw that Judy Miller and her daughter Karen had stepped through the gap in the hedge, and now stood in a corner of his yard.

Kevin let the mower die as he smiled at the sexy thirtyish blonde and her teen daughter. "Hey, ladies, what's up?"

Judy smiled at him. "Mister MacDonald, Karen's spring band concert is tonight, and I invite you to come with us."

" 'Us'?" Kevin said. "Is Sam coming too?"

"Nope," Judy said cheerfully. "Hubby's at some hospital in Eugene, Oregon, waiting for parts. Gone three more days, at least." Sam was a traveling X-ray-machine repairman.

As Kevin walked across the lawn, he said, "I'd love to go to your concert, but there's a problem. Karen, you still play flute, that right?"

"First section, third chair!" redheaded Karen said, beaming.

"Oh, I'm sure you're good," he said to Karen. "The problem is, Vietnam gave me high-frequency hearing loss. I've heard you practice through an open window, and half the notes you play, I hear quiet, and lots of notes I can't hear at all. So thanks, but I'll pass."

Kevin wasn't telling the whole truth. It was almost painful for him now, being around high-school kids. They all had so much youth, and energy, and optimism! When he'd been drafted in 1970, he'd had youth and energy too, but he'd lost the optimism forever in 'Nam.

But Kevin was *not* declining because he didn't like his neighbors. Judy kept herself looking hot for Sam; and whereas Millicent had rationed sex to Kevin with an eyedropper, Judy the MILF gifted Sam with sex by the bucketful. Meanwhile, Karen was the kind of good student and happy person that comes from knowing that her parents are devoted to each other.

Now Karen said, "That sucks, losing your hearing."

Kevin laughed. "No lie. The original reason I became an Electrical Engineer was so I could design better stereos."

"We can't talk you into coming?" Judy asked. "Karen graduates in two months. It's your last chance to hear great flute-playing!"

Kevin smiled and shook his head.

Judy squeezed his arm. "If you change your mind before six o'clock—"

Karen blinked. "What is *that?*" she said, pointing. A second later, the sun was blotted out by something in the air.

"Shit, it's a flying saucer!" Kevin exclaimed.

The yellow-orange spacecraft circled overhead twice, then slowly dropped to land in the street, right in front of Kevin's front yard. The whole time, the flying saucer moved as silently as a soap bubble.

After the saucer landed, Kevin could tell it was about forty feet in diameter. Little rectangular metal things on the saucer hull moved sideways, to reveal—*speaker grilles?* Then a big rectangular metal thing on the saucer hull moved sideways, to reveal a rectangular orange door. That door swung down, becoming an orange ramp.

A dozen four-foot-tall gray aliens, all with big black eyes, walked down the ramp.

****

Kevin stared at the aliens. But at the same moment as the first aliens walked down the ramp, Judy and Karen started chanting with flat voices—

"The Zlarians are good. You trust them. You want to help the Zlarians. You go to them. The Zlarians are good. . . ."

Actually, it was hard to hear Judy and Karen, because every dog in the neighborhood started to howl in pain. On Marty's and Sally's front porch, their poodle suddenly laid herself flat, and tried to cover her ears with her paws.

Then the Miller women started stiff-legged walks toward the spaceship.

"*Hey!*" Kevin yelled.

Judy and Karen acted like they hadn't heard.

Meanwhile, other neighbors came out of their houses— Marty Carlin was naked—and sleep-walked toward the spaceship. Everyone's face was blank with a thousand-yard stare, and everyone was chanting the same thing.

Minutes later, when many tranced neighbors were standing at the curbs, suddenly the dogs stopped howling. Then the little rectangular things on the spaceship moved sideways again, covering up the speaker grilles.

Chapter 2
Aliens Need Women

Each of the aliens was holding in one hand what Kevin assumed at first was a tablet computer—a red flat rectangle. Except that one corner of the flat rectangle had a tiny red convex bulge. Near the opposite corner of the rectangle was an orange button.

But now the aliens spread out and walked toward Kevin's silent neighbors. Each alien pressed the orange button on his flat rectangle, then held his rectangle up above his head, so that it was near a human's ear. Immediately after, the human did something.

Most of the aliens' gizmos were making the humans turn and go back into the house, chanting as they walked—

"The spacecraft does not interest you. The Zlarians do not interest you. What other Earthlings do with the Zlarians does not interest you. You go back into your dwelling."

Most gizmos were causing that, but not all.

One alien wore something like a big red necklace, except that down at the center of the necklace was an orange electronic box. When Red Necklace held his gizmo up near a human's ear, that human walked to the orange ramp, stripped naked, then walked up into the spaceship.

Only women between eighteen and forty-five were selected by the red-necklace alien, Kevin saw.

****

Since the UFO had landed, Kevin had been flabbergasted again and again, and his poor brain was too overloaded to think about moving. At last Red Necklace noticed that Kevin hadn't moved from the corner of his front yard in all this time.

Red Necklace pointed at Kevin. "*Klexip uaneh!*"

After Red Necklace spoke, a minion-alien walked toward Kevin, gizmo in his hand. The alien seemed to be unarmed.

Come to think of it, no alien seemed to wear a weapon of any kind. *They expected a cakewalk*, Kevin realized.

Kevin looked away from the approaching minion-alien just in time to see Karen and Judy remove their panties, then walk up the ramp.

"You trust the Zlarians, and you want to help them. You enter the spacecraft," Karen and Judy chanted.

"HEY!" Kevin yelled. He thought, *C'mon, you guys, snap out of it.*

Again Judy and Karen did not respond. Then they disappeared from view.

This shit stops now! Kevin thought. He bolted for his house. When he came outside, he had a rifle in each hand, and boxes of ammo in his shorts pockets.

He dropped to the grass on his stomach, and began loading his weapons. Briefly he recalled the smell of Vietnamese mud.

By now, the minion-alien was standing near the lawn mower. He (She? It?) was looking back and forth between the spaceship and Kevin, clearly undecided.

"FREE MY NEIGHBORS! LET THEM GO!" Kevin yelled.

The minion-alien started to walk toward Kevin. He held his gizmo out from his body and facing Kevin, like a priest fending off a vampire.

Kevin mentally rolled his eyes. *This guy's more stupid than an REMF supply officer.*

"DON'T COME CLOSER! GET BACK!" Kevin yelled.

The alien kept coming.

"LAST WARNING! YOU ALIENS GET OFF MY LAWN."

The minion's response was to touch the flat screen on his gizmo, then thrust the gizmo toward Kevin again.

He still thinks he can hypnotize me like my neighbors? Open your eyes, E.T.

Kevin pulled the trigger. BANG!

The alien spun a quarter-turn and fell back onto the grass. The alien's hypnotizer-gizmo landed a foot away from the lawn mower.

Meanwhile, Red Necklace was yelling. Immediately all the minion-aliens hurried inside the flying saucer. The minion-aliens in their haste actually pushed naked Debbie Snodgrass into the spaceship.

Red Necklace remained outside, eyeing Kevin with that unblinking stare the entire time.

Kevin waited to see what would happen next.

He decided that he was going to claim that hypnotizer as a spoil of war. But he wasn't about to snake-crawl across the grass to claim it now. Guys in Vietnam who'd stopped to loot dead bodies often became dead bodies themselves.

Not quite a minute after the minions had rushed inside the spaceship, they came out again. Each of them was holding a dark-red ray-gun. (Either that, or they all were holding gun-shaped flashlights.) One minion was holding two ray-guns; he handed the spare to Red Necklace.

"RELEASE MY NEIGHBORS!" Kevin yelled.

"*Smarbiva! Puitonoj akreefa!*" Red Necklace yelled at his people.

In response, the minions moved sideways, then slowly advanced on Kevin. Three of the aliens walked side by side, not spread out, which was amateurish.

Strangely, the minion-aliens held off firing, and several were letting the "barrels" of their ray-guns droop.

Kevin suspected that the minions, whatever else they usually did, had no training as soldiers.

Still, Kevin should have been dead many times over. He was outnumbered, and the range between the closest aliens and himself was no more than twenty yards.

But twenty yards meant that he couldn't miss either.

BANG! BANG! Down went two of the minions.

Z-zap! Kevin ducked his head. The ray-gun shot missed him (mostly), but he felt the sole of his right shoe get hot.

Things were about to get exciting: Kevin now had a clear shot at Red Necklace, but now all the minions were finally aiming their ray-guns at him.

****

That's when a rocket-propelled grenade came from somewhere to the right, and slammed into the flying saucer.

B-b-b-brap! B-b-brap! Automatic-weapons fire tore into the gray aliens.

Then humans wearing Army battle-dress uniforms ran toward the aliens from the right, weapons firing as they came.

In seconds, it was all over. Kevin was 100 percent alive, the aliens were 100 percent dead, and the United States Army was responsible.

Kevin shrugged. *First time in my life the Army's done something that wasn't at least a little clusterfucked.*

Kevin stood up, stretched the tension out of his muscles, then sauntered over to the lawn mower. He picked up the alien hypnotizer-gizmo.

He looked up to see a brunette woman in battle-dress uniform; she was frowning at him.

Chapter 3
Hurray for the Army?

Kevin noticed the Army woman's huge tits, but he also noticed the flat-black Captain's bars on her collar tips.

"*Sir!*" she called out to him. She began striding toward him—

—in the process, stepping onto his lawn without his permission.

He noticed she was wearing "Mickey Mouse ears" firing-range ear protectors around her neck. *Huh?*

"Mickey Mouse ears" looked like hard-plastic earmuffs. They were designed to completely cover the ears. Kevin was puzzled why this Army captain would be wearing those big ear-protectors around her neck. *Did her unit rush here straight from firing-range practice?*

She stepped over the lawn mower, merely glanced at the dead alien, and pointed at the hypno-talker in his hand. "Sir, what you are holding is alien technology of danger to the United States government and its people. I ask you to surrender such to me immediately."

"Not gonna happen, Captain Taylor," Kevin said, reading her Velcro'd-on name tag. "This is a spoil of war. Besides, I'm the property owner and he intruded on my property. The law's on my side."

Kevin noticed, while he was arguing with Captain Taylor, that soldiers were going into the spaceship. That the soldiers carried weapons, he expected. But the soldiers' hearing all being protected by Mickey Mouse ears, that was a surprise.

"That's not correct, sir," the woman replied. "The Alien Invasion Act gives me the authority as a military officer to impound what you're holding. I'd prefer not to point weapons at you, so hand it over. Now, please."

"The *What* Act? I think SoldjrFindr.com would have discussed such a law. You're lying to me, Taylor."

Soldiers emerged from the spaceship. Each hearing-protected soldier was carrying his weapon in only one hand; the other hand was carrying out one or two of the alien hand-held hypno-gizmos. These were loaded into an Army truck.

Meanwhile, Captain Taylor was glaring at Kevin. "Mister, I am an officer of the United States Army—"

"And that means you don't lie? Pfft. Army officers lie to grunts all the time, so you'll certainly lie to a civilian."

"I do not lie, cheat, or steal, nor tolerate those who do. But buster, you'd better hand over that alien technology now, or else—"

Kevin said, "First Lieutenant Padraig C. O'Donnell. Volunteered his platoon for a dangerous mission. It went bad, seven guys killed just in my squad. If he'd come clean and told us he'd volunteered us and he was sorry for what happened, we would've shrugged off all the shit. But no, the fucker told us he'd done it on *orders*. Then he ordered the RTO"—radio operator—"to keep quiet. So don't give me that 'don't lie, cheat, or steal' bullshit, hm?"

"Are you disrespecting me because I'm a woman? Given your age—"

"You're on my property without my permission, Captain Taylor. Leave now, or I'll have you arrested."

She left then, without the alien gizmo. But she stopped in front of his mailbox, pulled a notebook out of her pocket, and wrote down his house number. As she put the little notebook back in her pocket, she gave Kevin a long look.

Investigate all you want. My DD-214's on file at the county courthouse, Captain Taylor. Which means there ain't shit that the Army can do to me now.

Just to make that point, Kevin walked to the front door of his house with his alien trophy in hand. He gave Captain

Taylor a big smile and a sloppy left-handed salute, walked into his house, and emerged seconds later with a can of beer in hand.

Pop! Fuff. The can of beer now was open. Kevin mockingly toasted Captain Taylor with it.

****

By now the soldiers were carrying stretchers around, and were loading the dead aliens onto them. Soon Captain Taylor and two stretcher-bearing soldiers stopped at the curb in front of Kevin's yard.

"*May* we collect the exoplanetary invader from your property, Mister MacDonald?" she asked with sarcastic-voiced formality.

Kevin waved them forward and they loaded up the dead alien. As they were leaving, the officer said sarcastically, "*Thank* you."

Captain Taylor and the stretcher-bearers went over to the Army truck. Seconds later, she walked away from the Army truck, toward the spaceship ramp. But now she was wearing the Mickey Mouse ears on her head, not around her neck.

Also, she *was carrying a rectangle that, except for its Army paint job, looked almost like the aliens' hypno-talker!*

Kevin was so shocked, he dropped his beer.

Taylor boarded the spaceship. Seconds later, Kevin's naked neighbors started coming down the ramp. But they were chanting again. This was *not* good.

Captain Taylor gestured toward a second Army truck. Naked, zoned-out women walked to the back, stiffly climbed up the olive-drab wooden stairs, and took seats in the bed of the truck. The women did not look around, nor did they talk to each other.

Kevin called out, "JUDY! KAREN! COME OUT OF THERE. GO HOME."

His naked neighbors looked at him with thousand-yard stares. They droned in chorus, "The Army needs you. You want to help the Army."

Captain Taylor eyed Kevin, as more and more naked women got in the truck. She then spoke to two soldiers. They put the olive-drab stairs in the bed of the second truck, walked to the cab of that truck, and drove away.

"*WHAT THE FUCK?*" Kevin yelled. "FIRST THE *ALIENS* KIDNAP THEM, THEN THE *ARMY* KIDNAPS THEM?"

Captain Taylor's response was to give Kevin a *fuck off and die* smile.

****

A chocolate-chip-pattern crane soon showed up, and began to load the spaceship onto a chocolate-chip-pattern flatbed truck.

Meanwhile, Kevin finished mowing his front yard. But he was paying much more attention to Captain Taylor and her crew than to what his mower was doing.

After the flying saucer was loaded onto the flatbed truck, the spaceship then was covered with a big, chocolate-chip-pattern tarp that—isn't this amazing?—fit over the flying saucer perfectly.

Only then did a soldier come out with trash bags, and casually tossed Kevin's neighbors' stripped-off clothing into the trash bags.

First you kidnap my neighbors, then you get rid of the evidence, Kevin thought.

At that point, disgusted Kevin went inside his house.

****

A minute later, Kevin's doorbell rang. When he opened the storm door, he saw Captain Taylor standing there, with two soldiers behind her.

What the fuck? She's wearing Mickey Mouse ears again!

Kevin made no attempt to unlock the screen door. He could see and hear the captain, and she could see and hear him, but for *damned* sure she wasn't getting into his house except by force.

She said to him (through the screen door), "I ask you to please give us the alien technology"—

Then she help up the Army version of that technology, right in front of his face! She looked smug.

The Army's version of the hypno-talker, Kevin noticed, had two convex disks, not one disk like the alien version, and two push-buttons instead of one. Seen up close, the two convex disks were actually speaker grilles.

Taylor's triumphant smile turned to puzzlement when Kevin started laughing.

He held up a finger in a *Wait here* gesture, and walked away from the screen door. Seconds later he returned, with a smile and a piece of paper. Written in big letters, so that both she and the soldiers behind her could read it, was:

Your toy doesn't work on me, honey.

When Taylor's expression, and the two soldiers' expressions, all changed, Kevin let the paper drop to the floor. Then two-handed, he gestured *Take off the ear protectors*. When she and the soldiers did so, he stopped smiling.

"Captain Taylor," Kevin hold her menacingly, "I'm about to go to my closet, get out my rifle, and load it with ammo. Then I'm gonna come back here"—he pointed straight down— "and point my rifle at you through the screen. Then one of two things'll happen. You will die, or I'll die and you'll go to Leavenworth. Now, if you don't like those two choices, you and your men be gone when I come back. *Got me?*"

"I got you," she said sullenly.

"Good. One more thing: *Where the fuck are you taking my neighbors?*"

"Fuck you, Corporal Kevin MacDonald," she replied. "That's on a need-to-know basis, and you lost the need to know in August, 1972."

"Fort Carver, I'll bet that's where you're taking them," Kevin said, watching her face.

She said nothing; one of the soldiers frowned.

Kevin did indeed load up his rifle with ammo. Seconds later, he jerked open the storm door, ready for anything.

But Captain Taylor and the soldiers had disappeared from his front door.

Chapter 4
Reverse-Engineered

AUTHOR'S NOTE: This chapter is necessary to lay out technical info about how a hypno-talker works, but it has no dramatic tension. In short, geeks will love it, but it is deadly dull reading for everyone else. I won't be offended if you skip to the end of the chapter.

****

Kevin thought, *Judy and Karen need me to make this work!*

Somewhere out there, probably somewhere in Fort Carver, Judy and Karen were being held captive by the Army. And only Kevin could rescue them.

If he could figure out how to work the alien hypno-gizmo, or build his own.

Kevin had earned a Bachelor of Science degree in Electrical Engineering in 1977, and he'd been interested in electronics since the 1960s. As a result, his basement had every kind of electronics in it, from a 1960s pocket transistor radio to a Dell 64-bit computer motherboard.

He also had lots of testing equipment. He didn't have a vacuum-tube tester—that was before his time, professionally speaking—but he did have an oscilloscope and a microscope capable of eyeballing the microcircuits that were burned onto computer chips.

Kevin didn't know if Zlarian computer chips were similar enough to Earth-made chips that he could look at them under the microscope. He hoped so, else he'd have a big problem.

By now, Kevin had a theory: The alien hypno-gizmo and its Army clone both "spoke" at a very high frequency that a human conscious mind didn't hear, but the human's subconscious mind heard and obeyed.

That would explain why dogs in the neighborhood were howling at times, and it would explain why Kevin was unaffected by the hypno-gizmo. Whatever ultrasonic frequency that the aliens (and the Army) were using, Kevin couldn't hear!

He decided to test that theory. He plugged a microphone into his basement computer's "MIC" jack, loaded up the sound-file editing software, clicked that software's "Record" box, then pressed the gizmo's orange Playback button.

Kevin couldn't hear a thing. But the software-generated graphs showed him that something was being recorded—at the far-right (ultrasonic) end of the right-channel graph.

Once Kevin finished recording, he tried to use the sound-file editing software to play his recording at half-speed. But the playback at half speed just sounded weird and distorted. Duh, the sound-edit software had not been designed to handle ultrasonic frequencies.

What to do, what to do? Somehow Kevin had to bring the gizmo's ultrasonic speech down to a frequency he could hear!

Too bad the aliens didn't put their recording onto an LP. Then I could just rub my thumb against the turntable—

Kevin's head whipped around. He looked at the dustcover that said "AKAI," as he stroked his chin.

****

On a shelf in Kevin's basement, under a dusty dustcover, was a Japanese-made reel-to-reel stereo tape recorder.

The very last thing that Kevin had done, before he'd left Vietnam to return to the World, was to order that tape recorder from the AAFES catalog. Other grunts in Vietnam who were "zero and a wake-up" had gotten drunk; Kevin had celebrated still being alive by buying electronics.

He hadn't touched that tape recorder in decades, but this was about to change. *Shit, I hope the rubber parts haven't gone bad*, he thought.

On his basement workbench three minutes later, he had the hypno-talker's orange button mashed down, while quarter-inch magnetic tape whizzed from one reel to the other at 7-1/2 inches per second.

Kevin recorded for one minute, stopped the machine, then rewound the tape to the beginning.

But when it came time to play back the recording, Kevin changed the speed setting to 3-3/4 inches per second. Now the magnetic tape moved at a calm and placid speed.

Kevin now could hear words: robotic, speaking slowly, but squeaky-pitched. Alas, Kevin couldn't make out what the words said.

Kevin rewound the tape, then changed the playback speed to 1-7/8 i.p.s. The magnetic tape *crawled*.

Now played at one-fourth of their recorded speed, the tape-recorded words were spoken very slowly but still were very high-pitched, like a stoner who'd inhaled helium:

"The spacecraft does not interest you. The Zlarians do not interest you. What other Earthlings do with the Zlarians does not interest you. You go back into your dwelling."

These were the same words that many of his neighbors had chanted, when they'd walked back into their houses.

****

It took Kevin only a few more seconds to nail down the hypno-talker's original sound frequency, and to find out that a microphone could "hear" the hypno-talker clearly from five feet away.

Which meant that when Kevin built his own hypno-talker, his hypno-talker had to play at that same ultrasonic frequency, and be loud enough to be (subconsciously) heard at least five feet away.

Having finished discovering what the alien device would do, Kevin went to work discovering how the gizmo worked.

The alien screws were ass-backward; to get them off, he had to create a rule of "Lefty-tighty, righty-loosey." Once Kevin got the cover off, he discovered that the small convex bulge covered up a tiny tweeter (high-frequency speaker). A small hole in the case that had puzzled Kevin turned out to be an input jack.

What, no Wi-Fi input? It's probably a security feature— no Wi-Fi input makes it almost impossible for an enemy to subvert the message.

Kevin's big worry had been how to figure out the mysteries of alien computer hardware and an alien operating system. Luckily, he dodged a bullet: All of the gizmo's doings were hard-wired circuits, not software commands.

Most of the circuitry was designed so that the gizmo could be used as a simple writing tablet. Once Kevin figured out that part of the circuitry, he ignored it thereafter.

As for the circuitry within the gizmo that played back ultrasonic speech, the "form follows function" rule meant that the alien circuitry was designed the same as Earth electronics. Well, Kevin had thirty-something years working with Earth electronics circuits that created or reproduced sound.

So in less than a day of peering at the alien chips through his microscope, Kevin had uncovered their mysteries.

The hypno-talker was very simple, really (when you disregarded the writing-tablet part). The gizmo downloaded an ultrasonic sound file (in a compressed format that was the Zlarian version of an MP3 file) from the mothership. Then when a Zlarian pressed the Play button, the gizmo decompressed the sound file, converted that output to analog, and ran that analog output to the tweeter-speaker.

If you disregarded the ultrasonic part—and the whole "trying to mind-control nubile Earth women" part—the alien hypno-talker worked the same as any "press the button and I talk" doll that Wal-Mart sells.

****

Kevin had spent an entire day successfully uncovering the hypno-talker's mysteries. That meant that Judy and Karen, and his other female neighbors, had been held prisoner by the Army for an entire day.

Kevin urged himself, *The clock is ticking! Get this done!*

Kevin had discovered what the hypno-talker did, and he'd discovered how it had been built. The last step was for him to build his own hypno-talker.

That's when Kevin recalled something about the Army hypno-talker: it had two push-buttons, not one; and it had two speaker grilles. Kevin guessed that the second grille was a built-in microphone, and the second button was to Record.

For Kevin's gizmo to do what the Army's did, he would have to add a recording ability—piece of cake!—and the ability to change a voice's playback frequency.

Kevin himself didn't know how to do that, but he knew the task was doable. Wal-Mart, besides selling talking dolls, sold battery-operated toys that could make a ten-year-old boy sound like a pro wrestler. Or like Mickey Mouse.

A few hours of research, and he had the answer to how to change the frequency of a voice.

A few hours more, and Kevin had written a C program that would record in MP3 format, then play back with the voice at the same ultrasonic frequency as the alien gizmo.

Kevin made a trip to Fry's Electronics, then did an hour of puttering in his basement. The result? Kevin had (he believed) his very own built-from-scratch hypno-talker.

****

Kevin celebrated his accomplishment by going upstairs to the kitchen and making himself a ham sandwich.

Now I need to test the hypno-talker I built, he thought.

He was weighing his options when his doorbell rang.

Chapter 5
Kevin Test-Drives His Home-Made Gizmo

When Kevin's doorbell rang, two peaceful days had passed since Judy and Karen had been hypno-kidnapped by aliens, then had been whammied again by the Army.

So Kevin wasn't worried (much) that he'd find Captain Taylor and a company of soldiers waiting to jump him when he opened his door. If the Army were going to break in and steal his gizmo, they would have done it already.

Kevin was right. Standing on his front porch were a young man and young woman. The young man was holding a folder, while the woman was holding a clipboard.

The young man had pasty skin, a bad haircut, horn-rimmed glasses, a t-shirt that said "Nurd's Comics & Gaming," and a potbelly under the t-shirt.

The blonde had a light tan, large tits, and light-blue eyes in a pretty face. She was dressed in a t-shirt and denim skirt that showed lots of her arms and legs; this showed that her muscles were toned. She gave Kevin a practiced smile—

"Good afternoon, sir. I'm here for the Unicorns Marching Band"—meaning that she, at least, attended Kanssouri University. "I want to give you the opportunity to help a worthy cause, while providing yourself with hours of entertainment and education."

"You want me to buy magazines," Kevin translated.

"I offer an excellent selection," the blonde said.

Kevin unlocked the screen door. "Then come on in!"

She didn't touch the door handle. The young man peered closely at Kevin, nodded at the blonde, then walked in ahead of her.

When both young people were standing in Kevin's foyer, he slapped his forehead. "Hold on, I need to get something!"

Kevin rushed back to the kitchen, grabbed his cloned hypno-talker off the kitchen table, pressed the red Record button, then he spoke some words. After Kevin released the Record button, he then rushed toward the young people.

****

The young man, Kevin saw, was trying to talk to the young woman, who looked bored with everything.

As Kevin got close to the foyer, he mashed down the Playback button, which still was orange in his version—

Both young people's faces went blank.

They started chanting, "You trust the old man. You believe anything the old man tells you, you feel whatever the old man tells you that you feel, you'll do anything the old man tells you to do, and you'll answer any question the old man asks with the whole truth and nothing but the truth."

After they had chanted Kevin's words three times, in chorus, he took his finger off the Playback button. It took ten seconds or so before their blank faces got lively again.

"I'm Kevin," Kevin said. "What are your names?"

"Egbert Whitehall," the young man said.

"Mabel Brown," the blonde said, "but I tell everyone my name is Bethany."

Egbert shook his head, confused. "Bethany, why are you saying this?"

She said woodenly, "I'll answer any question the old man asks with the whole truth and nothing but the truth."

Holy shit, it works? Calm down, maybe it works. I need to run more tests.

Kevin said, "Bethany, why don't you take off your t-shirt? I'm harmless, and it might get me to buy magazines."

She shrugged. "Sure, makes sense," and pulled off her top. Egbert's eyes got big.

YES! Kevin thought.

Kevin asked Mabel/Bethany, "Why are you selling magazines for Band? What do you yourself get out of it?"

She replied, "I belong to Alpha Sigma Sigma sorority, and I made a bet with Delilah Monescu over who could sell the most magazines. I plan to be a rich man's wife someday, and charity fundraising gets my husband and me good press, so I need to develop my fundraising skills."

"Uh-huh," Kevin replied. "By the way, Bethany, don't you feel sort of weird, being halfway dressed on top?"

"Yeah, now that you mention it, I do feel kinda weird."

"So take your bra off too. Egbert won't try anything, I'm harmless, and you won't feel weird anymore."

Bethany took off her bra, then smiled at Kevin. "You're right, sir, I feel better now."

So did Kevin. Bethany's naked tits were large and well shaped.

Kevin nodded, and turned to the boy. "And you, Egbert? Why are you here?"

Egbert was looking at Bethany's chest the entire time: "I'm hoping that if I'm a really nice guy for her—beyond the math tutoring, I mean—she'll like me and she'll go on a date with me."

Bethany laughed. Egbert looked like he'd been kicked in the stomach.

"What's so funny, Bethany?" Kevin asked.

"It's just that—hee, hee—I asked Egbert to come with me and be my bodyguard today *not* because I'm attracted to him, but because I know he's easy."

"How so?"

"He's giving up his entire day just because I asked him to, and he'll do it for free. Whereas Mark or Albert would expect a blowjob, and then I'd have to fix my lipstick afterward."

Kevin asked, "And Mark and Albert are. . . ?"

"Jocks I date. Mark is on the Unicorns baseball team, and Albert is on our soccer team."

Kevin nodded. He decided that Bethany strongly reminded him of Millicent, his ex-wife.

He said, "I think you're kidding yourself about him not being attractive. Admit it, he's *very* attractive, in a nerdy sort of way."

Bethany looked Egbert up and down. "Yeah, I guess he is. Very attractive, I mean."

Kevin said, "So since he's attractive, it's really turning you on that he's looking at your naked breasts, am I right?"

"Oh yeah, I'm getting wet right now."

"Why don't you show us? Take your skirt off. Egbert won't touch you, and you know I'm harmless."

"Sure, I can do that," Bethany said. She unzipped her denim skirt and let it fall to the floor.

"I see a wet spot on your panties," Kevin said, "and now Egbert can see it and smell it. I'm sure knowing this is getting you even hotter."

Bethany gave Egbert a smoky look. "*Ooh*, yeah."

"So tell us, Bethany: Your jock boyfriends, how would they behave if you were wearing nothing but panties and sandals, and your panties had a wet spot?"

"Mark would be trying to pull my panties off and fuck me, and Albert would be fingering me and trying for a blowjob."

"And yet Egbert isn't trying either of those. He's acting restrained. That shows maturity. You admire Egbert's maturity, don't you?"

"Yeah, I suppose," she said. She sounded bored.

"Bethany, you don't get it. The best possible boyfriend you can have is someone you find attractive, who also is mature. You're tired of dating boys, right? Even boys with muscles, right? You prefer Egbert as your boyfriend, right, because he's so mature?"

"Well duh," Bethany said, "what girl wouldn't?"

"Then you're lucky that Egbert likes you. Now, I'm going to talk to Egbert now, but Bethany, think hard about this: What would your life be like if Egbert stopped liking you?"

"*Awful,*" she said, sounding horrified. "All I could date would be college athletes with lean bodies and high status."

Kevin turned to Egbert, with was looking amazed at how events were unfolding. "And you, Egbert, what's your claim to fame? Are you on any school teams?"

Egbert stared at the floor. "Nope, the closest I've ever come to being a jock is being bullied by them."

"That's so sad," Bethany said. "Let me help you feel better." She started rubbing Egbert's cock through his pants.

Then Egbert looked up. "But I'm getting straight A's in my Mechanical Engineering major, and I do a real good job of tutoring Bethany in college algebra."

Kevin said, "So you're an engineer, too? I've been learning or doing Double-E since 1973. Give me five, kid."

Kevin and Egbert high-fived each other—

While Bethany looked puzzled. "Being an engineer, that's good? I thought all engineers were nerds and geeks."

Kevin laughed. "I don't know if I'm a geek or a nerd, but I'm an engineer. Which means I've got money—you should see the RV I've got parked out back. It's *huge*—it's built on a bus chassis."

Kevin didn't mention to the college kids that every time he got a raise or promotion, he shared that news in a short note to Millicent. *You sues, you lose, Millie.*

"A *huge* RV? Wow," Bethany said.

Kevin laughed again. "It's not because I'm special. Bethany, twenty years from now, Egbert himself will be pulling down serious coin—"

"*Really?* Wow."

"—while women like you will all be divorcees whose kids have all grown up, so your child-support payments have run out, not to mention your looks have faded. Twenty years from now, there'll be packs of you ex-hotties, all desperate to marry Egbert. But he'll remember how all you women sneered at him when you were young and desirable, and he won't give you the time of day."

"That's so awful," Bethany said. "Especially since we'll all deserve it."

Bethany looked at Egbert and said with feeling, "Egbert, I've treated you so *wrong* for so *long*."

"Not now, you're not," he gasped. His face was flushed, probably because almost-naked Bethany still was rubbing his hard-on through his pants.

Kevin said, "He's not the only one who's really turned on, right Bethany? You want to fuck Egbert so bad, you can't think straight."

"You got that right," Bethany growled. "Egbert, I need you so much."

Kevin said, "Bethany, remember how I told you how Egbert will be earning serious money in his forties?"

"Yeah?" she said. She still was rubbing Egbert.

"As soon as he graduates here, he's going to start earning good money, with steady raises and promotions coming—"

"And you'll *deserve* all those raises and promotions, I know you will!" Bethany said to Egbert with shining eyes.

"But there will be one little cloud on forty-something Egbert's horizon—"

"There will?" Egbert said.

"I hope it's not extra bad," Bethany said.

"Egbert in his forties really, truly wants the job of Vice President of Engineering. But getting that promotion requires schmoozing bosses and coworkers, and it requires political finesse, which Egbert just can't do."

"Poor Eggy," Bethany said. "He's a geek nerd to the core."

Kevin smiled—someone might even uncharitably call it an evil smile.

Then Kevin said, "But Bethany, you can help your future self, while you help Egbert with his future problem. You marry Egbert now, in your early twenties. You never divorce him, and you make the sex for him always so good that he'll never divorce you when cuties give him the eye."

Bethany nodded. "Because if he's got money, cuties *will* give him the eye. Those whores!"

"Also, when you socialize with people he works with, always you politick for him and you schmooze for him."

"I can do all that," Bethany said with resolve. "Especially when it means I get to fuck him all the time."

Kevin said, "Just so you understand, let me spell out what I mean: The way for you both to have a happy life is for you, Bethany, to be Egbert's wife till one of you dies. Always you have to be his arm-candy, his dress-up doll, and his ambassador outside the house, and be his eager fuckdoll in the bedroom."

Bethany said, "Do all this and we both will live happily ever after?"

"Yes. But first you have to convince Egbert to make you his wife. Use my bedroom."

Bethany grabbed Egbert's shirt. "Let's go! Fuck me now, and I'll make it *soo* good for you."

"Hold on," Egbert said to Bethany.

Then he turned to look at Kevin. "Is there anything *I* need to do, to have a happy life?"

"You bet there is," Kevin replied. "Take charge, Egbert, starting with Bethany. A man can't be happy in his life if he doesn't take charge of it."

Egbert's eyes got distant and thoughtful. In the silence, Bethany said, "*Please*, Egbert, fuck me."

"Not so fast," he said. "Call up those two jocks. Tell each of them it's over. Make it convincing. *Then* I'll fuck you."

Egbert looked at Kevin and mouthed *Never happen.*

But it *did* happen. Bethany yanked her smartphone out of her purse and made two phone calls—while rubbing her pantied crotch against Egbert's leg.

Mark started swearing over the phone, and Albert kept telling Bethany about the great sex she was giving up. It made no difference; in only six minutes, Bethany was boyfriendless.

Now Egbert was willing to fuck Bethany, and so Kevin led them to his bedroom. Kevin handed Bethany's discarded clothing to Egbert.

Just before Kevin shut the bedroom door, he said, "Remember, Egbert: Take charge."

Two minutes later, Kevin was sitting in the hallway outside his bedroom, reading *Popular Electronics*. Kevin heard Egbert yell, "Oh yeah, babe, that's right, take *all* of me in your mouth!"

Ten minutes after that, Kevin heard, "Oh yes, *yes!* Fuck me, my engineer, fuck me with your hard engineer cock!"

****

When Egbert and Bethany walked out of the bedroom, Kevin noticed something. "Bethany, you're not wearing a bra."

As Bethany blushed, Egbert said, "I told her to put it in her purse, and not to put it on till I tell her to. Which will be right before we leave here."

As Kevin high-fived the newly confident Egbert, Kevin thought, *My hypno-talker definitely works.*

****

Kevin didn't buy any new magazine subscriptions from Bethany, but he did renew *Popular Electronics* for one year. What the hell, Kevin could spare the money; and besides, at the moment he was in a *wonderful* mood.

THE HYPNO-TALKER OF ZLAR 31

Chapter 6
Finding Out Stuff

Kevin smiled. *Captain Taylor, I know all about you now. I even know where you live.*

****

SoldjrFindr.com was a subscription website to help active-duty Army people find other active-duty Army people.

The good news for any member was that he could get information through SoldjrFindr that Google never heard of.

The bad news was that before a member could get all this juicy info, he had to *become* a member, which was a hassle. Besides prepaying the annual fee, a membership-applicant had to snail-mail a *notarized* photocopy of his active-duty ID card, his retiree ID card, or his DD-214 discharge. SoldjrFindr wanted all spies, scammers, and spammers kept *out!*

Kevin had joined the site years ago, in order to keep track of his Vietnam buddies who also had joined the site, as well as Vietnam friends who had gone "the full thirty" and retired. Kevin also enjoyed reading the discussion threads.

Now, with his neighbors kidnapped by Army Captain Taylor, Kevin had a new use for his SoldjrFindr membership.

After Egbert and Bethany left the house, Kevin went to SoldjrFindr.com and logged in. Only a few minutes later, Kevin was eyeing a photo of Captain Lourdes Taylor. SoldjrFindr told Kevin that Lourdes Taylor was company commander for Antares Company, Fourth Special Missions Battalion, Fort Carver.

One minutes after finding this datum, Kevin had Lourdes Taylor's home address. Thanks to Google Earth, Kevin even knew what her house looked like.

Alas, searching for info about the Fourth Special Missions Battalion got Kevin zilch, even when he used SoldjrFindr. Kevin couldn't find out so much as a whisper about that outfit. Not a surprise, if they were assigned to fight Zlarians.

****

After the Army had gotten its hands on nineteen-year-old Kevin, he'd been sent to Fort Lewis in Washington for Basic, then to Camp Crocket and Fort Benning in Georgia for jump-training. After all that but before going to Vietnam, he'd taken leave, and Kevin had felt zero interest in finally seeing the inside of his hometown's Army post.

Private MacDonald had set foot in Fort Carver exactly once in his Army career, to shop at the PX. The next time that Kevin had seen the main gate of Fort Carver, he'd become a Vietnam vet and a civilian.

What did Kevin's own history mean for rescuing Judy and Karen? Kevin had been on-post at Fort Carver only once. If the Fourth Special Missions Battalion had even been present in 1971, which was doubtful, Kevin hadn't noticed it.

All of which meant that now Kevin had no idea where the 4th SMB was headquartered on post, and what kind of facilities they had.

He'd never ever laid eyes on the 4th SMB, Google was no help, and SoldjrFindr wasn't telling him shit. How was he supposed to get near Judy and Karen, much less free them, when he was suffering from a total intelligence failure?

Kevin sighed. He had already planned to hypnotically "recruit" Antares Company's first sergeant, in order to create confusion and diversions. Now it looked like Kevin would need to pump the guy for information too.

After three minutes of using SoldjrFindr, Kevin had the home address of Sergeant First Class George McGuy. Fortunately for Kevin, McGuy lived off-post.

****

McGuy was in his forties, and fit. He stood in the open doorway of his house and repeated dully, "You trust the old man. You believe anything the old man tells you, and you'll do anything the old man tells you to do. You'll answer any question the old man asks with the whole truth and nothing but the truth, even if the truth is Top Secret."

"Did you say something, Georgie?" a woman's voice called out from inside the house.

This was bad for Kevin. *Shit, if she gets a look at my face, but she's too far away for me to hypnotize, I'm fucked!*

Kevin murmured, "Make her think everything's fine, but you need to leave the house for a while."

McGuy called back, "Heather, the Duty Officer's got a wastebasket fire, and he needs me to put it out."

"Gotcha," the woman's voice said. "Call if you'll miss dinner."

Hearing those words, Kevin relaxed. A little.

****

Five minutes later, the RV was parked in the parking lot of a Burger Johnny's. A minute later, McGuy's pickup truck drove onto the lot. Twenty seconds after that, McGuy was sitting in the passenger seat of Kevin's RV.

Because Burger Johnny's had gone bust, no customers, employees, or surveillance cameras were watching the RV or the pickup at the moment. Kevin had no wish to harm McGuy's career if he could avoid it, which meant that Kevin and McGuy must not be seen together.

Not *seen* together, but Kevin needed to spend time with McGuy, to pump him for information.

Kevin offered McGuy a cold can of Coke from the RV fridge. After all, if Kevin was going to maybe ruin McGuy's

Army career, the least that Kevin could do in return was to be a good host!

****

Kevin had never expected, when he'd started questioning McGuy, to hear *too much* information. Five minutes in, Kevin was saying, "*The FBI* has gizmos?"

McGuy said, "Orders of the president. We were ordered to make copies of all plans and technical manuals for the A-667KPK, and hand the copies over to the FBI."

Kevin sighed. "Anybody else have the Army-version hypno-talkers besides the FBI?"

"Officially I don't know. But we've given our one-day training class to FBI agents, CIA agents, and a hot blonde who was working for the Obama reelection campaign."

Kevin, stared, appalled. Then he shook his head. "Tell me about you guys chasing Martians."

As 1SG McGuy explained it, usually the Special Missions Battalions had fifteen minutes' warning when a Zlarian spaceship landed. Usually the landing site was in another state, so fertile women had long since been kidnapped when the 4th SMB showed up. But this time, the fool Zlarians had landed a spaceship in the 4th SMB's hometown.

Kevin was confused. "If you get there long after the Zlarians have taken the women, then how do you rescue the women? Isn't that your mission?"

McGuy shrugged. "Yes, except we usually *don't* rescue the women. This is the first time we've managed it. Our secondary objective is to cover up all evidence of alien kidnappings, and usually that's all we achieve."

Kevin stared, openmouthed.

Then he shook his head to clear it. "So where are my neighbors being held at?"

McGuy shrugged. "At the captain's house, off-post."

Kevin blinked. "Why is Taylor holding them *there?*"

The sergeant's voice turned wooden: "Captain Taylor is a graduate of West Point. She knows what she is doing. I will not question her orders with regards to the debriefees."

Kevin slumped back against the driver's seat. "Holy shit."

****

A few minutes later, Kevin had squeezed Sergeant McGuy for all the good information he could.

Kevin took a few seconds to think about what he'd just learned. Then he scooped up his home-made hypno-talker and freshened McGuy's obedience programming.

Kevin gave new orders to Taylor's first sergeant.

Fifteen seconds after Kevin finished that, McGuy was walking across the Burger Johnny's parking lot to his pickup. Meanwhile, Kevin and his huge RV were driving away.

Kevin drove back to his own house, and shut off the engine. Kevin wouldn't start up the RV again till around eight o'clock that evening.

When it would be full dark outside.

****

Kevin's land-line phone rang at 5:01. The only reason that Kevin answered it was because he loved to mess with telemarketers. Everyone else called him on his smartphone.

Kevin went to the kitchen, answered the phone, and said, "I don't want any."

"Kevin? Thank god you're home! This is Sam Miller."

"Hey, guy, you at the airport? Need a ride?"

Sam said, "No, I'm still in Oregon. But what's the deal with Judy and Karen? They're not answering their phones!"

Oh shit, Kevin thought.

Aloud he said, "Sam, there's a problem, but I'm handling it. Don't worry."

"What problem? What's going on? What's wrong with my wife and child?"

"Guy, if I told you now, over the phone, you'd think I was lying to you. Or joking. Or crazy."

"Stop right there. I'm Judy's husband and Karen's father, and I deserve to know what's going on."

"I have everything covered. Trust me."

"*No.* I need more than that, I need answers. What if whatever happened to *them* happens to *you?*"

Oh, I doubt very much that Captain Taylor would make me a sex-slave in her house. Nah, she'd just kill me. Aloud Kevin said, "Tell you what. On my back steps is a molded concrete frog. If you don't hear from me again, when you get back home, come into my backyard. Under the frog will be an envelope, which will explain everything."

"Jeez, Kevin, you're scaring me. Are they dead?"

"I don't think so. But *I* might be dead in a few hours, which is why I'm leaving you the envelope."

Chapter 7
Rescue?

Kevin used a pocket-sized LED flashlight to lock his back door, to slip the sealed envelope under the concrete frog, then to walk to the dark RV.

He didn't want to think about Sam retrieving that envelope, or what that would mean for Kevin.

At 7:52 p.m., Kevin started the RV and drove out of his driveway, with only the streetlights enabling him to see. Kevin didn't turn on headlights till he was a block from his house.

Kevin's home-made hypno-talker lay on the passenger seat.

At 8:02 p.m., Kevin was where he needed only to drive fifty feet, make a left turn, then drive half a block, and Lourdes Taylor's house would be on his right. But instead of doing any such driving, Kevin pulled the RV over to the side of the road, and dug out his smartphone.

There was one text message, from McGuy: SHE'S GETTING DRESSED.

Everything is on track so far, Kevin thought.

Five minutes later, Kevin put the RV back on the road. Seconds later, he was coming up on Taylor's house.

He was moving slowly, because he was looking for an empty beer can to be reflected in the headlights.

If the beer can were laying in the street, this meant that Sergeant McGuy had persuaded Captain Taylor to get in his car. But the beer can on the grass would mean, "She refused to come with me."

Now in front of Taylor's house, Kevin spotted the beer can next to the curb. Kevin breathed a sigh of relief. *The plan is still "Go."*

The plan was that McGuy, in full dress uniform, was to ring Taylor's doorbell at eight o'clock, tell her that Colonel Brooks insisted she meet with him *now*, and then McGuy would drive her to the 4th SMB compound. Captain Taylor wouldn't dare leave the compound until she was absolutely sure that Col. Brooks wasn't there; by the time she got back to her house, Kevin would have long since freed his neighbors.

****

That was the plan, which seemed to be working so far. Kevin didn't want to recall the old military saying, "No battle plan survives engagement with the enemy."

The main reason that Kevin didn't want to think about things going bad, was that things were already bad enough. Kevin was in his sixties, out of shape, needing glasses, and it had been decades since he'd practiced hand-to-hand combat. Kevin had chosen not to rope any old Army buddy into this mad scheme, so tonight Kevin had no partner and no backup.

Try as he might, Kevin hadn't been able to cook up any kind of Plan B. So what he was about to do, had to work!

****

Less than a minute later, Kevin stood at Taylor's front door.

"Kilo Mike Delta, commence operation," he murmured to himself.

With his right hand gripping a corner of his gizmo, and with right thumb resting on the orange button, he reached across and pressed the doorbell button with his left hand.

Answering the door was Debbie Snodgrass. She was wearing a pink miniskirt and pink high heels, but was otherwise naked. Debbie was holding a stopwatch.

Her eyes went wide, and she said, "Mister MacDonald! I'm sorry, but I can't let you in Mistress's house. She is my Mistress, and I must obey—"

As Kevin pressed the orange button on the gizmo, he thought, *Something about her voice is strange.*

A second later, Debbie was blank-faced and reciting with a robotic voice, "You trust the old man. You believe anything the old man tells you, you'll do anything the old man tells you to do, and you'll answer any question the old man asks with the whole truth and nothing but the truth."

"Who are you talking to, Slave Debbie?" called out a woman's voice from inside the house. Kevin's blood ran cold—

—till he realized that whoever's voice it was, it wasn't Captain Taylor's.

"Let me in, Debbie," Kevin ordered. Debbie opened the front door for him, he walked in—and stared.

****

In the living room, he saw over a dozen women, all of whom he recognized as his neighbors. All of them were dressed like Debbie: pink miniskirts, pink high heels, and nothing else. Pink panties were scattered around the room.

Half the women had their pink skirts hiked up, and were lying on their backs, moaning. The remaining women were eating their pussies.

Kevin saw Judy getting licked by L-Something, the brunette part-time paralegal who lived three houses to the right of Kevin.

Karen—sweet, innocent Karen—had her head between the legs of "BB" Carlin, who had dyed-blue hair and tattoos on her arms and legs. BB was pushing on Karen's head.

BB said, "*Ohh,* Slave Karen, be proud. Pleasuring a woman well is indeed what we take most pride in, and is our greatest purpose."

There was something odd about how BB said that last sentence, but Kevin couldn't spot what it was.

While Kevin was stunned into silence, Debbie Snodgrass called out, "Time! Switch places."

Debbie set about adjusting the stopwatch, as the lickers around the room lay back, hiked up their skirts, and became the lickees.

****

At last Kevin got over his shock at the lesbian orgy, and remembered why he was there. *We have to all get out of here before Taylor gets home!*

Now he pressed the orange button on his gizmo. Debbie, and four women whose names he didn't know, all froze, and started reciting the gizmo-mantra.

Kevin commanded, "*Stop the lezzie stuff!* Get up, get dressed, I'm here to take you home. *Hurry!*"

But the gizmo had only a five-foot-radius range. Most of the women in the room were unaffected by that first blast—

—including L-Something, the brunette paralegal. She glared at Kevin. "You've done something to those slaves! Plus, Mistress forbids you to be in here. I'm calling her!"

The paralegal raised her upper body up (while keeping her hips on the floor; Judy continued licking). The enslaved paralegal reached up, grabbed a smartphone that had been laying on the coffee table, and started punching squares.

"*No!*" Kevin yelled, and raced toward L-Something—or tried to.

Another still-enslaved pussy-lickee grabbed Kevin around his ankles, tripping him.

Kevin fell down, but he made sure to keep his grip on his gizmo. Once he was on the floor, a press of the orange button got his captor to free him.

Kevin stood up, and hurried over to the paralegal as fast as his over-sixty legs could move. But by then, the woman was on the phone—

"Mistress, this is Slave Levina. Our neighbor, Mister. . .You trust the old man—"

Fuck! Now Taylor knows I'm here!

Kevin grabbed the smartphone out of the paralegal's hypno-frozen hand, jammed the gizmo under his arm, and turned Levina's smartphone off. He tossed the smartphone on an end table, which he noticed already had the Army-version gizmo laying on it.

Kevin tossed the Army gizmo to Debbie. "Debbie," he said, "hold on to this, and don't give it to anyone but me."

She nodded.

He said to Debbie and the other four women in his first batch of Hypnotized: "Go outside to the RV and get in. Do not come out unless *I personally* tell you to come out. Get going!"

The five women shuffled out the front door. *Jeez, they need to move faster!*

Kevin looked around then, with his hypno-talker in hand, and noticed something odd: The lesbian orgy was still going on. Even Judy and Levina, who'd been gizmo-hypnotized a minute earlier, were still licking and getting licked.

Looks like the hypno-talker doesn't undo previous programming, it just enables me to paint over it with my own commands. Useful to know.

Just about the time that Kevin was figuring out how to use the lesbian orgy to get the women out faster—

The kitchen phone started to ring.

Immediately all the lickers (including Judy!) jumped up, and started walking toward the kitchen.

Kevin said, "Judy, *stop!* What are you doing?"

Judy stopped, but in an *Isn't it obvious?* tone, she replied, "That could be the Mistress, trying to call us. We must answer the phone."

"No, *don't* answer the phone. In fact, Judy and Levina, stop *them* from answering the phone." Kevin pointed to the women hurrying into the kitchen.

Judy rushed into the kitchen and grabbed a woman around the waist, trying to drag her out. Levina, meanwhile, was herself heading for the kitchen.

Kevin started to hurry into the kitchen himself—but arms wrapped around his ankles, and he went down.

His gizmo flew out of his hand. *Oh, fuck!* Fortunately, it didn't hit the carpet hard.

Kevin looked back. Holding his ankles was—*Karen?*

Kevin's young neighbor was glaring at him. "Mister MacDonald, you're intruding in Mistress's house. Whatever you're trying to do, I'm stopping it."

Kevin thumped the carpet in frustration. Oh, he could easily escape, but he'd hurt Karen. And Karen and Judy were the two women here whom he wanted most *not* to hurt.

Everything is going wrong! Without his hypno-talker in his hand, he was helpless. Meanwhile, only five women had boarded the RV! Dammit, he'd never figured that Taylor would tell her slaves to resist intruders; he'd figured that he'd be able to hypnotize one batch of slaves after another, without the other women causing trouble.

Worst of all, the clock was ticking. Taylor was coming!

Well, *one* problem he could fix. "Levina, pick that up and hand it to me," he said, pointing.

Levina handed Kevin his gizmo, and he reprogrammed Karen enough that she let go of his ankles. He stood up, as his knee-joints made noises.

Hurry! We're almost out of time! Fuck the kitchen phone, get back to packing your neighbors into the RV.

But before he'd taken one step—

Katie, the real-estate salesman's wife who lived half a block to Kevin's left, now stood in the kitchen doorway. "Mistress says that she already was on her way home, and will deal with the intruder."

"*You bet your ass I will*," a female voice growled behind Kevin's back. Kevin recognized that voice.

He spun around. In the front doorway stood Lourdes Taylor, in dress uniform, with a handgun pointed at him.

****

Her free hand brought Mickey Mouse ears from her neck to around her ears in a swift motion.

Which meant, Kevin had lost his chance to use his gizmo on her.

Now with her free hand, she pointed to his home-made hypno-talker, then put her hand out flat. *Gimme.*

"You'll have to come take it from me," he said, with stomach in, chest out, and chin up. *Show no fear*, he had learned long ago.

"Whatever you just said, I can't hear you," she said.

She pointed to his gizmo. "I can't hear *that*, either." She smirked.

She pointed her handgun at his chest, but didn't fire it. She smiled in triumph. "By the time the police show up, you'll be dead, your homemade A-667KPK will be hidden from policemen's eyes, and all my honeys will be reprogrammed to say that you burst in here and I had to shoot you dead to save us all from ravagement. You fucked up, *corporal*."

Kevin's shoulders slumped then, his head bowed, and he squeezed his eyes shut. His left hand dropped limp at his side; his right hand brought up the rectangular gizmo to cover his nose and mouth, as a geisha would use her fan.

To Capt. Taylor and other woman in the room, Kevin looked despairing and defeated.

****

But Kevin only *appeared to be* despairing and defeated. With his lips hidden from Taylor's view, he was speaking quietly, so that with ear-protection on, she couldn't hear:

"Karen, drop to the floor and roll into Taylor from behind; knock her off her feet. Judy, pull the ear-protectors off her ears. Karen, *now*."

Kevin opened his eyes then, and looked into Taylor's eyes. But Kevin's gaze now was not that of a coward, but that of a warrior. Taylor's expression changed from contempt to confusion—just before Karen knocked Taylor on her ass.

"*Hey!*" Taylor yelled.

She was dazed and confused for half a second, which was time enough for Judy to bare Taylor's ears.

Seeing that, Kevin rushed forward.

Taylor jerked her gun arm up, with murder on her face—

But then, Kevin's gizmo got close enough. Taylor's face went blank, and she started reciting.

Chapter 8
Taylor, Remade

Kevin's first order to Lourdes Taylor was, "Tell the women that it's okay for me to be here, and not to attack me."

Only then did Kevin say to her, "Give me your piece."

Then he ordered her, "Take me into your bedroom. Bring nobody else."

Kevin had no interest in bedding Lourdes Taylor. However hot her body might be, her *mind* was ugly enough to erase all her appeal to him. Kevin was getting her alone to ask her questions that none of his neighbors could hear.

Once in her bedroom, he asked, "How did you get back so quickly? I expected you to be gone for at least an hour."

She replied, "When the First Sergeant told me that the colonel wanted to see me, his voice was wooden. I knew then that he'd been hypnotized, but I played along. Before I changed into my dress uniform, I ordered my slaves to practice their pussy-licking, and reminded them of my standing orders about intruders. Once we got to the compound, I ordered Sergeant McGuy placed in protective custody, and I ordered the Duty Driver to bring me home. I already was on my way home when Slave Levina called me. As soon as she mentioned 'the old man,' I knew you had to be the intruder. Just before I walked into the house, I got my ear-protectors from my car; I figured I'd need them."

At last Kevin realized what was so strange about his hypnotized neighbors' speech: They all talked normally. None of them had ever sounded wooden.

He asked, "You said that First Sergeant McGuy's speech was 'wooden,' and your speech now is wooden. Why do the women out there sound normal?"

"I discovered a neat trick last night. After I've used the A-667KPK to program someone, I ask her a question that relates to her programming. The first time I ask, she'll repeat her programming word for word, except she'll say *I* instead of *you*. She'll still sound wooden, though. If I ask the question again, she'll give the same answer but in different words, and she won't sound wooden."

"Have you ever asked the same question a third time?" Kevin asked. He had a theory about what would happen to the programmed person's brain then.

"No," Taylor replied, "Last night I was in a hurry."

Now it's time to practice what I've learned, Kevin thought. Aloud he asked, "Lourdes, if I tell you to do something, what should you do?"

She looked at him unblinkingly, and in a robotic voice replied, "I trust the old man. I believe anything the old man tells me, I'll do anything the old man tells me to do, and I'll answer any question the old man asks with the whole truth and nothing but the truth."

Kevin nodded, then repeated the question: "Lourdes, if I tell you to do something, what should you do?"

She looked at him and said in a normal tone of voice, "I trust you and I believe what you say, so I'll do anything you say and I'll answer any question you ask."

Kevin asked the question a third time.

Taylor replied, "Well, it occurs to me that you're older than me, so you've seen more than me about how the world works. Plus, you're obviously smart enough to build your own A-667KPK from scratch. Not to mention, you came here to rescue damsels in distress, which tells me you're a good person. So I figure I can trust you and believe anything you say. The smart thing for me is to do is whatever you tell me, and the smart thing for me is to never ever bullshit you."

"You realized all that on your own, Lourdes?"

She smiled at him. "Uh-huh, just now. I'm embarrassed that I didn't realize it the day the Zlarians landed in your neighborhood. I gave you shit that day, which was wrong."

Kevin thought to himself, *Wow, the three-questions trick really works.*

He stepped over to a corner of Taylor's bedroom, recorded new instructions into his hypno-talker, then walked over to Taylor and pressed the orange Playback button.

Chapter 9
Decision Time

Kevin got Taylor to tell him exactly what she'd programmed her lesbian slaves to think, say, and do.

Right after he learned all that, Kevin deprogrammed Taylor's lesbian slaves, point by point. In the process, he used the question-and-answer trick on them, so that no outsider could tell that the women had been twice programmed.

When all the women were back to normal, they dressed in the clothes they'd been kidnapped in, then Kevin loaded them all into his RV and headed for home. The trip was standing-room-only for everyone but blue-haired BB Carlin (who'd claimed the passenger seat), but no woman complained.

While Kevin was driving his neighbors across town, the women decided on their own to tell their families only "We were kidnapped, our neighbor Mr. MacDonald rescued us, and we don't want to talk about what happened."

The trip across the city took eleven minutes.

Just before Levina, the brunette paralegal, left the RV, she came up forward. Levina shared a look with BB, then Levina said to Kevin, "Mr. MacDonald, I'm a married woman, but you deserve to be 'thanked' for what you did."

BB nodded. She eyed Kevin and said huskily, "Let Levvie or me know when you have an evening free."

Judy and Karen were the last to leave the RV, and Kevin accepted grateful goodbye kisses from them.

Kevin parked the RV beside his driveway, then retrieved the envelope from under the concrete frog.

****

Soon Kevin was sitting in his favorite recliner with a cold beer in his hand.

But Kevin wasn't lounging, he was thinking. Hard.

The Army, the FBI, and the CIA all had hypno-talkers; should Kevin do something about that? His choices seemed all to be difficult.

But when Kevin recalled the week after he'd received his draft notice, his decision became easy.

In 1970, he'd been told he had to fight and maybe die in Vietnam. He'd asked why. The answer he'd received had been: "To protect democracy."

Eventually he'd been ordered to protect the Republic of Vietnam's democracy; but by the "domino theory," he also had been fighting to protect U.S. democracy.

Supposedly. So the potbellied politicians had claimed.

So Democracy was supposedly such a great thing in 1970 that it was worth maybe killing young Kevin MacDonald, but now the U.S. government was *fucking* with Democracy?

Buzzer *I'm sorry, but that answer is* <u>*not*</u> *correct.*

****

Two days after making his decision, Kevin had written a "cookbook." It was short and simple.

"This is <u>what the hypno-talker does</u> to people, and here is <u>a quick guide how you use it</u>. Here is <u>how to build</u> it, from <u>parts</u> you can buy at any <u>big-box electronics store</u> or <u>electronics website</u>. If you want to burn the unmodified circuit into a computer chip, here is <u>the circuit diagram</u> and here's <u>how to burn it into a chip</u>. Or if you want to 'edit' the circuit diagram, start with the <u>C-program source code</u>, then use the excellent C-to-circuit 'silicon compiler' that is available from <u>Jillsoft</u>. If you need help, check out the <u>FAQ</u> and the <u>Hypno-Talker User Manual</u>. NOTE: One piece of <u>protective gear</u> you absolutely must wear, <u>because here's what happens to you if you don't</u>."

The cookbook very deliberately did *not* mention either alien invaders or U.S. government secret mind-control. Posting info about such things would come later, if at all.

****

Kevin desk-checked his cookbook five times. Then he uploaded it to four websites: in New Zealand, in Russia, in Sweden, and in Canada.

All four sites were not only outside the United States, but any official demand that came from the USA to any of these sites was rudely ridiculed, when it wasn't simply ignored.

The result? Now anyone with access to the internet and knowing some electronics, and who could read English, could build his own hypno-talker.

And the United States government couldn't do jack shit about it.

Chapter 10
Lordy, Lordy!

Saturday night, April 6

Kevin paid the cover charge at Dance The Army, and walked into the smoky darkness.

Shit, strip clubs are a lot more expensive now than they were in the Seventies, Kevin thought.

Kevin had never been in here before. No surprise, since the joint was two blocks from the main gate of Fort Carver, which put it on the other side of town from where Kevin lived.

Kevin got himself a beer (wincing when he was told the price), then he wandered around. He watched lap-dancers from a distance, and he overheard a few snatches of conversation (and lots of conversations about snatches).

Out of nowhere, the DJ's voice boomed out, "Now, men, making her Dance The Army debut—give a warm welcome to Private Parts!"

The new dancer was in her thirties—ancient, so far as strippers went. To Kevin, her big tits looked real, but her short purple hair looked ridiculously fake.

Private Parts had come on stage in a Victoria's Secret parody of an Army battle dress uniform, that was too skimpy to be Regulation, and which had an E-2 private's single chevron sewn above each nipple. Private Parts also was wearing black open-toed stilettoes instead of black boots.

By the end of the first song, Private Parts had stripped down to camouflage-pattern panties and high heels. Her legs, arms, and abs all were muscular, even though this was supposedly her first day stripping.

By then, Kevin was leaning against the wall, behind two seated men with Army haircuts. The big-boned seated man blurted out, "Lordy, lordy, that's Lourdes Taylor! What the fuck is *she* doing as a stripper?"

The tall seated man replied, "I'd heard that she'd resigned her commission yesterday—but shit, I never figured she'd wind up *here!*"

Kevin glanced over. Both men were wearing West Point rings. Word would travel fast.

Minutes later, the woman herself was standing in front of them. She said, "John, Norman, good to see you here. If you get your wallets out, we'll have fun."

The big-boned officer said, "*Christ*, Lourdes—"

"Please, if you see me here, call me Private Parts."

The tall officer said, "I can't believe this. You graduated West Point, you were an Active Army captain, and now you're offering us lap-dances?"

She smiled at the men. "Lap-dances and blowjobs both. One man for twenty bucks"—now she leered at both men—"or I suck off both you and your buddy for thirty-five."

Ten seconds passed while the two men stared at her, and Private Parts stood there with a smile and raised eyebrow.

The tall officer said, "*Why* are you doing this? Did your Battalion Commander 'suggest' you resign your commission for some reason?"

Her smile disappeared. "You're close. I *did* do something very bad. Nobody in the Army caught me, but I realized on my own that I was a disgrace to the officer corps. Once I realized this, resigning my commission, and becoming a stripper and cheap whore, all were entirely my own idea."

Lourdes Taylor, a.k.a. Private Parts, hadn't noticed Kevin, who still was leaning against the wall. He was smiling.

TO BE CONTINUED

BOOK 2

Chapter 1
The Company Sold

Monday Morning (April 8)

Omaha, Nebraska

Everyone who knows me, calls me "Oddy." No, it's not an insult, it's the short version of my name, Odysseus. Theoretically, Arnie Bluteau and Janice Wellington should call me "Mr. Popeil," since I am Information Technology Supervisor for Fleischer Transport, and thus their boss. But nope, Arnie and Janice call me "Oddy" too. We're relaxed that way.

At the moment, the three of us were listening as Mr. Fleischer gave his last speech to his employees.

Since there was no one room in Fleischer Transport that could contain all us employees, the ceremony was being held in the parking lot.

Which means that I was wearing my "driving" bifocal glasses instead of my "reading" bifocal glasses. An optometrist could tell them apart, but to anybody else, they're glasses with big, black, dorky-looking frames. Don't ever get pinkeye.

". . .From the bottom of my heart, I thank you all," Mr. Fleischer was saying. "It has been your hard work and your dedication, each one of you, that has made Fleischer Transport an organization that people want to do business with. Over and over, you have made me proud."

I murmured just loud enough for Arnie and Janice to hear, "The guy isn't even gone yet, and I miss him already. He made every one of us employees feel like a king."

Arnie murmured back, "Fleischer *paid* us like a king, too. Think the new lady is going to keep our great salaries?"

Janice shrugged. "We'll find out, soon enough."

Soon Mr. Fleischer finished his speech, to whistles and long applause. Then he stepped aside as the new owner, Olivia Olson, stepped to the podium.

I muttered, "Well, at least she'll be nice to look at." Ms. Olson was a brunette with her hair in a bun, which was the same color and hairstyle that one of my long-ago babysitters had worn. Okay, fine, I have a unusual fetish, which Olivia Olson just happened to hit.

Arnie nodded. "*Oh*, yeah. Check out her skirt. Long skirts do it for me."

Janice whispered, "Are you two *crazy?* Look at her! Flat-chested, she's skinny, she has no curves at all. Worse, she's in her *thirties*."

Such a description was every way different from Janice's own. Natural-blond Janice had worked as a Hooter's waitress when she'd been twenty-two—but that was five years and thirty pounds ago.

Now I grinned at Janice. "I think you're jealous."

"Pfft."

"Then say something *nice* about how she looks."

"I like her pearl earrings."

"That's *it?*"

Janice said, "Guys, she's looking at us. I think she wants us to shut up."

Indeed, Ms. Olson was still standing at the podium, giving her speech. But her eyes were looking daggers at the three of us.

But I must tell you that, however much I enjoyed looking at Ms. Olson, her speech was painful to listen to. Olivia Olson has a screechy voice.

****

Eventually Ms. Olson stepped away from the podium, handed Mr. Fleischer a white envelope, and the two of them shook hands. The old owner was grinning (as he often did); the new owner wasn't smiling at all.

The show was over, so we employees drifted inside.

Two minutes later, Arnie, Janice and I were back inside Information Technology's open bay, and I'd just switched back to my "reading" bifocal glasses.

There was a knock at the door.

Standing there was Mr. Fleischer and Ms. Olson. He was saying to her, ". . .since I'm the only Level Six user in the company, I'm the only one who can upgrade you to a Level Six account."

Ms. Olson didn't even look at Arnie, Janice, or me. "I understand that part, Maximilian, but why do we have to do it here? Your computer in your office is much more convenient."

She hadn't addressed the question to me, but I answered it: "So that there's less harm if somebody put a keyboard-logger on his machine. For you to get a Level Six account, Mr. Fleischer has to personally log in and assign it to you, *and* he has to do it from my computer, *and* two people from I.T. have to type in their user names and passwords as witnesses."

Then Ms. Olson asked me an oddball question. "What level of account do you have, Mr. Popeil?"

"Level Five: All Departments," I said, as I wondered why she'd asked me that. "I can't read Mr. Fleischer's email, or peek inside his BIGBOSS folder; but other than that, I can look at, or change, anything that he can."

"I see," she said. Her face revealed nothing.

Then Ms. Olson turned to Mr. Fleischer. "Shall we do what we came for?"

Two minutes later, I was typing in my user name and password. "Okay, who's the other witness? Arnie, Janice, do I have a volunteer?"

"I guess I will," Janice said with a shrug.

As Janice was typing at my keyboard, Ms. Olson asked her, "How long have you worked here, Ms. Wellington?"

"Me? Almost five years."

"Do you know your job?" Ms. Olson asked Janice.

I thought, *Don't ask me, lady. Janice have never worked hard enough for me to find out if she knows her job or not.*

Meanwhile, Janice was shrugging again. "I know it well enough, I suppose."

When Janice backed away from my keyboard, Ms. Olson asked the room, "So are we done now? I want to get started."

Mr. Fleischer put a hand on her skinny shoulder. "Hold your horses, Olivia. We're almost done."

Now Mr. Fleischer looked at me. "Oddy, you need to change the combination for the BigBoss keypad." Mr. Fleischer was referring to the keypad to get into his big office.

I nodded, then Mr. Fleischer turned back Ms. Olson. "Is there anything else I can help you with, before I leave?"

Olivia put on what looked to me like a very fake smile. "Thank you, Maximilian, but I'm good. Enjoy your retirement."

Mr. Fleischer grinned, shook the hands of Arnie, Janice, and me, wished Ms. Olson good luck, then he was gone.

No sooner had he left, but Ms. Olson turned to glare at Arnie. "*You!* You work here in I.T.?"

Arnie's face said, *I can't figure out what is going on.* Aloud he said, "Yes, ma'am. I'm Arnold Bluteau."

"When was the last time you shaved, Mr. Bluteau?"

Arnie's face started turning red. He's very sensitive about his heavy beard. (So I'll never mention to him that I know that, because of that heavy beard and his big size, Arnie had been called "Caveman" in college.) Anyway, Arnie replied to Ms. Olson, "Six-thirty."

"Six-thirty this morning, 6:30 last night, or June 30th of last year?"

There was complete silence in the room for two seconds. I was thinking, *What the hell, lady?* Then Arnie said, "Six-thirty this morning, ma'am."

"Starting tomorrow, I want you to have some kind of shaving device in your desk. I expect you to shave during every lunch break. Is that clear?"

By now, Arnie's face and neck all were bright red. "Yes, ma'am, very clear."

Ms. Olson spun around to look me in the eye. "Tell me again about the computer systems in the building."

So I did. I told her about the computers and the software for the S&D (scheduling and dispatch) and warehousing systems, and the state-of-the-art security system ("Complete with motion detectors and motion-analysis software!") for the outer doors and the grounds.

Janice interrupted then. "But before you think everything is up-to-date and modern, ma'am, let Oddy tell you about *inside* security."

I smirked. "Ms. Olson, the places that have keypads—your office, this place, Personnel, Payroll, the Warehouse Manager's office—all that runs off a DOS computer. A *Russian* DOS computer, running *Russian*-written DOS software."

Ms. Olson's eyes were wide. "How did *that* happen?"

"It happened in 1990, a year after the Soviet Union broke up. Russia need hard currency, so Mr. Fleischer got the whole shebang for practically nothing."

I led Ms. Olson over to a computer and monitor that looked like something out of a museum. I said, "Take a good look—the Chekhov Model Two. Now for your keypad. Write down a number between six and eight digits. Sorry, can't be less than six, nor more than eight."

She grabbed a sheet of source code out of the trashcan, thought a moment, then she wrote down—

11247635

One minute later, I handed the piece of paper back to her. "Here you go. All done."

"Does this number get me into only my own office, or is it good for the other places you mentioned? Payroll, et cetera?"

I said, "All of them. You have the run of the building now."

Ms. Olson nodded. "I assume you have a shredder here?"

Janice led Ms. Olson to the shredder. By then, Ms. Olson had the paper folded double, so that Janice couldn't see the keypad code.

Ms. Olson fed the paper into the shredder, then she left, without another word.

The very last thing that I saw of Ms. Olson was her sexy brunette bun.

Little did she know that, despite her paranoia about her keypad code, it was already compromised. You see, if I switched the *76* in the sequence with a *19*, I'd get 11-24-1935, which was Grandpa Harry's birthday. And I certainly could remember the *76* easily, since 1976 was the year I was born.

No lie, fifty years from now, I could write down the eight digits that Ms. Olson had just shredded.

But why would I want to remember Ms. Olson's keypad code? After all, that door was unlocked during normal business hours.

****

Thirty seconds later, I was back at my desk, in my glass-walled office. Arnie came to my open doorway, gestured to the floor by my desk, and asked, "Um, would you mind. . .?"

"Go right ahead," I said.

By my desk were two sixteen-pound dumbbells. I use the dumbbells, plus sometimes I do push-ups in my office, and this is how I deal with stress. As a result, my legs are skinny, my abs are ordinary, and my pecs are ordinary, but my shoulders and arms are badass!

As Arnie was doing curls with the dumbbells, he asked, "Is my five o'clock shadow really that bad?"

I shook my head. "She was out of line, embarrassing you like that. That shit wasn't called for."

A minute later, he put the dumbbells down, then walked to the doorway. At the doorway, he turned around and looked me in the eyes.

Arnie said, "You're my boss. I wish you'd said something."

****

Just before lunch, the laser printer started to hum. When I saw that it was Janice, not Arnie, walking toward the printer, I got alert. Janice doesn't work more than she has to. So she had to be up to something.

Janice scooped up the pages, then walked straight toward my open office door. Once she crossed my doorway, she put her finger on the first page, as though she were pointing to particular text.

Brace for heavy seas, I thought.

When she was only two feet away from my chair, she leaned forward, giving me a peek at pudgy cleavage. Murmuring quietly, as though Arnie might overhear, Janice said, "I left my lunch at home. Can I borrow five bucks from you? It's for Lean Cuisine and a yogurt."

"Here we go again. Why can't you carry plastic in your purse?"

"If I carry a credit card around, sometimes I act stupid. *Please?* I'm hungry."

"You're into me for fifty-three dollars already, Janice. Do you *ever* plan to pay me back?"

"I swear, I'll pay it all back next Monday. Well, maybe not Monday."

I didn't believe her, but I loaned her the five bucks anyway. Yeah, I know, sometimes I'm not assertive.

Ha-ha-ha-ha, I have to laugh when I think back on that visit. Janice mooching me was a problem, but it was a *normal* problem; she'd done it before. This was just about the last moment that my life would be "normal."

****

An hour after lunch, there was another knock at I.T.'s door.

"Ha-ha-ha-ha, we sure are popular today," I said.

Arnie went to open the door. Walking in were Hamilton Garvey, our Personnel Director, and the most sourpussed old woman I had ever seen. She was wearing a black pantsuit, and had close-cropped gray hair. A flesh-colored hearing aid filled her left ear.

I stepped out of my office and walked up to the pair. "Hey, Hamilton, what's going on?"

Hamilton's face showed lots of emotions, none of them happy. "I have been . . . replaced. This is Cecilia Jones, the new Director of Personnel—"

"It won't be called 'Personnel' anymore," the woman said. "Now it will be called 'Human Resources Management.' "

Arnie was standing close by now. To Hamilton he said, "Hold on, Olivia Olson fired *you?*"

The already frowning old woman frowned more deeply. "Call her *Ms. Olson,* young man. *Olivia* is disrespectful, and suggests a pattern of sexist behavior on your part."

Hamilton said, "Well, *I* sure as hell can call her *Olivia*. Because number one, I went on two dates with her in college. And two, *I'm* the guy who PM'd her through Facebook, when I heard she was looking for an investment opportunity. Yessir, *I'm* the guy who told her, quote, 'Fleischer Transport is going great. Check us out.' "

I said, "And then she fired you? That sucks, Hamilton."

He shrugged. "New directions, needs new blood, blah-blah-blah. I should've seen it coming, she was the same in college. Anyway, my stuff is all in the car, I'm here just to tell you that Personnel—"

"Human Resources Management," Cecilia the Hag corrected.

"—needs a new keypad combination. Good luck, everyone."

Then without a word to Cecilia the Hag, or a handshake, Hamilton Garvey walked out of I.T.

I looked at the sourpuss and, keeping my own expression bland, I said, "Now if you'll just step over here—"

She gestured toward Janice, who was nearby (and wide-eyed), but who hadn't spoken a word. Sourpuss said, "I would prefer that the young woman handle this task, if at all possible."

The words were a request. The tone of voice was an order.

Sometimes I'm not assertive. I didn't object to Janice doing the Chekhov Computer stuff with Sourpuss Cecilia.

The task should have taken only one minute. If Janice were being fumble-fingered, it would have taken two minutes. It took five minutes, with them talking the whole time.

By then I was back in my glass office, so I couldn't hear what was said. But what I saw reminded me of an New York City police detective questioning an unwilling witness.

****

The time was one minute till five o'clock. I was logging off my computer, Arnie was logging off his computer, and Janice? She was already standing by the front door.

There was a knock at the door. I thought, *This is getting ridiculous.*

I walked out of my office, calling out, "Nobody leaves till we find out what this is about."

Janice pouted.

I opened the door, and one of the warehouse guys walked in. I couldn't guess what he was doing here.

Neither could Arnie. "Steve, what are you doing here?" Arnie had worked two Christmas Breaks in the warehouse when he'd been a college undergraduate, so he knew many of the warehouse guys.

Steve looked at Janice, who was only two feet away. His voice dripping with sarcasm, Steve said, "Miss Wellington, Ah wish to thank you right kindly for what you've done."

Then Steve turned to Arnie. "Ah just been fired. 'Sexual harassment.' Because supposedly Ah groped her ass."

"Shit!" Arnie said. "Thanks a lot, Janice."

"Guys, I didn't say Steve had *groped* my ass," Janice said. "I specifically said he 'patted' my ass. And I told Ms. Jones that this was at the Christmas party, over two years ago, and we were both drunk at the time."

Steve said, "Whichever word you used when you tattled, Ah'm out of a job."

By then the clock said 5:01. I said, "Let's go home, people."

By then I wanted above all, just to *get away from* all the melodrama.

Chapter 2
Something New On The Internet

Monday Evening

I hate the smell of cigarettes, so I don't smoke cigarettes. I think cigars are ridiculous, every possible way. But I've liked the taste and the smell of pipe smoke, ever since I started smoking a pipe during college poker games.

So once I'd arrived home, changed clothes, and had poured me some soda from the fridge, I lighted my pipe. *Ahh.*

God, what a day. I *needed* to smoke my pipe as I fixed myself dinner (translation: as I nuked some ostrich pot pies from Discontinued Den).

After I ate and rinsed off my dishes, I got on my laptop and played with the internet. Eventually I visited the pirated-files discussion website, FreeAndUncontrolled.ky. It was F&U that had first recommended the game show "¡Viva Argentina!", which is now my favorite TV show. And I watch episodes of it for free!

(Yes, the things that "¡Viva Argentina!" has contestants doing are silly. But mainly I enjoy watching the show because the spokesmodel, Maria Anna, is so hot. Plus, Maria Anna doesn't speak much, but what she does say is, once I pause the video and translate the closed-captioning, absolutely hilarious.)

Anyway, eventually I went to the F&U forum called "Hot Topics," which I knew would certainly be interesting. The most recent posting was a debate about the man shown banging a woman in a hotel room in a pirated video; was he really North Korea's Rot Kim Chee?

Then, reading down the thread list, I saw this thread: "DIY HYPNO-TALKER—real deal or fake?"

Hold on, what? I thought. I clicked the link for that thread—

> *SverigeCowboy255: This soon ago went up. Does anyone know anything about a "do-it-yourself hypno-talker" or VietVetElecEngnr51?*

> *NigelFrBrighton: Never heard of either of them. Sounds dodgy.*

> *[two Chinese characters]: Baidu and Google know nothing.*

> *MusashiLives: Has anyone downloaded the ZIP file? It is nice if it works.*

> *ILuvPonies: It would also be nice if Nigerian banks would send me millions of dollars, but I'm not going to give out my bank-account details.*

> *LionRoar925667: Why do you say bad to Nigeria?*

The thread had many more posts, but all the comments looked like variations on *How stupid does this guy think we are?* So far as I could tell, nobody had bothered to even download the ZIP file, much less try to build the thing.

Which was too bad. Reading somebody's report on this "hypno-talker" would have added some entertainment to my stressful day.

Chapter 3
I Get A Negative Raise

Tuesday Morning

I.T. doesn't have its own coffeemaker. Putting hot liquid in the same room as multi-million-dollar electronics is just asking for trouble. So when any of us wants coffee, we have to go down the hall to the I.T., Personnel, Payroll, and Warehouse breakroom.

At ten o'clock or so, I'd drunk up my first coffee of the day, and needed a refill. I walked into the breakroom and saw Jessie Carter, the assistant warehouse director. I didn't know many people in the warehouse, but *her* name I knew.

Mainly because she had a habit of coming to work wearing a tight black miniskirt, with the top two buttons of her blouse unbuttoned.

Rumor was, Mr. Fleischer had personally called her into his office three times, and had ordered her to dress more professionally, or else. The first two times, so rumor said, she'd made vague promises; the third time, she'd threatened to sue for wrongful termination.

Now she was standing in a corner of the breakroom, looking sexy as hell except for the frown on her face. She was sipping her coffee and watching two big guys by the coffeemaker.

Warehouse guys are often loud, but these two men were talking quietly.

Just as I got close enough to the coffeemaker that I could overhear the men's conversation, Jessie Carter called out, "Frank, you've been on break long enough. Get back to work. Dave, I give you one minute."

Two very meek *Yes, Ms. Carter*s greeted this command. The blond man dumped his coffee in the sink, squirted a little water in his cup, dumped that into the sink, and rushed from the breakroom as if his pants were on fire.

The remaining man chugged his coffee, wincing as he swallowed big gulps of hot liquid. Though he was big enough to snap Jessie Carter in two, his shoulders were hunched.

By the time that I had filled my coffee mug, Dave the warehouse guy was washing out his own coffee mug at the sink. I didn't know him and he didn't know me, so I was surprised when he spoke to me (very quietly)—

"You're head of I.T., aren't you? Head computer guy?"

I smiled. "Sure am. You need something computed?"

"Watch yourself," Dave said. "The Bitch Goddess fired Mike this morning."

"Um, which Mike?"

"The Used-To-Be Warehouse Manager. He got fired, totally bullshit reason, and now Warehouse Slut is running—"

"Dave," Jessie Carter called out, "get going. Unless you want to get fired too."

Dave rushed out of the room without finishing his sentence.

****

Just before lunch, the phone rang on Janice's desk. She talked briefly, hung up, then walked around to the doorway of my office.

"Ms. Olson wants to talk to me in her office," Janice said. "Right now."

I said, "Huh. Any idea what this is about?" I was annoyed that Ms. Olson had pulled Janice off her work without talking to me first.

Janice replied, "*No* idea what she wants. Anyway, I'm leaving."

Fifteen minutes later, Janice was back. As soon as she walked in, she caught Arnie's eye, made a *Come with me* gesture, then walked into my office.

As soon as all three of us were in my office, Janice said, "Ms. Olson asked me a lot of questions about technical stuff. What I knew, and what you guys knew. Oddy, she asked *lots* of questions about *you*. At first I thought she was just testing my loyalties, you know? But now I think she was being serious. maybe she's writing up our résumés?"

"Or she wants to know what to put in the want ad," Arnie said. "After she fires us."

"Arnie, that's dumb," Janice said. "Why would Ms. Olson fire any of us?"

Arnie gave Janice a long look, but said nothing.

Janice said, "Um, one other thing. Ms. Olson said I'm getting a 10 percent pay cut, but it's nothing personal."

Arnie said, "*What?*"

I said, "So what did you say when she told you that? Did you argue to keep your salary?"

"No, I just said 'Okay.' Didn't argue."

Arnie shook his head. "Janice, you're wimpy."

****

Right after lunch, I got the summons from Ms. Olson; I was told to bring Arnie with me.

"Oh, *shit!*" Arnie said when I told him. "Does my face look okay?"

"Your face looks fine. Didn't you shave ten minutes ago?"

Instead of answering 'Yes' to that, Arnie turned to Janice. "My face look okay?"

"Your face looks fine," Janice said. Then she laughed. "But maybe you should consider electrolysis, hm?"

Arnie gave Janice a dirty look, but didn't reply.

****

Mrs. Smithson, who had been Mr. Fleischer's grandmotherly receptionist, was gone. Mr. Fleischer used to joke that Mrs. Smithson had been the model for the original "Have a nice day" smiley face of the 1970s, because she was always so happy. But now, Mr. Fleischer and Mrs. Smithson were both gone.

Instead, Ms. Olson's receptionist was a twenty-something woman with short black hair and a scowl.

Arnie and I walked up to her. I said, "Popeil and Bluteau, here to see Ms. Olson."

"Is she expecting you?" the receptionist asked, in a tone of voice that suggested she was convinced otherwise.

Arnie said, "No, we were just taking a leisurely stroll around the building during working hours, and whaddayaknow, we wound up here."

"I don't like your sarcasm," Ms. Black-Hair told Arnie.

Arnie replied, "If you weren't told we were coming, maybe you're not as important as you think you are, princess."

I said, "Just tell Ms. Olson we're here."

Ten seconds later, Ms. Blackhair hung up her desk phone. "You may go in," she said, in a tone of voice that stated she was doing me a favor. As for Arnie, he got glared at.

****

Ms. Olson didn't offer us coffee; instead, she gestured for us to take seats in front of her desk.

"I'll get right to the point, " she said. "Maximilian was a soft touch, and he overpaid you both. I'm reducing your salary by 10 percent."

At first I thought that Ms. Olson was ignoring me and talking only to Arnie. Then I realized that Ms. Olson wasn't merely giving Arnie long looks, she was *studying his face.*

"This is bul—nonsense, ma'am," Arnie said. "Yes, you pay more in salary for people here, but you don't have to spend money training new people. Our turnover is almost zero."

For several seconds, I said nothing. Sometimes I'm not assertive. Then I thought, *Arnie is counting on me.*

I said, "Ms. Olson, Arnie is right. He works hard, he knows his stuff, he's quick to debug programs, and he's worth every penny he gets."

She replied, "It's good that he was an asset to Maximilian. But Mr. Bluteau, you are arguing with me, and you're not high enough up the ladder to argue with me. What's worse, I've made it clear that I don't like your facial hair, but you're not shaving it. I like defiance even less than argument."

"*What?*" Arnie said. "I shaved fifteen minutes ago."

"He did indeed," I said. "I saw him."

"You're lying," she said. "You're *both* lying."

Then she looked at me. "But it's to your credit as a supervisor to protect your employee, so I'll overlook it."

Now she looked at Arnie. "But *you?* You're fired."

Arnie said, "Since I'm no longer your employee, will you go on a date with me? I like your skirt."

"*What?* No!"

Arnie looked at me and shrugged. "It was worth a shot."

He looked at Ms. Olson, and now his voice was angry. "I have only one more thing to say—"

I've mentioned that Arnie is both tall and muscular. Before, when I've seen him angry, all he's done is pound a desk, or pound a wall. Now he stood up, walked to Ms. Olson's desk, and leaned forward to put his hands on her desk—and the man radiated sheer primeval menace.

Arnie's deep voice was cracking with fury held back. "It's not my beard that bothers you, Ms. Olson, it's my penis. We both know this, so don't insult me by lying."

By then, Ms. Olson was pressed back in her chair, looking terrified.

She took a deep breath, then said to me, "You have ten minutes to get him out of the building. Or by god, I *will* see him tasered on the floor."

****

At four o'clock, Cecilia the Hag delivered to me Arnie's replacement: Priscilla, who had just graduated from Wellesley College with a double major in Women's Studies and Computer Science.

I was impressed by Cecilia's speed, finding a replacement computer person only three hours after Arnie got fired. I mean, perish the thought that poor Arnie had been set up from the beginning.

Priscilla's first words to me, her supposed boss, were the disdainful "You're the one in charge? Figures."

I talked to her for half an hour, finding out what her technical knowledge was. By then it was four-thirty, and I was tired of everything.

My office phone rang then. It was Ms. Olson calling.

"Is Priscilla there with you?" Ms. Olson asked.

"Yes, she's in my office. I'm explaining her training schedule to her."

"Training is fine, but I want her to show you what she can do. Give her an assignment."

"Ms. Olson, with all respect, this isn't like someone getting hired at the loading dock—"

Her voice got dangerous. "Mr. Popeil, are you being *defiant?*"

I caved. "Okay fine, I'll give her an assignment."

"Today," Ms. Olson said. "Before she goes home."

"Yes, I'll give Priscilla an assignment, before she goes home."

I hung up the office phone and sighed. Then I look at Priscilla, who was sitting three feet away.

I said, "Here's your first assignment. Our workhorse scheduling program has a small bug in it. Program's written in C, and originally written in 1990, so it's small and simple. Last month, Mr. Fleischer asked us to make some improvements. I gave that job to Arnie. A little after midnight this morning, we found out that if a truck arrives at a site before midnight but doesn't depart the site till after midnight, that truck disappears off our map. So print out the source code, start looking through it till five o'clock, and tomorrow start hunting for the bug."

I scribbled the file name and handed the paper to her.

"Piece of cake," she said, and walked out of my office.

God, I missed Arnie.

I can't tell you what work I did between four-thirty and five. Because all the time I was keeping busy, I couldn't shake the thought, *No matter what I do, or how well I do it, that might not save me in the end.*

Chapter 4
All The Internet Is Chicken

Tuesday Evening

Ah, home sweet home.

After I checked my mail and lighted my pipe, I put a frozen burrito in the microwave. Specifically, I zapped a burrito made of Peking rabbit, brussels sprouts, and mangos.

Discontinued Den has great prices, but their frozen foods are weird.

****

Fifteen minutes after my microwave chimed, I was surfing the internet. Eventually I wound up at the pirate-torrent discussion site FreeAndUncontrolled.ky.

I was curious about the "do-it-yourself hypno-talker," so I went to "Hot Topics" and hunted up the hypno-talker thread. The results were completely disappointing. Not only had nobody built the thing, nobody had even admitted downloading the ZIP file.

There was only one new comment in the last twenty-four hours—

SouthernCrossSam8402: Oh, yeah? If this thing were real, it'd be all over the news, mate. The bloke who uploaded this is a liar, and he thinks we're stupid. What a shithead!

I posted a comment—

NamedAfterASailorMan: So nobody at all believes this thing might be real? Where is your sense of adventure?

An hour later, somebody replied—

PhuqueTheMPAA: I don't care if it's a con job. I lost interest when I read the blurb. The blurb says I have to buy a chip burner. No way Jose, not till I know this thing works.

****

The bottom line: Every way I could imagine, Tuesday was a shitty day. I went to bed early.

Chapter 5
The "Rewards" Of Being The Boss

Wednesday Morning, Just After Midnight

The land-line phone rang by my bed, blasting me out of a sound sleep.

My first waking though was, *Oh god, is Pappy in the hospital?*

The very first thing I did, awake, was to knock my glasses off the nightstand. Then, while I was trying to talk on the phone, I also was squinting my right eye, with my left eye shut, so I could pick up my glasses before I blindly stepped on them. Don't ever get pinkeye.

Meanwhile, I was speaking into the phone: "Hello?"

The clock by the phone said 12:11; no wonder I was groggy.

"Mr. Popeil? This is Luke Baxter, Chief Scheduler on Graveyard Shift. We have a disaster."

That woke me up instantly. "What's wrong?"

"All our trucks disappeared off the map at midnight."

"*All* of them? Shit. Okay, I'm getting dressed and heading in."

"*Thank you*, Mr. Popeil."

****

I came in to find a note on my desk—

Found the bug, fixed it, out the door by 7:30.

Sisterhood is powerful (and smart!)

P

I cursed Priscilla long and loudly—too bad she wasn't there to hear it—then I headed to the breakroom for coffee. Lord knows I was going to need that coffee.

****

Priscilla hadn't used the History feature, which would have enabled me to open the source-code file and go directly to her changes. Instead, I had to print out the source code the way she'd left it, and eyeball the printout. *Shit, this will take hours.*

I kept falling asleep in my chair. One time, I woke up to discover that just before falling asleep, I'd typed—

if IsLeprechaun(Pat)
while (GoldNotFound)
FindGold();
else;

—in the middle of our scheduling program.

Sometime during the night, the janitor came in, and started dumping wastebaskets. When he got to Priscilla's desk, he dumped from her wastebasket a large number of 8-1/2-by-11-inch sheets.

"*Wait!*" I called out.

What had been in Priscilla's wastebasket was the program source code as it had existed yesterday afternoon, before her changes. What I had on my desk was the source code as it existed now, after her changes.

When I compared each pair of pages, it took me only a half-hour more to figure out what lines of code she'd changed. I typed yesterday's lines of code back in, then started looking for the bug that Priscilla was supposed to have fixed.

****

At 6:30 that morning, I phoned Luke Baxter. "I think I've got everything fixed. I've tested it under simulation. I'm uploading the new version to the system computer now. If you don't tell me it's fucked up in the next fifteen minutes, I'm going home."

Once I told him this, I hung up my office phone and waited for ten minutes. Actually, I hung up the phone and waited for thirty seconds, then fell asleep in my chair for nine minutes.

My ringing phone woke me up. Luke Baxter told me, "Everything seems to be fine."

"Glad to hear it. Call me at midnight if things go bad again."

I wrote a note each, to Janice and to Priscilla. Each note explained briefly what had happened, stated that I would not come in till the afternoon, and that Priscilla wasn't to do *anything* without Janice's supervision. Finally, I wrote, "I will not answer the phone. Any phone. So don't bother."

I kept my note to Priscilla free of profanity and sexist language. I'm amazed.

****

When I got home, I turned my smartphone off, and set it to charge. Then I took the handset of my kitchen land-line phone and draped it over a chair.

Soon I was hearing BEEP-BEEP-BEEP-BEEP...

By then I was in my bedroom. I got nearly naked, crawled into bed, then went into a coma.

Chapter 6
Hump Day Fucks Me

Wednesday Afternoon

I stepped out of my car in the employee parking lot at 1:30. I didn't have eight hours of sleep, but I could function (if I drank enough coffee).

A casually dressed man had walked out of the building, carrying a cardboard box. Now he was walking across the parking lot, toward a pick-up truck at the far end of the parking lot.

By now, after three days of Ms. Olson's management style, I had an idea what that cardboard box meant.

As he walked past me, I said, "You got fired, huh?"

He stopped walking. "What the fuck? I got fired for telling a joke to the Warehouse Slut?"

"What was the joke?"

"Okay, a nun and a stripper are standing in the same checkout line at Wal-Mart. The nun says to the stripper—"

When he'd finished the joke, I said, "Yeah, that joke is more than enough to get you fired from here, these days."

"*Really?* I've been driving a truck since Sunday, so I'm out of touch. Have lots of people gotten fired?"

"Lots of *men* have been fired. And the reasons are a crock, in at least one case. But the only woman to lose her job has been Mrs. Smithson, Mr. Fleischer's receptionist."

"So the new lady is looking for reasons to fire men, you're saying."

I nodded. "Seems that way."

"But she hasn't fired *you*," the trucker said to me. He was giving me a look that said *Why are you so lucky?*

"I haven't been fired *so far*. But there are still 3-1/2 hours left in the workday."

****

The moment I walked into Information Technology, Janice looked up. "Ms. Olson wants to talk to you. She's pissed."

"What's wrong? Did the scheduling program crash again?"

"No, she called your office phone at 8:30, and I had to tell her that you weren't coming in till later."

Priscilla told me then, "If you'd wanted me to waste time testing the software, you should have told me beforehand. Really, this software crash was your fault, not mine."

I didn't call Priscilla a fool, an airhead, or a princess. I'm amazed.

Two minutes later, I was on the phone with Ms. Olson: "This is Odysseus Popeil. What do you need?"

She screeched, "I need for you to work the hours you're supposed to work. I pay you to be in your chair at eight o'clock."

"No, you pay me to *think*. And there's no point in my sitting in a chair if I can't stay awake to think."

"I don't like men arguing with me."

I almost replied *You don't like men, period.* Instead, I said, "I have a lot of work to do, and only three-plus hours to do it in. Is there anything else we need to discuss?"

She was silent for ten seconds. "Nothing else. Get back to work."

Frankly, I'm surprised that Ms. Olson didn't fire me, then and there, for my disrespect. But at the time, I was too groggy and pissed off to care what I said.

****

I hung up my office phone, then I hit the dumbbells. Through the glass of my office, I saw Janice explaining my impromptu weightlifting to Priscilla. Priscilla rolled her eyes.

While I was curling the weights, my eyes fell on my ink-jet printer. I saw that my printer was almost out of paper.

Late-night printing-out of the scheduling program's entire source code will cause that, I suppose.

After I put my weights away, it turned out that I had only a few sheets of paper left of the ream that I kept in a desk drawer. So I needed to go to the supply room to get another ream of paper.

To get to the supply room, I had to walk down a dead-end hallway, past Personnel a.k.a. Human Resources Management (on my right), and Payroll (on my left). Where the supply room was, there was only the janitor's room (across the hall), and a fire exit at the end of the hall; an alarm would melt eardrums if the fire-exit door were opened.

In other words, nobody ever happened to wind up in this part of the building, or walked here on their way to someplace else. Only the janitor, and people wanting supplies, came here.

The supply room had a keypad, even though its security was only Level Two. Once I went through the door, a spring at the top of the door pulled the door shut.

Once inside the supply room, I discovered that there were no wrapped reams of paper on a shelf, but there was an unopened twenty-ream box of paper on the floor.

I eventually found some scissors, cut off the ratchet straps, lifted the lid off the box, and (because I'm a nice guy) I put nineteen reams of paper on the shelf.

In all, I was in the supply room for two or three minutes.

I grabbed the twentieth ream of paper out of the box, walked to the door, and was just about to open the door when I heard women's voices.

****

I recognized Ms. Olson's screechy voice. "We have a problem, Cecilia. With Popeil."

"Livvie, sweetie, you're in charge. If Popeil causes problems for you, fire him."

"You don't understand. He's the only person in I.T. who's good at his job. What's worse, you know what Scheduling & Dispatch is saying today? Quote, 'Popeil manned up,' unquote. It's said to me with a smirk. They're on to me, Cecilia."

"He's part of the Patriarchy, Livvie. Just by sitting in his glass office, he's holding back Janice and Priscilla from reaching their potential. And what if he finds out about the Project? No, Popeil needs to be gone. Like Bluteau, that big, hairy brute."

I thought, *The Patriarchy? Jeez, you believe that nonsense?*

Meanwhile, Ms. Olson was saying, "I have no good reason to fire him—"

"What about harassment?"

"You talked to Janice as much as I did. To fire him for harassment, I'd have to make stuff up. And what if he puts her on the witness stand and she says none of that happened? I'd be disgraced and ruined."

I thought, *A good thing I never acted on my urges, back five years ago. God, Janice was luscious when she was slim as well as stacked.*

Meanwhile, Cecilia was saying to Olivia, "You'd be 'ruined'? Sweetie, you exaggerate."

"Not a bit. It's one thing to fire a few warehousemen, or a few truckers, to scare the rest of those men. But I am really afraid that if I fire Popeil when everyone knows he doesn't deserve it, every *man* who works for me will quit. Soon."

I thought, *Thanks for the idea.*

Cecilia the Hag said, "Their wives would never allow all of them to quit."

"If the men here got convinced that sooner or later they'd each be fired themselves, just because they *are* men? Warehousemen, truck drivers, dispatchers, schedulers, the goddamn janitor—god, what better way to screw me over than if all of them quit, all on the same day?"

That's an even better idea, I decided.

Cecilia said to Ms. Olson, "Men don't just quit their jobs. They're wired like that."

"And after they all quit, then what? What if that makes the news? Even if it doesn't, what would that do to Olson Transport's reputation, when we stop meeting our commitments?"

"That's a lot of conjecture, Livvie."

"I don't want to go broke because I screwed up. Nor do I want to give the Patriarchy a propaganda victory."

Oh jeez, I thought, *again with the Patriarchy? Next you'll be ranting about alien abductions.*

Ms. Olson continued, "Besides. . ."

" 'Besides,' what?"

Ms. Olson spoke so quietly that I almost couldn't hear her. "Besides, Popeil has balls. Him and Bluteau both. It bothers me, firing Bluteau that *manly* man, and it would bother me firing Popeil."

I thought, *That's great, she doesn't want to fire me. I can relax now.*

Cecilia said, "Livvie, let me point out what you're forgetting. One, aliens are kidnapping Earth women and getting them pregnant—"

"You don't know that for sure."

"Dammit, Livvie, I watched my own granddaughter walk into a spaceship. Where was I? Two, the Patriarchy is not stopping any of this alien abduction. So Three, it falls to the Sisterhood to figure out when and where the aliens will land, so we can prevent our sisters from becoming brood mares for aliens."

I thought, *Wow, "the Patriarchy" and "alien abductions" both? Next you guys will be saying the U.S. government is part of the conspiracy.*

Ms. Olson said, "I can't help but wonder why the U.S. Army would be covering up these alien visits. Well, the ones that happen in the USA."

"Because the Patriarchy runs the Army, Livvie. The same Patriarchy that Popeil is part of."

"I've met him too, Cecilia. Popeil doesn't strike me as the type—"

"Sooner or later, he's going to discover Priscilla working on the Project. Then what? Either he'll sabotage it directly, on orders from the Patriarchy; or he'll tell the Patriarchy, and the Patriarchy will destroy the Project's effectiveness somehow."

"You're saying, so long as Popeil is head of I.T., the Project to predict alien kidnappings can't succeed?"

"As long as Popeil is in the same room as Priscilla, the Project is in danger. He has to go, Livvie. *Be strong.*"

Ms. Olson was quiet for a long time.

I held my breath.

Eventually Ms. Olson said, "I'll demote him. He'll be humiliated, having to answer to Janice. Maybe he'll quit then. If he quits on his own, there won't be any mass resignations."

"He won't quit, I guarantee it. You'll have to go to Plan B."

"Which is?"

"Do you really want to know? Tomorrow, you raise up Priscilla's clearance to the same as Popeil's is, and Priscilla and I will do the rest."

"Um, what do you have in mind?"

"Child porn. Put pictures on the network in places that he can reach, such as Human Resources Management— *those* pictures, I'll be sure to find. You call him, show him the pictures, point out that only he and you have clearance to put pictures in all those different places, and tell him he has a choice to make: he quits, or he's arrested."

After a pause, Ms. Olson said, "If he won't quit, I won't fire him. He deserves better than that."

Cecilia paused, then said, "If he's still with the company, I'll go to Plan C. Best for you that you not know what Plan C is, just that it involves a friend of a friend who knows how to make up fake letterhead stationery. One way or another, by five p.m. Friday, Popeil will be no longer your employee."

Ms. Olson didn't say yes; she didn't say no. Instead, she said, "I need to get back to my office." I heard footsteps walking away.

I waited two more minutes before I walked out of the supply room.

****

At ten till five, Ms. Olson called Janice and me into her office.

Ms. Olson told us that I.T. needed "new blood," and so I was getting demoted and Janice would be my boss.

Janice was utterly shocked. Ms. Olson looked at me hopefully.

I smiled at both of them. "Wonderful, that's great. Before I leave work, Janice, I'll go upstairs to S&D and give them your phone number. I *think* I got the problem with the scheduling program fixed—but if not, Janice, you might want to go to bed early, just in case that phone rings at midnight. Wow, working only eight to five again, that's such a deal."

Ms. Olson didn't know what to say.

Janice knew what to say: "Um, Ms. Olson, can we postpone my promotion till eight o'clock tomorrow morning?"

I "let" Janice and Ms. Olson talk me into that.

****

Janice and I were walking back to Information Technology.

"Oddy?"

"Yes, Janice?"

"This wasn't my—I didn't ask for this."

"It's okay, Janice."

"I'm not ready to be a boss."

"Maybe you'll grow into it. I did."

Janice didn't reply.

When Janice and I returned to I.T., we found Cecilia the Hag talking to Priscilla. I pretended to not know what that was about.

By then it was five o'clock. Janice and Priscilla (and Cecilia, thank heavens) were soon gone.

****

When I was sure I was alone, I opened up the filing cabinet and pulled out the external hard drive.

Normally, we do a backup of the network once a week. But I broke from that routine in two ways.

Normally, someone in I.T. does the backup on Sunday. This time I did the backup on Wednesday night.

Normally, when the backup is finished, the external hard drive goes back in the filing cabinet. This time I picked up the external hard drive with my left hand, draped my sports coat over it, and carried it out to my car.

Chapter 7
Desperate Times, A
Desperate Measure

Wednesday Evening

I'd started my car in the employee parking lot, being so pleased with myself for putting one over on the conspirators. But by the time I'd arrived home, reality had sunk in.

Technically, I had stolen the external hard drive.

Now I realized that if I wound up suing Ms. Olson for wrongful termination, her lawyers might be able to keep what was on that external hard drive out of evidence, because it was stolen. Worse, her lawyers could use the fact that I'd "stolen" it to black-mark my character.

If those women wanted to lie and create fake evidence in order to force me to quit, or to have an "excuse" to fire me, they could. I couldn't stop them, all I could do was embarrass them afterward.

God, that sucked. Just the thought of losing a job that I was damned good at, for no good reason at all, made my balls shrink.

****

With the commute completed, I walked into my house, external hard drive in hand. The first thing I did was to go to my freezer and decide about dinner.

Sigh It looked like I'd be eating another weird pizza tonight. Thankfully, this one wasn't quite as weird as the anchovy-and-sauerkraut pizza I'd bought six months ago. *But jeez, is it too much to ask that Discontinued Den sell a normal pizza once in a while? Pepperoni and mushroom would be nice.*

I started the pizza cooking. I lighted my pipe; *ahhh.*

Then I powered up my laptop at the kitchen table, and typed out the conversation between Cecilia and Olivia that I'd overheard. This wouldn't help me much legally, I knew, since I couldn't prove that such a conversation ever took place.

Still, that file was the only legal hope I had, so I spent a lot of time on it. By the time I was satisfied with what I'd written, the pizza was cooked and was cooling on the kitchen counter.

I sliced the pizza into six wedges, went back to my laptop, and got on the internet.

****

Less than a minute later, I was reading the "DIY HYPNO-TALKER—real deal or fake?" thread.

No change from yesterday. Nobody had posted that they'd built it, nobody had posted that they'd downloaded it, and now nobody wanted to discuss it. Drat.

But I realized at that moment: *I have no other options. None. Zero.*

I posted a comment—

NamedAfterASailorMan: I'm going to try it. I already have a chip burner, and if it isn't good enough to build this, I know where to buy a good chip burner really cheap. I'll let everyone know how things turn out, even if I have to admit tomorrow that I was a fool.

I went to where the pizza lay on the counter, put two wedges of pizza on a plate, then brought the plate back to the kitchen table.

Then I got back on my laptop, and typed the location for the hypno-talker's ZIP file into my File Transfer Protocol software. I chose the Canadian website (I had a choice of four) so that the electrons wouldn't have to travel so far.

I put my pipe in the ashtray. With hands and mouth free, I picked up a wedge of double-spinach pizza and took a big bite, as my other hand double-clicked the "Download" button.

****

I unpacked the hypno-talker ZIP file, and started looking through the collection of files. I didn't spot anything as phony or made up. The guy who wrote the user manual talked like he believed what he was saying.

He wrote that the key to this thing working was that it turned a human voice ultrasonic. The circuit diagram, as best as I could make it out, seemed to go along with that.

Nearly every page in the user manual had a warning like "BE WEARING EAR PROTECTION WHEN YOU USE THIS ON SOMEONE ELSE!"

At least the guy was consistent. He'd given the same warning in the download-description blurb.

If this was a fake and a fraud, the guy had spent a lot of time cooking it up, for no payoff. Nowhere did he ask for money, or provide contact info.

I couldn't shake the feeling that this "hypno-talker" was genuine.

I forced myself to eat the rest of the pizza—jeez, who *volunteers* to eat spinach?—then I got in my car and drove to Baste's Electronics, a big-box store.

****

At Baste's Electronics, I bought all the parts that the hypno-talker's user manual said to buy. I also bought a new external hard drive for Olson Transport, to replace the one I'd stolen.

On my way home, I stopped at a drugstore and bought a box of ten bright orange, foam-rubber earplugs.

Soon after that, I was home. I immediately started to burn the hypno-talker's main chip, as per the diagram.

Please, please, please, this has got to work.

****

I worked on building the hypno-talker till after midnight. Thankfully, the phone didn't ring, which meant that I'd fixed the scheduling program.

I paused for an internet break. First thing, I hit the hypno-talker discussion thread, to see what comments there were to my "I'm going to try it" post.

I found two—

SouthernCrossSam8402: Why wait? I'll say it now: NamedAfterASailorMan, you're a fool.

> even if I have to admit tomorrow that I was a fool.

MusashiLives: Please you say soon, if this does truthly work.

Chapter 8
The Hypno-Talker Is Tested

For any number of reasons, I didn't sleep well that night.

Still, next morning I was, other than being groggy, fully healthy.

Yet at seven that morning, I called Janice. I told her I was "sick."

"Uh-huh," Janice replied, her skepticism plain. Janice is lazy, but she isn't stupid.

I then said, "I ask you to come to my house after work. There is something I need to give you, and something I need to show you."

Janice said, "Ooh, what are you going to give me? What will you show me? Are they a nice surprise?"

"I'm sorry, but I think it would be unwise to tell you that. I don't trust Priscilla, and I don't trust Ms. Olson. What you don't know, you can't tell."

"Ms. Olson would go ballistic if she found out that I'd gone to a male coworker's house by myself. Do you know the lectures I would be forced to listen to? How about you give me the . . . whatever . . . at work?"

I laughed. "Janice, in an hour you'll be my boss. If a female boss goes to a male subordinate's house and has sex, that isn't harassment, it's empowerment."

"Duh, you're right. Second rule of feminism: 'Nothing a woman does is bad, except to help a man.' Okay, I'll be over at your house at five-thirty. Um, will I need to wear a surgical mask?"

"No, of course not. Why—"

"Bingo. Caught you. But don't worry, I won't share my suspicions with Ms. Olson. That woman scares me."

****

My phone rang at 8:05 a.m. I'm guessing that Priscilla had wasted no time alerting Ms. Olson of the wrinkle in their plans.

Ms. Olson's first words to me were, "This is the second day in a row you've not been here at eight o'clock. Get your butt in here."

"I'm sick. Won't be coming in."

"Nonsense. What you are, is goofing off. Malingering. I ought to tell Payroll to not pay you for today."

"Enough! Stop right there. Are you a doctor? Are you qualified to say whether I'm sick or not?"

"*Of course* I'm not a doctor. But you think I don't know shirkers—"

"One word: slander. I'm mad enough to sue you for slander—"

"How *dare*—"

"—and if you say to *anyone*, even your nail technician, that I'm only pretending to be sick, I *will* sue you for slander. You *know* I have the motivation to hurt you."

Yes, I know, I *was* malingering, so I couldn't possibly win a slander suit. But I was thinking back to college, where I'd once bluffed a pair of fours into a winning poker hand.

Ms. Olson took a breath, then tried a new tack. "Look, I *need* you to come in. I'm not sure that Ms. Wellington can handle everything by herself—"

"Not my problem, boss lady. *You* fired Arnie, *you* promoted Janice, *you* demoted me, and you or the hag hired Priscilla. Who, if it were up to me, would be fired as well. You made your bed, and it's not my job to stop you lying in it."

"How about you come in for just an hour? That's not too much to ask, is it?"

I thought, *Priscilla can't plant the child porn unless I'm in the building. But you don't know I know that.* Aloud I said, "And when I refuse to come in even for an hour, what will you do? Threaten to fire me? What a surprise."

"I'm not like that. You don't understand. I'm just trying—"

"Excuse me, Matt Lauer is on. Goodbye."

****

"No, Ms. Olson. *No.* Why have you called me again? I'm sick, I'm a flunky now, and I'm not coming in for any part of today. Goodbye."

I turned off my cel phone, and dumped it back in my pocket with a frown. Ms. Olson had called me at *precisely* the wrong minute.

The time was 1:27 that afternoon. Every part of the hypno-talker was built, and each part had been double-checked. Now it was time to test.

I would run the first test without me wearing earplugs. I got the impression that the hypno-talker's "inventor" had never hypnotized himself with the device, so I was curious what would happen.

For the test, I had inserted a timer circuit that would shut off the hypno-talker after fifteen seconds.

In front of me was a battery-operated alarm clock; beside me was a kitchen chair with the hypno-talker laying on the cushion. (I figured it wouldn't be smart for me to be holding the hypno-talker and then go into a trance.) I looked at the clock, flipped the toggle switch on the timer circuit, and—

I saw the second-hand jump ahead by fifteen seconds.

Then I got the urge to cluck like a chicken.

I fought the urge, even putting both my hands over my mouth—

—for five, maybe ten seconds. Then I yanked my hands away from my mouth and said, "Awk-buk-buk-buk-awk!"

I couldn't *not* cluck like a chicken.

Fortunately, after I quite clucking, the urge disappeared.

Now I did a fist-pump. "Well, knock me down! It *works!*"

I pressed the hypno-talker's black button to record new orders, then I ran the test a second time—again, without my wearing earplugs. Once again, the second-hand of the clock jumped ahead fifteen seconds. This time I couldn't remember my own name till 1:30. Which was strange to live through, let me tell you.

I decided to run a third test, this time with my orange earplugs in my ears. It turned out that these orange earplugs were for serious noise reduction; I rolled them between my fingers like a joint, then I pushed an earplug all the way into each ear canal.

After I inserted the earplugs in my ears, I ran the third test. This time the clock's second-hand moved normally, and I felt zero urge to sing "I'm A Little Teapot."

****

At three-thirty, I got another phone call from Ms. Olson. Could I please, *please* come in? She told me that she wouldn't mind if I walked into the building, quote, "wearing a ratty bathrobe and Homer Simpson slippers."

For the third time that day, I told Ms. Olson, "I'm not coming in today."

****

By 5:37, all my electronic equipment was back in my garage, and my battery-operated alarm clock was back in the guest bedroom. My kitchen table was bare, except for—

1) the replacement external hard drive,

2) my home-made hypno-talker, and

3) a pair of orange earplugs by the hypno-talker.

I was pacing the floor, and glancing often at my smartphone clock, when the doorbell rang.

Janice was here.

I had very special orders for Janice recorded on my hypno-talker. Special orders that I'd refined over a four-hour period.

Life was about to get interesting.

Chapter 9
Janice In A Trance

When Janice had first started working for me, five years ago, she'd worn skirt-suits for the first four days. For Casual Friday, she'd shown up wearing blue jeans and a t-shirt, and she hadn't dressed-up for work since then.

After that first Casual Friday, Janice had begun wearing denim skirts often, till she'd gotten fat.

After she got fat, Janice wore plus-size women's slacks Monday through Thursday, and women's jeans on Friday.

Five years ago, newly hired blond, skinny, long-legged, and big-breasted Janice wearing any kind of skirt had really been something to see. God, how I'd wanted to fuck that woman! Alas, when Janice had gained the weight, she'd ditched the skirts.

So you can imagine my utter shock now, when I opened my front door: Janice stood there wearing heels, stockings, a black blouse, and a cranberry-colored wool skirt-suit.

"Wow," I said. "You look good." I meant it.

She sighed. "Officially, I'm a supervisor now, so I have to dress the part," she said, as I gestured her inside.

"So I guess I can wear blue jeans and a t-shirt for Casual Friday. Of course, this assumes a lot." I made myself laugh.

I started to walk toward the kitchen. "Please follow me."

****

Janice and I were standing at my kitchen table. She said, "You told me you were going to give me something, and show me something?"

I picked up the external hard drive. "Things may soon get ugly. To save my ass, last night I did an unscheduled backup and then I stole the external hard drive. This is its replacement; take it to work with you tomorrow. Hopefully without anyone seeing you bring it in."

"By which you mean Ms. Olson."

"Or Priscilla, or Cecilia the—the Personnel Director."

Janice looked into my face for several seconds, then nodded. "I hear what you're saying," she said somberly.

Then she gestured toward the hypno-talker. "Is this what you want to show me? It looks sort of like a tablet computer, but with speaker grilles and pushbuttons."

"Uh-huh, it does," I said.

Then I started putting the earplugs in. I explained, "Something's loose somewhere, so it makes a buzzing sound that drives me nuts. Sorry if this bothers you."

Once I had the earplugs in, I picked up the hypno-talker, looked at Janice, and pressed the orange button.

****

Janice's eyes lost focus, her face went slack, and she started chanting. With my earplugs in, I couldn't hear well what she was saying; but lip-reading told me that she was saying the words I'd recorded.

The hypno-talker was built to repeat the recorded message till the batteries ran down, or until I released the orange button. When she mouthed "That is all" for the third time, I took my finger off the button.

Janice's face got normal. She said something—but by then I was pulling my earplugs out of my ears, so I couldn't hear what she was saying.

Once my ears were undeafened, I said, "Would you repeat that?"

She said, "It didn't work. It didn't light up, or buzz, or do *anything*."

I pretended to look embarrassed—which is a hard trick when inside my head, I was high-fiving myself. *It works on Janice, whoo hoo!*

"Back to the drawing board," I muttered.

She put a finger on my kitchen table, next to a brass door key. "Is this the key to the glass-walled office?"

"Yes, but ask for it tomorrow, don't take it now," I said.

She nodded, and pulled her hand away. She didn't argue one bit.

Yes! The hypno-talker works!

I said, "Janice, what do you think of me, as a person? As a man? Not as a boss."

The hypno-talker User Manual had claimed that this kind of questioning would "invoke her programming," so I was anxious to hear Janice's answer.

The User Manual was correct. Janice's face lost expression again, and her voice got robot-flat: "I trust you. You are completely sexy to me. I will do anything you request, I will answer any question you ask, and I will believe anything you say. I will help you keep your job and become I.T. Supervisor again. That is all."

Only after spouting all that did her face return to normal.

"I'm sorry," I said, "but pulling those earplugs out too fast messed up my ears. What is it you think about me?"

"I think you're trustworthy. You're A-1 hot, despite being bald. Tell me what to do and I'll do it, ask me anything and I'll answer with as much as I know, say something to me and I'll believe it. I won't let Ms. Olson or anybody destroy your job, and I'll even go beyond that and help you become I.T. Supervisor again."

I said, "Janice, you just realized stuff about me. What did you just realize?"

She said, "I just realized that in five years, you've never given me a reason to distrust you, even when you were hot for my body. So just now I connected the dots, and realized I absolutely trust you. And by the way, your big, muscular arms and shoulders, they get me *rrreally* hot!"

"I like that," I said.

"Because I trust you, and you're older and wiser than me, it's okay for me to do anything you tell me and to answer any question you ask, and of course I can believe anything you tell me. Meanwhile, so far as your job goes, just one day as I.T. Supervisor shows me that this is the job that *you* deserve, not me. It's just plain wrong to cheat you out of being I.T. Supervisor, and I stand with you there, 100 percent."

"That's really nice," I said, "all those nice thoughts you have about me." *Every one of which, I planted in your head.*

Janice smiled at me. "All those nice thoughts get thought because you're a great guy, and a great boss."

"In that case," I said, "wanna fuck?"

"I'd love to," Janice replied.

As we were walking into my bedroom, I said, "Tomorrow is payday. How about tomorrow you pay me back the fifty-eight bucks you owe me?"

"Sure, no problem," Janice said calmly.

Needless to say, with Janice being this cooperative, I really enjoyed the sex.

****

I'd always wondered, how much of Janice's tits were her, and how much was padding. Now I got to find out. Her shoes, she took off herself. Then I removed her cranberry wool skirt-suit. I made myself act calmly when I unbuttoned her black blouse.

Underneath everything, she'd been wearing black panties and a huge black bra. I ran my hands over the bra cups—in the interest of collecting data, you understand. She gasped at my touches, and my fingers detected only thin, unpadded satin. I felt her nipples get harder, as they poked my hands.

I kissed Janice, as my hands took hold of either side of her panties and pulled them down off her hips. As her panties dropped to the floor, I smelled Janice's arousal.

When I broke the kiss, she gave me a sexy smile. "The practical thing now would be for me to unfasten my bra. The sexy thing would be for you to unfasten it. Which do you want?"

I said, "Be both, sexy and practical. You unsnap your bra, but make it a striptease, you taking it off."

That's what she did. When the bra was unsnapped and the cups only loosely covered her tits, she turned around and pulled the bra straps down. When she turned back around, the only reason her bra cups were covering her boobs was that her hands were holding the bra cups in place. Slowly, at a speed of only millimeters per second, she pulled the bra down.

"Well, knock me down," I breathed. "Your boobs are amazing, Janice. True works of art."

I'd undressed Janice; now Janice returned the favor by undressing me. Not much to tell there, except that undressing me was done with lots of stroking and licking.

Her removing my shorts, this she left for last. When my erection was exposed to light and air, I learned something new about Janice—

Janice had a weight problem because she liked to put things in her mouth.

****

I couldn't keep my hands off her tits. I couldn't keep my mouth off her nipples. When Janice lay on her back, those big tits flattened out (as much as they could)—Janice's big tits were the real deal. *Yes!*

Janice's own hands were busy too, caressing my arms and shoulders. "Mm, I love those strong arms and shoulders you have, Oddy. They get me hot."

"You want me to fuck you now," I said.

"Yes, Oddy! I'm so horny. I will gladly pay you Monday for a good fucking right now. Well, maybe not Monday."

I turned down her offer of money for sex, but I fucked her anyway. I'm a swell guy that way.

When I was fucking Janice, her hands went between our bodies, and she started squeezing and pulling her nipples. I've never seen a woman do that outside of porno movies.

Her pussy got wet when I fucked her. *Really* wet, slurp-slurp wet. I don't know if the hypno-talker caused that, or my clit-stroking technique did. I'd like to think the latter.

Janice wasn't a screamer. When she came, her arms around me squeezed tightly enough to nearly break my ribs, as she went rigid and gasped. This happened at least four times.

The big news about that sex session? About nine o'clock or so, I got to enjoy my first-ever titty-fuck.

"Fuck my tits, cream on my tits," Janice kept saying then.

The only downside to the whole fucking-Janice thing? I couldn't shake the feeling that, even though Janice was ten years younger than I was, she'd done this more than I had.

Chapter 10
Yankee Doodle Goes To Town

Early Friday morning

I walked into Olson Transport at 7:02 a.m., an hour before I was required to be at work. In my left hand I carried what most people would assume was a blue tablet computer.

I'd timed it perfectly: The night security guard was missing from the front receptionist's desk. Nobody would know I'd come in early (unless he/she recognized my car in the parking lot), and nobody would see me bring the hypno-talker in.

A minute or two later, I was inside I.T. and using the brass key to unlock the glass-walled office. I turned on the desk computer, then I lay the hypno-talker on a corner of the desk. With my hands free, I logged in.

"Let's see what Priscilla has been up to," I said into the silence, "while I was gone."

Less than a minute later, I laughed. "Well, knock me down! Priscilla, didn't your mother tell you that impatience would get you in trouble someday?"

****

After I'd turned on my computer and had logged in, the very first thing I'd done was to try and access the PRISCILLA folder. If she still had a Level Four clearance, I could peek inside that folder with no problem.

No dice. I was sternly informed, "YOU MUST HAVE LEVEL FIVE CLEARANCE TO ACCESS THIS FOLDER."

This meant that Priscilla had a Level Five clearance, like Janice now had, and like I'd had until yesterday. Priscilla could upload files to the computer network without Janice's knowledge or permission.

****

Olson Transport has its own proprietary operating system. Sometimes for us in I.T., that's a pain in the ass. But what this also means is that Priscilla would not know how to do some things unless she'd ask Janice or she'd wander over to the system manuals. Neither of those options would be a good choice if Priscilla was trying to be sneaky.

On our system, whenever a user searches for some specified group of computer files, those files are listed by, among other things, the date that the file was modified.

It turns out that for any of us in Information Technology, the Date Modified can be easily edited. *Edited* as in *falsified*.

But any file in our operating system has a second date-stamp: the Date Created. *That* sucker, Priscilla would have to ask the system to list.

To sneak-change the Date Created, Priscilla would need a Level Five clearance *and* some knowledge of our operating system's fine points, *without* hitting the manuals. Plus, of course, she'd have to know about the operating system slapping a Date Created aspect on the file in the first place.

****

After I tried unsuccessfully to peek in the PRISCILLA folder, I did a search for all files in the network with Date Created being yesterday. Amid all the files I knew were legit, I found fourteen JPG files.

I opened all fourteen JPG files and made myself look at them. The pictures were all of elementary-school-aged boys, all naked.

All fourteen JPG files had Modified dates of last Christmas Eve. Two of the JPGs were in the Warehouse folder, three JPGs were in the S&D folder, two were in the Payroll folder, three were in the Personnel folder, and four JPG files were in the I.T. folder.

Meaning that, if you naively accepted those Christmas Eve modification-dates as true, only Mr. Fleischer and I had had the clearance to upload those files and put them in those places. But if Mr. Fleischer had uploaded those pictures, he could have put them inside his Level Six BIGBOSS folder, and nobody would have known they were there. In short, the modification-dates plus the files' scattered locations "proved" that I was the files' uploader.

Now I couldn't mark those files for deletion fast enough! Of course, since I had only a Level Four clearance now, the files wouldn't actually disappear till Janice disappeared 'em.

Ms. Olson and Priscilla had goofed, big time. The child-porn pictures had Dates Created of yesterday, when I'd missed work all day.

I needed a legal witness that Priscilla had framed me. Janice was officially my boss, but also was now my hypnotized fuck-buddy, so she was the perfect candidate.

****

I called Janice on my smartphone. "How far from here are you?" I asked. I'd "requested" that Janice come in early.

Janice said, "I'm nearly there."

"Priscilla is a Level Five now."

"Not after I sit down at my computer!" Janice said.

"Priscilla used her Level Five to make mischief. I'll show you after you get here."

"I just turned into the parking lot," Janice replied.

I looked at my computer's clock. The time was 7:14.

****

I showed Janice what I myself had recently discovered: that Priscilla had a Level Five clearance, that our network had child-porn pictures on it, and that those pictures had been uploaded yesterday after four o'clock—

"Hold on," Janice said, "she uploaded that shit from I.T., while I was sitting five feet away? That snooty bitch!"

I asked, "Were you checking up on her work yesterday? Or were you being lazy as a supervisor?"

Janice's face fell. "Lazy, very lazy. I didn't come over to Priscilla's desk once."

Then Janice's face brightened. "If she's stupid enough to not think about the Date Created file aspect, and she's stupid enough to major in Women's Studies, maybe she's stupid in other ways."

Janice went to Priscilla's desk and started searching it.

Seconds later, Janice grinned. "Aha, a USB stick."

A minute after that, Janice was back at her old desk, staring at her computer screen. "The new girl has pictures of naked boys, how sweet. This Cornhusker girl is about to make the Wellesley girl her bitch."

At that, I walked into the glass-walled office, picked up the hypno-talker, and walked out to the I.T. open bay. "I'm going to talk to Ms. Olson now. I might not be back for a while."

Janice looked puzzled. "Why are you going to show her your whatchamacallit, when it doesn't work?"

I replied, "The 'whatchamacallit' is unimportant. Don't think about it."

Janice gave me a half-lidded look. "How about I think about how to best suck your cock? We've got half an hour."

I smiled. "Nah, I really need to be there waiting when Ms. Olson gets in. Find something else to think about."

Janice nodded, then turned her face back to her computer screen.

The time on my smartphone said 7:22.

I was in a good mood. As I walked through the door and away from Information Technology, I was whistling "The Sailor's Hornpipe."

****

When I was standing in front of the locked door to Ms. Olson's office, I looked around. *Am I being watched?*

I couldn't see anyone, which meant that nobody could see me. *Whew!*

Less than thirty seconds later, I had punched in Ms. Olson's keypad combination (11247635) and, with thumping heart, I stepped through the door.

The receptionist's station was empty, as I expected. Next to the receptionist's station, the door to Ms. Olson's private office was shut.

What will I find when I open that door? I didn't know Ms. Olson's habits; for all I knew, she might already be at her desk. The hypno-talker User Manual had told me that this device had a range of only five feet, whereas the distance between this door and Ms. Olson's desk chair, I knew, was more like fifteen or twenty feet.

Meaning that if I walked through the private door and Ms. Olson was already there, things would get ugly.

Here goes nothing. I yanked the door open and stepped inside.

Ms. Olson's private office was empty. All the lights were off; the only light came through the blinds. *Whew!*

The private office had its own bathroom, I knew. I stepped into the bathroom, shut the bathroom door, and pulled out my right earplug just enough that I could hear almost normally.

Now I wait.

****

Sometime later, I heard the private-office door open and shut, I heard the click of a light switch, then I heard footsteps on the carpet. I heard the sound of a garment landing on the leather executive chair, then I heard more footsteps.

I had just shoved the right earplug back into my ear when the bathroom door opened up.

There stood Olivia Olson. She looked into my face, and her eyes went wide.

She dashed for the desk phone. I ran after her.

****

I wasn't there for what happened in I.T. (I was busy with Olivia at the time), but Janice told me later what had happened with Priscilla.

After the hypno-talker and I left Information Technology, Janice deleted all the child-porn pictures. Then she downgraded Priscilla's clearance from Level Five to Level One.

When Priscilla walked into I.T. at eight o'clock, the door to the glass-walled office was wide open, but Janice wasn't in the I.T. Director's office. Nor was Janice at her old desk. No, Janice was sitting at Priscilla's desk.

The USB stick with the child-porn pictures lay on Priscilla's desk, next to the mousepad.

"Good morning, Priscilla," Janice said sweetly. "We need to talk."

The last time that Janice had used that same super-sweet voice? The day that her ex-boyfriend had come into her Hooters restaurant and had sat at one of her tables.

Now Priscilla said, "Um, hello, Janice. What do we need to talk about?"

"It's 'Ms. Wellington,' dear. Remember, I'm your boss."

By now, Priscilla looked nervous. "What do we need to talk about, Ms. Wellington?"

"Oddy came in early today. He found child porn on the network. He marked the files for deletion. I agreed with him, so I deleted them all. Any comments, dear?"

"*Of course* he deleted them! He must have heard about Ms. Jones finding them, and he destroyed the evidence! With your help."

"No, dear. These same files are on this USB stick, but with 'date modified' dates of Wednesday night. *You* uploaded them, not Oddy. Somehow you got a Level Five clearance, and you *planted* these files yesterday. But you made a mistake, dear."

Janice said no more. Finally, Priscilla broke the silence. "What mistake did I make?"

"Bingo. Caught you. I'm not going to tell you what your mistake was, so that you can't successfully pull that trick at your next job."

"Janice—Ms. Wellington—"

Janice picked up the USB stick, then stood up. "You're fired, Priscilla. Come with me; we're about to talk to Personnel."

"It's Human—"

Janice gave Priscilla a look, and Priscilla shut up.

During the walk to Personnel, Priscilla whispered, "Why are you helping him? We're women, and all women have a common enemy—"

Janice's laugh was scornful. "Every Women's Studies major should be *required* to work as a Hooters waitress, dear. In order to make enough tips to pay for your education, you'd have to learn what men are really like."

A minute later, the two women were in Personnel. Janice basically dragged Priscilla in front of Cecilia the Hag.

Cecilia said, "Ms. Wellington, you're just the person I want to talk to. Yesterday I found disgusting child-porn pictures—"

Janice said, "What a coincidence, that's what I'm here about."

Then Janice spoke loudly enough so that everyone in Personnel could hear: "PRISCILLA HERE PLANTED THOSE CHILD-PORN FILES, AND I CAN PROVE IT. ODYSSEUS POPEIL FOUND THOSE FILES, I DELETED THEM, AND PRISCILLA IS FIRED, EFFECTIVE IMMEDIATELY."

Janice caught Priscilla shooting Cecilia a look: *Do something!*

Cecilia said to Janice, "I think you need to step back from this. Whatever friendship you have with this man has clouded your judgment. He's a pervert, he's been caught, and you need to talk to Ms. Olson before you do anything rash."

Janice said, "Are you countermanding my authority to dismiss my subordinate, *bitch?*"

Janice stepped forward, invading Cecilia's space. "This morning, Priscilla had a Level Five clearance. Oddy didn't give it to her before his demotion, and I sure didn't give it to her after, so that leaves only Ms. Olson. You suggest I talk to her? Fine, I'll ask her why *she* gave Priscilla a Level Five clearance that Priscilla then used to frame Oddy. I'm not part of your little conspiracy, and I don't *want* to be, you got me?"

Then Janice raised her voice a second time. "IF PRISCILLA ISN'T ESCORTED OUT OF THIS BUILDING IN THE NEXT TEN MINUTES, I'M GOING TO START WANDERING THE HALLWAYS, TELLING EVERYONE ABOUT THIS INTERESTING USB STICK I FOUND."

Cecilia caved. "Very well. You want her marked 'Ineligible for rehire'?"

Janice said, "Is there an even lower ranking? Maybe 'The Company spits at the mention of her name'?"

Chapter 11
Oh, Popeil!

Olivia Olson's Office

Friday, 7:56 a.m.

I was standing in the bathroom. The bathroom door opened up.

There stood Olivia Olson, wearing a smoke-gray skirt-suit. She looked into my face, and her eyes went wide.

She gasped, then she dashed for the desk phone. I ran after her.

Too bad for her, her long skirt slowed her movements. Just as she laid her hand on the handset, I pressed the orange button on the hypno-talker.

She froze for an instant. Then she remained in that pose, but her lips started moving.

****

Just like with Janice, I played the ultrasonic message three times, then I took my finger off the orange button.

(Did I need to play the message three times, instead of one time? I don't know, but I figured it couldn't hurt.)

Then I pulled my earplugs out of my ears.

Just like with Janice, I asked the same question, in nearly the same words, three times, so that my ultrasonic programming became Ms. Olson's own ideas.

When I was confident that I had defanged Ms. Olson, I laid the hypno-talker on a corner of her big desk.

Since Monday, I'd seen her often angry; a few minutes ago, I'd seen her frightened. But now her face showed no anger and no fear.

"How did you get in here?" she calmly asked.

"That's not important—"

"Oh, sure," she said, nodding.

"—but what *is* important is that I overheard you and Cecilia the Hag talking, Wednesday afternoon. I was in the supply room."

Her face went white. "You heard *everything* we said? Did you tell anyone?"

The private door opened up, and Ms. Olson's black-haired receptionist walked in. "Ms. Olson, I'm—"

She came to a complete stop when she saw me. "You're supposed to call first and make an appointment," she told me.

"That will be all, Gloria," Ms. Olson said. "Make sure we're not disturbed."

Gloria the receptionist gave me a suspicious look, then left the room as she'd been ordered to do.

I continued the conversation from before: "No, I didn't tell anyone, Ms. Olson. You can trust me."

"I know that. I trust you completely, Popeil."

I asked her, "Did you mean what you said, that you find *me* attractive?" I didn't mention Arnie.

"Yes, I find you attractive. You have strong arms, but otherwise you're skinny. I like skinny men."

"So why haven't you shown me this? Why are you a *bitch on wheels* around Arnie and me?"

She looked at the floor. "Because I knew I'd get my hopes up, for nothing. Men don't find me attractive. Never have."

"You're kidding me!" I exclaimed. "Arnie and I both—Ms. Olson, you have a pretty face, and how you wear your hair really gets me going."

Her hand swatted air. "*So why am I still*—pretend I didn't say that."

"Why are you still *what*, Ms. Olson? What did you start to say?"

"I'm thirty-three, Popeil. Goody goody, I have an M.B.Λ. But not only am I not married, but—why has no man except total strangers ever wanted to fuck me?"

"*I* want that, Olivia. *I* want to fuck you very much."

"*Really?*" Olivia replied. She looked at me with longing.

****

I walked forward to where I stood close to Olivia. "Now is the perfect time to have sex," I told her.

"Oh sure," she said, agreeing because of the hypno-talker.

"I like your perfume. It smells nice," I told her, my face only inches from hers. "I like your pearl necklace. You're very girly."

"Except I'm not shaped girly," she said. "Please don't laugh when I'm naked."

"Olivia, believe me, everything will be fine." She relaxed completely.

"Touch me," I said. "Put your hand on the front of my pants."

By then, I had a boner. Even if nobody else found Olivia attractive, *I* certainly did. Plus, having sex with the Lady Boss in her office—this had long been a fantasy of mine.

She obediently put a hand on my pants—and gasped. "Did *I* cause that?"

"Yes, I—"

I couldn't say any more before Olivia threw herself at me and kissed me hard on the mouth.

****

Mr. Fleischer had known that employees would feel uncomfortable, attending meetings in the company owner's office. So he had furnished one part of the room to make people feel more comfortable in meetings.

At that end of the room, the gray room carpet was covered with a large, multicolored Persian rug. Atop that Persian rug, four overstuffed chairs and a blue couch faced each other, in roughly an oval shape.

Many times when Mr. Fleischer had been the owner, I'd attended meetings in this room, either sitting on the blue couch or facing the blue couch. But never once had I imagined *having sex on* the blue couch!

Now I walked Olivia across the room to the Persian rug. There I undressed her slowly and carefully; because damaging someone's clothing at work, when coworkers might notice, is just plain stupid.

Her bra and panties were white, practical, and not in the least sexy. However, I didn't tell her that.

"I don't know why I bother," she said, when I removed her bra.

"They don't sag. That's a big plus," I replied.

Then I started sucking on her nipples. She liked that, or so her moans and arching back told me.

I undressed myself, as Olivia watched me. When my chest was completely bare, she bit her lip.

"Wow, your muscles," she said. "*Mmm.*"

My naked self led naked Olivia to the blue couch, and sat her down on it. I asked her, "Are you ready to be fucked now?"

She nodded, but said nothing. Her eyes were wide.

I reached around behind her head, cupping my hand around her sexy brunette bun. "Lean back. Relax," I said. I lowered her upper body, spinning her a quarter-turn in the process, till all of her was lying on the couch.

She reached over and stroked my hard cock. "Does this feel good? I've touched a dick only once."

"Yesss, Olivia, that's niiice," I hissed.

She bit her lip again. "Please, fuck me now! Wait, I'm going to bleed, aren't I?"

I jumped up and ran to the bathroom, my hard-on swaying back and forth. I grabbed about a half-dozen paper towels, and, with my hard-on again swaying back and forth, I ran back to the blue couch.

Olivia and I managed to get the paper towels placed so that there would be no bloodstains on the blue couch.

"We pause for station identification," I said. Then I reached into my pants pocket, pulled out a foil packet, and condomized myself.

Olivia frowned, looking at my cock. "I think all this running around has softened it a little. We can't have that."

So saying, she sat up and gave me a blowjob—or tried to. She was inept, to be honest. Her teeth scraped.

But it didn't matter. Simply knowing that, without any hypno-order from me, Olivia Olson had chosen to put her lips on my cock—this got me hard as granite.

After several minutes, she pulled her face away from my cock. "Fuck me. Please. Please do it now," she said.

So I did.

After I broke her hymen, I said, "That bad part is over with. Now you'll enjoy what I do." I meant that as reassurance, but I forgot something: Thanks to hypno-talker programming, my statement became prophecy—

Instantly Olivia's pussy started getting slurpy-wet, and she started thrashing, thrusting, clutching, and moaning.

I didn't last long after that; Olivia's sugar-walls were both tight and slick, and they were really doing a number on my cock.

But apparently my cock was returning the favor. About five seconds after my balls tightened and I started shooting into my condom, Olivia arched her back and—

"Oh, Popeil!"

—screamed into my shoulder.

Chapter 12
Strong To The Finish

Later Friday morning

After we climaxed, we spent one minute kissing.

Then Olivia cleaned herself off, and she and I got dressed. I put the used paper towels and the used condom and foil pack into the bathroom wastebasket.

Then Olivia looked at me with a bedroom smile. "Oh, Popeil! Tell me what you want me to do now."

I did, I told her what I wanted her to do next. (No, it's not what you think.) Ten minutes later, I was sitting in one visitor's chair in front of Olivia's desk, and Cecilia Jones was sitting in the other visitor's chair. Olivia had kindly hidden the hypno-talker in a desk drawer.

Cecilia the Hag glared at me, then turned back to Olivia. "I'm glad that all of us are in the same room. I've just received a letter from the registrar at Georgia Tech, stating that they have no record of awarding any degree to this man."

Cecilia the Hag gave me a cruel smile. "I recommend—"

Olivia put her hand up. "Odysseus, remind me: When did you get your degree from Georgia Tech?"

I said, "June, fifteen years ago. Got a B.S. in Computer Science."

Cecilia said, "That's a lie, Popeil, and I have written—"

Olivia said, "I agree, someone is lying." She picked up the handset. "I'm calling the registrar's office."

Cecilia gasped.

****

The phone call took ten minutes, most of that consisting of Olivia being put on hold.

Olivia's "replies" pretty much consisted of *Uh-huh* and *I see* and *Would you repeat that?* I couldn't guess what the person at the other end was telling her.

As soon as Olivia ended that call, she punched buttons on her desk phone and spoke into the handset.

I heard Olivia's voice both from her mouth and from the speaker overhead: "Security, please come to Ms. Olson's office; Security, please come to Ms. Olson's office. Code Twelve."

Cecilia the Hag gave me a triumphant smile. "Code Twelve is when a former employee is about to be escorted off the property."

"Exactly," Olivia said.

Totally unworried, I said, "Well, *somebody* here is about to have a sucky day."

A minute later, there were two knocks on the door, then the daytime security guard stepped in. He was built to make warehousemen worry.

Olivia turned to Cecilia, her hands clasped. "I've decided that this company needs old blood, that we need to go in an old direction. You can pick up your paycheck from the front receptionist, two weeks from today."

"But—"

Olivia looked at the security guard. "Peter, her office is in Personnel. Give her ten minutes to pack up, but don't let her touch the computer."

****

I didn't stay long after Cecilia the Hag was escorted out of Olivia's office. In fact, I was there only long enough for Olivia to phone Janice and apologize for demoting her, then Olivia gave me my Level Five clearance (and my Supervisor position) back.

Just before Olivia handed me back my hypno-talker, I reached around to the back of her head and caressed her hair bun one more time. God, that bun is so sexy!

Don't ask me how I know this, but right after I left her office, Olivia continued making apologetic phone calls. The second person Olivia called was Arnie Bluteau; then Olivia called Mrs. Smithson, Mr. Fleischer's former receptionist. Next, Olivia phoned Hamilton Garvey, former Personnel Director. Each person got their old job and old salary back.

In fact, everyone in the company got their old salary and/or former job back. Except for Jessie Carter, also known as Warehouse Slut; Olivia had her escorted out of the building before lunchtime.

Nobody but me knows this, but I'll mention it here: Olivia completely lost interest in tracking any supposed "alien abductions."

****

Friday afternoon, 4:55 p.m.

"I've decided I'm going to start exercising," Janice announced. "Next year, I plan to run in the marathon. And not only—"

"Marathon? *You?*" Arnie said.

Janice said, "Not only do I plan to run in the marathon next year, I plan to be exercised enough that I'll be strong to the finish."

I said, "Janice is exercising, Arnie is back with us, and I'm I.T. Supervisor again. Things are *perfect.*"

Arnie said, "Do you think it's too late to ask Ms. Olson if she's free tomorrow night?"

Chapter 13
I Tell The World

Friday evening

Soon after I got home, I went to the "DIY HYPNO-TALKER—real deal or fake?" thread, because I knew that MusashiLives was anxious to hear back from me.

I posted—

NamedAfterASailorMan: I downloaded the hypno-talker, I built it, and I tried it. Two things you should know. One, that guy wasn't shitting about needing the earplugs, so don't forget to wear them. Two, does the hypno-talker work? FUCK YES, OMG!!!

Chapter 14
Meanwhile in Wheat City, Kansas

Friday, April 12, 1:07 p.m. CDT

Lourdes Taylor noticed the geeky young man working on his laptop.

Young men work on their computers all the time. But there he was at El Toro Blanco, at an outdoor table, but was he listening to Mexican music? Was he actively enjoying the Mexican food in front of him? Nope. *He should have stayed at his office and bought a cardboard pizza for lunch. Would've been cheaper,* Lourdes thought.

Lourdes wasn't optimistic about getting money out of him, but as one of her West Point professors had said, "Fortune *doesn't* favor the brave. Nope, it favors the bold. Be bold, gentlemen. And ladies."

So now Lourdes pasted on a wanton smile and sauntered up to the geek, putting one high-heeled foot in front of the other, in order to wiggle her hips. But he never noticed.

"Hello, tiger," she purred when she got close. "Want some company?"

His head jerked up then. He turned to look Lourdes up and down—noting her short purple hair, her purple high-heeled mules, her pink denim miniskirt, and a cutoff black t-shirt that covered her ordinary tits and that displayed her extraordinary abdominal muscles and her muscled arms.

"Naw, I'm good, thanks," he said cheerfully. "I've got a great lady waiting for me at home. Sorry we can't do business."

"Not a problem," she replied.

He slapped his forehead. "Where are my manners? I'm Egbert. Would you like some chips?" He picked up the basket of tortilla chips and held it out to her.

Lourdes wondered how a guy who looked like a geek, and who was focused on his computer like a geek, could be so confident. Very few men, Lourdes had discovered, could talk to a prostitute and be totally relaxed throughout. *This guy acts like he's fucking some hot sorority girl every night.*

Lourdes took one tortilla chip. With a genuine smile, she said, "You're sweet, Egbert. I'm Bernadette."

He grinned. "That your real name?"

Rather than answer that, Lourdes said, "Honey, give me enough money and you can call me 'Hillary Clinton.' "

Egbert laughed. "Sorry, I'm just a poor Unicorn"—Kanssouri University—"mechanical engineering major. I need all my money to hold down my student loans."

She gave him a girly-wave. "In that case, I'll let you get back to your homework." Her lower body turned to leave.

"Oh, I'm not doing homework right now, I'm watching the noontime news."

He spun the laptop around so she could see the screen. He gestured: "See? There's a flying saucer over Topeka."

"What?"

****

Egbert pressed a key, and the television image switched from mute and closed-captioned, to sound: "—just tuning in, there is a flying saucer floating motionless over a high-school football field in Topeka. Here's Sharon Kildare of Topeka station WIBW with an update."

Lourdes gasped when she saw the TV image. She had personally captured a flying saucer identical to it—shit, had it been only a week and a half ago? So much had happened in that time.

Meanwhile, a woman's voice was saying on TV, "—flew over Topeka an hour and a half ago. All witnesses whom I've talked to, tell me that it moved quickly and in absolute silence. Now it's hovering over the football field at Topeka West High School. The Kansas Film Board tells me that this is not connected with any movie."

"Whoa," Egbert said. "Just think, Bernadette, you and I get to see a real flying saucer on TV."

Lourdes thought, *A week ago Tuesday, I saw a flying saucer for real. Back when I was an Army officer.* Aloud she said, "You'll never forget this, I'm sure."

Meanwhile, the TV image had changed from an underview of the yellow-orange flying saucer, to a helicopter-camera view of a highway. A Kansas Highway Patrol car, its lights flashing, was racing toward the camera; behind the patrol car followed a caravan of chocolate-chip Army vehicles. It was a *long* caravan.

The TV-woman's voice said, "I have just been informed that the president has ordered a special Army unit from Fort Carver to deal with the flying saucer, should it attack Topekans. As you can see, the Army unit is now arriving in Topeka."

Lourdes nodded. Considering the distance from Wheat City to Topeka, it would take the Fourth Special Missions Battalion one and a half hours to get to Topeka, even with the Highway Patrol clearing the path.

The helicopter-camera was now moving along the highway, its direction opposite to how the Army was moving. Egbert whistled. "Those are *a lot* of Army vehicles."

"Yep," Lourdes said, truly amazed.

It sure looked like Col. Brooks had sent Antares Company *and* Betelgeuse Company *and* Capricorn Company to Topeka. Which was great for the people of Topeka, if the Zlarians started any shit.

The only trouble was, Lourdes realized, nobody from the 4th SMB was left at Fort Carver if—

"Shit!" the woman's voice said on TV.

The picture switched from Army vehicles on the highway to a picture of blue sky and clouds. The clouds moved quickly sideways till there was a yellow-orange dot in the middle of the screen. That dot was shrinking as Lourdes watched.

"Folks," the TV-woman's voice said, "the flying saucer just *left*. No warning at all."

Then the camera swung down and around, to show a brunette woman holding a microphone. She was standing in an empty football stadium.

The TV reporter continued, "You just saw how fast it moves. Now it's moving in a . . . direction?"

"South-southeast," said a male voice from off-camera.

Hearing that, Lourdes's blood went cold. Wheat City and Fort Carver were south-southeast of Topeka.

TO BE CONTINUED

BOOK 3

Chapter 0
Previously

Day 1

(Tuesday, April 2)

Fort Carver Post Hospital, Kansas

Army Captain Lourdes Taylor climbed out of the chocolate-chip Army truck that had backed up to the loading dock.

For this task, it was important that as few strangers as possible see what she was delivering, so entering the hospital through a regular door was out of the question.

Captain Taylor pounded on a loading-dock door. A second later, it was opened by a man in his forties. He was dressed as an Army doctor.

Captain Taylor saluted. "Doctor Renfield? I'm Captain Lourdes Taylor of Antares Company, Fourth SMB, making delivery in accordance with Plan Fifty-one."

Major Frank Renfield, M.D. returned the salute. Then he put on an embarrassed smile and lowered his voice. "It's been so long since I got the briefing, I've forgotten what Plan Fifty-one is in regards to."

Then seeing her worried face, he added, "I remember that it's rated Top Secret. All these medics with me have Top Secret clearances."

Captain Taylor gave the doctor an impudent grin. "Then it's time I remind you what Plan Fifty-one covers. You *do* have twelve gurneys ready, correct?"

Seconds later, a medic and a gurney waited near the truck. Two Antares Company men brought a Zlarian corpse out of the truck, and plopped it onto the gurney with no more reverence than if it were a sack of flour.

"Holy shit," Doctor Renfield said.

"*Now* I get the joke," the medic said. "It's Plan *Fifty-one*. As in 'Area Fifty-one.' "

"What's Area Fifty-one?" Doctor Renfield asked.

While the alien corpses were being loaded onto gurneys, Captain Taylor said to Doctor Renfield, "They're Zlarians, from Zlar. Z-L-A-R. I don't know whether that's a planet or a star. Anyway, now it's your job to cut these guys open and figure out how their bodies work."

Doctor Renfield sighed. "Yeah. Such a simple task I have."

****

Day 4, 0815 hours
(Friday, April 5)
Office of Col. Louis Brooks, Battalion Commander

Captain Lourdes Taylor was standing at attention, as Col. Brooks slapped the paper that lay on his desk. The same paper that Captain Taylor had just handed him.

He said, " 'Effective immediately'? You really are resigning your commission, effective immediately?"

"Yes, sir. As soon as the Army can cut me loose."

"*Why*, for fuck's sake?"

"Conduct unbecoming, sir. I am a disgrace to the uniform and these captain's bars, so I should no longer be wearing either of them."

Captain Taylor was staring at the point on the wall that was directly in front of her nose, so she didn't see the colonel's reaction. But he was silent for a while, before he spoke.

"Are you under investigation?"

"Not yet," she replied. "But sooner or later, I would be."

Lourdes Taylor had turned seventeen unlucky civilian women who'd been hypnotized by the Zlarians, into Lourdes's own hypnotized lesbian harem. But then old Kevin MacDonald, a Vietnam-era ex-draftee, had counter-hypnotized those women. If Lourdes stayed in the Army, she *would* be arrested, and she *would* be given a court-martial. While talking things over with Kevin, Lourdes had realized that resigning was not only the tactically smart thing to do, it was the *right* thing to do.

He said, "I could order you to tell me what this is about."

"Yes, you could. *If* you order me, I will tell you."

He said, "I told Brenda a month ago, I hope I live long enough to see you make General. Dammit, your men respect you, you throw yourself at problems instead of avoiding them, you're creative, you're resourceful, and your sense of tactics is excellent."

Captain Taylor said, "Yes, sir. At West Point I dreamed of one day being a general. But at West Point I also was taught the Honor Code, and I've gone against it now."

Col. Brooks sighed. "Very well, I will accept your resignation, effective 1600 hours. For the rest of the day, you are to teach Lieutenant Henderson whatever he needs to know, in order to be Acting Company Commander."

"Thank you, sir."

"At ease, for fuck's sake! Have you given any thought to what you'll do next?"

"I have, sir," Captain Taylor replied. "Even though I won't be in the Army anymore, I've figured out a way to still support our men in uniform."

She didn't mention that her planned way to "support our troops" was to become a stripper and streetwalker. The idea for that had come to her while she'd been talking with Kevin MacDonald.

Which in turn was right after Lourdes had realized that men were *at least* as attractive as women were.

****

Day 11, 1:11 p.m.
(Friday, April 12)
Wheat City, Kansas

"Oh, I'm not doing homework right now," the college student told Lourdes. "I'm watching the noontime news."

He spun the laptop around so she could see the screen. "See? There's a flying saucer over Topeka."

"What?"

Streetwalker Lourdes Taylor had been flirting with a college student, trying to drum up some business, when he'd mentioned that he was watching the "noontime news."

This puzzled Lourdes, because the time was after one o'clock, so the noontime news should be long over.

Then Egbert showed Lourdes *why* the local affiliate was broadcasting news instead of a soap opera—

There was a Zlarian spaceship floating over Topeka!

Now Lourdes learned that the spaceship had been there long enough for the entire Fourth Special Missions Battalion to go racing off to Topeka. But as soon as the 4th SMB *got to* Topeka, the spaceship flew away.

At high speed.

Straight toward Wheat City and Fort Carver.

Five minutes later, a TV station in Topeka discovered that the spaceship was flying at cloud-height, even though for a human pilot this is the stupidest act imaginable. Because the spaceship flew at cloud-height, it showed up on Doppler weather radar.

Lourdes watched, spellbound, as a live weather map showed a traveling magenta segment moving south-southeast across eastern Kansas.

The magenta segment moved fast, about seven miles a minute, and it kept heading straight for Wheat City.

Ten miles from Wheat City, the traveling magenta segment disappeared off the weather map.

Had the spaceship crashed?

Would it reappear in a few seconds?

Had it turned invisible to radar?

For the first time Lourdes realized, *really* realized, that she was a female of childbearing age, and that she carried no hypno-talker-blocking earplugs in her purse.

Just a few minutes from now, Lourdes could be a hypnotized thrall walking naked into that spaceship.

Chapter 1
Jerry Asks Cindy For A Date

Friday, April 12, 1:26 p.m.
English Building, Kanssouri University
Wheat City, Kansas

The class had just ended, and Jerry Green was pulling on his Pizza King windbreaker. Jerry couldn't remember anything about footnotes, today's lecture topic. Instead, Jerry had been thinking all period about Cindy Hope.

This was the day that Jerry would ask sorority hottie Cindy for a date! *Will she say yes? Will she say no?*

Jerry figured that the worst that would happen was that maybe she'd laugh at him. That's why he was going to ask her out when nobody was around, just in case.

Cindy stood up now and was gathering up her books. *Look at her, 67 inches of big-breasted, blue-eyed lusciousness!* "Cindy! Wait!" Jerry called out.

Cindy looked in Jerry's direction and frowned slightly. "Yes?"

Jerry dumped his *The Modern Term Paper* textbook, his notebook, and his pen into his bookbag, put his bookbag on his back, and hurried over to Cindy.

By now the classroom was empty, and Cindy's frown was bigger. She glanced at the clock on the wall.

Jerry had practiced in the shower what he was going to say to Cindy, and how he was going to say it. But when he was actually standing two feet in front of her, he blurted out—

"Cindy, I think you're pretty and you dress nice and you act confident all the time and would you go out with me tomorrow night?"

Cindy pasted on a fake smile. "Listen, um . . . what is your name again?"

"Green. Jerry Green, and—"

"Jerry, I'm sorry but I already have plans for tomorrow night."

"Not a problem, because I work tomorrow night. What about Monday or Tuesday?"

Cindy didn't answer his question; instead, she asked a question of her own: "Is Pizza King where you work?"

"Yeah. Every weekend, Friday night and Saturday night and Sunday night, I'm delivering pizza."

Cindy looked thoughtful for a moment, then asked, "Do you work around here? Do you deliver to Alpha Sigma Sigma sorority house?"

"Yeah, sometimes, though usually it's the frat houses who order the pizza. Anyway, what do you say about going out with me on Monday or Tuesday?"

Cindy gave Jerry another fake smile. "Let me think about that, okay? But in the meantime, you're definitely working tomorrow night? Delivering pizza?"

Jerry couldn't guess what Cindy was thinking. "Yeah?"

Now Cindy gave Jerry a brilliant smile. "Tomorrow night, Alpha Sigma Sigma is throwing a lawn party, and we *will* need pizza. I will make sure we ask for *you* to deliver it, Jerry Green."

So saying, Cindy gave Jerry a girly-wave, then she sashayed out of the empty classroom.

Jerry thought, *That didn't go as bad as I feared. True, I didn't get the date, but at least she didn't embarrass me.*

Chapter 2
Women Walk Out Of The Spaceship

Meanwhile, across town

Friday, 1:26 p.m.

Outside of El Toro Blanco Mexican Restaurant

Two minutes after the spaceship disappeared off weather radar, Lourdes Taylor spotted it for real.

The spaceship was several miles to the west, too small for her to make out its shape. But she recognized its color: halfway between daffodil and sunflower. The spaceship was high in the sky, like an airplane; but it moved slowly, like a helicopter.

Then the flying saucer stopped dead in midair, directly over what surely must be Fort Carver. For a few seconds, the flying saucer made no movement in any of the six directions.

Then the spaceship started to move slowly east, descending as it came.

The spaceship was heading right straight, directly toward, Lourdes.

She felt fear. *Do the Zlarians know I'm the person responsible for their people's deaths?*

"Motherfuck," Egbert said. Lourdes had completely forgotten he was around. Egbert added, "If anything happens, I'll protect you." He sounded as if he believed his big words.

Lourdes thought, *Do you know five ways to kill a man while unarmed?* But what she said aloud was, "Go pay your restaurant bill first, Egbert."

****

Lourdes was wrong: The spaceship wasn't heading *directly* toward her. It hovered over a vacant lot a half-block away from the Mexican restaurant, then slowly descended.

Egbert had taken her advice, had gathered up his laptop computer, and had just walked inside the restaurant to pay his bill.

Meanwhile, Lourdes looked at the slowly dropping spaceship, felt cold fear grip her mind, and—

—ran *toward* the spaceship, as fast as her high-heeled mules would allow. She had graduated from West Point; she would *not* give in to fear!

But she was running with a finger stuck in each ear. She suspected she looked ridiculous.

By the time Lourdes reached the vacant lot, the flying saucer had touched ground. Lourdes kept expecting the spaceship's speaker grille-covers to move aside, but that never happened.

But the door-cover did move aside, and a mango-colored door opened downward, becoming a mango-colored ramp.

Lourdes expected Zlarians to walk down that ramp, carrying either hypno-talkers or ray-guns.

Instead, fifteen or twenty naked human women walked down the ramp.

Since the speaker-grilles were covered, and the naked women weren't chanting, Lourdes took her fingers out of her ears.

****

The youngest naked woman looked nineteen. The oldest was in her forties, with individual gray hairs.

The naked women were of every ethnicity, and included a tall African woman with ceremonial scars on her face.

Every woman belly's showed stretch marks.

Every woman had the overdeveloped musculature of a female bodybuilder. Lourdes exercised hard every single day, and she didn't have a body as good as most of these women.

"*Où sommes-nous?*" a brunette woman exclaimed.

A bottle-blonde with six-inch brunette roots pointed to a billboard that read, "Stylish shoes in the latest colors." The bottle-blonde asked, "Are we in the United States?"

The bottle-blonde spoke with an Australian accent.

Lourdes stepped forward and replied, "Yes, you're in Wheat City, Kansas."

The Australian woman turned and spoke to the other naked women, in some kind of pidgin. Lourdes, meanwhile, was fetching her smartphone from her purse.

Lourdes snapped a photo of all the naked women. Then Lourdes stepped up close to the Australian woman and asked, "What's your name?"

When the Australian woman turned to face Lourdes, Lourdes snapped a close-up of her.

The Australian said, "I'm Sheila. Why are you taking our pictures? We're all in the nuddy!"

Lourdes said, "I haven't much time. The U.S. Army will be here soon, then I can't help you."

"The *Army?* Why—?"

"Hurry, give me an email address of someone who'll recognize your face."

"Why should we worry about the Army—?"

"We don't have time! I need to send this email before the Army shows up, trust me. Email address, please!"

Sheila gave Lourdes the email address of her sister Lizzy in Darwin. Lourdes sent the two pictures, along with a message—

Sheila is in Wheat City, Kansas, USA. She just walked out of a UFO.

"Ahem!"

Lourdes had just finished sending the email when the African woman cleared her throat, and looked pointedly at Sheila. "*Less Zlaren las Exexas necesarok,*" the African said.

Sheila said, "Right. We've been asked to give Earth's people a message: Zlar needs women."

Lourdes said, "Yeah? 'Zlar needs women' for *what?*"

That's when Lourdes heard Zlarian speech coming from the spaceship.

****

With smartphone still in hand, Lourdes looked up to see what was happening.

Two ray-gun-carrying Zlarian males had appeared at the top of the ramp, with a third Zlarian between them.

From the watermelon-wide hips, Lourdes figured out that the middle Zlarian was female.

The female was carrying something in one hand, and she was wearing a translator-necklace.

The two Zlarian males lifted up the female, carried her down the ramp, and set her on the ground. The object in her hand was immediately put to use as a forked, two-handed cane. The males spoke to her briefly, then they walked back up the ramp.

The female didn't look like the Zlarian males, and not only because of her shape. Her dove-gray skin was covered with navy-blue blotches. Also, it immediately became clear that she *needed* her two-handed cane, in order to walk.

Meanwhile, the spaceship's mango-colored ramp-door lifted up, and the door-covering slid back to cover the ramp-door.

Seeing that, Lourdes rushed up to the Zlarian female, in order to snap her photo with the smartphone.

Lourdes looked over her shoulder at Sheila. "Who is she?" Lourdes asked.

"She was our midwife. Humans can't pronounce her name."

The spaceship rose, in complete silence, then moved south.

Lourdes asked Sheila, "What's wrong—"

****

"—with her?" Lourdes asked.

Lourdes heard running footsteps approach, then Egbert showed up. "Motherfuck, I missed the spaceship," he said, with eyes on the sky.

Then he looked at Lourdes. "Why didn't you wait for me to protect you? Whoa, that is one sick alien."

"A *bloke!*" Sheila exclaimed.

Sheila started walking toward Egbert, hips swinging. "I want a baby with you, mister man! Give me a baby!"

Lourdes couldn't understand the other naked women's words, but clearly they were saying the same thing as Sheila.

Fifteen or twenty shapely, instantly horny, and naked women were sashaying toward Egbert.

Lourdes called out, "Sheila, what's wrong with the female alien?"

"I'll tell you later," Sheila replied, "after I get up the duff."

"Why did they put her off the ship? Is this punishment? Exile? Is she *infectious?*"

"That's not important," Sheila said. "Getting preggers, that's what's important now."

"Dammit, *the Army is coming!*"

"No worries, mate," Sheila replied.

Now Lourdes looked over at her "protector." She yelled, "Egbert, the flying saucer has messed up these women's minds. I need you to leave now."

"*Right now?* Can't I—"

"It's important. I don't have time to explain." *Fuck, I miss being able to just give him a direct order and be done with something.*

"What a day. First I miss seeing a spaceship, and now I'm walking away from hot, naked pussy."

But Egbert was true to his word. A minute later, he was gone—to the disappointment of all the naked women.

Then Sheila took a breath. "That was strange. I don't know what came over me, I'm not that kind of—"

"Later. Tell me about this Zlarian female."

"Zlarian women all have a disease. Zlarian men don't catch it; and lucky for us, *we* don't catch it. So we Earth women get turned into surrogate mums."

Lourdes was stunned. *This explains why the Zlarians are kidnapping fertile Earth women. This also means that the Zlarians will refuse to stop.*

Lourdes asked, "What causes this disease? A virus? Bacteria? Is it genetic? How close are the Zlarians to a cure?"

****

Lourdes never got an answer to those questions. A First Lieutenant and some soldiers showed up then—driving an old farm truck. *What the fuck?*

(Lourdes then sleuthed out that the spaceship, while it had paused overhead, had hit Fort Carver with a directional electromagnetic pulse. *Everything* electronic got fried.)

As soon as the first soldier stepped out of the truck, Sheila got stuck again on "I want your baby."

Soon the naked women, and the sick alien female, all got put in the farm truck to be driven away. Blah-blah-blah, "national security," the First Louie explained to Lourdes.

Sure, buddy, maybe somebody did indeed give you orders that invoked national security. Or maybe you just want to stick your dick into all those women who've turned into pregnancy-nymphos again. I know how sexual temptation can corrupt an Army officer.

As soon as the Army left with its prisoners, Lourdes emailed Sheila's sister in Darwin a second time, attaching a photo of the sick alien female. Along with the picture, Lourdes wrote out everything she'd seen and heard this day.

Lourdes made sure to quote Sheila saying, "Zlar needs women."

Lourdes might well get Gitmo'd for this, but Lizzy in Darwin deserved to know what had happened to her sister.

Then Lourdes thought about the sick alien woman. Lourdes said aloud, "It would be lots better for Earth and Zlar both, if somebody found a cure for that disease. Hm, if she's in Army custody, maybe the Army will find a cure?"

Lourdes then recalled her impressions of Doctor Renfield.

"Not gonna happen," she sighed. "Not by Renfield."

Chapter 3
At The Pizza Store

Saturday, April 13, 2:14 p.m.

Pizza King Delivery Store, Wheat City

Two blocks from Kanssouri University

Between two and five in the afternoon, this is the slowest time of the day in any restaurant. At the moment, only one driver was out, and that was with only one delivery order. Bob (the store manager) and Dave (the other driver) were prepping for the dinner rush.

That's when the babe and the rich-dressed frat guy walked in. The hottie was wearing a very wide black hat.

The frat guy looked around, then looked at Dave. "Jeez, why are you working on a Saturday afternoon? That's when the best sports is on TV."

Dave shrugged.

"Quiet, Willy," the babe said. "I need to talk to the nice man."

Meanwhile, Bob had *hurried* over to the counter, and not just because his position required it. "Hello, may I *help* you?"

The girl's long hair was an ordinary brunette color. But that was the only thing ordinary about her. She had a beautiful face, enormous tits, and Bob was sure her blue eyes actually glowed in the dark. *What a hottie!*

The coed gave the manager a warm smile. "Hi, there"—she glanced at his nametag—"Bob, I want to order pizzas for a party tonight, and I have a *big* favor to ask."

Bob smiled back. "What's the favor?"

The busty babe crossed her arms under her big tits, then leaned on the counter. Undoubtedly she was unaware that Bob was getting a great view of her cleavage.

"First," the girl said, "can you please tell me when Jerry Green comes in to work tonight?"

Bob said, "He comes in at five o'clock."

She said, "I have six pizzas to order for later today, I want them to come out of the oven just as Jerry walks in the door, and I want *him* to deliver them to my sorority."

Bob shook his head. "Sorry, but Pizza King policy is that no certain driver gets a certain order. This way, your pizza is hot—"

Now she was looking at him like a blue-eyed puppy. "*Please*, pretty please with a cherry on top? I'd *really* like it if you could do me this favor."

"Okay," Bob said. "Just this once."

Bob knew that the district manager would clean his clock if word got back to him about this. But on the other hand, Pizza King's district manager wasn't oh-my-god *fuckable* like this girl was.

After that, it was just a matter of ordering the six pizzas and the babe paying for them.

As Bob was handing "C.H." her change back, she once again smiled at him. She summarized the order: "Delivery time 5:15, and *Jerry Green* will delivery all six pizzas. You're so sweet, Bob."

As soon as she and Frat Boy left, Dave looked over from where he was folding pizza boxes. "She *played* you, Bob. The way you had your tongue hanging out, she could have asked for all the money in the register."

Bob laughed. "No lie. But *damn*—a girl who looks like that, asks for Jerry *by name*? He is one lucky sonuvabitch."

Chapter 4
News About The Hypno-Talker

Meanwhile, across town

Saturday, 2:14 p.m.

1408 Ewen Drive, Wheat City

Jerry Green sat down at his computer and web-surfed. Eventually he came to FreeAndUncontrolled, the piracy-discussion website. Jerry started reading its threads.

Minutes later, curious Jerry clicked on the thread "DIY HYPNO-TALKER—real deal or fake?" He started reading.

Two minutes later, an amazed Jerry murmured, "Whoa!"

Jerry downloaded the ZIP file that the thread had linked to, unpacked the ZIP file, and started reading documentation.

" 'Whoa' squared," Jerry murmured a half-hour later.

Jerry decided he wanted one of those hypno-talkers for himself. He didn't have the tools to build one, but he knew who did—

Al Bayer, who'd started a company, "Computer Wizard On Wheels." Al's company did on-site computer repair, fixing both hardware and software.

For sure, Al would have a chip-burner.

Jerry tried calling Al on his cel phone, but the call went to voicemail. Which meant one of two things—

Al was on site somewhere, restoring the usefulness of some computer-user's machine; *or*—

With this being Saturday afternoon, Al maybe was playing poker. If so, Jerry laughed, Al was probably losing.

Chapter 5
Urine Trouble

Saturday, 5:12 p.m.

Jerry couldn't find parking closer than a block away from the Alpha Sigma Sigma sorority house; but he'd long ago learned this was normal for Greek Row on a Saturday night.

When Jerry stepped out of his car with two bulging pizza bags, music was blasting from behind the sorority house. Even a block away, the music was bass-thumping and loud.

> *I like to say it,*
> *"I'm such a good girl,"*
> *But put me with you,*
> *You make my toes curl!*
>
> *Don't get me drunk, just*
> *Help get me undressed.*
> *Maiden's on fire now,*
> *Got brand-new unrest.*
>
> *This maiden needs it,*
> *This maiden needs you.*
> *You're the man I choose,*
> *I will bleed with you.*
>
> *Please kiss on me now,*
> *Not like your sister.*
> *Then I'll kiss you back,*
> *Right on your mister.*
>
> *I crave it right now,*
> *First penetration.*
> *Like what you see, my*
> *Deforestation?*

This maiden needs it,
This maiden needs <u>you</u>.
You're the man I choose,
I will bleed with you.

As Jerry was walking around the sorority house to get to the backyard, he saw that a yellow garden hose was attached to a faucet on the side of the building. The garden hose ran off into the backyard.

Jerry didn't give that yellow garden hose much thought.

As soon as Jerry and his pizza bags walked into the backyard, two frat boys pointed to him and yelled something.

The music went silent. Jerry heard a young woman say, "Ohmigod, a year ago I was getting crowned Prom Queen, and now I get to drink beer and talk to studly guys. Life is *soo* good."

Jerry frowned. He hadn't been able to get a girl to go with him to his own Prom. It had become a joke among the girls of his school: *If you want to stunt your social status, take Jerry to the Prom.*

Jerry shook his head to clear the memory. Back in the present—

Cindy was dressed in black shorts and a yellow plunging-neckline t-shirt, and was wearing cork wedges. She and a frat boy were standing almost under a big tree.

Cindy had Jerry give the pizzas to the frat boy (who was named Willy). Willy walked away, handed the pizzas to another frat boy, then returned to Cindy's side.

Meanwhile, Jerry was looking at Cindy, hoping for a tip.

Cindy said, "Oh! I forgot about tipping you, and I locked my purse in my trunk. But I know something that's just as good."

Jerry thought, *Like what? Asking your boyfriend Willy to tip me? Talk about mixed feelings on my part!*

But instead, Cindy moved to stand near the trunk of the tree, and put her left arm out. She said, "Here, stand next to me and let Delilah take our picture."

"*Really?* Oh, wow," Jerry said.

Jerry put his empty pizza bags down, walked over to where Cindy had suggested, and moved to face a girl with thick black hair, who was holding a digital camera.

That's when Willy strolled about ten feet away. Jerry didn't care why.

For some reason, frat boys and sorority girls began to gather, encircling Cindy and Jerry. A girl moved to stand next to Delilah the photographer; the newcomer had green eyes and a helmet of curly brunette hair that hid her ears.

Delilah raised her digital camera to being in front of her face, then immediately she brought it back down. "You are out of the focus," Delilah said to Jerry. She spoke with a slight accent. "Forward come about one foot."

He did so, and Delilah brought her camera back up.

Delilah said, "I now down count. Four . . . three . . ."

"At "two," Cindy let go of Jerry's hand, then darted toward Willy. Jerry stared at her retreating back, confused.

"One . . . *zero!*"

Jerry heard a *kl-klank* noise overhead. His brain was just starting to wonder what the sound might be, when—

He was doused in yellow liquid, and everyone burst out howling with laughter.

He wiped the liquid out of his eyes, where it was running down from his hair. Then his nose told him the truth: He reeked of cat pee.

Meanwhile the circle of young men and women were still laughing at him.

He finally thought to look up. He was standing under a tree limb, on top of which a galvanized-iron bucket lay sideways. Cat piss dripped down from the lip of the bucket.

A woman's voice said, "Guys, he stinks. He needs to be cleaned up."

"Not a problem, Cindy," a male voice said behind him.

Jerry felt cold water spray the back of his body.

He whirled around. A frat boy was holding a green garden hose with a sprayer attachment at the end. The guy was smirking.

The guy said, "Your face needs cleaning." Then he started spraying Jerry in the face.

This made the crowd laugh anew.

Jerry threw his arms in front of his face, and spun around to the front again, facing Delilah the photographer—

Only to get blasted with water again. It turned out that Willy was holding the yellow garden hose, with a sprayer attachment at the end.

"Sprayers off, guys," Cindy said. By now, Jerry was getting water-blasted in stereo.

"Aw, Cindy, I can still smell him," Willy said.

"Oh, well," Cindy said with exaggerated disappointment. "I guess *we'll* just have to live with it."

The water-spraying stopped. Cindy walked up close (but not too close) to Jerry. The laughter of the crowd got quieter.

Cindy said, "Jerry Green, the way you asked me for a date yesterday was totally loser-pathetic. There are seventh-grade boys right here in Wheat City with more social skill than you've got. Sheesh, you're a nerd."

Jerry dripped, and shivered, and said nothing.

"I mean, you didn't even *ask* if I had a boyfriend. Isn't that Step One in learning how to ask a girl out?"

Jerry said nothing.

"And even if that spaceship landed *here* and the Martians grabbed Willy *right now*, I wouldn't go out with you."

Jerry said nothing.

"I'll bet you still live at home with your parents."

Jerry still didn't speak, but he frowned. Jerry's father had "gone out to get cigarettes" when Jerry was in diapers, and had never returned. But yes, Jerry lived with his mother.

Cindy continued: "I am totally out of your league. Especially when you don't know the first thing about asking a girl out."

Jerry broke silence: "It's not a crime to ask a girl out. It's not a crime to ask a pretty girl out. You could've just said no."

"A crime? Hell, *yeah,* it's a crime!" Willy said. "When a *loser* asks her out."

"No, *this* is a crime," Jerry said, jerking a stinky thumb toward the bucket. "As in handcuffs, Miranda rights, and 'don't drop the soap.'"

This made Cindy laugh. "Really? Where are your witnesses, loser? Not one person here will ever see the back seat of a police car."

A muscular young man walked up to Jerry, carrying the two pizza bags. "You're on the clock, loser boy, and I'll bet your boss is wondering about you. Leave now."

A cold, wet, and angry Jerry Green walked out of the sorority house's backyard, as frat boys and sorority girls jeered him.

****

The Pizza King store had gone dead silent as soon as Jerry had walked in.

Then Bob broke the silence: "What the hell happened to you?"

Jerry told him.

Bob sighed, then said, "Go home. You're off the clock, as of now."

"What, you're *firing* me?"

Bob sighed again. "Of course not. But you're taken only one run, that order was prepaid, so you don't owe Pizza King any money tonight. So—"

"But, *Bob*—"

"Jerry, I'm sorry, but right now you're *disgusting*. I can't let you get anywhere close to customers. Go home, so you can get your clothes clean."

When Jerry got into his car to go home, he was hit hard by the stench. The back of the driver's seat smelled like cat piss.

Saturday night was Jerry's best-tipping night. But *this* Saturday night? Total suck! Zero tips, earning less than an hour in wages, Jerry might have to go buy new pants, socks, and shoes, when he had no money to spare—

Not to mention, today being played for a fool, being publicly humiliated, and getting laughed at.

Curse Cindy, Jerry thought as he smacked the steering wheel.

Curse Willy.

Curse all those pretty Greeks with their better-than-thou attitudes.

I want payback!

Chapter 6
Jerry Talks To Al

Saturday evening

"So how did you do?" Jerry Green asked over the phone. "With your poker?"

"Not too bad," Al replied.

Jerry knew this meant *I went in the hole, but it's not a disaster yet.* However, Jerry kept his thoughts to himself.

"So what can I do you for?" Al asked. "Not to rush you, but the wife and I were about to head out to a restaurant."

Translation: *My wife is pissed, and I'm trying to smooth things over. So don't take too long, because that'll piss her off more.*

Jerry said, "Check your email. There's a widget I'll pay you to make for me."

Jerry had sent the email that afternoon, because he'd wanted the hypno-talker that afternoon. Now after his urine-drenched humiliation, Jerry *really* wanted the hypno-talker.

Seconds later, Jerry heard, "Sure enough. Let me call you back in a few minutes, when I can give you an estimate—"

Jerry heard a woman say over the phone, "Albert Michael Bayer!"

"—or maybe I'll have to call you in the morning," an embarrassed Al said.

Al then murmured into the phone, "I went in the hole $157 today. The wife is pissed."

****

Sunday morning

Al had just called Jerry on his smartphone.

Al asked, "Can you tell me what this thing is for? Your email didn't say."

Jerry said, "How about I tell you later?"—while hoping that "later" would never come. "Anyway, how much?"

"Two hundred and fifty. Have it done by Wednesday."

Then Jerry got a fiendish idea. He said, "Let's talk about a volume discount. What's your price for five of 'em? How much for me to buy ten?"

Chapter 7
Raising The Money

The deal that Jerry wound up making with Al was that the *second* hypno-talker would cost Jerry only a hundred bucks. Ditto the third one, the fourth one, and the eighty-seventh one. But the *first* one would set Jerry back $250, and Al wouldn't budge from that price.

So Jerry needed to get his hands on $250, which he absolutely did not, no way in hell, have in cash.

****

Jerry punched in the phone number for Steve Prince, who was not only Jerry's mom's sister's husband, but who also was the richest of Jerry's relatives. Uncle Steve owned a fleet of garbage trucks.

"Prince residence," Jerry heard on his smartphone.

"Hi, Uncle Steve. I have a favor to ask."

Jerry heard a sigh over the phone. "I'm fine, Jerry. Your Aunt Naomi is fine, and your Cousin Carrietta is fine. Snowstorm's ringworm is getting better. *How much do you need?*"

"Jeez, Uncle Steve, just because—I haven't mentioned money at all."

"So I can tell you goodbye now, and hand the phone to your aunt?"

"No! Okay, yeah, I'm calling to ask you for money."

"How much?"

"Uncle Steve, the other day an entire sorority humiliated me. I'm on stupid *YouTube*, and—"

"I'm guessing: a lot of money. How much?"

"Two-fifty."

"That's gonna be hard—Snowstorm's vet-bill kicked us in the teeth. Why do you need it? Car repair?"

"No, the car's limping along."

"Wait, you said something about a sorority. Are you in legal trouble? Are you calling from jail?"

"Duh, check your caller ID."

Two seconds later, Uncle Steve said, "Fine, you're calling from your smartphone. Are you being sued? Is the money is to pay some lawyer?"

"No."

"Then what's the money for? You're not telling me squat."

"Uncle Steve, please don't ask me that."

Silence.

More silence.

Jerry said, "Whatever you think it's for, it's not that."

"It's drugs, isn't it? You've gotten hooked on drugs."

"*What?* No, uncle, I could never do stuff like that!"

"There was a girl in my high school. A good Christian girl, goody-two-shoes. But in college she got into shit. I don't know the details, but I know she flunked out of college and had to go into rehab."

"Uncle Steve, I'm not—"

"So don't tell me that this couldn't happen to you. For all I know, it already has."

"I am not into drugs. I. Am. Not."

Silence.

Uncle Steve said, "I'm sorry, but no money from me. We can't afford it now, but I'd send it if you'd given me a good reason. To put it mildly, this hasn't happened."

****

Jerry walked up and down the hallway of Bennett Hall, which was the biggest Kanssouri University men's dorm. Jerry knocked on doors and repeatedly asked—

"Hey, you want to buy a twenty-inch LCD TV and a Nintendo Wii? I need only $250 for them."

Everyone either didn't have the interest or didn't have the money.

****

Bubba's Friendly Pawn
Wheat City

"Hold on," Jerry said, as he pulled old receipts out of his front pocket. "I've got all the documentation right here."

The balding guy behind the counter picked up the receipts and glanced at them.

In a bored voice, he said, "For the TV and the Nintendo, I'll give you a hundred bucks if you sell 'em to me—"

"Are you *kidding* me? This is a high-def TV in perfect condition! It has a great picture. And with it is a *Wii*."

The pawn-shop man looked unimpressed. "It's one-fifty if you take out a loan."

"Um, how much does the loan cost?"

"Four percent interest a month. So six bucks a month. You go ninety days without paying, they go up for sale."

Minutes later, Jerry walked out to his car, $150 "richer" but without the TV and Wii he'd carried in. *At least I have some hope of getting my stuff back.*

Driving back to his house, Jerry sighed. He had skipped all the pawnshops near the Kanssouri University campus, to do business with a pawnshop in the affluent part of Wheat City. *But boy, was I wrong about getting a good offer for my stuff.*

****

The next morning
Pizza King Delivery Store

"I got most of the cat pee out," Jerry said. "Still, it's got an odor. Hope it didn't cost the store much."

Jerry handed over to Bob the store manager, Jerry's Pizza King shirt. That shirt was given neatly folded, with the nametag on top. Bob looked at the shirt like it were a purple poodle.

"I'm confused," Bob said. "What's going on?"

"I have to quit," Jerry said.

Bob stared. "Because of the prank?"

"Because I had to bicycle here to give you the shirt, and I'll have to bicycle here to pick up my paycheck."

Bob said, "That sucks. First the cat-piss prank, then your car craps out."

Jerry didn't tell Bob that the car hadn't died, Jerry had sold it.

Jerry had already biked to the bank and deposited the cash he'd received from his pawn loans and the sale of his car. Tomorrow, after the deposit was credited to his bank account, he'd Paypal Al, so Al could get started building Jerry's hypno-talker.

Then sometime after that, Jerry would start collecting payback from the people who had humiliated him.

Chapter 8
Cindy Gets A Phone Call

Wednesday afternoon
Alpha Sigma Sigma sorority house

Cindy Hope's smartphone rang. She recognized neither the phone number nor the area code.

She snarled into the phone, "Go call some other sucker, creep-ass!"

An old man's voice said angrily, "Do you know who you're talking to?"

"Yeah, a goddamn telemarketer. Goodbye!"

Cindy ended the call, but her phone immediately rang again. It was that same number, calling back.

She considered letting it ring. But instead, she answered with "Hey shithead, I already—"

"This is your Uncle Albert," the old man said.

By which he meant *Albert Hope, Miami wheeler-dealer*. His nickname behind his back was "Abandon Hope," because he so often forced his opponents to accept outrageously unfair deals. Uncle Albert was *loaded*.

"Oh, um, *hi,* Uncle Albert," Cindy now said meekly. "Sorry about the, um, misunderstanding. I thought—"

"Girl, I don't have time for chit-chat," the old man said. "I'm taking my yacht out on a cruise, tomorrow at sunset. I'm inviting you to be on that yacht when it leaves. If you're smart, you'll be there."

Cindy's first thought was *Hold on, you expect me to catch a puddle-jumper flight from Wheat City to Kansas City, then fly from Kansas City to Miami in the middle of the week, in the middle of the semester, for a <u>yacht cruise</u>?*

But Cindy already had shot off her mouth once to Uncle Albert, and wound up sounding stupid. Cindy *hated* sounding stupid.

So instead, Cindy calmly asked, "Why would I be smart if I went on your yacht cruise?"

"Because I'm gonna die soon. Albertine is dead"—by drug overdose, back in the Seventies—"Albert, Jr. is dead"—drunk as a sailor, he'd crashed his DeLorean against a tree in 1982—"Albert Benjamin is dead"—by AIDS—"Albert Charles is dead"—by suicide—"and no fucking way will there be another Mrs. Hope. So who the hell do I leave all my goodies to?"

"I'm sorry, uncle, I don't get it. What does your kids being dead got to do with a yacht cruise?"

"Girl, are you stupid or something?" the old man said. "I need to decide who to put in my will. So I'm inviting all my relatives, except for the pinheads, to ride on my yacht tomorrow. We'll go out to sea, no distractions, and you talk to me and try and make me like you. When we get back to Miami, I make out my will."

"What happens if I—"

"If you're not on the yacht, you're not in the will. The Golden Rule applies here."

Meaning *I have the gold, so I make the rule.*

Cindy said, "Can I bring a guest?"

"No problem. But just remember, if *he or she* pisses me off, *you* get cut out of the will."

Cindy told Uncle Albert that she was "thrilled" to spend time with him (which he didn't believe for a second), then it was just a matter of getting the where-and-when details.

As soon as Cindy hung up with Uncle Albert, she called Willy. "Pack a suitcase," she told him, "you and me are flying to Miami. As soon as we can get there."

Willy took the news calmly: "Are you fucking *nuts?*"

Cindy wound up promising to pay for Willy's round-trip airplane tickets, plus she promised to give Willy a bunch of blowjobs. Mentally she shrugged.

Chapter 9
Jerry Gets The Ball Rolling

The waiting was hell.

Jerry had had all the money he needed by Sunday evening. But now without a car, he couldn't pay Al in person. Which meant that Jerry had to deposit the cash into his checking account, wait for the deposit to be credited, then send Al the money electronically.

So Al didn't receive the money till Tuesday morning.

But Al had a day job. Al didn't buy the parts and start work on the hypno-talker till Tuesday night, and it wasn't till Wednesday night that Al brought the hypno-talker to Jerry's house.

Then for Jerry, the hours *crawled* until Friday afternoon, when it was time for Jerry's next English 201 class with Cindy.

Jerry walked into class with earplugs and a carefully written script in his shirt pocket; his hypno-talker was in his bookbag. Either before class or after class, whenever the opportunity presented itself, Cindy was going to get whammied!

Unfortunately for Jerry's master plan of vengeance, Cindy didn't come to class Friday.

Fuck!

****

During English class and after class, Jerry was keyed up, but had no good way to vent. He had no idea what to do next.

Now classes were over till Monday, which should have meant that he would be jumping on his bike and zooming home. But the sky was black with storm clouds, he saw lightning and heard thunder bearing down on him from the north, and so Jerry decided to wait the storm out.

Jerry pedaled hard to the Student Union building. As he was chaining his bike up, it started to rain. Just as he stepped inside the building, it started to rain *hard*. Within a minute, lightning flashed and thunder boomed right outside the building.

Jerry was stuck inside the building for a while, so he decided to go through the hot-food line and fill his stomach.

He was two steps away from the food-serving line when bright-pink color caught his eye. He turned his head and saw two girls who were wearing pink Alpha Sigma Sigma t-shirts.

One girl was a busty blonde, and the other was Delilah, the girl who had photographed his humiliation.

Eating can wait, Jerry thought. *Let's take some vengeance.*

By the food-serving line were dozens of tables. Most tables were empty. Some tables had people eating, some tables had one person reading or studying (while occasionally munching on food), and one table had four guys playing a table-top role-playing game. Delilah and the blonde were walking among all those tables.

Don't let those girls see you!

While following Delilah and the blonde from a distance, Jerry walked past the role-players' table. Jerry heard a geeky-looking guy say sarcastically, "*You bet* it's something to tell my grandchildren. I got to see a flying saucer *leave*."

Jerry walked up close to the two sorority girls, and—

The storm made the lights flicker. The blonde stopped walking, and quickly looked around. She looked right at Jerry for an instant, but her gaze didn't stay on him.

Delilah and the blonde now took seats at a table within the food court. That was a problem. There was nothing for

Jerry to hide behind now. He couldn't walk up to the table without Delilah or the blonde seeing him.

I'll just have to brazen it out then, Jerry thought.

He put his bookbag on a table, and opened it. By now he could hear both girls talking. Black-haired Delilah now was sitting with her back to him. Just as she'd done at the lawn party, Delilah now spoke with an accent.

By now, Jerry could see the blonde's face clearly (though Jerry pretended to take no special interest in that face). Oddly, even though she certainly had to have attended Saturday's lawn party, Jerry didn't recognize her. And hers was a face he would have remembered: She had blonde hair, pale blue eyes, a pretty face, a golden tanning-bed tan, and enormous tits.

The blonde quit looking at Delilah for a moment, to idly look around the room. Again she looked straight at Jerry, and his heart almost stopped. But again she showed no sign of recognition, and then her gaze moved on. Maybe she didn't recognize him without his Pizza King hat and shirt?

B-BOOM! said the sky above. All the lights in the Student Union building went out (except for the red EXIT lights).

Which meant, now it was time for vengeance against Alpha Sigma Sigma Sorority.

Jerry picked up the hypno-talker and, by feel, pressed the Record button.

"You trust me completely," he recorded. "It's good to answer my question with the complete truth. You believe what I say, and you'll do whatever I tell you to do."

Then Jerry put the earplugs in his ears, picked up the hypno-talker, found the Playback button with his thumb, and stood up. *It's time, bitches.*

By the dim light of the dining-room skylights, Jerry started sneaking up on the two sorority girls (who were still talking in the near-darkness).

****

Delilah Monescu's smile was condescending. "Sweetie, if you want to help the not-blessed, organize a black-tie charity event. There is no need to *date* the not-blessed."

Bethany Brown glared at Delilah. "Egbert will be rich one day, I will be married to him, and I will be happy."

The lights went out. Delilah shrugged. She couldn't *see* well, but she could still *talk.*

Delilah laughed scornfully. "Bethany, I am come from a heroic prince of Wallachia. I will have the rich husband too, but he also will be handsome and brave. Your geek is neither one."

"Egbert *intended* to protect that woman from the spaceship."

"Really, dear? As I recall, when he sawed the spacecraft, he ran *into the restaurant.* He not comed out till the flying saucer was *gone,* did you not tell me?"

Bethany's voice was angry: "Delilah, you are twisting—"

Then Delilah realized that first, the lights were back on; and second, there was a guy standing by her table, pulling earplugs out of his ears.

Then Delilah gasped, as she recognized him. "Hey, you are the geek on whom we poured—"

"Perhaps I'm that guy, or perhaps I just look like that guy. Believe that I'm not him unless I tell you otherwise."

Delilah said, "Yes, now I look, I see many little differences between you and the pizza boy."

"What do *you* think?" the guy asked Bethany. "Do you think I look like the pizza man?"

"How would *I* know?" Bethany said. "I was already mad at them because they didn't want Egbert at the party. When Cindy got everyone planning to mess with the pizza guy, I *left.*"

The guy said, "Hold on, you didn't help plan dumping cat piss on the pizza guy, you didn't help set it up, and you didn't watch it happen, right?"

Bethany nodded.

The guy said to Delilah, "But *you* not only were in the thick of things, you took photos of the pizza man and put them on the web."

Delilah shrugged. "So what? He was the loser nerd."

****

Jerry asked the two girls where Cindy was. Neither girl knew where, beyond "on a yacht."

Jerry next looked at the girl sitting with Delilah. "You, the blonde, what's your name?"

"Mabel Brown, but here everyone calls me Bethany. That's what I prefer."

Jerry looked at Bethany and felt torn between desires. This girl was blameless—but she was also *hot*. He thought, *Those are excellent tits.*

But virtue edged out vice. Jerry said to her, "I need to talk to Delilah alone. Now is an excellent time for you to go talk to your boyfriend, or to wait outside his classroom."

Bethany stood up then, and pulled her purse onto her shoulder. Jerry expected her next to walk out of the Student Union—without an umbrella, poor girl. But instead, Bethany walked across the room to the role-players' table. She walked behind the geeky guy and reached down to caress his chest, two-handed.

Jerry stared. *How on earth did a guy who looks like that, score a babe who looks like her?*

****

After Jerry watched Bethany and the role-player geek, he snapped his thoughts back to the task of revenge. "Stay here," he told Delilah, "I have to go do something. Ignore everyone till I come back."

Jerry stood up and picked up his hypno-talker. He had to find someplace where he could be alone—just him, his prewritten script, and the hypno-talker's Record button.

Five minutes later, Jerry walked back to Delilah's table with the new message recorded on his hypno-talker. Delilah was such a lucky girl, she would be the first Alpha Sigma Sigma sorority girl to hear Jerry's script.

As earplugged Jerry sat down, facing Delilah, Jerry was smiling. A shark would worry, seeing that smile.

Jerry said to Delilah, "Just so you know, I'm the pizza guy who got the cat piss poured on him."

As soon as Jerry quit speaking, he mashed down on the hypno-talker's orange button.

Delilah's face went blank, and she started to chant along with the ultrasonic words.

A minute later, Jerry stopped pressing the orange button, then he reached up to pull the earplugs out of his ears.

The first thing that Jerry heard clearly was Delilah saying, "I am so much sorry for what I doed. How can I to you make up it?"

Chapter 10
Delilah Obeys Her Programming

A few hours later

1408 Ewen Drive, Wheat City

By the time that Jerry had left the Student Union, the thunderstorm had blown through. Jerry had bicycled home without a problem (except for a wet bicycle seat and slippery bike pedals).

Now Jerry was in his bedroom, listening to music—and waiting. That's when his mom Julianne knocked on his door, waited two seconds, then opened the door without invitation.

When Julianne saw Jerry, she frowned. "A girl is here to see you. Her name is *Delilah*."

Jerry said, "Relax, Mom, she isn't *that* Delilah." Jerry's mom was a bit of a Bible-thumper.

"Are you going on a date?" Julianne asked. After all, it was Friday evening.

"Nuh-uh, no date." Then Jerry said, "Delilah and I will probably be spending a lot of time in the basement—"

"No you will not, young man! I will not abide my son sinning with a girl under my—"

Jerry said, "*Mother dearest,* when I spend time with a girl in the basement, that's just harmless fun. *Mother dearest,* you don't need to go downstairs to investigate."

Julianne's face got robotic. "Understood," she said.

Then her normal face and normal tone of voice returned. "Well, you two kids have fun doing wholesome and Bible-approved activities down in the basement."

Jerry smiled. "Mom, the King James Bible even has a word for what Delilah and I are gonna be doing."

****

Jerry opened the front door. "Yes Delilah, you wanted to see me?"

Delilah said, "Yes, I doed thinking, and I—"

Then a special part of her programming kicked in, now that she was at his house. "Oh my," she breathed. "I never realized how much *manly* you are. I *want* you."

Jerry opened the door wider. "Please come in. I want to show you something in the basement."

Delilah bit her lip. "I am sure that I want it to see."

****

Once Jerry and Delilah were in his basement, he pretended innocence. "What did you want to talk to me about?" he asked.

"I thinked I want to say sorry to you," Delilah said. She opened her purse and took out a thick wad of bills. "I want to give to you money, as the way of I make the apology."

He tested her: "You haven't asked your parents for this money, have you?"

Her face went blank and she replied woodenly, "I not asked my parents for this money. I not committed a crime to get this money. This money is for my own use, and I sacrifice by giving to you this money."

"Wow, how much is here?" he asked with genuine curiosity. He'd programmed her with a hundred-dollar minimum.

"I bringed two hundred forty-seven dollars," she replied.

"And gifting me with $247 is your idea of how to make amends?"

Her voice got wooden again. "I give you this money, this is entirely my own idea."

Then her voice got husky. "But you are so much sexy, I think of another way to apologize."

Delilah pulled her pink Alpha Sigma Sigma t-shirt up and off, cast it aside, then reached back to unsnap her bra.

****

Whoever invented the hypno-talker, Jerry wanted to shake his hand. Delilah sucked Jerry's cock like he were a rock star—and jeez, her pussy was *wet!*

Delilah also did this *Ha!-Ha!-Ha!-Ha!* thing when she was being fucked close to orgasm, which Jerry had never heard of before.

****

After the sex, Delilah stretched, then started getting dressed.

Jerry said, "Don't you want to know why I brought you down here?"

"Not only so I could leap on your bones?" Delilah said with a smile.

"Not only," Jerry said, laughing.

He reached behind the basement couch and, with a flourish, revealed his blue device. "Ta-da!"

Delilah shrugged. "That is not the new. That is the tablet computer that you holded when you sat down with me and Bethany."

"But that's the big news, this *isn't* a tablet. It's my hypno-talker. I can use it to program people without them realizing."

"It really works?" Delilah asked. She was blocked from realizing that such a device might already have been used on Delilah herself.

Jerry said, "Yeah, I've tested it on my mom." *And on you, and on Bethany.*

Delilah said, "I have the idea." Jerry knew that Bethany would swear up and down that it was her own idea, what she was about to say.

Delilah continued, "Please you tell me how to buy this—"

"Why?"

"—then I use it to make other Alpha Sigma Sigma girls to know that you are the sexy, and to hypnotize them to make to you the apology."

Jerry thrust his hypno-talker into Delilah's hands, as a "gift." He said, "What a great idea! But Cindy has to be the first girl you use this on."

Delilah shook her head. "Cindy still not is in the Wheat City. Cindy is somewhere on the yacht."

"Just don't use that on Bethany Brown," Jerry said.

"Oh no, that is wrong," Delilah said. She didn't know *why* it was wrong to use the hypno-talker on Bethany; Delilah just was sure that it was.

"Wow," Jerry said, "you offering to do this for me is such a complete surprise." *Not!* Jerry asked Delilah for her email address, and scribbled it on a piece of paper. "I'm going to email you the user manual —before you whammy anyone, read it. And buy some earplugs."

"Earplugs, you mean like—I am sorry, I forget what I about was talking," Delilah said. Jerry had erased from Delilah's memory that Jerry had been wearing earplugs for some of the time he'd talked to Delilah in the Student Union.

Then Delilah said, "I have the another idea."

Jerry pretended ignorance: "What idea?"

"I will use this, Ronaldo to hypnotize. He at the party was, and he at you laughed. I will use this and make him for all days imp—impo—his penis will not come up."

"Why would you do that?"

"So I not do be required to give to him the blowjob anymore."

"You really hate blowjobs? Because a half-hour ago—"

Delilah smiled at him, and then knelt down in front of him. "I not hate for *you* the blowjobs. You are the sexy."

Delilah gave Jerry one-and-a-half blowjobs, then he fucked her again. Her pussy still got wet, hooray.

Chapter 11
Jerry Wrestles With His Conscience

Two minutes after Delilah drove away, Jerry was handing two hundred dollars in cash to his mother.

"What's this for?" Julianne asked.

"I need you to Paypal two hundred dollars to this email address"—Jerry handed her a slip of paper—"then deposit this cash into your checking account to make up for it."

"Fine, I'll do it, but what's going on?"

Jerry was sorely tempted to use the *Mother Dearest* code phrase on his mom, so she'd stop asking embarrassing questions.

But then Jerry realized, *If I do that enough times, she won't be my mom anymore. Which would suck, because I'm already without a father.*

So Jerry related to his mom the hard way: "The Paypal thing is nothing you need to worry about."

Julianne looked hard at him. "Something is troubling you. Give it to Jesus, whatever it is."

"Nothing is troubling me, Mom. Really." *Well, except that what I've done to Delilah—hypnoing her to give me sex and money—sort of feels like rape and armed robbery.*

But dammit, it's nothing of the kind! If I sued those girls and sued the sorority, I'd win. But this way, I am getting all the money, no lawyers are; and it's a girl who's wronged me who is handing me money, not her insurance company.

Besides, these bitches owe me, big time!

Julianne shook her head. "If you won't give it to Jesus, give it to me. I'm your mother, talk to me."

What the hell, let's tell her. "You know I quit Pizza King, and I sold my car."

"And you've never told me why you did those things."

"Some sorority girls pulled a nasty prank on me. Which got me so mad, I would've burned their sorority house to the ground if I'd had telekinetic powers."

"When was this?"

"Last Saturday. The day before I quit Pizza King and sold my car. Anyway, so far as the nasty prank goes, I'm handling things, Mom. Without calling the cops, or lawyers, or getting cops or lawyers called on me."

"So what's bothering you?"

"I'm not playing by the rules. A lawsuit would be slow, and expensive, and might not work, but it would be playing by the rules. I've gone outside the rules."

"If the police knew all the facts, would they arrest you?"

"No. What I've done isn't against the law. In any case, they can't prove anything."

"Would I be disappointed if I knew all the facts?"

Jerry was deciding how to answer when his mother spoke again—

"Stop, don't answer that question! But I'm here if you need me."

Then Julianne walked to her computer and pulled up her Paypal account.

Jerry suspected that his mother had told him not to answer her question because neither mother nor son would have been happy if Jerry had answered honestly.

She doesn't know the half of it! How do you tell your mom that you've already hypno-programmed her, twice?

****

As soon as Jerry was in his bedroom and on his computer, he emailed Al—

"The money just sent is for two more hypno-talkers. I need them ASAP."

Chapter 12
Cindy Makes A Phone Call

Saturday, 8:37 a.m. Eastern
Yacht Pier 2
Savannah, Georgia

Cindy *needed* to talk to someone who wasn't treating her like a bimbo (Uncle Albert), and who wasn't trying to stab her in the back (her other relatives).

So Cindy walked off the yacht, then walked far enough away that she couldn't be overheard. Cindy dug her smartphone out of her purse and called Delilah.

"Good morning, sailor girl!" Delilah said cheerfully. "Are you enjoy your world cruise?"

"Am I *enjoying* sailing on Uncle Albert's yacht?" Cindy sputtered. "Are you fucking kidding? Uncle Albert spends hours of every day on his cel, yelling at one worker-bee or another. Jeez, why'd he even leave the office? As for my other relatives, Aunt Trudy is nice, but I would gladly feed everyone else to the crocodiles."

"That is sad," Delilah said. "So where you are now? New York? London? Paris? *Bucharest?*"

"We're in Savannah, Georgia, loading up on diesel fuel and food. At the moment, I'm off the boat. Thank god."

"Is Willy with you? You not have him mentioned."

"Willy is on the yacht," Cindy said with gritted teeth. "He says it's because he has no interest in Savannah. But the real reason, I think, is because my cousin Penelope is on the yacht. Willy and I had a big argument a half-hour ago."

"That too is sad," Delilah said.

"So tell me what's new at the sorority house and on campus, *please*," Cindy said. "God, I miss Wheat City, even with all its snow and tornadoes."

"Not much is new. A big thunderstorm comed yesterday. Susie Ross misses her period and is scared to buy a pregnancy test. And yesterday, to Jerry I talked—remember the pizza man on who we dumped the cat urine?—and I thinked, 'He is so much the sexy.' "

"Wait, *what?* Run that through again."

"Yes, it was forty-five days ago when Susie—"

"Not *that*, Delilah! The dork nerd, you think he's *sexy?*"

"You let me start to the begin. Jerry comed to our table at the Student Union when I was to Bethany talking. Somehow I not noticed him to the table walk—he appeared from air. Then Jerry talked with me and Bethany for some minutes—"

"About what? *What* could you and Bethany possibly talk with that nerd about?"

"About the lawn party. In the honest, I don't remember much about the talk, only that I trusted him. So whatever he asked me, I told him the truth. Anyway, he suggested after a few minutes that Bethany leave. Then Bethany leaved, then Jerry leaved, then Jerry comed back, then I thinked, 'I am so much sorry for what I to him doed.' "

"Hold on, Bethany left, then the nerd left, then he came back? Where'd he go, and what did he do while he was gone?"

Cindy could hear Delilah's shrug. "He not sayed why he leaved, or why he comed back. I trust him; I am certain that he had the good reason."

Cindy said, "Where is this story heading? I *hope* that when Jerry asked you for a date, you told him that you and Whatzisname-o, the soccer player, are an item."

Delilah giggled. "Actually, yesterday I telephoned Ronaldo and told him that I was feeling sick, and I stopped our date. After I and Ronaldo talked, I goed to the ATM machine, then I goed to Jerry's house."

"Good god, Delilah," said Cindy, "*why?*"

"To give to him the money for to show that I am sorry. But once I was in his house, I thinked that he is so much the sexy." Delilah giggled. "Before I leaved, we fucked like the hares."

Cindy noticed Uncle Albert then; he was making big, angry gestures that said *Get your ass back on the yacht.*

By the time that Cindy was indeed back on the yacht, she had said goodbye to Delilah and had stowed her smartphone.

Once back on the yacht, Cindy ignored Willy talking to Cousin Penelope.

****

Cindy thought about her conversation with Delilah, then made another smartphone call to Wheat City—quickly, before the yacht moved out of range of a cel tower.

"Hey, girlfriend, enjoying the ocean?" Cindy soon heard Colleen Bennett say.

"Yeah, I've having a blast," Cindy said, her tone of voice declaring the opposite. "Listen, can't talk long. You noticed anything strange about Delilah?"

"Hm, yeah, her English is all goofed up, and she's always talking about she's descended from some prince back in Romania. Hold on, she does that already. Why are you asking me this?"

"Well, it's that she's . . . just let me know if she starts doing or saying anything weird, okay?"

Cindy could hear the unasked question in Colleen's voice: "Sure, Cindy, not a problem."

Chapter 13
Bertrice and Linda-1

1408 Ewen Drive, Wheat City

Jerry in his house was like a caged lion on Saturday, between waiting for Delilah to send over hypno-programmed sorority girls, and waiting for Al to deliver two more hypno-talkers.

Then both things happened, one right after the other.

That afternoon, no sooner had Al driven away from Jerry's house, but two cars drove up.

Jerry watched through the gauzy curtain. Two young women each got out of her car, then came together. They spoke briefly, then they walked together toward the front door.

It was more accurate to say, they walked sorta-together. The auburn-haired girl didn't let the blonde with the big tits ever get closer than four feet from her.

The auburn-haired girl, it turned out, was named Linda Collins. Linda had the smoothest, most flawless skin that Jerry had ever seen. If she ever moved to Manhattan, she could model cosmetics. Linda had a toned figure; but alas, her tits were ordinary.

Bertrice had blond hair, which was either natural or very expertly dyed. Alas, that blond hair had been hacked short by a dull machete—or so it seemed. But making up for her ridiculous haircut, Bertrice had blue eyes and enormous tits.

Bertrice had brought exactly one hundred dollars as "apology"; Linda had brought $226.00.

As before with Delilah, the two girls had that "special moment of realization" within a few seconds of laying eyes on Jerry. While each girl was handing him cash, it turned out—

Linda gasped as Jerry was counting her money. "Oh my god, you're *hot*," she said.

Bertrice held out five twenty-dollar bills, then her face changed. "Yes, you *are* hot. This is very confusing."

Jerry gestured, "Ladies, follow me." As he was walking toward the basement, he asked over his shoulder, "Why is you being attracted to me confusing?"

Linda said, "Because she's a *rug-muncher*."

This pissed Bertrice off. "Like you didn't know from the start." To Jerry, she said, "I told them during the first day of Rush Week. Alpha Sigma Sigma shocked the shit out of me when I got the invite anyway."

By now everyone was going down the basement steps. Linda said, "Duh, *look* at you! We figured it would be a howler, watching all the frat boys trying to get you naked."

Jerry shook his head. "Letting unsuspecting guys hit on a stacked lesbian, *that* is cruel."

****

They got undressed. That is to say, Linda stripped, Jerry undressed, and Bertrice started to get undressed. Linda said, "You're doing it wrong. Take your clothes off so he wants to fuck your naked body."

Lordy, those are big tits! Jerry thought, watching Bertrice learn how to strip. *Wow, the carpet matches the drapes.*

Linda had been the teacher, and Bertrice the student, during the striptease lesson. But now Bertrice took the lead: She walked over to Jerry, kissed him, then walked over to the bed and knelt on it, facing Jerry. Bertrice's hands started to stroke her boobs and pubic hair. Linda copied all of Bertrice's sexy moves.

"Fuck us with your hot, fresh pepperoni, Mr. Pizza Man," Linda Collins said.

Jerry, needless to say, had never been in a threesome before. Now he not only was about to have a threesome, but the women involved were gorgeous. His cock was pointing straight up.

Jerry walked up to the edge of the bed. As soon as he was within Bertrice's reach, she asked, "Can I—can I touch it? I've never wanted to touch one before."

"Or have one touch you," Linda said. "You're a virgin, right?"

Bertrice laughed. "Technically."

****

When Jerry pulled out of Bertrice, he had blood on his dick.

He was surprised when Linda Collins came forward to lick him clean. Everyone was surprised (including Linda, it seems) when Linda then kissed Bertrice on the mouth.

****

Bertrice said, "I've never done a titty-fuck before."

Jerry said, "Neither have I. Neither Anna nor Georgia had the equipment you've got."

****

Linda was good at giving head. Bertrice wasn't, of course, but she was a fast learner.

Bertrice's pussy was tight. Linda's pussy, not as much.

Bertrice was tactful when she gave Jerry tips how to lick pussy.

****

After everyone got dressed, Jerry asked, "So do you feel better about dumping the cat piss on me?"

Linda said, "Yes, even though Bertrice and I didn't do all that much. It was Cindy, Delilah, other-Linda, Colleen, and Debra who were the ringleaders there."

"*Who?* Give me their full names, please."

Linda Collins said, "The ringleaders were Cindy Hope, Delilah Monescu, Linda Tanner, Colleen Bennett, and Debra Chin." Bertrice nodded.

Then Bertrice said, "I thought it was wrong, myself. But I wasn't strong like Bethany, who left, not caring what anyone said."

Jerry snapped, "Yeah, Bethany is the only one who actually spoke up and backed up her words with actions."

Then Jerry calmed down enough to think. He said to Bertrice and Linda, "You two think you could help me get a little payback? Let me show you something."

With that said, Jerry led Bertrice and Linda over to his two just-received hypno-talkers.

****

Linda Collins drove off, having tossed her brand-new hypno-talker onto the front seat of her car. Jerry watched through the gauzy curtain as Linda left, then he turned to Bertrice. "You know, as long as you sent a steady stream of Alpha Sigma Sigma girls to my house, I wouldn't mind if you used this awesome device for personal gain, one time."

"You mean, lure some straight-as-a-ruler sorority-sister hottie to the Ellen Degeneres side?" Bertrice's smile was lewd. "*Oh,* yeah. . ."

Jerry asked, "Have somebody in mind?"

Bertrice grinned. "Marybeth Wells, the cutest, sweetest girl in the sorority. She has blue eyes in a cute face, and chestnut-colored hair—she's stacked, but not as big as me.

She tutors the rest of us, because she's smart in math and science—she says she got that from her famous grandfather. And she makes a *killer* coconut cream pie—she says she got *that* from her grandma. And *innocent?* If innocence were perfume, you could smell Marybeth a mile away! *Which*, she says, she *also* got from her grandma."

Chapter 14
Bertrice Wastes No Time

Forty-five minutes later
Alpha Sigma Sigma sorority house, Wheat City

Bertrice spotted Marybeth wandering through the upstairs hallway of the sorority house, talking to sorority sisters. Marybeth was sipping from a bamboo cup. Presumably Marybeth's grandmother had brought the cup back to the United States, fifty years ago; also presumably, Marybeth's grandfather had made that cup.

When Bertrice got close, she saw that Marybeth's cup had *Roy* carved into the side. Marybeth's famous grandfather was named Roy.

Bertrice said to Marybeth, "Hey, can I show you something interesting in my room? I think you'll like it."

Marybeth's frown was pretty. "Can it wait till tomorrow? Kenny is picking me up in an hour and a half."

"C'mon, it'll only take a minute," Bertrice said, already walking toward her room.

As Bertrice was frog-marching Marybeth toward her room, Bertrice saw Linda Collins leading Cheryl Parkinson into her own room. Bertrice and Linda winked at each other.

Jerry had given a suggested script to Bertrice. When Bertrice read that script, the words seemed oddly familiar. To Jerry's script, Bertrice had added a paragraph that was custom-tailored for Marybeth Wells. It had taken Bertrice twenty minutes to write one dinky paragraph and to phrase it the way she wanted it.

But now it was time to begin Operation Sappho. Bertrice walked over to her desk and picked up the hypno-talker.

"What is it?" Marybeth asked.

"What does it look like?" Bertrice replied with a smile.

"If Grandfather had built it, it could be anything." It had once been said of Roy that he could build a nuclear reactor from a coconut shell.

(This was of course an exaggeration of Roy's cleverness. But not by much.)

Now Bertrice said, "Well, let me show you what I've got. But first I have to put these earplugs in. This gizmo beeps sometimes, which drives me nuts."

Bertrice put down the hypno-talker, fished the earplugs out of the desk drawer, put the earplugs into her ears, then picked up the hypno-talker again.

Bertrice pressed the orange button. Marybeth's face went blank, and she started chanting.

****

A minute later, Bertrice took a deep breath, then took her finger off the orange button. Marybeth blinked, looked around, then looked at Bertrice.

By then, Bertrice was taking the earplugs out of her ears.

Marybeth blurted out, "Oh, that poor pizza man! We were *so* wrong to him! I'm going to make it up to him."

Bertrice nodded. "I've already gotten square with him, and you should too."

Then Bertrice shut up and waited.

"Um, Bertrice?" Marybeth said. "I never noticed before but . . . you have pretty eyes."

"So do you. Your blue eyes are expressive, always," Bertrice said. She stepped a foot closer.

Marybeth's hands went to her stomach. "My stomach muscles are fluttering, with you close. What does that mean?"

"You don't know what you're feeling?" Bertrice put her hand on Marybeth's stomach; indeed, the innocent's abdominal muscles were twitching.

"Grandma said that her stomach muscles fluttered the first time she saw Grandfather. But she didn't find out what that meant till her wedding night."

"And what did the flutters turn out to mean?" Bertrice asked. Her hand started caressing Marybeth's stomach.

"Grandma wouldn't tell me! She said a man would show me on my wedding night, and it would be glorious!"

"I'll give you a clue, sweetie. It has to do with this." Bertrice's hand slid down Marybeth's body and inside her jeans and panties, in order to stroke Marybeth's nubbin.

Marybeth gasped. "That—oh, yes!—feels nice."

Bertrice said, "A few women, like me, like to give nice feelings like this to other women. *Pretty* women. Pretty women like you."

"Is it okay if I kiss you?" Marybeth asked. "Would you mind?"

"I wouldn't mind one bit," Bertrice said. Bertrice used her other hand to pull Marybeth's head toward hers.

When Bertrice broke the kiss, Marybeth said, "I should pay you back. I should do to you what you're doing to me."

"If you want to, I won't argue."

Marybeth's hand went to the top of Bertrice's shorts, paused, then slid inside Bertrice's panties. It turned out that Marybeth wasn't *completely* innocent: She knew how to stroke a clit.

"That feels nice, young lady," Bertrice said, and kissed Marybeth again.

For several minutes, things continued like this, with Bertrice and Marybeth kissing each other and stroking each other.

Bertrice broke the latest kiss to say, "You have a decision to make. I want to make you feel even better than this, but you have a date with Kenny tonight."

"Kenny!" Marybeth said scornfully. Then her expression got wooden: "He laughed at the pizza man. He deserves no special favors from me or anyone else."

Marybeth pulled her smartphone out of her jeans pocket. A few seconds later, she said into the phone, "Kenny, something's come up. I'm breaking our date . . . . No, I expect to be at the sorority house all night."

As Marybeth was putting her smartphone back in her pocket, Bertrice said, "Kenny's going to be broken-hearted."

Marybeth shrugged. "But it won't kill him." Then she looked at Bertrice nervously. "Okay, my evening is free. Now what?"

Then Marybeth added, totally unnecessarily, "You should know, I'm a—I've never—Kenny and I only kiss and hold hands."

Bertrice didn't reply with words, she just kissed Marybeth again.

Then Bertrice reached for Marybeth's pink Alpha Sigma Sigma t-shirt, to pull it up and off Marybeth. "You asked, 'Now what?' *Now,* I get a look at you up close. And what I see, I am gonna touch."

Marybeth's eyes were half-lidded. "*Mm,* sounds nice."

"After that, you'll lie right back and I'll tell a tale, a tale of a happy clit. . ."

****

Bertrice was eating Marybeth out, and the innocent naked girl was moaning and thrashing. Then Marybeth said, "I think Grandfather does this. I just figured it out."

Bertrice raised her head. "You think your grandfather eats your grandma's pussy? Many men refuse to." Bertrice went back to what she was doing.

Marybeth gasped out, "Grandma once said that she was really, *really* glad that Grandfather had married *her,* and not Whatzername, the big-name actress."

Chapter 15
Caught By Colleen

As soon as Marybeth got dressed, she kissed Bertrice goodbye, and left Bertrice's room. Bertrice lay naked in bed, thinking how lucky she was. But after a minute of that, Bertrice also got dressed.

Bertrice went looking for Marybeth. Who, it turned out, wasn't in her room.

Bertrice found Marybeth in the sorority-house kitchen. Marybeth was eyeing the spice rack, while a package of chicken fillets waited on the kitchen counter.

No one else was around.

Bertrice walked up behind Marybeth and put her arms around Marybeth's waist. "Hey, honey, what are you up to?"

Marybeth replied, "I need food. I'm thinking about Wok Chicken. Now the question is, what spice to use. Ginger or—?"

Since no one else was in the kitchen, Bertrice spun Marybeth around and kissed her.

"Oh my god, that's so gross!"

Just because the sorority-house kitchen was empty one moment, Bertrice learned, did not mean that it would *stay* empty. Standing just inside the doorway was curly-haired Colleen Bennett, and she had a disgusted look on her face.

****

Off the coast of Florida, Cindy's smartphone's Caller ID told her that it was Colleen Bennett calling her. The first thing that Cindy heard after she answered the phone was, "I've been trying to reach you for an hour!"

Cindy said, "Uncle Albert brought us back close to shore. Because God forbid that he stay out of reach of a cel tower for very long. Anyway, what's up?"

"You won't believe this. You absolutely will not believe it. I caught Bertrice necking with Marybeth in the kitchen."

"Wow. It's the ones you never expect."

"Really truly," Colleen agreed. "A few girls here have given off vibes like they walk both sides of the street, but Marybeth was never one of them."

"That is so weird. All this weird shit is happening," Cindy said, "and I'm here on this yacht and can't get to the bottom of it."

"Weird shit like what?" Colleen asked.

Cindy said, "Well, first you got Delilah gushing how Jerry the pizza guy is so sexy and she fucked him, and now Marybeth turns lezzie? It's like a Weirdness Virus is going around our sorority."

Chapter 16
Girls Gone Weird

On Sunday, things got amazing for Jerry, in terms of getting revenge.

****

Sunday morning, Bertrice the stacked lesbian came by, bringing with her Marybeth Wells in the flesh. And if Bertrice was only "technically" a virgin, Marybeth was the real deal.

A virgin in a sorority? Isn't that against the law?

Marybeth, so Jerry was told, was a pie-baking virgin. (In fact, Marybeth had gifted Jerry with a pie at the beginning of her visit.) Marybeth was *so much* a virgin that she didn't even know what a blowjob was. When high-school boyfriends had said to her, "Put your mouth on me," Marybeth had kissed each boyfriend on the *lips*.

So not only did Jerry bust Marybeth's hymen in his basement, but he also took her blowjob-cherry; all of this happened with Bertrice cheering Marybeth on.

Jerry liked Marybeth; she was the only Alpha Sigma Sigma girl who didn't come across as spoiled, stuck up, or bitchy. So when Marybeth offered him $549 in "I'm sorry I clapped while you got cat-peed on" money, Jerry refused most of the cash.

Jerry kept only a hundred dollars, then gave the rest of the money back to protesting Marybeth. Jerry explained, "Take Bertrice out to dinner sometime. She is so happy to have you as a girlfriend."

Jerry was telling only the truth. Whenever Marybeth touched Bertrice or came close to Bertrice, Bertrice *glowed*.

Besides, Jerry was feeling generous. It wasn't often that a girl ever gifted him with her virginity *and* a blowjob *and* a hundred bucks in cash *and* a coconut cream pie.

****

Linda Collins, whom Jerry had given a hypno-talker to, had ensorcelled Linda Tanner, who was one of the ringleaders of the cat-piss prank.

Sunday afternoon, Linda Tanner was standing in Jerry's living room—

". . .Ohmigod, other-Linda was showing me her new tablet, and suddenly I realized that I had *so* treated you like shit! I drove to the bank, and then I came here to give"—Linda Tanner's voice suddenly got sexy. "Oh wow, you're a *stud.*"

"I'm a board in the wall?"

She slapped his arm. "No, Jerry, you're *sexy.* I want you to jump my bones."

That was an unfortunate turn of phrase. Linda Tanner was skinny—correction, she was anorectically gaunt. That, plus the fact that her hair had no shininess to it, meant that Jerry felt no desire for her at all.

Not to mention, it had been Linda Tanner who had figured out how to collect all that cat piss.

Now Jerry put his hands on both of Linda's bony shoulders. "Linda, do you trust me?"

She went blank-faced and robot-talking: "I trust you completely. I will do anything that you tell me to do, I will believe anything you tell me, and I will answer any question you ask with the complete truth and nothing but the truth."

Jerry smiled with relief that Linda had been programmed properly. With his hands still on her shoulders, Jerry looked into her eyes. "Linda, I don't want to have sex with you. Your body disgusts me."

Linda gasped. "Because I'm too fat, right? I knew it."

"Linda, Linda, believe what I say. You are not too fat, you are too *skinny*. You need to eat more. *Much* more."

"How *much* more?"

"Believe me, Linda Tanner, until I tell you to stop, you are too skinny and you need to keep gaining weight."

He snapped his fingers. "In fact, come with me." Jerry led Linda into his kitchen.

Jerry opened up the fridge and took out Marybeth's coconut cream pie. A big wedge was missing, but there was still plenty of pie to eat.

"Try some," Jerry said. "You need to eat."

Jerry cut her a thick wedge of pie, and she wolfed it down. Then she stared at the remaining pie.

Jerry's smile was as wide as a carnival barker's, or a used-car salesman's. "Of course you can have seconds! A third helping too, if you've got the room."

Linda Tanner didn't rush to eat the second wedge of pie, but she did eat all of it. "Oh my god," she said, "do you know how long it's been since I've *enjoyed* the taste of food?"

"That's another reason why pigging out is the *right* thing for you to do, till I tell you to stop. Because pigging out means you're free to enjoy your food."

Five minutes later, Jerry let Linda kiss him goodbye at his front door. As soon as she broke the kiss, she burped.

As Linda Tanner unlocked her car and slid behind the wheel, Jerry watched her and thought, *In six months, you'll be obese. And then you can forget getting a rich husband.*

Jerry grinned.

****

Debra Chin was another of the cat-piss ringleaders. Sunday afternoon, an hour after Linda Tanner left Jerry's house, Debra Chin showed up.

Debra Chin, it turned out, was tall and shapely, and could have been a runway model in Hong Kong.

Debra Chin too had been hypno-talkered into feeling sorry for her terrible deed, and she too now stood on Jerry's doorstep with cash in hand, as apology.

She also had been hypno-programmed to believe anything that Jerry told her, do anything he told her to do, and—

Answer any question he asked.

"Why did you do this to me?" Jerry asked her.

"Because Cindy said you were a nerd, and I thought that girls like us deserve better than to be hit-on by nerds."

"Girls like you? What do you mean?"

"Hotties. Babes."

"Do you still think that nerds shouldn't hit on girls like you?"

"No, I realized that I've been mean and snobby. I need to make it up to you!"

He took the proffered cash, pocketed the money without counting it, sidestepped her sexual offers, then gestured behind her to her car—

"Dig your keys out of your purse. We're going somewhere."

****

Fifteen minutes later, they were in downtown Wheat City.

Jerry parked Debra's car across the street from the Daughters Of Christ Soup Mission. Jerry turned off the engine.

"What are we doing here?" Debra asked.

Jerry said, "Now we watch who goes in."

Maybe ten minutes later, a man shambled up the street with a paper-bagged bottle in his hand. He had a long, graying beard, hair that had gone uncut for at least six months, and his clothes didn't fit right—

"*Eww,* he's wearing a striped shirt with herringbone pants," Debra said. "And that coat is *all wrong* for his complexion."

—plus the guy didn't dress fashionably, it seemed.

The man tilted the bottle all the way back, dropped the bottle into a trash can, then entered the soup kitchen.

Jerry said, "You know who has lower status than even nerds? Winos and homeless guys. How discouraged they must feel! Debra, believe me, you can help these guys in a way that most people can't."

"How can *I* help them? And"—Debra's voice sounded disgusted now—"why would I want to? The guy's a *wino.*"

"They need to feel like *men.* Getting a blowjob from a hot woman would do wonders for their self-esteem. For some of them, that alone would be enough to blast them out of their rut."

Debra's voice definitely sounded disgusted now: "You're saying I should give blowjobs to winos and homeless guys, as an act of charity?"

"Debra, realize that you want to do this. When you go to sleep at night, you don't want to think, 'I helped dump cat-piss on a guy who did me no harm.' No, you want to go to sleep thinking, 'I'm a caring, generous person.' Right?"

Debra frowned. "Can't I show I'm caring and generous by writing a check to the soup kitchen, or cooking there for an hour a week?"

"Debra, realize that this is the best way. *You* would give these guys a unique gift. If you suck off enough winos and homeless guys, believe me, you will feel really good about yourself."

"How much is 'enough'?"

"You should suck off two down-and-out guys every week for every time you go down on a rich guy that week. Or suck off three homeless guys or winos that week—whichever is *more*."

A man in his twenties stepped out of the soup kitchen then. He had a week's growth of beard, and his shoulders were slumped.

Debra opened the passenger-side door. "I want to believe I'm caring and generous. He'll be the first guy I prove it on."

Jerry stayed in the car. He watched Debra sashay up to the guy and talk to him. The homeless guy and Debra talked for a few minutes, then they walked together into the alley.

Ten minutes later, Debra walked out of the alley. Her knees were red, her lipstick was smeared, and her smile was stuffed with smugness.

Jerry thought, *Any woman who regularly blows winos in alleys, will find it hard to land a rich husband.*

Jerry grinned.

****

After Jerry and Debra returned to his house and Debra drove away, Jerry called up Delilah Monescu.

Twenty minutes later, Delilah stood on Jerry's doorstep. "You do want me to see?" she asked hopefully.

Delilah wasn't the only Alpha Sigma Sigma girl with a hypno-talker; Linda Collins, Bertrice Anderssen, and Marybeth Wells now each had one. So Delilah wasn't needed as a recruiter anymore. Meanwhile, Jerry had not forgotten that Delilah had been one of the plotters.

Jerry had taken cash from Delilah, and he'd fucked her. But Jerry wanted more revenge, and now he would take more revenge.

Now at his front door, Jerry smiled at Delilah. "I want to congratulate you. I'm told that you're descended from Count Dracula."

Delilah glared. "Prince Vlad the Third of Wallachia was not the Count Dracula. That is a lie that the Englishman's story telled! Prince Vlad is the hero because he beated the Islamists and castrated the boyars, he is not the vampire!"

Jerry smiled. "But the stories about Prince Vlad impaling captured Turks on thick, pointed stakes, that part of his story is true, right?"

"How you do think is that Prince Vlad beated the Islamists?"

Jerry said, "My point is, Bram Stoker's Count Dracula would do the same thing as Prince Vlad."

Delilah frowned. "I suppose, yes."

"Anyway, since you are proud of Prince Vlad your ancestor, I thought of a way for you to honor him."

"How? Please you tell me."

"You dress yourself like a female Count Dracula."

Delilah took an angry breath.

Jerry continued, "I know, he isn't really Count Dracula. But now your clothing will give you something to start a conversation with."

"Is true, you think I must dress as the vampire?"

"Delilah, believe me, the more you look like a vampire, the more that a potential husband will know that family is important to you."

"I this will do. I want the rich husband to marry, so I will dress as the vampire."

"Good. But believe me, you never know when you will meet this rich husband, so you should dress like a vampire *every day* until you marry."

"I see it. I will this do."

"Don't forget the make-up. Believe me, Delilah, the more you look like a vampire, the more that rich man will be impressed by you."

"Oh, I see it. I will all this do."

Two minutes later, as Jerry stood in the doorway and watched Delilah drive away, he thought, *I doubt that a woman who dresses like a vampire seven days a week will be someone a rich man wants to marry.*

Jerry grinned.

****

As Jerry lay in bed that night, he smiled. Linda Tanner, Debra Chin, and Delilah Monescu now had no chance of snagging a rich husband—

• Linda, because soon she would be disgustingly fat;

• Debra, because she'd get a reputation for slutting around with "losers"; and

• Delilah, because her vampiric appearance would make potential mates think she was "freaky."

But then Jerry's smile changed to a frown. The woman whom he most yearned for vengeance on, Cindy Hope, was out of his reach.

So far.

Jerry thought, *Well, at least Cindy has no idea what nasty shit has been going on in her absence.*

Chapter 17
Cindy Burns A Bridge

Monday morning
Near the Transient Boat Pier
Vero Beach, Florida

For three and a half days, Cindy had been trapped in the company of her asshole elderly *rich* uncle, her gold-digging relatives, and her tomcatting boyfriend. By now Cindy wanted to scream, because Uncle Albert showed Cindy no respect.

Suddenly Uncle Albert turned away from paralleling the shore; now the yacht was pointed toward land.

"What's here?" Uncle James asked.

"We're here to get fuel and potable water," Uncle Albert said.

Then Uncle Albert looked directly at Cindy, while raising his voice loud enough for everyone to hear: "We'll be here only thirty minutes. *Don't* make me wait for you."

Cindy glared at her uncle. "I'm not a child."

Cindy's smartphone rang then. It was Colleen Bennett calling from Wheat City.

"Cindy, you have to get back here to the sorority house!" Colleen said. "It's a mess, and I need your help to straighten everything out."

"What's wrong?" Cindy asked.

"What *isn't* wrong? Start with Delilah. Now she's telling everyone she's Dracula's granddaughter. She just left for her first Monday class—dressed like a vampire."

"Maybe it's just a Romania thing?"

"Then there's Debra Chin. This morning at breakfast, Debra announced that Jerry the pizza guy convinced her to start blowing winos and homeless guys as a charity project—"

"*Fuck?*"

"She says, now she likes herself a whole lot better."

"*Jerry the nerd* told her that? And she *bought* it?"

"*Totally* bought it. The other weird thing about breakfast was that Linda Tanner was gulping down every food she could reach. She told us that Jerry said she shouldn't diet anymore."

"Shit, *Jerry* again?"

"Yeah. I forgot to mention, but Delilah said it was Jerry's suggestion that she start dressing like a vampire."

"Jerry is wrecking my sorority! This shit has to stop."

Colleen said, "And there's more—"

Cindy said, "I'll see you soon, believe it!" Cindy ended the call with a stab of a fingertip.

By now the yacht was alongside the pier, and Uncle Albert was just shutting down the engines. Uncle Matt and Uncle James, along with a guy on the pier, were doing stuff with ropes.

Parked on the pier was a fuel-tanker truck; by that truck stood two guys in matching gray coveralls. One guy held the end of the fuel hose in his hand, waiting to attach it to the yacht.

Cindy made a snap decision. She rushed from the deck to the cabin that she shared with Aunt Trudy. Cindy then grabbed her suitcase, opened it, and dropped it onto her bed.

****

As soon as Cindy could throw all her clothes into her suitcase and could roll her suitcase to the gangplank, she was ready to leave the ship. Fortunately, by now the yacht's gangplank had been lowered, so she didn't need to wait any longer. With her purse hanging from her shoulder, Cindy grabbed her suitcase's handle—

"It seems you want to be disinherited," Uncle Albert sneered, behind her.

Cindy turned around and eyed everyone. "No, I want to spend no more time around an *asshole* like you, ditto my *gold-digger* relatives, likewise my *horn-dog* boyfriend."

Cindy's relatives gasped.

Cindy continued, "Frankly, I'd rather be in a car that's flipping over at high speed than spend another minute with you jerks."

Aunt Agatha—the brown-noser of the century—said, "Cousin Albert isn't always charming, but at least he's *rich*. I don't see *your* yacht anywhere around here."

Cindy's laugh was scornful. "Aunt Agatha, suck up to the asshole enough, maybe *you'll* own a yacht someday. *This* yacht. But if you get it by groveling and being a whore, will you ever enjoy it?"

That wiped the smug smile off Aunt Agatha's face!

"Anyway"—Cindy gripped the handle of her suitcase harder—"I'd like to say that it's been fun, but it sure as hell hasn't. Goodbye, everybody."

As Cindy was walking down the gangplank, she heard Uncle Albert say behind her, "If she's leaving, William, you're off the ship too. Get packing."

Willy yelled out, "*Cindy, wait for me!*"

Cindy heard Penelope say, "You choose *her?* I hate you!"

That made Cindy grin.

By now, Cindy was stepping off the gangplank onto the pier. The two refueling-truck men were staring at her like she'd fought a rabid dog to the death—and won.

****

It was fun letting Willy grovel. Cindy made it clear that he was forgiven for nothing that had happened since he'd first laid eyes on Cousin Penelope.

Cindy insisted that Willy buy her lunch in Vero Beach. He did.

Cindy insisted that he pay for the taxi rides. He did.

The trip back to Wheat City took hours, both due to having to wait hours for a flight, and due to riding on slowpokey Greyhound buses.

By the time that Cindy and Willy caught a cab at the Wheat City Greyhound station, it was nearly dark; by the time that Cindy and Willy climbed into Cindy's car at the Wheat City airport, it was full dark.

Cindy's car then zoomed through the city, the car's headlights slicing the darkness. Destination: Alpha Sigma Sigma sorority house.

Chapter 18
It's The Tablets!

Since they were in Cindy's car and she wasn't about to let Willy drive, he was free to pull out his smartphone and make a call—

"Yeah, we're back in town. Cindy's kinda mad at me—"

"FOR GOOD REASON!" Cindy yelled into his phone.

"—I'll tell you about it later. So what's new in Wheat City? . . . You're shitting me! *All* of them?"

After Willy ended the call, he said, "That is weird."

"You gonna tell me, or do I have to guess?"

"Every girl in Alpha Sigma Sigma who was dating somebody in my frat, broke up with him. Tom Snell is super bummed out, because he really likes Susie Whatzername."

"Susie *Ross*. Her name is Susie Ross. And Tommy *better* like her, because he's maybe gotten her pregnant."

Willy shrugged. Cindy knew why: Pregnancy wasn't *his* problem.

Then Cindy thought back to what Willy had said. "Why did my girls break up with your guys?"

"Because all the guys supposedly are pigs for laughing at the poor pizza guy after he got cat piss dumped on him."

Cindy said, "Jerry again! Dig my phone out of my purse. Colleen needs to know I'm back."

"Yes, *ma'am*," Willy said, his voice dripping with sarcasm.

"What's *your* problem?"

"That you've been giving me shit once an hour, since we walked off the yacht. You haven't hit me yet with *It's over*, but I figure that's only minutes away now. So since we're still technically a couple, you think you can give me orders?"

"Dammit, Jerry Green has done something to my sorority sisters, and he needs to be dealt with!"

"Not my problem, lady. I did my part last Saturday at the lawn party, remember?"

Cindy drove in silence, while Willy called Colleen, said only "We're back in town," and hung up.

Cindy was frustrated. She *needed* Willy's help now, but he was correct: He had no reason to help her.

Cindy had never joined Debate Club in high school—and wouldn't have, not even with a gun to her head—so she didn't know how to win Willy over with clever arguments.

And no way in hell would Cindy ever *beg*.

So how the fuck could she get him to back her up now?

By now Cindy's car was driving by the Alpha Sigma Sigma sorority house, about to turn into the driveway that connected the parking lot in the back. Facing the street, there was a banner hanging from the second-story windows, but outside was too dark for Cindy to read it. Possibly it said *Yay, Unicorns!*—but more likely, it said *Too bad, Unicorns!*

Suddenly Willy said, "Stop the car! Now!"

"Why? We're almost there." Cindy meant the rear parking lot. But in the meantime, she had stopped the car in the middle of the street.

Willy yanked open the glove-compartment door, started pawing through everything till he found the LED flashlight, then opened the passenger-side door.

Willy jumped out of the car and turned on the flashlight. Now Cindy could read the banner: JERRY GREEN, WE'RE SO SORRY.

"*Fuck*," Cindy breathed.

Seconds later, Willy was back in the car, and putting the flashlight back in the glove compartment. "That is weird," he said.

Cindy was out of time now, and now she *had to* get Willy helping her. Then inspiration hit.

Cindy didn't drive her car into the rear parking lot—which at night, was lit up like a sports stadium. Instead, Cindy moved the car over to the curb of the street—the dark, dark street—and shut off the engine.

Willy's voice was confused. "What's going on?"

Cindy's hand reached over in the darkness and unzipped Willy's pants.

Willy made no move to stop her.

Cindy said, "I need your help now, Willy."

Both of Cindy's hands were on Willy's belt now, unfastening his belt and undoing the snap of his jeans.

Willy made no move to stop her.

Soon Willy's hardening cock was exposed to the moonlight.

Cindy bent down. "I really, really hate Jerry Green."

Then Cindy said nothing more for ten minutes.

****

After Cindy parked her car in the sorority-house parking lot, she and Willy entered the sorority house through the parking-lot door.

Which put them in the kitchen. They found Linda Tanner in the kitchen, eating an entire chocolate cake by herself.

"Look who's back," Linda said, with no warmth in her voice. "Are you ready to tell Jerry you're sorry?"

"Are you ready to get clean and sober?" Cindy replied.

Cindy pushed through the kitchen door and walked into the sorority-house living room, with Willy following in Cindy's wake.

Cindy got greeted by a vampire—

"Enter freely and of your own will," Delilah said in a disapproving tone. "Or do the better, and walk out where you came in."

"Quiet, or Willy here will stake you," Cindy said.

Neither Willy nor Delilah said anything in reply.

The big-screen TV was turned off. Cindy didn't know what to make of that. Come to think of it, the stereo was off too.

Cindy looked around. "Where is Debra Chin?" she demanded.

Colleen replied, "She's volunteered to cook soup at the mission." Brunette, curly-haired Colleen rolled her green eyes. "Those poor do-gooders are letting a slut guard the henhouse."

Colleen was wearing her bubble-gum-pink Alpha Sigma Sigma bookbag. Cindy figured that Colleen had just returned from the university library.

Susie Ross demanded, "Are you ready to call up Jerry and make nice? Tell him you're sorry?"

"Gee, Susie, wouldn't you rather talk about the baby you might, or might not, be carrying?" Cindy said.

"This is more important," Susie said. "You haven't gotten right with Jerry, so you embarrass the rest of us."

So saying, Susie pulled out her smartphone. "Putting you on speaker," she said.

From Susie's smartphone, Cindy heard, "Hello, Jerry here."

Every woman in the room—except for Colleen, thank god—and Cindy, each said "Hi, Jerry!" (or similar) in a warm, cheerful voice.

Cindy looked at Colleen, who shrugged.

Bertrice called out, "Cindy is here. And Willy." Bertrice and Marybeth were sitting together on the couch—shoulders and hips touching, and each woman had a hand on the other's knee. Nobody but Cindy seemed bothered by this.

Speakerphone-Jerry said, "Welcome back to Kansas, Cindy. Now you can give me your apology in person."

Cindy said, "I'm not saying jack shit to you! What have you done to my sorority?"

"Not nearly so much as I've wanted to, Cindy. I've had fantasies of that building burning to the ground, with everyone trapped inside. Lucky for you, I don't the power to do that."

"You're evil, Jerry. You've done something to my sisters."

Through Susie's smartphone, Jerry laughed. "Indeed I have. To your entire sorority in general, and four of the cat-piss ringleaders in particular. But now it's time for me to finish this. Soon as my mom gets home, I'm borrowing her car, I'll drive to the sorority house, and I will *deal* with you two. Which I am really looking forward to!"

"Oh, yeah? I—"

"See you soon. Bye." Then Jerry hung up on her!

Cindy said, "I am *not* waiting for that evil loser clueless nerd to come *here!* We—"

Linda Collins held up a hand. "Um, before you go running off, can I show you my new tablet?" Linda picked up a blue tablet computer that had been leaning against a flowerpot.

"Linda, are you crazy? The last thing I want to do now is talk about computer stuff."

Linda Collins said, "*Please?* I'll need only a few minutes to show you what it does."

Bertrice reached down beside the arm of the couch, and brought up an identical blue tablet. "They're really cool. See, I've got one too."

Marybeth mirrored Bertrice's motion. "Me three."

Delilah shrugged. "Mine in my bedroom is. By my coffin."

Behind Cindy, Willy's voice sneered, "When did you guys all become computer geeks?"

Cindy figured it out: "It's those blue things! *That's* how Jerry took over the sorority. I don't know what they are, but they're not the blue tablet computers they look like."

"That is—it's ridiculous," Marybeth said, her face looking worried. Marybeth was still a terrible liar.

Abruptly Cindy turned around, running straight into Willy. "Out the back door, Willy! We're going to the nerd's house and I'll straighten this out, once and for all."

Colleen jumped up off the couch and glared at all the Jerry-fans in the room. "Hold on, Cindy, I'm coming with you guys."

Chapter 19
I'm Flooring It!

Monday night

Colleen didn't ask *Front seat or back seat?* She yanked open the left rear door of Cindy's car, shrugged off her bookbag, threw the bookbag on the back seat, then jumped in the back seat herself.

As soon as Cindy sat in the driver's seat, she immediately heard a zipper-sound from the back seat. "What are you doing?" she demanded.

"Jesus, just getting my smartphone out of my bookbag," Colleen replied, "Chill out."

****

Seconds later
In Cindy's car, Wheat City

"*Arrgh!*" Cindy yelled in frustration.

From the back seat, Colleen's voice said, "What's wrong?"

Cindy said, "I left in such a hurry, I didn't ask anyone what the nerd's address was. You guys, get your smartphones out and hit-up Google."

Colleen said, "He lives at 1408 Ewen Drive."

Willy asked suspiciously, "How do you already know that?"

****

1408 Ewen Drive, Wheat City

Jerry watched his mother's car drive up the driveway. Immediately Jerry took out his smartphone and punched-in Cindy's phone number (which Delilah had given to him).

Alas, the phone call didn't go the way that Jerry expected—

Once Cindy answered her phone, Jerry gloated: "I'm leaving now, Cindy. I'm coming now for you and Willy, and your sorority sisters will let me in."

But Cindy's voice replied, "You waited too long, loser. *We* are coming for *you!* Soon we'll be at 1408 Ewen Drive. And Willy is *really* looking forward to pounding on you. Unless you hide in the house and won't come out, coward."

Several seconds of silence passed, then Jerry said, "I'll make it easy for him. I'll be standing in the street, in front of my house."

****

In Cindy's car, Wheat City

After Cindy ended the phone call, Willy repeated his question to Colleen: "How do you already know the geek's address, sweetheart?"

Colleen's voice was scornful. "You got any idea how many of our sorority sisters have been to his house to *fuck* that guy? By the way, fella, my name is *Colleen*, not *sweetheart*."

Cindy said, "So, Colleen, *you* haven't been to Jerry's house, *right?*"

"God, no."

"You haven't fucked him?"

"Ugh."

"You haven't apologized to him, over the phone or in person?"

"No."

Cindy nodded. "Good."

Colleen said, "Change of subject. We're still close enough to campus that there are lots of stop signs around, and lots of

Wheat City cops who like to ticket college students. So don't run any stop signs, okay?"

Cindy said sarcastically, "Yes, *ma'am!*"

Colleen's voice sounded annoyed. "Do you want the cops to have an official record tonight that your car was at a certain place at a certain time?"

Willy said, "She's got a point."

"*Fine*," Cindy said, "I'll stop at the damned stop signs."

Cindy couldn't clearly see Colleen in the rear-view mirror, but now Colleen was doing something to make her curly hair shake. "What are you doing, Colleen?" Cindy asked.

"What?"

"I said, 'What are you doing, Colleen?' "

"My earrings hurt. I'm pulling on them, trying to make them comfortable."

"Ha, like anyone can even tell you're wearing earrings, what with that hair of yours."

****

1408 Ewen Drive, Wheat City

Julianne had just walked in the door. Jerry greeted her with this request: "Mom, I have a big problem, but I want you to let me handle it."

"That depends. How big is this problem?"

"I can't tell you now, don't have time, but it's *big*. I just ask: Don't call the cops unless things really turn to shit."

"Language, young man," she said automatically. Then she said, "You actually think I might need to call the police?"

Jerry looked her for nearly a minute, trying to decide what to say. Finally he walked up to her and kissed her on the cheek. "Talk to you later, Mom. I love you."

Then Jerry turned and walked out the front door, into the darkness.

Out of his mother's hearing, Jerry said, "If things *really* turn to shit, Mom, you'll need to call an *ambulance*."

****

In Cindy's car, Wheat City

Less than a minute after promising to stop at every motherfucking stop sign near the campus, Cindy had stopped at her fifth stop sign in less than a mile. No sooner had Cindy stopped, but she was rattled by the honking of a car right behind her.

That's weird, how I didn't notice that car come up behind me, Cindy thought.

In the rear-view mirror, Cindy noticed that Colleen's hands were back at her ears again, and Colleen's curly hair again was shaking.

****

1408 Ewen Drive, Wheat City

Right after Jerry walked out of his house, he pulled his smartphone out of his pocket and called Delilah. Jerry asked only one question: "Who's in the car with Cindy?"

When Jerry heard Delilah's answer, he thanked her, then ended the call.

At least there is only one man in the car, Jerry thought. *On the other hand, Delilah thinks it's Cindy who's driving, and Cindy is really pissed at me.*

Jerry still had his smartphone in his hand. He looked down at the time-display. *Cindy, Willy, and Colleen will be here in less than fifteen minutes.*

Which meant that Jerry probably was less than fifteen minutes away from disaster and pain. But he had one slim hope.

Jerry walked down to the curb and waited. He checked the time-display on his smartphone roughly twice a minute.

He got a text message, and he immediately replied to it. But that didn't make the time pass more quickly.

****

In Cindy's car, Wheat City

Cindy was zooming across town to Wheat City suburbia, where the nerd lived.

From the back seat, Colleen said, "Are you speeding? . . . Shit, slow down! We want to avoid cops, remember?"

Cindy said, "I want to get there! *Not* drive 30 mph every fucking inch of the way."

"If you don't care about the cops, how about this? I don't want to get killed during my last week as a college student."

"Huh? You lost me."

"I haven't had time to tell you," Colleen said. "I'm dropping out of college, and next week I'm starting a new job in Nevada."

"*What?*" Cindy said. "Why are you dropping out? What's the job? Bennett Hall was named after your grandfather!"

Willy said, "How about we get to the runt's house, I pound his face in, and you two share gossip later, hm?"

****

1408 Ewen Drive, Wheat City

Jerry phoned Delilah again. "When did they leave the sorority house?" he asked her.

After he ended the call with Delilah, he stepped off the curb into the street.

Jerry said to the stars and moon, *almost* calmly, "Cindy and them ought to be getting to my house this very minute."

****

In Cindy's car, Wheat City

Cindy's car turned onto the nine-hundred block of Ewen Drive.

"We're half a mile from giving that runt some payback," Willy said.

"Oh my god, there he is!" Cindy exclaimed.

Far ahead of Cindy's car, a figure stood in the street. He was brightly lit by a street lamp.

"What's he doing?" Willy asked, puzzled. The man in the street was paying no attention to Cindy's approaching car.

"He's texting," Colleen answered.

Cindy laughed with delight. "What a perfect target." She sped up her car.

A second later, Colleen said, "Speed limit here is thirty. *Cops*, remember?"

Cindy chortled. "Oh honey, I'm *way* past worrying about speeding tickets." Cindy sped up again, from 40 mph to 45.

Soon the car was coming up on an intersection, and Jerry was only one-block-and-change away.

"Stop sign, stop sign!" Colleen said.

"*Fuck* the stop sign, *fuck* the speed limit," Cindy replied. "I'm flooring it!" Cindy mashed the gas pedal to the floor.

****

Colleen gasped as Cindy's car flew through the stop-signed intersection.

Jerry the nerd finally looked up from his smartphone.

Willy said, "*Fuck*, Cindy, you really—?"

"COLLEEN TO CINDY: Stop the car!"

And with a screeching of brakes, Cindy did.

"What the fuck did you do *that* for?" Willy said. "I almost hit my head on the motherfucking dashboard!"

Cindy said, "Colleen *made* me stop, somehow."

The click of a seatbelt being unfastened was like a rifle shot. Willy spun around to look Colleen full in the face. "You're one of *them!* He's—"

"COLLEEN TO WILLY: Face forward, get calm and stay calm, and say nothing till I give you permission."

All of which, Willy did. Now Cindy was frightened.

Quietly Colleen said, "Colleen to Cindy: Drive slowly till you get to Jerry, then stop the car."

A minute later, after Cindy had unwillingly done those things, Jerry put his smartphone back in his pocket, then walked up to Cindy's car.

Through the glass, Cindy heard Jerry say, "JERRY TO CINDY: Pull the car over to the curb, roll down all the windows, then shut off the engine. JERRY TO CINDY, WILLY, AND COLLEEN: Stay inside the car till I give you permission to leave."

After Cindy had (again unwillingly) done all those things, Jerry walked up to her car again. Cindy figured that Jerry was going to talk trash to her. Instead, Jerry walked to the back-seat door, and his next words were for Colleen.

****

1408 Ewen Drive, Wheat City

Jerry was sweating, and his muscles were rubbery. It was all he could do to speak in a normal voice.

He'd looked up from his texting to see the car zooming straight at him, the pitch of the engine climbing higher and higher.

For two seconds, Jerry was sure that he was seconds away from death.

Then the car came to a loud, screeching halt, which was matched with the smell of burnt rubber. Jerry wondered, *Did my emergency plan work?*

Then when Cindy's car came ahead slowly and then stopped a few feet away from Jerry, like a well-trained dog, he finally let himself believe: *The emergency plan worked!*

But now Jerry had a few loose ends still to straighten out, and some revenge still to take.

Jerry walked up to the back door of the car. Colleen Bennett was staring back at him with green eyes.

Jerry said to her, "Jerry to Colleen: Hand over the blue tablet and your earplugs, and I permit you to show your true feelings now."

When Cindy saw what Jerry was receiving, she yelled, "You two-faced *bitch!* You had one of those blue thingies, and you used it on us!"

Colleen was sniffling now. She said to Jerry, "She hates me! You made me betray her, and now she hates me."

Jerry said, "Colleen, look at the bright side: Next week you'll be a *Nevada brothel whore*, and you'll have worse things to bother you than whether Cindy hates you."

Then Jerry turned to look at Cindy: "If you're angry at Colleen, you should be angry at Delilah too. Delilah lied to you about where her hypno-talker was, and it was Delilah who loaned this to Colleen to use on you."

Cindy asked, "What happens now?"

Jerry said, "I've dealt with Delilah, Linda, Debra, and Colleen. Now it's time for me to deal with you and Willy."

****

In front of 1408 Ewen Drive, Wheat City

Cindy wanted desperately to start her car. She couldn't.

Cindy wanted to yank on the door handle, open the door, and run away. She couldn't.

Cindy heard sniffling and sobbing behind her. In the back seat, Colleen was weeping.

The difference between Cindy and Colleen was, Cindy wasn't sad, she was *scared*.

Willy hadn't said a word since Colleen had told him to be quiet, and now he still seemed unbothered by everything. It was like Willy was on horse tranquilizers.

Jerry walked away from Cindy's car to stand under the street lamp. He pulled a paper out of a pocket, unfolded it, and then read aloud from it, as he held a corner of the blue thingy close to his mouth.

By the time Jerry had walked back to Cindy's car, he'd folded up the paper and had put it back in his pocket.

As soon as Jerry was standing beside Cindy, he ordered, "Jerry to Cindy and Willy: Go stand in front of the car."

Cindy couldn't stop her muscles from obeying. Within seconds, her butt was touching the hot hood of her car. Willy meanwhile still acted as calm as a statue.

Jerry said to her, "I've decided that you two are going to live in Portland, Maine. I don't know anything about Portland, except that it's way north on the map, so I figure it has to be damned cold in winter. It seems to me that if somebody was rich enough to live anywhere he wanted, no way would he choose to live in Portland, Maine."

Then Jerry paused to put earplugs in his ears, picked up the blue thingy, and looked at Cindy with the seriousness of an executioner about to pull the switch.

"When I asked you out, Cindy, you should have turned me down gently."

Jerry did something with the blue thingy, and—

Cindy's whole outlook changed.

Chapter 20
In Portland, Maine

June 22

Exactly two months had passed since Cindy had tried to run over Jerry Green with her car. Now Cindy and Willy were living in Portland, Maine, just as Jerry had suggested.

Cindy and Willy had packed up and left Wheat City so quickly, they had actually left town before Colleen had herself moved away (to Nevada's Pussycat Fantasyland brothel).

Cindy couldn't explain to anyone—not her professors, not her sorority sisters, not her family—why she'd made this change in her life. At least she didn't need to explain to Willy, because he shared her compulsions.

The time now was 8:27 in the evening. Willy lisped, "Let's go, bitch." He was impatiently slapping his left hand against his red-leather Bible.

Cindy replied with a fake-British accent. "I still can see a bit of the sun. I shan't go outside yet."

Only when all of the sun had disappeared below the horizon did Cindy open the front door and step outside.

Cindy opened her car door with the car-door remote, using her right hand, while her left hand adjusted her fangs.

Before Cindy started her car, she wiped crumbs off the front of her gown. Willy tightened the knot of his purple tie.

****

Ten minutes later, Willy and Cindy were walking around downtown Portland. They each had a mission now—or to be more exact, a compulsion.

Now they heard a loud male voice with a Southern accent: "Your lifestyle is sinful! I call upon you all to repent of your wicked ways."

Cindy knew, without asking, that wherever that voice was coming from, was the place where Willy wanted to be. Cindy hurried toward the preaching as quickly as her platform stilettos would permit; still, Willy had no trouble keeping up.

Cindy and Willy rounded a corner. Thirty feet away, a pompadoured man, who was holding a black-leather Bible, was preaching to two drag queens.

"Oh mercy," said the blue-dressed drag queen when she spotted Cindy and Willy. "It's the gay street preacher and the Whore of—"

"I am not a homothexual," Willy said. "God'th power cures homothexuality. Repent, and Jesuth will cure *you* too."

"Yeah, right," the red-dressed drag queen said, "Jesus obviously hasn't cured *you,* honey."

The red-dressed drag queen then remarked to the blue-dressed one, "Ain't nothing more pathetic than a self-hating faggot."

The blue-dressed drag queen then said to Willy, "Let me fuck you up the ass right now, in that alley. We *both* will feel much better afterward."

The other street preacher, Cindy decided, had been too amazed by recent events to say anything till now. Now he turned to Willy and asked, "What's your name, brother?"

Willy's shaking-hand shot out, as eager as a puppy. "I'm Willy. Or you can call me William, that's fine too."

The Southerner put his hand on Willy's shoulder. "Brother William, thanks for your help, but I've got this."

"But I want to help you! I love to preach God's Word, ethpecially Hith power to cure homothexualth."

"Right, we believe you," the blue-dressed drag queen said.

"Brother William," the Southerner said, no longer smiling, "I do believe that you are acting as a stumbling block for these two sinners. Please leave."

"You *really* don't want—?"

"Please leave *now*."

As Cindy and a slump-shouldered Willy started to walk away, the Southerner preacher spoke to Cindy for the first time: "You! You in the . . . costume, do *you* know Jesus?"

Cindy replied in her fake British accent, "Do I *look* like someone who knows your god, priest?"

The red-dressed drag queen said, "What you *look* like, honey, is someone who needs to let the seams out on that outfit. You've been enjoying Blood Pudding way too much." Both drag queens laughed.

Cindy snapped her fingers, as if just now remembering something. She turned back to the Southerner. "Say, would you like me to suck your dick? Only three bucks. For five bucks, I'll even swallow."

"*What?* No! Begone, evil woman!"

"It's the costume," the blue-dressed drag queen said to Cindy. "You can't convince Reverend Dixie that you're just a little lost lamb when you're dressed like *that*."

Cindy and Willy walked away. When they could no longer see the Southerner and the drag queens, Cindy and Willy stopped and looked at each other. Cindy had never been the type to console a sad person, and Willy had never been that type either. So neither one spoke words of comfort.

Instead, Cindy and Willy both said the same words at the same time: "Let's find some winos."

****

Two blocks away, in an alley, Cindy and Willy found a wino (whom they recognized) and a homeless man (whom they had never seen before).

"Hey, look," said the wino, "it's the chubby vampire chick and the faggot preacher!"

"I am not homothexual," Willy said.

"I am not fat," Cindy said.

"Are you two shittin' me?" the wino said. "Look at you, fella, you're wearing a purple shirt and a purple tie—"

Willy said, "I will have you know: The shirt's color is *thistle*, and the tie's color is *orchid*."

"—and as for you, sweetie," the wino continued, "I can see you've put on weight from three weeks ago."

"Perhaps," Cindy begrudged. For the past two months, Cindy was constantly hungry, especially for sweets. Not an hour went by that Cindy was not eating something. *Of course I'm gaining weight, duh!*

The homeless man looked at Cindy. "Are you—are you a real vampire?"

For the first time since sundown, Cindy spoke without a British accent: "I'm not a vampire, I just dress like one."

The wino cackled. "Be *glad* she's not a real vampire, George. The fangs come out when she sucks your dick."

George the homeless man looked confused. "She's sucked your dick, Robby?"

The wino cackled again. "Pay Chubby Vampire Girl five bucks, and she'll suck *your* dick too."

Cindy gave George a sexy smile. With the British accent back, Cindy said, "I must pay the rent somehow. So stud, are you up for a go? I will do you for three bucks if you wish, but then I shan't swallow."

****

Across the street, an old red pick-up truck was parked. It was ten years old, had sun-faded paint and a salt-eaten body, and there was a big dent in the passenger-side door. The old truck burned oil, and the air conditioner didn't work at all. The pickup truck's one mechanical virtue was that the heater worked like gangbusters.

Which was great in winter, but this wasn't winter.

The truck was prized by the driver, precisely because it was old and beat up. The driver liked to pay attention to strangers, but the beat-up truck ensured that he himself went unnoticed—

If the "vampiress" and the street preacher even noticed the driver, they would take him for a workman who was waiting for a coworker.

The driver had rolled both windows down. With the windows down, the driver clearly heard Cindy say, "I'm not a vampire, I just dress like one."

The driver thought, *But she sure looks like one, ayup. Suppose she were indeed a vampire? Why would a vampiress and a street preacher be hanging out together?*

Then the driver's eyes went wide, as ideas came to him.

He scooped up the steno pad that was always within his reach, flipped the notepad to a blank page, and started scribbling.

Portland's most famous resident had a great idea for his next novel.

Street-lamp light glinted momentarily off the scribbling driver's wedding ring, and he had a moment's thought: *That man is a flaming homosexual street preacher, and the woman is a fat five-dollar whore who dresses like a vampire. Neither of those two has any hope of marrying well, ayup.*

TO BE CONTINUED

BOOK 4

BOOK 4 OF
THE HYPNO-TALKERS
OF ZLAR

NERD
SAVES
WOMEN

DOCTOR MC,
MAD SCIENTIST

AUTHOR OF
THREE MORE WISHES

HYPO TO HELIO BOOKS

Chapter 0
Previously

Tuesday, April 2
Wheat City, Kansas

An alien spaceship from Zlar landed in a Wheat City suburban neighborhood. Then the spaceship (briefly) kidnapped fertile Earth women, all of whom were neighbors of old Kevin MacDonald.

Former Vietnam veteran Kevin MacDonald killed a Zlarian who was trying to use a hypno-talker on him. Kevin then took the hypno-talker as a spoil of war.

A U.S. Army company from Wheat City's Fort Carver—a company that was led by Captain Lourdes Taylor—killed all the other aliens, captured the Zlarian spaceship, and "rescued" the human women. However, Captain Taylor, instead of returning the rescued women to their homes and families, brought them to her house and turned them into her own personal lesbian harem.

However, Captain Taylor wasn't completely derelict in her duties: She turned the twelve Zlarian corpses over to Doctor Frank Renfield at the Fort Carver Post Hospital, as part of Plan Fifty-one. Doctor Renfield didn't impress Captain Taylor as very bright.

Thursday, April 4

Kevin MacDonald reverse-engineered the alien hypno-talker that he'd taken. His Earth-made copy of the hypno-talker got tested on two college students who came to his house to sell magazines: nerd Egbert Whitehall and big-breasted sorority babe Bethany Brown. Kevin programmed Egbert to "take charge of his life"; Kevin programmed Bethany to be horny for Egbert and to marry him for life.

Then Kevin MacDonald went to Lourdes Taylor's house, and freed his lesbianized neighbors from Taylor's hypnotic clutches. Kevin then used his hypno-talker to "convince" Taylor to first resign from the Army, and next to become a stripper and streetwalker.

Friday, April 5

Lourdes Taylor resigned her Army commission.

Saturday, April 6

By then, Kevin MacDonald already had learned that the U.S. Army, the FBI, and the CIA all had hypno-talkers. That offended Kevin.

So Kevin uploaded to the internet, schematics, computer source code, a parts list, and a user manual (and other help files) for his own hypno-talker. Specifically, Kevin uploaded these files to four pirate sites so that anyone in the world could download Kevin's files, and the U.S. government couldn't say jack shit.

Friday, April 12

Streetwalker Lourdes Taylor, who was calling herself "Bernadette" at the time, was unsuccessfully soliciting a young man (Egbert) at a Mexican restaurant. That's when Lourdes learned that a second Zlarian spaceship was headed for Wheat City—this time openly.

The spaceship landed half a block from where Lourdes was. But rather than capturing human women, the spaceship *released* nineteen human women, plus a sick Zlarian female.

One of the released human women was an Australian, Sheila. Lourdes took two pictures of Sheila and emailed the photos to Sheila's sister Lizzy in Darwin.

Egbert showed up just in time to see the spaceship leave. But his presence instantly turned the nineteen released women into "baby nymphos" who wanted nothing else but to get pregnant by him. Lourdes asked Egbert to leave, because with him around, Sheila was in no mood to answer Lourdes's questions.

Egbert left, as requested. Lourdes resumed questioning Sheila, who told her:

"Zlarian women all have a disease. Zlarian men don't catch it; and lucky for us, *we* don't catch it. So we Earth women get turned into surrogate mums."

But before Lourdes could ask Sheila more questions, the Army showed up and took the nineteen spaceship-released women, and the sick Zlarian female, to Fort Carver for secret Army experiments.

Friday evening, the first person who'd downloaded the internet plans for the hypno-talker, who'd built it, and who'd used it, reported back to the world: "[D]oes the hypno-talker work? FUCK YES, OMG!!!"

Chapter 1
Wheat City Reunion

Two-and-a-half days after the second spaceship landed

Just after midnight, Monday morning, April 15

Wheat City, Kansas

Egbert Whitehall woke up from a sound sleep with the thought blazing through his brain:

What happened to those women?

It was all over the Wheat City local news: The Australian government was claiming that:

• the Zlarian spaceship that had landed in Wheat City on Friday, had released Earth women,

• that one of the released women was an Australian, and

• that the Australian woman's sister, Elizabeth Smythe of Darwin, had received a mysterious email claiming that the U.S. Army had taken the women and was holding them at Fort Carver.

The Army denied everything.

The Wheat City news media then created stories implying that Australians were liars, the descendants of hardened English criminals, and kangaroo-fuckers.

Egbert hadn't really thought much about the spaceship-women, before now. And last night he hadn't thought about the spaceship-women *at all*; he'd been too busy getting sucked and fucked by Bethany.

And yet Egbert knew the spaceship-women were real— he'd seen them, heard them, and almost sired children with them. One of those women was *definitely* Australian—but if she wasn't already home in Australia right now, where was she? What had happened to her?

Egbert realized that the only person who might know (other than the Army) was Bernadette the streetwalker—but what if the Army had grabbed her as well?

Egbert *had to* find Bernadette. He leaped out of bed.

"You drank too much soda last night, Eggy?" a sleepy Bethany asked.

"I need to find out something," Egbert replied. "I'll be gone for a while, so go back to sleep." Egbert kissed Bethany's shoulder, then started getting dressed.

****

Egbert was cruising the streets, looking for Bernadette, but not having any luck. Then he started asking other hookers where Bernadette was. That didn't help him either—

"Hello, have you seen Bernadette? She's a prostitute with short purple hair."

"No, Sugar, but whatever she does for you, I can do it better."

"Hi, can you help me? I'm looking for a certain streetwalker with short purple hair. Name's Bernadette."

"I ain't seen her. What you want her for?"

"Maybe she's seen something important. I need to talk to her."

"Maybe she seed it, maybe she ain't—but if you drags her in front of the *police*, she ain't seen shit."

"Hi, I'm looking for a certain prostitute, named Bernadette, with short purple hair."

"You a cop?"

"Do I *look like* a cop?"

"I'm not saying another word to you! And for your information, I'm out here only to try and catch a taxi."

****

Finally at Joe's Burger Palace, Open 24 Hours, Egbert caught a break.

By the back of the restaurant was a picnic table, and sitting there were three women who were dressed like whores.

"I haven't seen anyone like that" was the reply given to Egbert by a young brunette with long, dark-red fingernails.

"I seed her," said a black woman dressed all in pink. "Friday night, she walkin' our street. Lucius, he pulled out a knife, walked up to her, and he told her either she gone be his bitch or she gone get took to the hospital. She did *sumpin'*—and then Lucius, he lying on his back with his wrist broke."

"Damn, what did she do?" asked the third woman there, a cigarette-puffing bottle blonde.

"Cain't tell you, even after I seed it. That bitch, she *fast*."

Egbert asked Miss Pink, "Any idea where I can find her?"

"She told me she strips at one of the clubs near Carver."

****

The bouncer at Dance The Army wouldn't let Egbert set foot inside the place, once he saw Egbert's I'm-only-nineteen driver's license. In any case, by then the time was only a few minutes before 2 a.m. closing time, so it didn't matter.

Egbert walked around to the back of the club, to the employees-only parking lot, and waited. Three argon lights made everything in the parking lot easy to see (if orangey).

Egbert had been waiting for ten minutes when the rear doors opened, and Bernadette and a blonde stepped out.

He called out, "Bernadette, is that you? It's me, Egbert."

Hearing those words, the blonde gasped, and ducked behind Bernadette—even though with her tall heels, the blonde actually was taller than Bernadette. As for Bernadette herself, she gave only a tiny gasp, then she frowned.

"Why are you here, Egbert? What do you want?"

He said, "The women who came out of the spaceship—where are they? What happened to them? I need to know."

"No you don't, Egbert. Trust me, drop this. Now excuse me, I'm going to walk . . ."

"Chinchilla," the blonde squeaked.

"Chinchilla to her car."

Just before Chinchilla got into her car, Egbert heard this very quiet conversation—

Chinchilla asked, "Are you going to be okay with him? Should I call the police?"

Bernadette said, "He's a good boy. But good boy or bad boy, I don't need the police. Thanks anyway."

****

Lourdes watched Wendy ("Chinchilla") drive away, then slowly she walked back to Egbert, the nerdy young college kid. Lourdes couldn't figure out why he was here.

"Egbert," she said to him when she got close, "the Army took those women away. I watched them do it. Let this go."

"No," he said. "*No*. I heard what you said over there: You called me a 'good boy.' A good boy doesn't make trouble. A good boy does what he's told. Well, I was a good boy that day. When you told me to leave, I left. Then what happened? Naked women got in trouble, they needed help, and I wasn't even there for them. But I'm here for them now."

"Egbert, *listen* to me—"

"Bernadette, I get it. You're scared, or you don't want to get involved. Just tell me what you saw and heard that day, then you can walk away and I'll take things from here."

Lourdes ignored the jab at being called "scared." How could he know he was talking to a former Army officer?

Instead, she said, "Dammit, you will get killed! Or Gitmo'd. Or thrown in Leavenworth for years, *if you're lucky*."

"My conscience bothers me, don't you get it? I know there's a problem with those women, and I haven't helped them, and I need to fix that. And as a wise man, Kevin MacDonald, told me a week and a half ago, "Take charge, Egbert, starting with Bethany. A man can't be happy in his life if he doesn't take charge of it."

"Who's Bethany?"

Egbert waved that aside. "My girlfriend, since the day that Mr. MacDonald told me to take charge of my life. She's *hot*; she could pose for *Playboy*. And because I've taken charge, she fucks me, she sucks me, and one day she'll marry me. So *excuse me* for not playing by the rules anymore, because the rules say geeks don't fuck sorority hotties!"

Lourdes went silent for a few seconds, then asked, "Have you ever served in the military? Are you in ROTC?"

He said, "No and no."

"Do you own a weapon?" she asked. By which she meant *a firearm of some kind.*

"Does a wooden practice sword count?"

Lourdes wanted to laugh, or to scream. Instead she said, "Okay, I'm in. Now please get in my car, and let's go talk to MacDonald."

"Wow, that's great!" Egbert reached into his pocket and pulled out a smartphone. "Hold on while I Google where he lives. I've forgotten."

"No need, " Lourdes replied. "I know *exactly* where he lives."

"You do?"

****

BAM-BAM-BAM-BAM! BAM-BAM-BAM-BAM!

Egbert stood on the front porch, feeling amazed, as the purple-haired prostitute pounded on Kevin MacDonald's front door with all the strength she had.

By streetlamp light, Egbert then saw her turn her head and look at Egbert with a serious expression. "My real name is Lourdes. Lourdes Taylor. You can call me *Lourdes* or *Bernadette* either one, and I'll answer to it."

"Which name would you prefer?"

"Nuh-uh, wrong question. That's 'good boy' thinking."

Then Egbert understood. "Why did you tell me your real name?"

"Because as long as you and I are in this little task force, I'm taking orders from you, and a subordinate should never lie to her superior officer."

Egbert thought, *That's a really strange answer for a streetwalker to give.*

Lourdes pounded the door again: *BAM-BAM-BAM-BAM! BAM-BAM—*

The porch light came on, and the screen door opened up. There stood old Mr. MacDonald, who was wearing a bathrobe and holding a rifle.

Kevin MacDonald didn't seem to have noticed Egbert at all. Instead he was glaring at Lourdes-slash-Bernadette.

"Captain Taylor," Kevin said coldly.

Egbert thought, *"Captain" Taylor?*

"Good morning, corporal," the streetwalker replied. "I'm sure you remember Egbert? He and I need to talk to you."

Chapter 2
Plotting Against The Army

Fifteen minutes later
Kevin MacDonald's living room

The old man yawned—the time was between two and three in the morning—then he glanced at Egbert, then turned to look at Lourdes.

Kevin said, "One thing I don't understand, Cap—Lourdes. Egbert has the least tactical knowledge of the three of us, and you have the most—"

"Because she used to be an officer?" Egbert asked.

"Not *just* an officer," Kevin said. "Notice, she's wearing a West Point ring on her hand."

"Wow," Egbert said. He looked at Lourdes with new respect.

"So why are you taking orders from Egbert?" Kevin asked.

"Two reasons, Kevin," Lourdes said. "The first reason is that I was told at West Point, 'Good officers lead. *Great* officers foster leadership in others.' Egbert is showing leadership, or trying to, and I want to encourage this. As for the second reason . . ."

Instead of saying more, Lourdes sighed, as she paused to stare at a psychedelic poster of a man on a motorcycle. Egbert saw Lourdes's shoulders slump.

Then after a time of silence, her shoulders straightened, and she looked at Egbert. "This isn't the first time the Zlarians came to Wheat City. The first time was two weeks ago—"

"The spaceship landed in front of my house," Kevin said. "That's when the captain and I met." He glared at Lourdes.

Egbert said, "Wait. Lourdes, you were an Army officer *two weeks ago*, and now you're a stripper and streetwalker? How did *that* happen?"

She said, "I resigned my commission because of this. I fucked up that day, I *royally* fucked up. The Zlarians had taken local women into the spaceship—"

"My neighbors," Kevin interrupted.

"And after my company liberated the women from the Zlarians, my orders were to take them to Fort Carver for medical and psychological screening. Exactly like what Lt. Cartwright did with Sheila and the other women you saw. My point is, Egbert, I never questioned those orders."

"But she didn't take my neighbors to Fort Carver," Kevin said. "She took them to her house and made them her own personal lesbian harem."

Egbert said, "*What?* My god, Lourdes, you took these women who were naked and had just been kidnapped by aliens, and you shoved a gun in their faces and told them they'd either lick your pussy or die? That's monstrous!"

Kevin and Lourdes exchanged a look. "There's something we haven't told him," Lourdes said.

"Yeah," Kevin said. To Egbert, the old man looked nervous for some reason.

****

Kevin MacDonald *really* wanted to avoid the topic of Zlarian hypno-talkers. He had reverse-engineered his spoil-of-war hypno-talker, and had then used his clone to reprogram both people in this room. Who each were smart.

What would happen if Lourdes or Egbert figured out that Kevin had whammied them?

****

"What are you talking about?" Egbert asked, an instant later.

Kevin said, "The Zlarians have a gizmo that they use to get Earthlings to do what they want. I call it a 'hypno-talker.'"

"Show Egbert what you took from the dead alien," Lourdes said to Kevin.

Kevin gave Lourdes a long look, but then he got up and walked toward the back of the house.

Lourdes then said to Egbert, "At the time, I tried to confiscate it. I was just following orders."

Soon after, Kevin returned, carrying what looked to Egbert like a bright-red tablet computer. Except that it had a small speaker in one corner, and an orange pushbutton.

Kevin pointed to a rectangular hole in the back. "This is for the Zlarian equivalent of a USB jack. This is where a Zlarian loads in a message. Then he presses the orange button, and an Earthling does whatever the message says."

Egbert says, "Wow, how jazzed you must be, an electrical engineer owning actual alien electronic technology."

Kevin frowned, then pointed to Lourdes. "But I'm not the only Earth person to grab up one of these. That day, Captain Taylor had an Army version of the hypno-talker."

Lourdes said, "Except the A-667KPK was more useful than that thing. It didn't need a cord, because it had a black Record button and a built-in microphone."

Egbert turned to look at Kevin. "Wow, that sounds *just like* your blue—"

Kevin said, "There's an Army version, an FBI version, and a CIA version. She used the Army version on my neighbors. She made them sex slaves!"

Lourdes shrugged.

Egbert got the feeling that his sleepy brain was missing something important. He put that thought aside and said,

"We need to move on. Lourdes, tell us everything you saw and heard three days ago with the spaceship."

When Egbert changed the subject, Kevin looked relieved.

****

Lourdes told her story about Sheila the Australian, the sick female alien, and the Army hauling them all away.

Egbert said, "Wow. So now we need to find out where the naked women and the alien woman are, and find out what the Army knows."

Lourdes said, "And find out what the Army plans with them. The Zlarian female might already be dead."

"Good point," Egbert said. "Do either of you have suggestions *how* we can accomplish these impossible tasks?"

Kevin said reluctantly, "I suppose I could clone the Army's hypno-talker, and use that *on* the Army to get info."

Lourdes said, "I thought you already made one. Didn't you bring a home-made hypno-talker into my house two weeks ago?"

Kevin stared at Lourdes for a second or two, and to Egbert, the old man's face sure looked panicky. Then Kevin broke his silence with, "Right, I did. I forgot about that."

Egbert said, "It doesn't matter. I don't like the idea of hypnotizing people, to get what I want from them—"

Now Lourdes looked as uncomfortable as Kevin. But she said, "I'm obliged to point out, Egbert, that this might be our only option."

Egbert shrugged. "But it's not our only option *now*."

Kevin said, "So, hypothetically speaking, you wouldn't have used a hypno-talker on Bethany if you had owned one."

Egbert shook his head. "That would be wrong."

Then Egbert said, "Anyway, I don't feel it's right to go around hypnotizing people, even if I can. Does anyone have any other ideas, how we can learn what secrets the Army is keeping about these people?"

Lourdes said, "You leave it to me. I'll get you that information."

"How—?"

"It won't be by hypno-talker," Lourdes said. But she didn't explain further.

Chapter 3
Perry Ringling's Bad Monday

Early Monday morning, April 15
Aboard a runway-bound, motionless airplane
Washington, D.C.

"Ladies and gentlemen, this is your captain speaking. A danger light has come on, so we're postponing takeoff till the problem's fixed. My apologies for the delay."

Great, passenger Perry Ringling thought. *Peachy.* He had missed sleep to be at the airport especially early—but at least he would arrive in New York early. Or so the plan went. But now some lazy airplane mechanic had ruined Perry's plan.

Then Perry thought, *If the president had ordered the Air Force to fly me around today, I wouldn't have this problem.*

But that would require more firmness with the Air Force than the man had in him. President Barry Buchanan avoided taking a stand, no matter how small.

****

The night before, Perry Ringling (28-year-old Assistant to the White House Chief of Staff) had watched while President Buchanan had paced back and forth on the Oval Office carpet.

Buchanan yelled, "Those aliens make me look like a fool!"

Chief of Staff Henderson made sympathetic noises.

"Then you have the other thing," the president ranted. "Some guy in Wheat City—the same Wheat City where the spaceship landed as easily as if they owned the place—he has published the plans on how to build a hypno-talker."

Perry asked, "Why don't you get a law passed making owning hypno-talkers illegal?"

President Buchanan pouted. "I wanted to, but the CIA, the FBI, and the Army all told me that such a law would cause them problems."

Of course, that problem would have ended instantly if President Buchanan would have replied, *Tough shit. I'm the president, and I will get this law made.* But Perry knew what the chances of *that* were.

Perry asked, "So who's the guy who published that stuff?"

Buchanan shrugged. "Beyond that he lives in Wheat City, we don't know. The FBI tells me they don't have the manpower to track this guy down."

Which of course wouldn't be a problem, Perry knew, if Buchanan would tell the FBI, *Too fucking bad. Track him down anyway.* But alas, Barry Buchanan was known as "the Indecider" for a reason.

The conversation shifted to what was going on in Fort Carver. President Buchanan had talked about releasing the rescuee women and the female alien, but then Secretary of Defense Buford started nattering about "national security." Buchanan stopped talking about releasing the women.

Then Perry spoke up: "Why don't I fly out to Wheat City and be the White House observer? Remind those Army people whom they work for."

"Would you, please?" Buchanan said. "That would be great."

"Plus I could investigate this other thing, while I'm in Wheat City. I could find out who VietVetElecEngnr51 is."

"Yes!" Buchanan said. "Perry, you're a lifesaver. Thank you for your dedication. I'll make the travel arrangements now." The president walked to his fancy desk and picked up the phone.

Perry said, "I do have one little request, for when I'm talking to all these different people."

"I'm listening."

"I need a hypno-talker. Of my own."

"No! Those things are evil—"

"I need one for *persuasion*, Mr. President. I really need it."

"You really do?"

"Yes, Mr. President," making his voice sound like what he was saying was obvious.

"Okay. I'll get the CIA to deliver one to the White House tonight."

****

Perry Ringling at twenty-eight was an almost-handsome man. And that explained much about him.

Perry had been born with a handsome face. As a small boy, his sister's friends and his female cousins had fussed over him. Even other girls in his school, at an age when girls supposedly didn't like boys, treated Perry as someone special.

As the saying goes, "Those who have, get." In fifth grade, Perry started growing. By eighth grade, he was the tallest boy in his school, and girls in middle school swooned when he talked to them.

Perry learned how to be charming, to make swoony girls swoonier. And it worked: In high school, not only was he bedding girls left and right his senior year, but he also was elected Class President.

When Perry was eighteen, he was a sex god. He was dating (and sleeping with) Sarah Ryan; every student in the school (except *possibly* the gays and the straight girls) wanted to fuck Sarah Ryan. And while Perry never did anything with Miss Baker, anyone in their English class could tell that the teacher wanted to fuck the student as much as Perry wanted to fuck Miss Baker.

Ah, those were the good old days: age eighteen. Because when Perry was nineteen and in college, he noticed: *His forehead was getting taller*.

By age twenty-two, balding Perry was already on the downhill slide. His bride, Sophie, was more attractive than 95 percent of other women. But Sophie wasn't a *stunner*, because the super-desirable women wouldn't date Perry anymore.

Now at twenty-eight, that part of Perry's life was over. Done. History. Below the eyebrows, Perry's handsome face and his tall build still said *movie star*. But what the top of Perry's head said was *middle-aged loser*.

And forget buying a toupee. Women could always tell, and they laughed at a man who wore one.

Alas, Perry had gotten spoiled by the time he was nineteen. He had come to enjoy special treatment, and he had come to expect sidestepping all the shit that ordinary men had to put up with. Baldy Perry *would not* give those things up! Not to mention, marital fidelity was for pencil-dicks. So if the only way for Perry to get world-class sex now was by cheating with a hypno-talker, that was not a problem.

****

Monday morning, the good news for Perry was, he had one of those notorious hypno-talkers in his briefcase. But that was the only thing to go right for Perry today.

At the moment, three men in green overalls were doing mysterious things underneath the quiet, motionless airplane. Perry heard a *clank-clank-clank* hammering sound come from below.

****

9:30 Monday morning (Eastern time)

Corporate headquarters, IEEE (Institute Of Electrical and Electronic Engineers)
New York City, New York

Perry Ringling walked into the headquarters of the organization for electrical and electronic engineers. These people would know the name of each and every such engineer in Wheat City, Kansas.

In the entrance lobby was a wide desk, behind which sat a security guard. Perry walked up to him, intending to ask for directions. But before Perry could say anything, the guard said, "Please put your briefcase on da counter and open it."

"*What?*"

Security Guard Carletti repeated the request, but no longer in a polite tone of voice. He added, "You got a problem with dat?"

Perry said, "Do you know who I am? I'm with the White House."

Carletti said, "I don't give a rat if you're da Indecider himself. You ain't getting past me until I look inside your briefcase, and dat's a fact."

With a sigh, Perry put his briefcase on the counter, dialed the "unlock" combination, unsnapped the briefcase, and lifted the lid.

Carletti's hand moved quickly, and he'd snatched the hypno-talker out of the briefcase before Perry's own hands had barely moved.

"Hey, that's mine!" Perry yelled. "That's my tablet computer you just grabbed!"

Carletti gave Perry a smart-ass smile. "Yeah? Dis place got guys who build *hypno-talkers* on weekends, so you think I don't know one when I see it? What's your name, Mr. White House, so I know what to write on da sticky-note?"

Carletti would not be reasoned with, and he could not be bullied. Perry simply was not getting his hypno-talker back before he was about to leave the building, "fuhgeddaboudit."

****

The young man in the IEEE Legal Department bit his lip. "Why does that name 'VietVetElecEngnr51' sound familiar?"

Another young man, who was typing on a computer nearby, replied, "He's the guy who uploaded the schematics and parts list for the hypno-talker. He also wrote a pretty good user manual, I hear."

The first young man turned back to Perry and said, "IEEE will comply with any subpoena that relates to VietVetElecEngnr51—that is, once a judge has ruled against our challenge to such a subpoena. But *without* a subpoena, you're out of luck, Mr. Ringling."

"Dammit, this man's action *helps terrorists!*"

The first man replied, "In that case, IEEE *definitely* won't divulge information without all due process being observed. The White House has cried wolf nonstop since 2001."

****

One o'clock Monday afternoon (Central time)
Office Of Vital Statistics, Kansas Department Of Health And Environment
Topeka, Kansas

A trip from New York City to Topeka that would have taken President Buchanan two hours at most, flying on Air Force One, had taken Perry four hours to make. But finally Perry was in Topeka.

For all the good it was doing him.

Perry figured that if VietVetElecEngnr51 lived in Wheat City, he might have gotten a divorce in Kansas. Since engineers make good money, his wife would have mentioned his job in the divorce papers. So Perry wanted to find all Kansas divorce decrees in which the husband was an EE and who had been born in 1951.

That had been the plan. But now Perry was being balked by a Kansas bureaucrat who wore horn-rim glasses: ". . .are not public documents. We give out copies only to the people named in the divorce decree, to their lawyers, to immediate family, or to those who can show a direct interest in needing a particular record."

Perry said, "I'm not asking for *particular* records, I want to search *all* the records."

The man replied, "In that case, you'll need to provide us with a warrant."

"Dammit," Perry said, pulling out his White House ID badge, "I'm with the president!"

The bureaucrat was unimpressed. "We don't take orders from the White House. So no warrant, no search."

Chapter 4
Perry Interlude 1

Ten minutes later

Perry was in a rental car, driving through Topeka on his way to a highway that would take him to southeast Kansas. During Perry's drive through town, he passed a cemetery.

Across the street from the cemetery were demonstrators, holding up signs—

God Hates Fags

God Has Judged Him

Burn In Hell, Fag

The signs looked like the handiwork of Wessex Anabaptist Church of the King. Then Perry remembered that the WACK congregation was based right here in Topeka.

About the time Perry realized this, he noticed that two of the women demonstrators were naturally blonde and *hot*.

Perry loathed preachers, and anyone else who was against sinning. Perry *liked* sin—the more pleasurable, the better. So Perry decided to take those WACK people down a peg.

Besides, it was about time that Perry test-drove the hypno-talker.

One minute after Perry decided to score some WACK babes, the car was parked nearby, Perry had earplugs in his ears, and he had the flat-black CIA hypno-talker in his hands. Perry pressed the black button and recorded this message—

You trust the bald guy holding the black tablet computer. You will obey his every order, you will believe anything he tells you, you will feel whatever

*he says you are feeling, and you will answer every
question he asks with the complete truth.*

With his heart pounding, Perry got out of his car and
walked toward the Wessex Anabaptist demonstrators.

****

Perry had been told that when he pressed the orange
button, everyone within five feet would start repeating what
they were ultrasonically hearing. If Perry didn't want to get
into trouble, he had to keep the blondes' WACK neighbors
from hearing what the blondes were saying.

So as soon as Perry got near the WACKs, even before he
was within five feet of the blondes, he started chanting,
"HALLELUJAH! PRAISE THE LORD! PRAISE JESUS!"

Loudly.

As he'd expected, the WACK churchgoers who were
unaffected by his hypno-talker started shouting back at him.
They completely failed to notice the two blonde women and
one man who were chanting words.

When Perry took his finger off the orange button, he
stopped yelling, and the three mind-controlled churchgoers
stopped chanting. But the others were still yelling.

Perry had to mouth the words, because no way could he
be heard over the shouting: "You and you, come with me."

"SINNER, GOD WILL SMITE—Sherry? Connie? Where
are you going?"

The blonde with the darker hair replied, "With him." She
gestured toward Perry.

"*Why* are you leaving with him?" the man asked.

"Because I trust him."

The surprised WACK members made no attempt to block
the blondes from leaving; Perry had gambled correctly.

By the time that the blondes had climbed into the back seat of Perry's rental car, he had noticed that they each were wearing wedding rings.

This should be fun, Perry thought.

****

"Tell me your names," Perry said.

"Sherry Phillips-Hemper," said the woman with honey-blonde hair.

"Connie Phillips-Smith," said the woman with bright yellow hair.

"You're both related to 'Brother Rod' Phillips?"

Both women laughed. Sherry said, "Mister, *everyone* in Wessex Anabaptist is related to Brother Rod, one way or another. Connie and I are second cousins."

****

Fifteen minutes later, Perry had registered at the Fantasy Nights Motel ("Hourly Rates Available").

As soon as Perry got Sherry and Connie in the motel room, he told them, "Take all your clothes off, and put them in a pile. Then take your rings off and put them on top of the pile."

Seconds later, Perry was amazed. *My god, they're actually getting buck-ass naked? This thing works!*

Bright-yellow-haired Connie asked (not angry, just confused), "Why are we getting naked with you?"

But meanwhile, she was getting undressed, as was Sherry.

Perry replied, "You're getting undressed because we're about to have sex. But it's okay, it's not wrong."

In less than a second, each woman quit frowning.

When both women were naked, Perry also got undressed. Long hours in the White House had given him a bit of a paunch, but the cousins didn't ridicule him.

Seeing the women naked, Perry was surprised to discover that both Phillips women had fake tits. Their boobs weren't stripper or porn-star sized, it's just that they were bigger than normal, and they didn't hang right to be natural.

All three adults now were naked; "Kiss me," Perry said.

Perry let Sherry, and then Connie, kiss him for a long time.

(Perry had zero interest in kissing; he wanted to go straight to the sex. But he'd learned the hard way that women didn't arouse without a lot of kissing.)

He interrupted kissing Sherry to look over at Connie. "Each of you stroke yourself while I'm kissing the other girl." Connie immediately (and unashamedly) started to masturbate.

Isn't the hypno-talker a great invention? Perry marveled.

Perry looked at honey-blond Sherry, whom he had stopped kissing. He said, "Each of you stroke my cock while I'll kissing you."

Perry went back to kissing Sherry, who immediately started to stroke his dick. Perry responded to getting his dick stroked by feeling up Sherry's fake tits.

By now, Sherry's nipples were stiff, and they were sticking out about half an inch.

A minute later, Perry switched to kissing Connie; so it was Connie's tits he pawed, and it was Connie's hands that stroked his cock.

Soon after Sherry started touching her pussy, she began to moan.

"Mmm, I feel so *good*," Sherry said. "This is *niiice*."

Perry kept kissing Connie for several minutes more, while Sherry's moans got louder. Then (judging by her sudden trembling and gasping), Sherry had an orgasm.

****

When Sherry had calmed down a little, Perry said to the honey blonde, "Sherry, you want to suck my cock now. It's okay to suck me."

Sherry's blowjob was so-so, even with her moaning while she was blowing Perry. But hey, Sherry's blowjob was free.

"Oh yeah, *suck* it, bitch!" Perry exclaimed.

Meanwhile, Connie had been kissing Perry; she now broke the kiss.

Connie asked, "Why are you insulting Sherry?" Once again, Connie's voice didn't sound angry, just puzzled. "That is not a nice word, what you called Sherry."

Perry replied, "During sex, it's not an insult if someone calls you *bitch*, or *slut*, or *whore*. In fact, it turns you on."

"Gotcha," Connie said.

Connie said to Sherry, "Suck him good, slut."

Then Connie went back to kissing Perry while he felt up her tits.

Sherry's cocksucking was inept, but the whole situation was exciting Perry. After a few minutes, he said, "I'm about to spurt. Swallow me, swallow me!"

Sherry did indeed swallow his cum, while Connie kept kissing him, and all this happened while Perry was still feeling up Connie's tits. Life was good.

When Sherry had sucked him soft, Perry said, "Sherry, go to the sink and rinse your mouth out. Connie, you get over here and suck me hard again."

Bright-yellow-haired Connie, it turned out, was a better cocksucker than Sherry was. Connie licked the underside of Perry's dick like it were a popsicle; Sherry had done nothing so fancy. Neither woman deepthroated Perry's dick, but Connie fell only an inch short of her lips reaching the end of his shaft.

Perry said, "Oh yeah, slut, that is damned good dick-slurping!"

****

When Perry was hard again from Connie's blowjob, by now Sherry was standing by the bed, jilling herself.

Perry moved off the bed. "You two lie side by side on the bed, with your hips at the edge of the bed. That way, I can fuck both of you, one after the other."

Connie said, "Did you bring condoms? I don't have any."

"Me neither," said Sherry, as she took her assigned place on the edge of the bed.

Perry replied, "I didn't bring condoms either. So you sluts better hope I don't get you pregnant."

Then Perry added, "By the way, it really gets each of you horny to have me fuck you, even though you've never met me before."

"*Ohh*, yes," Connie said, as she stroked her clit.

"*Mmm*, yeah," Sherry said, likewise fingering herself.

Then Perry fucked honey-blond Sherry till he climaxed. Her pussy was loose, but Perry coped. Sherry moaned as soon as Perry stuck his dick in; she immediately locked her ankles behind his ass. Sherry was already wet, which helped get Perry off.

Soon Sherry was yelling, "Oh god, oh yes, I'm—I'm—Take me, mysterious stranger!"

Perry's come felt *good*.

Once Perry was soft, after he'd fucked Sherry, he had bright-yellow-haired Connie suck him hard again. Connie made a face till Perry told her that she liked the combined taste of semen and pussy juice on his dick. Instantly her grimace vanished.

After that, Perry fucked loose-pussied Connie till he came. She also was wet when Perry stuck his dick in.

"This adultery is so delicious!" Connie yelled. "Fuck me some more!"

Anyway, Perry came twice, from fucking Sherry and from fucking Connie. Each woman climaxed at least once; but Perry didn't bother to keep count.

****

In the motel room, by the window, was a table with two little chairs by it. Perry slid off the bed and, seconds later, brought a chair back by the bed. He sat down on the chair and looked at the two women, who by now were sitting up.

"Lick each other," Perry ordered them. "It's okay to go lezzie with me watching, plus you'll enjoy it. Whatever weird tastes you taste, don't let them bother you. Take turns licking each other the way you each would like to be licked. Make each other cum, over and over. Connie, do you want to kick off, or receive?"

"I want to get a licking before I give it. So lick my slit, whore," Connie said.

Both Sherry and Connie had been lying so that their knees and lower legs were off the bed. Now Connie moved back, so that her head was on the pillow. Sherry rolled over onto her stomach, then moved up the bed till her face was just below Connie's bright-yellow-colored pubic hair.

Sherry went to work. Connie gasped. Perry couldn't see whether Sherry was using lips, or tongue, or both—but it didn't really matter, did it?

In less than a minute, Connie was yelling, "Agghh! Oh, *yes! Yes!* YES!" She thrust her hips off the bed, and Connie's hands pressed Sherry's head into her pussy.

Then Perry had Connie and Sherry switch positions. Whereas Connie screamed and talked dirty, Sherry was a woman who shook all over, like gelatin, when she climaxed.

****

Perry decided to use the hypno-talker's previous commands in order to make mischief. He said, "Sherry? Connie? After having sex together, you feel no tinge of conscience, right? What's more, you two realize you're each hot for the other."

Sherry said, "You are so right about that." Then she leaned forward and kissed Connie.

When they broke the kiss, Connie said, "Now I'm confused. Aren't we lesbians now? And doesn't God hate us?"

Perry said, "Believe me, it's okay to be lesbian with your second cousin."

"Okay," they each said. In less than a second, the worry on both their faces vanished.

Perry said, "Please, go back to kissing each other and feeling each other up."

They started kissing again. Sherry began stroking Connie's pussy, while Connie began stroking Sherry's tits.

Perry decided to make more mischief: "Sherry, Connie, you realize that you like sex with each other more than sex with your husbands. In fact, you realize that you're not interested in sex with your husbands at all."

Connie said, "Well, duh. He's lumpy and hairy, and he's going bald, and he's always pulling that 'Be submissive unto your husbands' shit on me. Whereas Sherry looks good, and she knows how to get me going."

Sherry said, "Agree totally. My husband is completely boring in bed—funny, I only now realized that."

Perry said, "Now you two women realize that you have no sex-interest in any man—your husbands, me, Brad Pitt, Clark Gable, anyone."

"Huh," Connie said.

"Wow, you're right," Sherry replied.

Perry continued, "You don't mind a man watching you two go at it. Actually, it turns you on even more, to make love to your cousin in front of a man. But each of you has zero interest in letting that man join in."

"Well, duh," Connie said. "A man doesn't know how to please my pussy the way that Sherry can, so why waste time on him?"

At that point, Sherry and Connie started kissing, then they starting caressing and groping, then they started licking. As before, Connie screamed and talked dirty, while Sherry trembled all over.

"*Ohh*, yeah," said Connie to Sherry, "you are *definitely* better than any man, slut! Keep licking me there!"

Watching the two women cousins have sex, Perry smiled. Wessex Anabaptist Church of the King, the "God Hates Fags" church, was soon going to be rocked by a lesbian scandal.

Which would be all Perry's doing. Perry enjoyed taking holier-than-thou people down a peg.

Chapter 5
Tuesday Is Worse Than Monday

Tuesday, April 16, 8 a.m. (Central time)
Gale County Office of Vital Statistics
Gulch, Kansas (15 miles from Wheat City)

For Perry, it was back to getting shit-on by local bureaucrats.

Perry didn't have a warrant, so he wasn't getting shit, so far as milking the county records for any divorce information.

****

Tuesday, April 16, 8: 30 a.m. (Central time)
Fort Carver Post Personnel Office
Wheat City, Kansas

Now Perry was in the Army personnel office that was attached to the Fort Carver Post Commander. Perry was hoping that VietVetElecEngnr51 was working for Fort Carver as a civilian employee or contractor.

Another wasted trip. A young woman in office Army uniform was now looking up at Perry. In a bored voice, she said, "Our records show only two civilians working on post who were born in 1951. One is a landscaper, and the other works at the bowling alley. Sorry we can't help you."

Perry said, "Maybe he isn't working for the Army *now*, but maybe long ago he was discharged from the Army here."

The young woman shrugged. "If he retired around 1999 or 2000, *maybe* we've got him. But if he served less than thirty, he won't be in our records."

She typed on the keyboard, and a second later announced in that same bored voice, "Sure enough, 'No record found.' "

It occurred to Perry that this woman might find the answers he wanted if she got a little more *motivated*. He told her, "I'll be right back."

Perry went into the men's room, removed the hypno-talker from his briefcase, and recorded a command:

"You trust me. You want to help me."

Then Perry put the hypno-talker back in his briefcase, shut the briefcase, and put earplugs in his ears.

Perry walked up to the bored-looking young woman, opened his briefcase, took out the hypno-talker—

And bedlam erupted in the personnel office.

****

Perry, with his earplugs in, couldn't hear what people were yelling; but it was a fact that suddenly people *were* yelling. Many people.

The young woman clapped her hands over her ears, then used her heels to roll her chair away from her desk.

Ditto everyone else within a five-foot radius.

Perry's peripheral vision caught a man standing up. When Perry looked at him directly, he saw that the standing man was an officer (he had a pair of silver bars on his collar), and the standing man was pointing a gun at Perry with his right hand. With his left hand, the officer was tossing what looked like big plastic earmuffs to a young enlisted man.

The officer was far enough away to be out of the five-foot range of the hypno-talker, but close enough that he probably wouldn't miss if he fired his gun. Perry was in deep shit.

The enlisted man put on the plastic earmuffs, then walked up to Perry along a path that kept him out of the officer's line of fire. The enlisted man snatched the hypno-talker away from Perry and laid it on a nearby desk. The woman whose desk it was, stared at the hypno-talker like it were a rotting poodle corpse.

The enlisted man pulled down his plastic earmuffs to wrap around his neck, pointed at Perry, then pantomimed removing earplugs.

Perry did so (which made his ears pop). The first thing Perry heard was the officer saying, "Give me one reason why I shouldn't have you arrested."

The bored young woman clerk (who by now was back at her desk), turned to the officer and said, "He's with the White House, sir."

The officer said, "Sergeant Wilkes, give him back his hypno-talker when he's outside. Make sure you're wearing ear protection when you hand it to him."

Then the officer said to Perry, "Mister, you're done here. Get out."

Chapter 6
Impressed

Later Tuesday morning, April 16

Fort Carver, Kansas

The only thing stopping Perry Ringling from getting into the conference room was one soldier with a sidearm. But that was enough, unfortunately.

The young man with boots and pistol said, "I say again, *sir*, that I can't let you pass into the conference room without your escort." Supposedly because Perry Ringling was wearing a Visitor badge.

Ringling replied, "I didn't feel like waiting, and Lt. Timbello is at this moment in the head—"

"This isn't the Navy, *sir*. That isn't what the Army calls it."

"Whatever. Bathroom, toilet, water closet—*latrine!* Timbello is in the latrine, and I'm from the White House, so I decided to go to the conference room early."

The soldier's smile was evil. "Well, *sir*, there's exactly one person from the White House who I'll let in here without a Visitor badge, and you look nothing like him. So you'll just have to wait till Lt. Timbello shows up."

Ringling gripped the handle of his briefcase all the harder.

Soon Lt. Timbello arrived, and Ringling finally was allowed to enter the conference room.

Only to have to wait some more, till General Jordan showed up. *Dammit, don't the words 'White House' mean anything to <u>anyone</u> in Kansas?*

****

Later Tuesday morning

General John "Sand Ghost" Jordan was hearing a whole lot of *It's not my fault* this morning. He didn't like it.

". . .no definite results to report yet, because of the obstacles we've been facing, but I and the medics feel we are making good progress," Dr. Renfield said cheerfully.

Of course he's cheerful, General Jordan thought. *He's not the guy getting phone calls from the White House.*

"Before you sit down, Major Renfield," the general said, "I hear there have been several sexual assaults of the rescuees by our medics? Care to comment?"

By *rescuees*, General Jordan meant the nineteen naked women who had walked off the Zlarian spaceship, only to be "rescued" at gunpoint, trucked to Fort Carver, and prevented from leaving and from communicating with their families.

Now Renfield made a fist in outrage. "General, I am as shocked as you at the lax discipline among this hospital's medics. Even our supposedly homosexual medic has been involved in these disgusting acts."

General Jordan let his face show nothing. "What have you done to stop further occurrences?"

"Every medic E-5 and below has been restricted to post for the past week and a half on my order, even those who live off-post. I would do more, but I've been told that court-martial is not an option."

Next to Lt. Timbello, Master Sergeant Kelly had the look of someone who was biting his tongue.

General Jordan, meanwhile, explained the facts of life to Renfield: "You can't court-martial a man for rape without mentioning at the court-martial who the rape victim is, and giving her a chance to testify. But our president *really* doesn't want the word to get out *officially* that we are holding those nineteen rescuees. The Australians already know way too much, thanks to whoever sent those emails."

Then General Jordan said, "Major Renfield and the medics, you are dismissed. Except for Master Sergeant Kelly, whom I wish to speak with about these sexual assaults. Master Sergeant, please wait in the hallway."

After part of the people in the conference room got up and left, General Jordan turned to Colonel Barkley. "And what have we learned about our captured spaceship?"

The Colonel sighed. "Other than some interesting things about metallurgy and plastics, nothing."

"*What?* How can this be? I understood that the spaceship was in near-perfect working order when we took it."

"The Zlarians pulled a sneaky on us. The short version is, somehow the *ship* realized that humans had taken over the ship, so the central computer and the backup computer both got auto-destructed with pre-aimed ray-guns. We've got no piloting software, no ship's logs, no user manuals—we can't even turn on the goddamn lights, sir."

"So we don't know shit about how to build that spaceship, or even how to fly that spaceship, you're telling me?"

"Yes, sir. Sorry, sir."

General Jordan let his face go blank again. "Everyone is dismissed; please send in Master Sergeant Kelly."

Everyone stood up except for the civilian, Ringling. General Jordan said, "You too, Mr. Ringling. Please wait outside in the hallway."

"I will not," Ringling said. "My job here is to observe and report *to the president.* You can't give me orders."

"Oh yes I can," Jordan replied. "You're a civilian allowed here by my sufferance. What I have to discuss with the master sergeant includes disciplinary matters that you need not see or hear."

"General, you can boss around these ground-pounders, but *I* don't have to—"

"Let me spell it out, Mr. Ringling. Either you walk out of this conference room, or you will be dragged out."

Ringling walked out, muttering, as Master Sergeant Kelly took a seat.

****

General Jordan got up, shut the conference-room door, then sat back down. He looked at Kelly.

"Rick, I've been watching you since Afghanistan. You speak honest truth. So tell me, what the fuck is going on with these sexual assaults?"

Rick Kelly replied, "Sir, they're going on, but Major Renfield—meaning no disrespect—has it ass-backward. Our men aren't raping the rescuees, the *rescuees* are raping *the men!* Soon as a soldier walks into the room with one of 'em, she starts yelling about 'I want your baby.' And if one of our soldiers comes across *two* of the rescuees, they'll rip his uniform off, hold him down, and take turns fucking him."

"And that's how the homosexual could be involved in one of these assaults?"

"Yes, sir. And don't even think of wearing a condom, because the rescuees will yank it off—painfully, I'm told."

In spite of himself, General Jordan grimaced.

Kelly added, "But around other women—nurses or female medics—the rescuees act perfectly normal. Well, except that Sheila Blackburn, the Australian, has started demanding to be released and is becoming uncooperative."

"I see," the general said. "Now tell me about the other project, trying to create a bioweapon against the Zlarians. Why is there no progress there?"

Kelly said, "Because we medics are out of our depth. I know all about field combat medicine in humans, but nothing about *this* stuff. Do you know that the Zlarian blood is gray, not red? And they have a four-leaf-clover-shaped organ where I'd expect their stomach to be."

"This four-leaf clover, what does it do?"

"Can't tell you, sir. I can't even guess. All I can tell you is that it has a whole lot of little blood vessels going in and out of the different 'leaves.' "

"And Major Renfield, is he out of his depth as well?"

"Sir, he is my ranking officer, and—"

"Master Sergeant, I give you a direct order to answer my question completely and honestly."

"Sir, he acts like the Zlarians are just short men in Halloween costumes. When I asked him what the four-leaf-clover organ might be for, he said, quote, 'I have no idea, but I don't think it's important.' We've spent way too much time testing bioweapon agents on Zlarian tissue samples, and Major Renfield seems puzzled that weapons engineered for humans won't harm Zlarians."

General Jordan sighed. "So Major Renfield is not suited to be in charge of Plan Fifty-one."

"Sir, I never said that."

The general said, "And who would be the perfect doctor to be in charge of this? Describe him."

"Sir, *she* would be a medical doctor, not a nurse or medic. She could talk to the rescuees without them going apeshit, and she wouldn't have to get info about the rescuees secondhand, like Major Renfield and I have to. The really blue-sky part, sir, is that this ideal lady doctor would have to know a lot about aliens. So she'd understand what she was seeing when she did the autopsies."

General Jordan nodded. "I have presidential authority to make personnel changes to Plan Fifty-one. Soon you'll have the boss you need, Master Sergeant."

Then General Jordan started writing on a pad. "In the meantime, I am making a written order that only women are to deal face-to-face with the patients of Isolation Ward Two."

****

As soon as Master Sergeant Kelly walked out, the pompous civilian Ringling rushed in. "General, the president needs your help."

General Jordan, knowing well that the president was fully equipped to give orders directly to any Army general, replied, "And what does he need my help *for?*"

Ringling pulled out a tablet computer; soon after, General Jordan was looking at an internet page, DataRFree.nz.

Ringling explained, "This is a pirate website. Mostly they offer Blu-ray movies, which costs Americans in the intellectual-property sector their livelihoods. But the site also has this."

Ringling did a little typing, to call up a new page, and then General Jordan hissed.

The tablet's screen read, "Do-It-Yourself Hypno-Talker," and the picture showed a device that, except for being painted royal blue, closely matched the Army's A-667KPK. Worse, the web page offered PDF files explaining *everything*.

Ringling pointed to the upper-right portion of the page. "See that name there, 'VietVetElecEngnr51'? The FBI believes he lives right here in Wheat City. The president wants him dealt with."

"So have the FBI go pick him up, if they know where he lives."

"They don't, not beyond what city. In any case, the FBI has only one agent for this entire county. But you're in command of hundreds of Army people."

"Forget it."

"*What?*" Ringling tapped the picture on the screen. "This could be an Army hypno-talker, repainted."

"Got any proof of that?"

"No, but—"

"Then catching this guy is the FBI's job. Or yours, if you've got a bug up your ass. But *not* the Army's job, and *not* mine. We clear?"

"Fine!" Ringling said. "If *you're* not going to find this guy VietVetElecEngnr51 and arrest him, then *I* will!"

****

Two days later
Thursday morning, April 18
Wahiawa, Oahu, Hawaii

Thirty-two-year-old Terri Rivers was just in the process of loading an Amy Hanaiali'i compact disk into the player, when someone started pounding on the front door.

Terri went to the front door and looked through the spy-hole. She saw two men in suits; and a third man in Army Class "A" dress-blue uniform.

She was not about to simply open the door. She called out, "Who are you, and what do you want?"

One of the men held up a gold badge to the spy-hole. "Are you Terri Rivers? We need to talk to you."

Terri couldn't begin to imagine what they had to ask her; still, she opened the door.

As soon as Terri opened the door, she saw that that the two men in in suits were big and beefy, and the man in Army uniform was an officer.

The two men in suits both showed her FBI identification cards. One man was taller, the other was almost bald. The Army officer introduced himself as Major Paul Saunders.

Bald Man asked her, "You are Theresa Rivers, novelist, with pen name of Terri Rivers?"

She said, "It isn't just my pen name. I've been called this since first grade. Why are you here?"

Tall Man asked her, "You are the author of *The Sword Of My Sharona*, also *Magic Kingdom For Rent—Cleaning Deposit Required*, also *Robot Riot In Colony 138*, also *The Third Alien Invasion*?"

"Twenty-two novels altogether. But what—?"

Now the Army officer spoke up: "And you served in the Army for six years as a medical doctor, specializing in internal medicine?"

"Is anyone here going to answer *my*—?"

"Please just answer the question," Major Saunders said.

"*Yes!*" Terri said. She looked at the three men expectantly.

Bald Man and Tall Man turned to look at Major Saunders. Saunders reached inside his uniform jacket and pulled out a folded piece of paper.

Saunders said, "Captain Theresa Rivers, you are recalled to Army military service immediately."

"*What?*" Terri took the paper but didn't read it. "I fulfilled my obligation! I've got a DD-214"—official military discharge—"in a filing cabinet in the other room."

"Doesn't matter," Major Saunders replied, "you're in the Army now, and now I'm ordering you to come with me."

" 'Come with me'? Without me even shutting down my computer, or phoning my husband? He'll think I was kidnapped!"

"No he won't," Tall Man said. He reached into his pocket and pulled out a three-by-five card, with some text on it and a picture of an eagle. Tall Man dropped the card on the carpet, just inside the door.

The card read:

This is not a kidnapping. _[Theresa Rivers]_ at this address has been NATIONALIZED ON SHORT NOTICE by an agency of the United States government, under authority of U. S. Secret Law 2002-17.

After Terri read the card, she said, "Well, I'm impressed."

To lock her front door, she had to get her key out of her purse. Bald Guy went with her when she went to her purse, and it was Bald Guy who actually locked the front door.

Parked at the curb, waiting for her once she was outside, was an Army-painted van.

As Terri was being rushed through the Honolulu airport, she had barely enough time to notice a newspaper headline: "AUSSIES TO WHITE HOUSE: WHERE IS SHEILA?"

Chapter 7
Welcome Back To The Army

Thursday evening

Fort Carver, Kansas

Whatever the Army wanted her for, Terri Rivers had quickly figured out, they wanted her *badly*.

She had been put on a military airplane, not a civilian airliner, so that when the airplane stopped in California (for refueling), nobody would have to go through Customs. Once the airplane had fuel, the airplane had flown straight from California to Fort Carver.

But what had really tipped Terri off that the Army seriously wanted her was that in the airplane had been Army dress and utility uniforms enough for a full issue for ten different women; the airplane had contained a first sergeant and a corporal, who each had worked at sewing machines. Terri had boarded the airplane in Honolulu wearing a t-shirt, shorts, and sandals; in Kansas she walked off the airplane in Army "dress blues" uniform.

Three minutes after her dress pumps touched pavement, Terri was standing in front of a general.

Good. now I'll finally get some answers, she thought.

****

In front of the general's desk, Terri saluted, but her salute was sloppy. *Deliberately* so. At the same time, Terri came only halfway to attention. (Her left hand wasn't pressing against her uniform skirt, and her stance had a slight slouch to it.)

Just to make her feelings clear, Terri's first words were "Reactivated Army Captain Theresa Rivers, here involuntarily. Sir."

The general (his nametag said "Jordan") sharply returned the salute, then replied, "Dr. Rivers, you have unique knowledge and skills, which I desperately need right now. That's why I reactivated you."

"You need me to write a novel set in an Army hospital?" she replied sarcastically.

"Dr. Rivers," Jordan said, "I remind you that I outrank you by quite a bit."

"And *I* remind *you* that I've been kidnapped."

"Legally, all legally," he replied. Before Terri could say more, General Jordan said, "Do you know where you are?"

"Fort Carver," Terri said. "Somewhere in Kansas."

"We're in *Wheat City*, Kansas," the general said.

Terri was stunned. Wheat City had been all over the news recently. She asked, "Does that UFO have something to do with my reactivation?"

Someone knocked on the door then, then someone entered. A man who was wearing a Major's oak leaf on one collar, a caduceus on the other collar, and a white lab coat over his uniform, walked up next to Terri and saluted the general. "Major Frank Renfield reporting as ordered, sir."

General Jordan said, "Major Renfield, I am relieving you of responsibility for Project Fifty-one. This is Captain Rivers, who now will head the Project."

"I see," said Renfield, in an angry voice. "Sir, I think she should have rank of Major at least, if you choose to put a woman in charge of Project Fifty-one."

Terri snapped, "What's this *woman* business? is the Army allowing sexism again?"

Jordan replied to the angry man, "Major, Captain Rivers here has unique knowledge and skills that qualify her to head the Project."

Then the general turned to Terri. "Major Renfield's comment about you being a woman isn't sexism. it's actually relevant to the Project."

Terri said, "With all due respect, sir, since I've clearly been drafted out of civilian life to head Project Fifty-one, I sure wish someone would explain what that is."

Jordan replied, "Easier to show you than to tell you."

Jordan picked up the telephone. "This is General Jordan. Tell my driver to bring my car around."

****

In the official car, Renfield said to Terri, "We haven't touched eight of 'em. All twelve are in the cooler, but that doesn't matter much. Our bacteria don't like them."

Terri shook her head. "I have no idea what you're talking about."

****

Five minutes later, the two men and Terri were in the post hospital, at the entrance to Isolation Ward Two.

General Jordan introduced Terri to the M-16-carrying soldiers who guarded the entrance to the isolation ward. Jordan told the soldiers that at first, Terri would have only civilian forms of ID; Jordan did not explain why.

Both guard-soldiers were women. Terri wondered about that.

Once in the isolation ward, Jordan walked Renfield and Terri to a pair of doors. By the doors was a numeric keypad, and two more woman soldiers with M-16s. Again General

Jordan introduced Terri, and again Jordan informed the soldiers that Terri at first would not have a military ID.

Each of the two doors had a small observation window, the kind that had chicken-wire embedded in the glass. Terri was amazed to see both men duck down so that they couldn't be seen by anyone on the other side of the glass.

Jordan said, "Inside, what you see is part of Project Fifty-one. Dr. Renfield will start your orientation tomorrow."

Inside, two-thirds of the fluorescent lights were turned off, and Terri saw women lying on tan Army cots. Most of the women were sleeping, but two pairs of women were talking.

One cot was empty.

Then Terri noticed that, off to the left of the cots, a woman stood, talking to someone much shorter. Terri's glance noted the other woman's hair—dyed-blonde, with six-inch brunette roots—and how the other woman was dressed—white t-shirt, blue jeans, and white sneakers.

Then Terri saw whom the woman was talking *to*.

Terri exclaimed, "You've got a *space alien* in there!"

Jordan said, "That is information that is Top Secret, *Captain*. Am I clear?"

"Yes, sir," Terri said absently. Then she said, "If the alien is leaning on a cane like that, it can't be healthy. Poor thing."

Renfield said, "It is an enemy civilian. It's receiving good enough care from us, considering."

Evidently the blonde had heard the voices just outside the doors. The blonde turned her face directly toward Terri's.

Terri gasped.

As Terri had told General Jordan, Wheat City had been in the national news lately. A *lot*. And always the news stories about Wheat City showed a photo of the Australian woman Sheila Blackburn.

The Australian government was claiming that the U.S. Army was holding Sheila Blackburn prisoner in Wheat City.

The Army was denying the Australians' claim—but there stood Sheila Blackburn, only twenty-five feet away.

Terri barely noticed what she was shown when Jordan and Renfield took her to the hospital basement to the (soldiers-guarded) morgue, to see the twelve alien corpses.

The only thought in Terri's head was, *What the Army is doing to those women is wrong, wrong, wrong!*

Chapter 8
Terri Meets Her
"Patients"

Friday morning, April 19
Isolation Ward Two, Fort Carver Hospital
Fort Carver, Kansas

Terri was not at all pleased with Major Renfield. Terri's promised "orientation" had lasted all of six minutes. In Major Renfield's office.

Which meant that Terri would have to start from scratch, despite all the time and money that the Army had already spent on the female alien and on the rescuees.

Well, Terri was planning on heading straight to Isolation Ward Two after her orientation, was she not?

The various nurses and female medics were already in the isolation ward, hard at work, when Terri stepped up to the inner doors.

Outside the doors, all four female armed sentries were watching her.

"Yell loudly if you need assistance, ma'am," said the woman to the left of the inner doors.

Terri didn't reply. She squared her shoulders, punched her PIN into the keypad, opened the doors, and walked in.

All nineteen rescuees went silent at the sight of her. Then Sheila said, "So you're the new dipstick doctor in charge? At least you don't leave the shithouse seat up."

Terri laughed. "Which is my main job qualification here." Terri walked over to Sheila and put out her hand to shake. "I'm Dr. Theresa Rivers. But please call me Terri."

"Can you get us released from this gaol?"

"Buchanan can, I can't. I'm sorry."

Sheila shrugged, then shook Terri's hand.

Terri then gestured to the other rescuees. "I want to introduce myself to everyone else. Sheila, I'll need your help."

The rescuees, understandably, were sullen. There was a lot of pidgin conversation between Sheila and the other rescuees that Sheila didn't bother to translate.

Minutes after the introductions started, Sheila said, "That's all of us."

"You forgot one," Terri said. She nodded toward the alien. "I want to meet *her* too."

So saying, Terri dropped down to the floor, so that she was eye-to-eye with the blue-blotched alien.

Sheila said, "We humans can't pronounce her name. But that whacker you replaced, *he* never asked her name. Plus to him, she was an 'it.' "

Terri now looked into the big black eyes of the alien, whose translator-necklace had remained silent all this time. Terri said, "Please tell me your name. My family name is 'Rivers,' which means *more than one river*. My given name is 'Theresa,' which means *harvester of grain.*"

The alien's translator-necklace said, "I am"—then came a string of strange sounds that were spoken with two voices. Then with one voice, the translator-necklace resumed: "I am named after a flower that blooms on Zlar only at night, and then only when both moons are full. So my name means *a female of rare beauty.*"

Terri said, "I will call you 'Night Flower' then. Is that okay with you?"

The translator-necklace replied, "Is this an insult?" But the alien was not looking at Terri, the alien was asking Sheila.

Sheila spoke to the alien in pidgin; again, without translating for Terri.

The alien female looked at Terri and the translator-necklace said, " 'Night Flower' is a good name."

Terri made a sweeping gesture to mean Night Flower herself, Sheila, and the other eighteen rescuees. "What can you tell me about why all of you are here?"

****

Night Flower, it turned out, was a Zlarian midwife, and her answer to Terri's question came wrapped in medical terminology. A lot of Night Flower's medical terminology had no earthly translation.

What *could be* translated, had Terri flabbergasted.

Five minutes in, Terri turned to one of the female medics and said, "Quick, run and bring me a Periodic Table Of The Elements. Hurry, fast as you can get it here!"

****

After talking to Night Flower, Terri left Isolation Ward Two and went looking for Major Renfield. When Terri found him, it took all Terri's effort to speak calmly.

Terri said stiffly, "I wish to confirm that you have not taken any blood or tissue samples from the female alien, except for bioweapon testing."

Renfield replied, "Yeah, pretty much. Once we established a medical baseline for the alien, we stopped benign testing."

"Am I correct that you've run no tests on the alien in order to enable diagnoses and courses of treatment for her obvious illnesses?"

"What are you asking? Have I tried to cure it of anything? Jesus, Captain Rivers, we're here to *kill* those aliens, so why should I spend the Army's money trying to heal one of them?"

After Terri left Major Renfield, she muttered, *What a blind moron. I've met* <u>*publishers*</u> *who are smarter!*

****

When Terri returned to Isolation Ward Two, she took blood and tissue samples from Night Flower, then Terri ordered medical tests.

Terri caught the medics exchanging puzzled looks. The medical tests that Terri was ordering, the medics had never heard of before.

Which wasn't at all surprising. The medical tests that Terri was ordering be done on Night Flower's blood and tissues, Terri's *med-school professors* had never heard of.

Friday afternoon, when the lab-test results started coming in, Terri realized that she had a decision to make.

****

Friday evening, Terri got the hospital's Duty Driver to take her to Bachelor's Officer's Quarters (even though Terri was in no sense a bachelor). Then she called Mark, long distance to Honolulu.

The phone call was awkward. Terri still could not tell Mark when she would be home, and she sure as hell could not tell him what she was doing. When Mark asked her flat out if Terri's work in Wheat City had anything to do with the spaceship landing in Wheat City, she had evaded the question. Nor could she warn her husband that she was thinking about doing something that probably would get her court-martialed.

After the call ended—God, she was frustrated! Terri wanted more than anything to get in her car, drive to the beach, and walk barefoot through the wet sand as she listened to the surf.

Alas, Terri's car was four time zones away, and the nearest beach with surf was a thousand miles away. So that left only one way to get stress-relief: *retail therapy.*

Besides, Terri *needed* new clothes. She had only one civilian outfit (t-shirt, shorts, and sandals), and even a *man* would agree that Terri needed more clothes than that.

On to Wal-Mart! (Via taxi.)

Chapter 9
Perry Interlude 2

Friday evening, April 19
Downtown Wheat City, Kansas

As Perry was driving down the street, he spotted the man leaning against the iron-barred door of a pawnshop. The black man's suit was well-tailored, but all the colors on display were too bright. No white man would ever wear that outfit.

The brightest thing that the man was wearing, however, was the white cast on his right hand.

The four women with the black man (two white women, one brown, and one black) also were dressed brightly, with their clothing hugging their bodies. But unlike the pimp, whose only visible skin was on hands and face, the women were showing *a lot* of skin.

Perry rolled down the passenger-side window of his rental car, and pulled over to the curb. The redhead broke away from the pack and sashayed over to Perry's car.

Perry already had his earplugs in. The CIA hypno-talker was laying on the front-passenger seat.

"Hey, sugar," the redhead said, "you looking for fun?"

Perry pressed the orange button on the hypno-talker.

The redhead started murmuring (though Perry couldn't hear her), "It is right to do what Perry says. It is right to do what Perry says. . . ."

After Perry released the orange button, he pulled one earplug partially out of his ear, and said, "I'm Perry. Tell me your name, girl—your real name."

She said woodenly, "It is right to do what Perry says. My name is Judy."

"Well, Judy, go tell your pimp I want to speak to him."

"Hey, Lucius! This guy wants to talk to you!"

Lucius smiled big as he walked to the car. Probably because he knew that usually when the john wanted to talk to the pimp, it was because the john wanted to hire more than one girl.

Lucius bent down and stuck his head in through the open window. "Hey, my man, you looks like you's trying to help out some friends. Some *lonely* friends. Or maybe *you* be lonely."

By now, Perry had shoved the halfway-out earplug back in his ear. He pressed the hypno-talker's orange button.

Fifteen seconds later, Perry released the orange button. Then Perry pulled the earplug halfway out of his ear again.

Perry said, "I need you to do me some favors. First of all, I want you to give me all the cash you have."

"You got it, my man," Lucius said.

Lucius reached in his pocket and pulled out a thick wad of cash in a money clip. He handed the cash to Perry, who tossed it in the glove compartment.

Perry said, "Second of all, I want you to loan me two of your girls for as long as I'm in town. I want Judy and the Mexican girl."

"Not a problem, man," Lucius said. "Except that ho, she from Nicaragua."

Then Lucius turned around and yelled, "Taffy! Fire! Get yo' asses over here."

Perry said, "Very good. Tell them to get in the back seat, then you walk back to that door."

Lucius said, "Taffy, Fire, get yo' asses in my man's back seat."

Judy/Fire opened the back door and got in the car. But Taffy said, "First you tell to us where we go, and what we do, and how long we go away." Taffy gave Perry a look that said *I don't trust you.*

Perry said to Judy, "Tell her I'm harmless and to get in the car."

Judy did this. Reluctantly, Taffy got in the car, as Lucius walked back to the pawnshop door. Perry rolled up the passenger-side window.

Perry shoved his earplug back in his ear, picked up the hypno-talker, and whammied Judy and Taffy with it.

After Perry let go of the hypno-talker and pulled the earplugs out of his ears, he said, "Taffy, I'm Perry. Ladies, we're going to my motel room to have sex. For a week."

"That's fine," Judy said. Taffy nodded. Both of them acted like spending a week in a motel room, just having sex, was all perfectly okay.

Perry moved the rental car back into traffic. As he did, he said, "So tell me, what do you think of Lucius?"

Taffy said, "He is the *pendejo!* I laughed when I seed him be beated up."

Judy giggled. "What's funny is, you saw that cast he's got? A *whore like us* gave him that broken wrist."

Perry said, "Sounds like Lucius has had some bad luck lately." Perry smiled at his own little joke.

****

For Perry, the sex with Consuela (Taffy's real name) and with Judy was no better and no worse than other sex he had had with other whores. But at least this time, he had not been stuck paying for it.

Not to mention, he'd never seen a live lezzie sex show before. And thanks to the hypno-talker, Judy and Consuela weren't faking. They really were getting each other off, right in front of Perry!

Hypno-talkers were marvelous technology.

Chapter 10
Egbert Meets Terri

Friday evening, April 19
Alpha Sigma Sigma sorority-house parking lot

Egbert was walking Bethany out to his car. She said, "I like how you're dressed up. You look good."

Egbert was wearing pressed slacks and a sports jacket. By engineering-student standards, he was indeed dressed up. But he replied, "Bethany, honey, I still don't look as good as you."

Bethany was wearing a sparkly dark-green dress with a high hemline and a low neckline. The message that it was sending was *I'm fuckable.*

Bethany's face was sending the same message. When Egbert opened the passenger-side door and Bethany got into his car, her smile at him promised *I'm going to melt your socks tonight.*

But seconds later, when he opened the driver's side door and slid behind the wheel, Bethany acted *embarrassed.*

"Um, Eggy sweetie, before you take me to the restaurant, could we stop off at Wal-Mart?"

"Okay. . .?"

"I want to clean up *afterward*, and, like, I can't very well use the shower in your dorm, right?"

"Not hardly," Egbert agreed. Baum Hall was a men-only dormitory.

"So is it okay if we stop off at Wal-Mart and I get some moist towelettes?"

"Good idea. Besides, I probably need to buy another box of condoms soon."

Bethany put her hand on his leg. "Yes, you probably do."

****

It turned out that the Wal-Mart was holding a parking-lot sale that was unique to Wheat City: an "Alien Visitors Sale." A quick glance showed Egbert that Wal-Mart was selling Halloween costumes of every kind of alien, plus science-fiction books and t-shirts.

"Oh, wow," Egbert said.

"Necessities first, *then* you can shop," Bethany said, dragging him into the store.

Five minutes later, with the "necessities" purchased, Egbert and Bethany walked out of the store. Egbert immediately dragged Bethany to the "Alien Visitors Sale."

Displayed where nobody could possibly miss them were Day-Glo green t-shirts that showed an alien's face and that were captioned, "Eat beans, Roswell! Wheat City, Kansas." And the t-shirts were for sale for only five bucks!

Bethany said, "Just so you know, I'm not starving *yet*."

Distracted Egbert replied, "Don't worry, we won't be here long."

"Whatever you say, sweetie."

The selection of science-fiction books was better than Egbert had expected from Wal-Mart. A thirtyish blond woman had just picked up *The Third Alien Invasion* in hardback. She flipped the book over, so that Egbert caught a glimpse of the author photo—

Egbert blinked. *No, it can't be*, he thought.

He walked up to the blond woman and said, "Pardon me, but you look *just like* Terri Rivers, who wrote the very book you're holding."

She smiled at him. "That's because I *am* Terri Rivers."

"You are? Wow, Bethany, this is Terri Rivers in the flesh! You know the tabletop role-playing game that me and the guys play in the Student Union Building? *The Galactic War*

Against Earth? Terri Rivers wrote the book that the game is from. This is so cool!"

"He's really glad to meet you," Bethany said politely.

Egbert realized something. "So why don't they have you out here behind a table, signing autographs?"

Before Terri Rivers could reply, Bethany looked at Egbert and Terri and said, "I'm going to go inside and shop for lipstick. Something *red*. Find me when you're done here?"

Egbert waved, distracted.

"Remember, she's wearing a wedding ring," Bethany said.

"*What?* Bethany, I'm talking to her only because she's a best-selling fantasy and science-fiction author. I'm not interested in her *that* way."

"You're so clueless sometimes," Bethany said. But then she kissed him on the cheek before walking inside the store.

Terri Rivers replied, "I'm not behind a table signing autographs because I'm not part of this promotion. I'm here only as a shopper."

This didn't compute. Egbert said, "You're on a book tour, and you stopped for the night in Wheat City?"

"No, I live here now. Well, since yesterday." Then Terri Rivers's voice got hard and she said, "You might say I was *persuaded* to move here."

"You moved to Wheat City from *Hawaii?* Did your husband come too?" Then Egbert realized something. "Wait, aren't you a doctor? I mean, *weren't you* a doctor before you became a famous novelist?"

Terri Rivers now was the person wearing the puzzled expression. "Yes, I once was an internist in the Army. I wrote *The Sword Of My Sharona* back then."

Keeping his face expressionless, Egbert said, "So are you back in the Army now?"

Terri sighed. "Yes."

"Holy shit, you're involved with the *aliens*. And Sheila and the other women that came out of the spaceship."

"I—um, let me remind you that the Army officially denies—"

"Lady, I *met* Sheila. She was naked and muscular, and she had an Aussie accent, and she propositioned me. So spare me the party line."

"I'm sorry, but I can't—it's classified."

"Not for me. So maybe I should walk into a local TV station and blab everything I saw, hm? Along with—with Bernadette. Bernadette actually saw soldiers with guns take everybody away."

"If you went and talked to a TV station, there's probably a Secret Law that you could be arrested with."

"So what? These women have done nothing wrong, but they're being held prisoner. That's *wrong*, you and I both know it's wrong, I'm going to fix that wrong, and to hell with what the law says!"

Terri Rivers was quiet for a while. Then she said, "This woman Bernadette, she actually saw the Army put the rescuees on trucks?"

Egbert said, "Yes, really you should talk to her." Then he pulled his smartphone out. "Let me text her, and set something up tomorrow. She works Friday nights."

Terri Rivers said, "Fine, I'll talk to her—but I'm not allowed to say much. Meanwhile, let me give you my email address—*terri AT terririvers DOT com*—so you can text me."

Then Terri Rivers said, "If your friend has actually seen stuff, it's too bad that I can't talk to her right now. I'm curious to find out what she knows."

Egbert said, "I'm not going to try and call her, sorry. I suspect she's busy right now."

Chapter 11
We Have Ways Of Making You Talk

Meanwhile

Behind Dance The Army strip club

Wheat City, Kansas

So Egbert wanted information about what the Army was doing with the rescuees? Lourdes was about to spy out that information.

Funny, Lourdes didn't look like Mata Hari!

Behind Dance The Army strip club was an employee parking lot. At the back of that parking lot was a smelly Dumpster. Standing just behind the Dumpster were Mess Sergeant Harvey McCabe and Lourdes.

Now Harvey was saying, "A *free* blowjob? What's the catch?"

"No catch," said Private Parts the stripper, also known as Lourdes Taylor. "I'm new at 'whore' stuff, and I need to practice blowjobbing. Tonight you're the lucky man."

"Nuh-uh, sister," said Harvey. "There's no such thing as a free lunch, and I oughta know, because it's my Army job to make the lunches."

"Then how about a trade? I ask you some questions, and if I like the answers, you get a free blowjob."

"What kind of questions?"

"You're the mess sergeant at Fort Carver Hospital, right? I'm really curious about some things there."

"Gosh, I don't know a lot, other than cooking. So am I gonna miss out on the free blowjob?"

Lourdes walked up close to Harvey, her hips swaying as she moved. Playing dumb, Lourdes said to Harvey, "So tell me about the aliens. I hear that there are aliens stashed in Isolation Ward One."

"They're in Two. Or at least, Isolation Ward Two is where all the heavy-duty, weird shit is happening."

"Weird shit like what?"

"Dunno. That's all super-secret, and mess cooks don't need a clearance. You know that, right?" Harvey sounded worried about his free blowjob.

Lourdes licked her lips. "So what can you tell me, Harvey? I want to get *good* at making a man come in my mouth. So I need *practice*."

"Well, I can't figure out what's going on. We deliver the food to guards outside Isolation Ward Two, and the guards deliver the food to the patients. So my guys never see the patients. But the patients aren't under quarantine, so why are the guards there?"

"Why do you say they're not under quarantine?"

"Because if they were, there's special procedures we'd have to do. Like serving their food on paper plates with plastic utensils. But no, the patients get plastic plates and cups and metal silverware, just like everyone else. Then when we get the dishes back, we wash 'em regular."

Lourdes dropped to her knees in the dirty alleyway. "You've got a keen eye, Harvey. Things are really looking good for your blowjob."

"Oh yeah? I'm hoping you'll start soon."

"Is there anything else strange that's going on in Isolation Ward Two?"

Harvey said, "Well, the guards, they're all women."

Lourdes replied, "*All of them* are women? Huh."

Meanwhile, she reached out and started to rub Harvey's dick through his pants.

Harvey gasped, bit his lip, then said, "They got rid of all of the men guards three days ago." He leered: "The men won't say why they left, but one guy told me he *liked* his assignment, and he's pissed he got kicked out."

Lourdes thought, *Guarding nineteen women who turn into baby-nymphos as soon as a man walks into the room? Yeah, I'm sure he liked his assignment.*

Harvey added, "Not just the guards got replaced. They replaced all the men doctors and medics too. The general kicked Major Renfield downstairs, and now supposedly there's a lady doctor in charge of . . . whatever."

Lourdes reached out and unzipped Harvey's pants. "I think you've earned a blowjob now."

Lourdes had had it drilled into her, years ago, *A cadet will not lie, cheat, steal, or tolerate those who do.* Lourdes interpreted that now to mean *If you give a man a blowjob, don't shirk at it.*

Evidently, Lourdes's best blowjob was good enough for Harvey. He came hard and he made strange noises when she swallowed him.

When she had finished and Harvey could talk again, he said, "Um, just out of curiosity, what would you have charged me? If I'd paid for it."

"Five dollars. I saved you five dollars."

"Oh."

Chapter 12
Perry Interlude 3

Late Saturday morning, April 20

Denny's Restaurant

Wheat City, Kansas

At the next booth over, the man's voice said, "Mm, food tastes better when my Snookum is near."

At the next booth over, the woman's voice replied, "My Eddie-Bear is someone I *want* to be near."

Then Perry heard a kiss. A brief one, admittedly, but you don't kiss in Denny's!

Perry, Judy, and Consuela were having a late breakfast, so Denny's Restaurant was nearly empty. But somehow Fate had stuck Perry with newlyweds at the next booth.

Being in love was fine with Perry—up to a point. After all, he'd been in love with Sophie when he'd proposed to her. And he still liked Sophie now (except when she got suspicious). But by his wedding day, Perry had remembered that all pussies are pink and all women can be bullshitted. Two weeks after Perry had returned from his honeymoon, he'd sweet-talked his way into sex with an old girlfriend.

Who had attended his wedding.

Now, Perry glanced over at the lovesick couple—and fell in lust. The woman had long, shiny, thick, chocolate-brown hair, like someone out of a shampoo commercial. She had perfect eyebrows, she had blue eyes, and she had tits. Not super large, but at least a C cup.

Perry had to listen to the lovebirds all through breakfast. When it came time to pay the bill, Perry passed on paying the waitress (using Lucius's money), in order to walk all the way over to the cashier, pay the cashier, then walk back to his table. At least this way, he got a momentary respite from the love-talk.

"Keep an eye on my briefcase," he'd ordered Judy and Consuela, as he'd walked away from their booth. "Don't let anyone else touch it."

When he returned to the booth, Perry's plan was to take a last sip of coffee, then the three of them would leave Denny's. But all that changed when Perry heard Eddie-Bear say, "Snookum, I need to head to the can. Be back soon."

"Don't take *too* long," the brunette goddess replied, "or I will die from . . . *missing* you."

Jeez, get a room, you two! Or a screenwriter.

Perry then got an Idea. He pulled out his rental-car keys, handed them to Judy, and said, "You two go to the car and get in the back seat. Wait for me."

After the whores left, Perry put his briefcase—he'd brought it to Denny's because he really, *really* didn't want it stolen—on the table. He dialed the combination, then quietly unsnapped the briefcase's latches. He took out the earplugs and put them his ears. Then he took out the hypno-talker.

The brunette was less than five feet away, but nobody else was anywhere close. Perry mashed down on the orange button.

He turned to look at the brunette, who was murmuring now. Perry didn't need to hear her words to know exactly what she was saying. ("It is right to do what Perry says.")

Perry released the orange button, pulled one earplug halfway out, and picked up the hypno-talker. Then he stood up and walked over to the next booth.

"Hello, I'm Perry. Tell me your name."

In a wooden voice, she said, "I am Betsy."

"Betsy, did you noticed the two girls I was with? You know what they look like?" When Betsy nodded, Perry said, "Leave Denny's now, and over there"—he pointed—"you'll find a rented silver Acura with my girls in the back seat. Get in the front passenger seat and stay there."

Betsy stood up and picked up her purse. Then she frowned and said, "But my husband—"

"If he opens the car door, don't talk to him and don't leave the car. Hurry, get going."

She got going. When Eddie walked out of the restroom, there was no sign of his wife anywhere. Instead, Eddie found Perry sitting where his wife had been.

"*What the fuck?*" Eddie said, loudly enough that Perry could hear the words even through earplugs.

Perry saw Eddie mouth something else, but Perry couldn't hear it. Perry pressed the orange button for twenty seconds, released it, then pulled his earplugs out of his ears.

He said, "I'm Perry. Listen to me, and do what I tell you."

Eddie said woodenly, "I am listening."

"Your wife is gone. You won't see her tonight. Maybe you won't see her ever. Don't worry about her."

Eddie said woodenly, "Don't worry about her."

"Don't ever fall in love again, Eddie. Believe me, love makes you weak. Bullshit a girl that you love her, if that will get you into her panties, but don't fall in love."

"Don't fall in love. Bullshit women."

"Right. If Betsy comes back, bullshit her and get her to fuck you a lot—but for pity's sake, don't stay faithful. Believe me, staying faithful is for chumps."

"Faithful is for chumps."

"Right. Now go on back to wherever you're staying, honeymoon suite or whatever. If Betsy isn't back by noon tomorrow, get an annulment and become a pick-up artist."

"Annulment. Pick-up artist."

Eddie walked out then, not even paying the check. (Whoops!) Perry put everything back in his briefcase, paid for

Eddie and Betsy's meal, and ten minutes later, his Acura was back at the motel and he was showing Betsy his motel room.

As soon as the motel-room door was shut, whores Judy and Consuela promptly got naked. Betsy looked confused.

Perry looked at Betsy and said, "Get undressed, then fuck me like you'd fuck Eddie. That includes a wet pussy."

Perry pulled off his shirt.

****

Perry started fucking Betsy, whose pussy was indeed wet, while Judy and Consuela watched.

Betsy's sugar-walls felt great on Perry's dick. The hypno-talker made her pussy be wet; but she also was tight.

Perry asked her, "When did you lose your virginity?"

"Eight days ago. A week ago Friday."

"*Sure*, bitch," said Judy. "With boobs like those, you stayed a virgin until eight days ago?"

"*Yes*, whore," Betsy said. "Except for. . ." Betsy looked embarrassed.

Perry ordered, "Finish the sentence."

"Except for me sucking the penis of a boy in middle school, who I thought I loved, and for giving two handjobs to Eddie. But afterward, Eddie apologized both times."

Perry grinned. "So I'm only the second man you've ever fucked."

"*Yes*," Betsy said, as tears formed in her eyes.

****

After ten minutes of Perry fucking Betsy's wet pussy, tears were still running down her face. He finally asked, "Why are you crying?"

Betsy sobbed, "Because it would break Eddie's heart, seeing me do this."

Perry said, "It's okay to cry over Eddie, but keep your pussy wet while I'm fucking you."

And such was the power of the hypno-talker, Betsy stayed as wet and aroused during sex as if she were fucking a rock star. Even as she wept.

****

Perry had a *great* come from fucking Betsy.

After Perry had climaxed, he asked Betsy, "What did you think when you sucked off that boy in middle school?"

"I felt all torn up. I loved him, but what I was doing was *eww*."

"So you think giving a blowjob is disgusting?"

"*Yes*," Betsy said.

Consuela said, "But it to you brings much money, if you sell it."

"If you do it right," Judy said to Betsy. "*I* do it right."

Perry looked in Betsy's eyes. "Suck my dick, Betsy."

Betsy nodded. "Yes, that sounds like the right thing to do now." Then she added, "But I still think it's disgusting."

A minute later, Perry sighed. Betsy was trying, but she'd only take three inches of his dick into her mouth.

"Deepthroat me," he commanded.

She did—for two seconds. Then she started choking and gagging.

Perry said, "Relax your throat muscles, and ignore your gag reflex."

Betsy instantly started sucking Perry like a porn actress.

"*Ohh*, yeah, this feels great," Perry said. He'd paid two hundred dollars apiece for blowjobs that didn't feel this good.

Judy and Consuela, who had been watching all this, were amazed.

"Oh my," said Consuela, "she understanded deepthroat on the *first try?*"

****

"You ever have sex with a girl?" Perry asked, when Betsy's mouth was no longer full.

"*Eww*, no," Betsy replied.

"You ever *kissed* girls before?" Judy asked.

"In seventh grade," Betsy replied. "Just for practice."

Perry said, "Then Betsy, today is your lucky day. Lie down on the bed and spread your legs."

As Betsy was obeying, Perry said, "Consuela, you're first. Give her the best pussy-licking you can give."

Perry said to Betsy, "Let yourself enjoy the feelings."

An hour later, after Betsy had screamed her lungs out (and after someone in the next room had pounded on the wall), Perry said, "Judy, get up."

The motel room smelled of pussy, and Betsy was flushed and sweaty.

It took Betsy thirty seconds before she could get her breathing under control enough to talk.

That's when Perry said, "You know what happens next, don't you, Betsy?"

Betsy shook her head, puzzled.

Perry explained it: "It's payback time."

Then Perry looked at Judy and Consuela. "You two do Rock-Paper-Scissors to see who gets eaten out by Betsy first."

****

The next morning, after buying the women breakfast (*not* at Denny's Restaurant), Perry took his three women back to his motel room. But once there, he said to Betsy, "Grab your purse and come with me."

Betsy obeyed Perry.

Perry drove to Wheat City's Greyhound station and parked across the street. He opened the glove compartment, counted out $250, and handed the cash to Betsy.

Then Perry opened up his briefcase, took out a notepad and pen, and scribbled a name and address from memory. Perry tore the top sheet off and handed this to Betsy.

"Betsy, go in the Greyhound station and buy a one-way ticket to Washington, D. C. Once you get to D.C., take a taxi to this address here. That's going to use up most of your two-fifty. Once you get there, pay the taxi, walk into the building, and ask for Miss Loretta. I've written her name at the top. Tell her that you want to work as a whore in her brothel, and that Perry Ringling recommends you. In six months or so, I'll look you up. When I do, repay this $250 with $500. Questions?"

Instead of arguing, she nodded as if Perry's order were reasonable. "I'm to start work in a brothel. That seems right. What do I tell my family and husband?"

"Nothing. Don't contact them. If they call you, write you, or walk up to you, say nothing."

Again Betsy nodded, as if all of this made perfect sense.

"Any more questions?" Perry asked.

"No."

Perry said, "Be the best whore you can be, so I don't get embarrassed for recommending you."

Betsy nodded. "That sounds right. Since I'm going to work as a whore, I should try to be good at it."

"Now get going. And when I see you again, six months from now, definitely have five hundred bucks waiting for me."

Betsy got out of the Acura, walked over to the doors of the Greyhound station, and went inside. Perry started up the Acura and drove away.

Chapter 13
Egbert Recruits Terri

Saturday afternoon, April 20

Stannum Mann Park, Wheat City, Kansas

Terri was sitting on a park bench near the tennis court, while Egbert stood watching a tennis match.

Terri and Egbert were waiting for "Bernadette," actually named Lourdes—anyway, the woman who had witnessed the rescuees walk naked out of the Zlarian spaceship, only to be captured and taken away by the Army. Since Terri was working with these same rescuees, she needed to know what this Bernadette/Lourdes woman knew.

Behind the park bench was a sidewalk that encircled the park, a feature that encouraged rollerbladers and power-walkers to use the sidewalk as a road.

Case in point: A purple-haired woman with muscular arms, legs, and abdominals was on the sidewalk and was quickly striding toward Terri's park bench.

But the purple-haired woman surprised Terri: She stepped off the sidewalk and walked up to Egbert. She gave Egbert a textbook salute: "Lourdes Taylor, reporting as ordered, *sir!*"

Then Lourdes turned toward Terri, her face somber: "So you're the Army doctor, huh? Is the lady alien still alive?"

Terri said, "I can confirm she's alive, but I can't—"

Suddenly purple-haired Lourdes was *grinning* at Terri. Then she turned her grinning face to Egbert and they high-fived each other.

Egbert said to Terri, "I'll skip working the math problem. You just admitted that you're working with the rescuees and the little lady alien."

Lourdes added, "And the twelve Zlarian corpses too, I'll bet."

Egbert said, "Wait, Lourdes. The other night, you didn't mention anything about alien corpses."

"That's because you didn't have a need to know that. She definitely has a need to know, if she's doing what we think she's doing."

Terri blurted out, "Who *are* you people?"

Egbert said, "I'm a college student who briefly met the women who came out of the spaceship, and who saw the lady alien but didn't talk with her. I think they're getting a raw deal now, and I won't stand for that."

Lourdes said, "In short, he's a do-gooder, who doesn't know diddly shit about the Army, so I've got his back. Me, I'm just your standard stripper and whore who used to be an Army officer."

Terri said, "You're *what*?"

Egbert said, "More importantly, she's someone who saw the spaceship land, saw the women walk out, saw the lady alien walk out—"

Lourdes said, "Actually, she was carried out."

"—and Lourdes saw Army guys load the naked women and the alien on a truck and haul them away."

"A civilian truck," Lourdes added, "not an Army truck."

"So what do you think?" Egbert asked Terri.

"I think you're telling me the truth," Terri said. She admitted this unwillingly, because Terri's job had just become a lot more complicated.

****

The American news media had spent very little time talking about the sick female alien; Terri had in fact forgotten about her until she'd looked through the glass and seen Night

Flower in the flesh. Probably some network-news poobah had decided that this part of the story was fake.

The news media was dealing with the rest of the story as "Our embattled president has to listen to ridiculous lies from those nutty Australians." Nobody could explain the emails that Sheila's sister had received, or the photos with them, but the news media implied that those had been lies too.

Speaking of which—

Terri looked at Egbert. "Which of you two sent the emails and photos to that woman in Australia?"

Lourdes replied, "To Lizzy in Darwin, you mean? I used a proxy—as far as the FBI knows, the emails came from Latvia."

Terri nodded, and went back to thinking. Egbert and Lourdes went back to silence.

Terri thought about lots of things, including hypothetical things—

• Being sent to the Fort Leavenworth Disciplinary Barracks in leg irons and handcuffs.

• Subpoenaed to testify before the House and Senate.

• Looking at the Hippocratic Oath that was framed on a wall of her Writer's Room back in Wahiawa, and feeling a deep sense of shame.

That last point was what decided Terri.

She looked at Egbert and Lourdes. "The sick female alien, I've named her Night Flower. The Army wants me to build a bioweapon that would kill her and all other Zlarians in this solar system. I refuse to do that. Whatever you guys are up to, I'm in."

****

"Welcome to the group," Egbert said.

But then he asked, "If you don't want to do bioweapon research, why are you still here? Why haven't you climbed into a hot-air balloon and flown away to a distant land?"

Terri replied, "Because *every* female on Zlar has a sickness. If I can help *at all*, I can't walk away!"

Chapter 14
Zlar's Problem Explained

AUTHOR'S NOTE: I put the Zlarian-illness infodump into its own chapter. Nothing happens in this chapter in terms of plot or characterization. Skip all of it if you want.

****

Saturday afternoon, April 20

Stannum Mann Park, Wheat City, Kansas

Egbert said, "So what can you tell us about this illness that Zlarian females get?"

Terri replied, "It depends. What do you know about amino acids?"

He laughed. "About what I know about medieval French literature. But please tell me anyway."

Terri said, "An amino acid is a carbon-chain molecule where somewhere in the molecule, there's a COOH group and an NH_2 group. In an alpha amino acid, which is the important kind for humans, the COOH group and NH_2 group come off the same carbon atom at the end of the carbon chain. That same carbon atom gets its two other places filled with a hydrogen atom and a carbon side chain."

"Gotcha."

"Humans use four amino acids to create their DNA. Zlarians use the same four. Human genetic code uses twenty-one particular amino acids to make proteins. Zlarian genetic code makes proteins from those same twenty-one amino acids. With me so far?"

Egbert said, "Gotcha. The Zlarians are really humans wearing Halloween costumes."

Terri rolled her eyes. "Gotta love nerd humor. Anyway, Zlarians of both sexes have one other amino acid that humans don't have. I'll call it *zlarine*. Zlarian females have a second amino acid that humans don't have; this I'll call *girlzlarine*."

"Can you get to the good stuff?" Lourdes asked.

Terri said, "Zlarian spaceships don't travel only to Earth and Zlar, they travel to other planets. From one of these planets, a spaceship brought back an alien virus. It modifies girlzlarine into *badgirlzlarine*."

Egbert asked, "Yet another amino acid that humans don't use?"

"Right. Since the spaceship had only Zlarian males on it, and Zlarian males don't have girlzlarine anywhere in their bodies, the crew of the spaceship didn't know they were causing a problem till it was way too late. Once the virus got into Zlar's atmosphere, Zlar had a worldwide medical crisis."

"*Fuck*," Egbert said.

"Yeah. There is no natural process on Zlar to modify badgirlzlarine into girlzlarine, either when the amino acid is floating free or when it's built into a protein."

Egbert said, "And when this girlzlarine gets turned into badgirlzlarine, it messes up the Zlarian females. So badly that they get blue blotches on their skin and they need to walk with a cane."

"Plus, it jams up their reproductive tissue so bad that Zlarian medicine can't do a workaround."

Egbert said, "Please tell me what exactly this virus does."

Terri said, "What the virus does is attack the third carbon atom from the end of the side chain. From that atom's point of view, it's got a polycarbon chain connected to it, an ethane (CH_2CH_3) chain coming off of it, a hydrogen atom coming off of it, and a hydroxide group coming off of it. What the virus does is pull that ethane chain apart and put it back together as a mirror image of itself, which gives the entire molecule a different shape. Before I came here, I would have told you that such a thing is impossible."

Lourdes asked, "So how do *our* women fit in? Human women?"

"The Zlarians feed them zlarine and girlzlarine, along with their food, and the Zlarians embed zlarine and girlzlarine into the human women's ovarian tissues, somehow completely suppressing all immune response. Then the Zlarians implant a Zlarian fetus into a human womb."

Egbert said, "But how do they prevent—"

"The Zlarians' solution isn't medicine, it's machinery: The Zlarians have fierce air scrubbers on all their spaceships now, so the human women aren't infected by the alien virus."

Lourdes said, "So the only way that the Zlarians can make little Zlarian babies now is by kidnapping Earth women and doing medical magic. There's no point in Earth asking nicely for the Zlarians to stop, because if they stop here, they die out there on Zlar."

"Unless either Zlar medicine or human medicine finds a cure," Terri answered. "Finds a way to turn all the bad amino acid into the good amino acid."

Chapter 15
Lourdes Faces Her Victims

With Terri's medical explanation ended, there was a moment of silence on the bench in Stannum Mann Park. Then Lourdes asked, "So what happens now?"

Egbert pulled out his smartphone. "I need to call Kevin, and set up a meeting of all of us at his house tomorrow."

Then Egbert looked Lourdes in the eyes. "You told me a week ago, you would obey my orders. How seriously did you mean that?"

****

Sunday afternoon, April 21
Kevin MacDonald's house
Suburban Wheat City, Kansas

Egbert couldn't miss how tense Lourdes was. But what was about to happen, needed to happen.

Terri Rivers asked Lourdes, "Why are you so nervous? What am I missing?"

Kevin MacDonald said, "My neighbors might lynch her. That's why she's nervous."

"Pretty much, yeah," Lourdes said. She looked at Terri. "You know about the A-667KPK hypno-talker, right?"

Terri shrugged. "One of the medics mentioned something Friday. Officially, I don't have a need to know."

Lourdes looked out the window and sighed. "The Zlarians use hypnosis on their spaceships to get women to go inside. The Zlarians also have a handheld hypno-gadget. Ask Kevin to show you his. Anyway, the Army copied the Zlarian hypno-talker, and designated it the A-667KPK."

"So . . . ?"

"I had an Army hypno-talker. I used it three weeks ago, when I was an Army officer. I used it on Kevin's neighbors."

"My *female* neighbors," Kevin added. When Terri looked blank, he added, "Lourdes made them give her sex."

Terri's eyes went wide. "Oh."

****

Egbert and Terri were in the foyer of Kevin's house, standing near Kevin as women from Kevin's neighborhood started arriving.

The fourth woman to arrive was a brunette in her thirties, whose hair was pulled back in a ponytail. Very seriously she said, "Kevin, be careful."

Kevin replied, "Be careful of *what?*"

Now the brunette looked fearful. "I can't tell you. Or else I'd get in trouble. *Legal* trouble."

Kevin and Egbert exchanged looks; meanwhile, Terri said, "You poor thing, I can tell you're scared."

Kevin said, "Debbie, what's this about? Did something happen in the neighborhood?"

Debbie shook her head. "This has nothing to do with our neighborhood."

Egbert asked, "Does it have something to do with your job?"

Now Debbie definitely looked fearful. "I . . . can't say."

Terri asked, "What *is* your job, honey?"

Kevin replied, "She works at the *Wheat City Telegraph*."

"I'm a researcher," Debbie said.

Kevin asked, "And does your researcher job have something to do with me being careful?"

Debbie looked scared again. "I can't say. I'd better not say. Please don't ask me anything else about this."

Terri, Kevin, and Egbert exchanged puzzled looks.

****

Egbert had ordered Lourdes to stay in Kevin's kitchen till he brought her out. Lourdes breathed deeply to stay calm.

In Kevin MacDonald's living room, besides Kevin, Egbert, and Terri, were most of (all of?) Kevin's neighbors who had boarded the spaceship three weeks ago. Who also had become Lourdes's lesbian sex slaves, soon afterward.

"The space aliens came *twice?*" Lourdes heard a woman say loudly.

Egbert said something in reply (though Lourdes couldn't make out the words), then three seconds later, the kitchen door opened. Egbert said, "Showtime, Lourdes."

"Executing Plan Echo," Lourdes replied, standing up straight. With her head held high, Lourdes followed Egbert out of the kitchen, through the dining room, and into Kevin's living room.

The first woman to see Lourdes said, "*What the hell?*"

The second woman to see Lourdes said, "What's *she* doing here?"

Lourdes recognized every face, of course. Every woman in this room (except for Terri) had licked Lourdes's pussy at least once, under hypnotic compulsion.

Through the yelling and insults, Lourdes walked toward the big-screen television, to an empty space between Kevin and Terri. Terri was looking at Lourdes with sympathy, but Kevin was looking at Lourdes with a cruel smile.

A second later, Lourdes was standing with her back to the television, at a spot that was between Egbert and Terri.

Kevin's neighbors were still yelling at her.

Lourdes stood straight, and looked straight ahead.

Egbert was holding his hands out, palms out, and he was repeating "Please let her speak," but Egbert was saying this *quietly*. Lourdes could barely hear him amid the racket.

When the room had finally quieted down, Egbert said, "Captain Taylor, is there anything you wish to say to us?"

Lourdes broke from her rigid stance to look into every neighbor's face. "I am no longer *Captain* Taylor. I resigned my Army commission Friday two weeks ago, because I had betrayed everything that being an Army officer stood for."

The women murmured at that.

Lourdes continued, "As a feminist, I took pride that I was better than men, whom I saw as thinking mostly with their dicks. But when I had you in my custody, I succumbed to the temptation to live out a sex fantasy of mine."

Lourdes made a point to look into each set of eyes. "I make no excuse for what I did. I wronged you all, I rewrote your minds, and I apologize."

A brunette said, "Yeah? What if we *don't accept* your apology? If I'd known you'd be here today, I'd have you served with a lawsuit!"

An eighteen-year-old girl—Kathy? Karen? Colleen?—said, "My first-ever sexual experience was not with a strong, handsome man, it was licking your pussy! I was robbed!"

Lourdes saw Kevin turn his face and give the young girl a sympathetic smile.

Lourdes had apologized, but some women here would not accept her apology. Lourdes had no clue what to do next.

****

Egbert stepped forward. "Ladies, I'm about to tell you something about Lourdes Taylor that you do *not* want to hear. But before I do that, let me remind you about what we talked about a few minutes ago. Most of you have no memory of the spaceship that landed here three weeks ago. The only three of you who do remember are Kevin and, um—"

"Judy and Karen," Kevin said.

Egbert continued, "And even Judy and Karen have gaps in their memories. Those gaps in your memories are the *only* reason you believe Kevin, right? Because nobody else on this street believes Kevin at all."

Kevin said, "Nope. All the men who got hypnotized three weeks ago, then went back inside—now when I talk about the spaceship, they think I'm crazy."

Egbert said, "Let's try to jog your memory. Kevin, please pull up that video of the spaceship again."

Seconds later, Kevin's big TV showed the yellow-orange spaceship from last week, hovering over a football field.

Egbert said, "You've seen it twice now on Kevin's TV. Everybody except for Kevin, Judy, and Karen, you're still sure that you never saw a spaceship like this on this street?"

"I'm an exception too," Lourdes said. "I've seen a spaceship like that twice."

"*Shut up*, bitch," the blue-haired young woman called out.

Egbert said, "Ladies, you've heard what Kevin told you and what Terri told you. Here's the thing you don't want to hear: Lourdes Taylor saved your asses. If she and the Army hadn't shown up that day, now every one of you would be orbiting Earth in the mother ship, pregnant with a Zlarian fetus. *Lourdes Taylor saved your asses.*"

The brunette said, "Fine, let's give her a stupid medal. *Then* I'll sue her."

Many other women muttered agreement with that. Clearly Lourdes had no friends among Kevin's neighbors.

Egbert asked Kevin, "Would you pull up the email pictures, please? The pictures of Sheila the Australian and Night Flower, the lady alien?"

A minute later, Kevin had, all three photos showing on his big TV: a picture of naked Sheila by herself, a picture of naked Sheila and other naked women, and a picture of the blotchy female alien.

Egbert said, "These are real photos. I recognize the vacant lot on Del León Street where the spaceship landed. I recognize all the people in those photos from nine days ago. But do you know what Fox News is saying about these photos? They're all *fakes*. Because—"

A woman interrupted: "Nobody's reported any alien kidnappings anywhere. So how did these women wind up on the spaceship that they supposedly walked off of?"

Terri said, "Yeah, it's a good argument. I bought it, till I came here."

Egbert said, "But we here know that nobody remembers their wives and daughters and sisters walking onto a spaceship, not because it didn't happen, but because everyone got his memory wiped. *You* know that's true because *all of you* got your memory wiped."

Judy (the thirty-something, sexy-shaped blonde with glasses) said, "Definitely."

Egbert looked around the room. "Ladies, we're the only people who know that there's a problem here—"

"The Army knows, so the White House knows," someone said.

Terri shook her head. "The Army is squelching the truth. Probably on orders of the White House."

Egbert resumed: "But the Zlar problem won't get fixed till the world knows about it. Well, I know a piece of the story, so does Kevin, so does Dr. Rivers. But Lourdes here is the person who knows the most about Zlarians in Wheat City having kidnapped fertile women. If Lourdes is going to be effective, she needs your help. *We* need your help."

"What kind of help?" the blue-haired woman asked suspiciously.

"When Lourdes speaks up publicly, none of you publicly trash her, and for god's sake, none of you sue her."

"But she wronged us!" young Karen said.

Egbert said, "Lourdes has already apologized. If you're still angry at her, a thousand more apologies won't be enough. I'm sorry, but my sympathy for you has limits."

"Because you're a man, and you want to get into Captain Taylor's pants," the blue-haired woman said. "Good luck."

Egbert said, "Lourdes has already resigned her Army commission—she's been punished enough."

"But not by *us*," the blue-haired woman replied.

****

Right then, there was loud pounding in the front door. "*FBI! OPEN UP!*" yelled a male voice.

"*Shit!*" exclaimed Kevin. "They're on to me."

Chapter 16
Kevin's Secret Deduced

Sunday afternoon, April 21
Kevin MacDonald's house
Suburban Wheat City, Kansas

"*FBI! OPEN UP!*" Egbert heard.

Seconds later, Kevin was saying, "Neighbors, stay here in my living room. Things are about to get ugly. Terri, you stay too. Lourdes and Egbert, please come with me."

Kevin and Lourdes moved out of the living room into the center hallway, with a confused Egbert keeping pace.

Egbert said, "What's going on?"

"Shh," Kevin said. He took a set of keys out of his own pocket and stuffed them into Egbert's pocket. Meanwhile, Kevin was saying, "I have to open the front door in a few seconds. Then they'll probably start searching the place."

In the hallway, Kevin stopped in front of a framed black-and-white studio photograph of a young man and woman. The young people had 1940s clothing and hairstyles. Kevin reached behind the frame and took out a CD or DVD disc, in a paper and clear-plastic envelope.

Egbert said, "Kevin, what the hell is—*hey!*"

Kevin had stepped behind Egbert, yanked Egbert's collar back, and now Kevin was stuffing the disc down the back of Egbert's shirt.

Kevin said to Lourdes, "Stand close behind him. Don't let the FBI see that Egbert is bulging where he shouldn't be."

The pounding on the door had resumed, so now Kevin was speaking as quickly as an auctioneer: "Lourdes and I have told you that I captured an alien hypno-talker. Using it, I built something very similar to what the Army has. Maybe it's identical, who knows? But I didn't *only* build something like what the Government has, I posted everything onto the web. *Everything*."

"Why?" Egbert asked.

By now, Kevin was at the front door, but he had not yet opened that door. "You ask *why?* Because the United States government, starting with Captain Lourdes Taylor, had royally pissed me off."

Then Kevin unlocked and opened the front door.

From just beyond the doorway, Egbert heard, "I'm FBI Special Agent Max Palmer. Kevin MacDonald, we have a warrant to search your house."

****

A man wearing latex gloves and an "FBI" windbreaker came up from Kevin's basement. He was carrying a clear plastic evidence bag. Inside the bag was the home-built thing that looked like a blue tablet computer. The latex-gloves agent showed the blue thingy to Special Agent Palmer.

Special Agent Palmer pulled out handcuffs. "Kevin MacDonald, you are under arrest for stealing U. S. military property, and for revealing classified information."

"Says who?" said Kevin, as he was being handcuffed. "Whose idea is this?"

A handsome-faced bald man answered, instead of Palmer. "You're being arrested by order of President Buchanan. He personally gave the order." The tall bald man held up a smartphone. "We heard him."

Egbert said, "He ordered Kevin's arrest, *really?* That doesn't sound like 'The Indecider.'"

The bald man shrugged. "I had to push him a little."

"And who the hell are *you?*" Kevin demanded. "You're not an FBI agent, I can tell."

The tall bald man replied, "*I* am Perry Ringling, and I work at the White House."

Lourdes said, "Never heard of you. You work in the basement there? I hear it's moldy." Lourdes's voice dripped with scorn.

"I am Assistant to President Buchanan's Chief of Staff."

"Hmph," Lourdes said to Egbert, "I was right, he's a flunky."

By now, Lourdes was standing next to Egbert, hip to hip, with her left hand pressing on the small of Egbert's back. Or to be more accurate: Lourdes's left hand was pressing on Egbert's shirt, which was pressing on Kevin's mysterious disk, which was pressing on the small of Egbert's back.

"What exactly are you arresting Kevin for?" Egbert asked Special Agent Palmer, even though Egbert already thought he knew the answer. (This was a trick that Egbert had learned, ironically, from watching cop shows.)

Palmer replied, "We suspect him of stealing government technology, reverse-engineering it, and posting the schematics on the web."

Lourdes said, "What he got wasn't government technology; and he didn't steal it, he won it."

Kevin was looking at Lourdes now, his expression surprised.

Special Agent Palmer said to Lourdes, "Why do you say that? What do you know?"

Lourdes said, "I can't tell you what I know, or why I know it. I signed a paper"—now Lourdes was smiling—"that says if I told anything especially interesting, the FBI could arrest me. Sorry I can't help you."

Palmer said, "The technology he reverse-engineered is used by the Army, the FBI, and the CIA. No civilian business uses it. QED, he stole it from the government."

Lourdes smiled. "You're overlooking one source, and that's where Kevin got it from. The government is not a victim. Except for President Buchanan being embarrassed."

Special Agent Palmer looked at Perry the White House staffer and said, "The search warrant might not hold up now. `Reasonable suspicion' is shot to hell."

Perry turned to Lourdes and asked, "Lady, did you vote for Buchanan?"

"Good god, no!"

Perry looked at Palmer. "Secret law 2001-38 applies here, *don't you think?*"

Palmer looked at Lourdes. "By Secret Law 2001-38, a witness's testimony that is helpful to the accused can be disregarded if there are questions about the witness's loyalties to our government. Yeah, here it applies. So whatever you wish to say on MacDonald's behalf, I don't need to hear it. Bob, take this traitor away."

By now two more FBI agents had come up the basement stairs. One had Kevin's laptop computer, bagged and tagged; the other agent was carrying the tower of a desktop computer.

As Kevin was being frog-marched out the front door by two other FBI agents, he yelled, "You won't find anything on those computers!"

After the front door was shut, Egbert said, "If that's true, that would clear Kevin's name, right?"

"No, it would prove he'd destroyed evidence by erasing files."

Egbert said, "Whatever he did on his computer can't be 'destroying evidence' if he did it before you showed up with your warrant. That's not allowed!"

Palmer looked at Perry; Perry looked at Palmer. Together they said, "Secret Law 2009-17."

****

Special Agent Palmer clearly was surprised to discover a group of women in Kevin's living room. He interviewed the women briefly. The interviews got even briefer when the women tried to tell the FBI how Kevin had rescued them.

Lourdes was asked nothing at all, except how to spell her name. Egbert got interviewed briefly; he always made sure to stand where an FBI agent could never walk behind him, so Kevin's disc was never discovered.

The tall bald man, meanwhile, was trying to talk up the blue-haired young woman. She ignored him.

Though each interview was brief, two hours passed before the FBI agents would let anyone leave the house. Egbert spent a lot of time bored and pacing around. He tried phoning Bethany, who talked sexy to him—but Egbert couldn't really get in a sexy mood with seventeen other women in the room, some of whom were obviously listening.

As soon as Egbert's call with Bethany ended, he started thinking hard.

The day that Egbert and Bethany had met Kevin—god, was it only seventeen days ago?—Kevin had gone back into another room and returned with, Egbert now knew, the hypno-talker.

Then things immediately had turned strange. One minute, Bethany had been ignoring Egbert; but after Kevin brought the hypno-talker into the foyer, Bethany had started answering all of Kevin's questions, she had stripped down to panties and sandals, and soon she had rubbed Egbert's cock through his pants and had begged him to fuck her.

Now Egbert added two plus two. He leaned over and whispered in Lourdes's ear, "*My god*, Kevin used the hypno-talker to reprogram Bethany."

Lourdes shrugged. "I wouldn't know, never having met her. But if so, she'll take every implanted thought as a compulsion, or else she'll think it's her own idea."

Egbert did the math again: "Lourdes, he's reprogrammed you too."

"No way! I decided to resign my Army commission and become a stripper and whore *entirely*—you think he did?"

"Are you kidding? it's obvious."

"Yeah. It is. *Fuck*." Then Lourdes looked at Egbert. "Maybe he also reprogrammed you."

Egbert looked at seventeen-day-old memories with new eyes—

Back then, Kevin had said to Egbert, "Take charge, Egbert, starting with Bethany. A man can't be happy in his life if he doesn't take charge of it."

Back then, it had sounded to Egbert like the Voice Of God had been speaking to him.

Now Egbert replied, "He did exactly that. Kevin reprogrammed my brain with just two sentences." Then Egbert reminded Lourdes of what the two sentences were.

Lourdes whispered, "If Kevin were here right now, I'd snap his neck."

Egbert replied, "If Kevin were here right now, I'd shake his hand."

****

The conversation with Lourdes had taken only a few minutes. Meanwhile, FBI agents still were interviewing people, and had not yet given permission for anyone to leave Kevin's house.

Egbert was still bored, still pacing around. Walking past Kevin's home stereo setup, Egbert noticed something—

"Lourdes, check this out. Kevin *made* this! By *hand!* He probably designed it too."

Egbert was looking at an AM/FM stereo tuner/amplifier. The case was made of folded sheet metal. The slots for the slider knobs had been made by moving a drill bit sideways, and all text on the front of the box had been lettered using a draftsman's stencil.

Lourdes started out unimpressed. "Big deal, he's an electronics engineer, what do you ex—holy shit."

" 'Holy shit' what? What do you see?"

"Look here at the whatchamacallit—where the slider knobs are."

Kevin's homemade stereo had a big round knob for overall volume control. But the home-made stereo also had a twelve-band graphic equalizer, for controlling twelve narrow bands of frequencies.

Egbert said, "Okay, I'm looking. What do you see?"

She said, "Look at the top two."

The first ten slider knobs had identical heights: each was a quarter of the distance from bottom to top. The next-to-last slider knob was halfway up, and the rightmost knob, which was labeled "10 kHz," was maxxed out.

Egbert said, "Okay, that's not what I'd expect to see, but it's not 'holy shit.' "

Lourdes explained that the Zlarians hypnotized Earth people by use of ultrasonic speech—

This was how the spaceship that had landed here three weeks ago, had gotten Kevin's neighbors to come outside.

Handheld hypno-talkers that used ultrasonics were how the Zlarians had made fertile women go into the spaceship. Other Zlarian handheld hypno-talkers that used ultrasonics had gotten Kevin's other neighbors to go back inside.

Ultrasonic speech was how the U.S. Army hypno-talker worked.

Now Egbert said, "Okay, fine, the hypno-talkers work off ultrasonics. But Kevin's stereo, what does—"

"Kevin was never affected by the ultrasonics—not by the spaceship, and not by the A-667KPK that I tried to use on him. He didn't need earplugs, he was immune to ultrasonics. I could never figure out why. But now I know why."

Egbert looked again at Kevin's basement-made stereo tuner, then nodded. "The sliders for the highest frequencies, he's got them cranked up. He's unaffected by ultrasonics because he can't hear them."

Chapter 17
Jailbreak 1 (Sort Of)

Sunday afternoon, April 21

As soon as the FBI allowed everyone to go home, Egbert locked up Kevin's house, then Egbert took Lourdes back to his dorm building.

"Shake it, baby, shake it!" a young man called out as Lourdes and Egbert walked down the first-floor hallway of Baum Hall.

"Don't let Bethany find out you're cheating, buddy," another dorm-neighbor called out. "You don't want a hottie like her cutting you off."

Lourdes looked back and replied in a sexy voice, "That would be *her* loss, not his. Trust me on this."

"*Ooh,*" young guys replied.

Seconds later, Egbert and Lourdes were in Egbert's dorm room. On his desk was a desktop computer, keyboard, monitor, and ink-jet printer. Egbert hit the Shift key; the monitor went from all-black to showing tiled selfies of Bethany wearing only purple bra and purple panties, in front of a lavender wall.

"Who's the big-breasted blonde?" Lourdes asked, not quite casually. "Bethany?"

Egbert grinned. "Yeah. She sent that last Thursday, when I had to cancel our date because I had a project due."

"She's . . . very lovely," Lourdes said, not quite casually.

"I don't think she's into girls."

"Fuck! I mean, *ahem*, why are we here?"

Egbert had long since removed Kevin's disc from the back of his shirt. Now he placed the disc in his desktop computer's disc tray.

To Lourdes he said, "I want to see what's on this disc, then I'll decide what to do next."

****

All the information was there: everything that possibly related to Kevin reverse-engineering the Zlarian hypno-talker, building his own hypno-talker, and putting his own-version hypno-talker on the Web.

Included in the disc's digital cornucopia was a low-fidelity MP3 file of an actual Zlarian message, that had been recorded onto a tape recorder and played back at one-fourth speed. Lourdes and Egbert listened to a very high-pitched voice speak very slowly; Egbert imagined Mickey Mouse stoned on a kilo of marijuana.

In one of Kevin's files on the disc, Egbert read, "Apr 4: Hypno-talker successfully tested." April 4th was the day that Egbert and Bethany had knocked on Kevin's door, intending to sell him magazines.

Egbert sighed now, reading that log entry. It was one thing to know *theoretically* that he and Bethany *maybe* had been reprogrammed by Kevin, but it was another thing to find strong proof.

On the disc, Egbert also found circuit schematics, a user manual, and a message signed by "VietVetElecEngnr51."

****

Lourdes had stood behind Egbert, reading over his shoulder but herself not saying a word. Now Egbert turned around and looked up at her. "I'm not strong on electronics, but I think I can build one of these. I can even improve Kevin's hypno-talker in one place, to get around the five-foot limit, using something I can buy at Wal-Mart."

"Why would you want to build a hypno-talker, after ranting how evil they were?" Lourdes asked.

"To bust Kevin out of jail, before they throw him in a secret jail that we can't get to."

Lourdes shook her head. "They arrested him for a crime. If we bust him out of jail, *we* become criminals too. Forget it, no fucking way I'll go to prison because of that *dickwad*."

Egbert said, "Can't you see? His arrest is a setup. They'll tell him that they won't prosecute him, *if* he takes all that stuff down off the internet, or if he denounces his hypno-talker as stolen technology."

****

Egbert and Lourdes went to Wal-Mart, where he bought a yellow camp flashlight that came with a 4 inch-diameter parabolic mirror to reflect the beam.

After Wal-Mart, Egbert and Lourdes went to Kevin's house, then downstairs to Kevin's basement.

Egbert laughed. "I've got a project due next Monday for Metal Fatigue class, but *this* is what I'm working on. Priorities, priorities."

Egbert used Kevin's notes to burn the chip for the hypno-talker, and then Egbert gathered up the other parts he would need, including a "tweeter" (high-frequency speaker).

But instead of installing those parts *on* or *in* a tablet-computer body, Egbert put everything into the camp-flashlight body. He put the tweeter where the flashlight bulb had been, and threw away the clear plastic disk that covered the parabolic reflector.

A little drilling and a little painting, and Egbert had what looked like a yellow camp flashlight, except that the "flashlight" had a one-inch-diameter speaker instead of a light bulb, had a little microphone grille next to the black pushbutton at the top, and had an orange button on the side.

Inside the casing, Egbert (after some trial and error) soldered a resistor in series with the tweeter, so that the tweeter sounded loud enough from two feet away, but sounded quiet at five feet away. This resistor saved the user of the hypno-talker from needing to wear earplugs.

Egbert knew that the parabolic shape of the mirror would turn the tweeter into a "sound spotlight." By running a 10-kiloHertz tone through the tweeter, and by putting Lourdes at the other end of the basement, Egbert was able to adjust the distance between the tweeter and the mirror. When Egbert had the settings right, Lourdes could not hear the 10-kHz sound at all if the mirror was pointing away from her; but if the parabolic mirror *was* pointed at her, Lourdes heard a high-pitched tone that was *loud*.

After that, it was a simple matter to connect the tweeter to the hypno-talker electronics, so that instead of the tweeter giving off a 10-kHz tone, the tweeter spoke ultrasonic hypnotic commands.

****

Sunday evening, April 21

Egbert and Lourdes walked into Wheat City's main police station.

Behind a very high desk, a police sergeant looked down at Egbert and Lourdes from on high. "May I help you with something?" he asked.

"Yes," said Egbert, as he pointed his "flashlight" at the policeman, "I hope you can help us *a lot*."

The policeman's face went blank, and he started to murmur, "The man in glasses who is holding the flashlight, I will believe whatever he says and answer whatever question he asks."

****

Later Sunday evening, April 21

The Yellow Brick Motel, Room 122
Wheat City, Kansas

Egbert, with Lourdes standing next to him, knocked on the motel-room door.

An FBI agent opened the door. His eye went wide. "I know you two!"

Before the agent could say more, Egbert blasted him with his "flashlight." The agent started woodenly reciting his instructions.

"*What the hell, Ramirez?*" Egbert heard from inside the room.

Egbert quickly moved to the left, so that he could see into the motel room. Egbert saw Special Agent Palmer, in t-shirt and boxers, bringing a handgun up to aim. Egbert was faster, hitting Palmer with ultrasonics before he himself got shot.

Egbert stepped back to where an ultrasonic beam aimed at one FBI agent would hit both men, even with Palmer being ten feet away from the other agent.

After Egbert reprogrammed the agents for thirty seconds, he took his finger off the orange button. Egbert said to the agents, "You have Kevin MacDonald in the Wheat City jail. When are you planning to transfer him to one of your regular jails?"

Special Agent Palmer said, "Tomorrow, we're transferring him to Topeka."

"And what crime do you think he's done?"

Palmer said, "He got hold of an Army hypno-talker somehow, either by stealing it or by receiving stolen property, he tore it apart and figured out how it worked, then he posted plans about how to build it on the internet."

"Do you have any proof of that?"

"None yet," said Agent Ramirez. "But our geeks have just started looking through his computers."

"I'm certain that proof will show up," Palmer added. "How else could MacDonald have put up schematics on the internet that almost exactly match the Top Secret schematics for the Army's A-whatever?"

"A-667KPK," Lourdes said.

Egbert said, "What about what he told you, that he got his hypno-talker from Zlarian aliens who landed in a spaceship in his neighborhood three weeks ago?"

Palmer laughed. "All criminals lie. Stupid criminals lie stupidly."

Egbert shook his head. "You should believe Kevin MacDonald in this. Lourdes here will tell you, she was in Kevin's neighborhood that day."

Lourdes glared at Egbert. "You know I don't like that creep."

"And I know why, but tell us the truth."

Lourdes looked at the FBI agents. "I saw Kevin pick up the red hypno-talker that was lying on the grass, right by a dead alien."

Egbert nodded. "That's what Kevin says too, so that's what happened. Kevin MacDonald got the hypno-talker legally, as an alien-technology spoil of war, and he rescued his neighbors, which means he's a hero. Bottom line: You should release him."

Agent Ramirez said, "I believe you. I'm convinced now that MacDonald is innocent."

Special Agent Palmer said, "We'll have to wait to release him till after the computer-forensics geeks make their report. Unless they find something bad, you'll have him back tomorrow or Tuesday."

Chapter 18
Worse Living Through Chemistry

Monday morning, April 22

When Egbert had handed in his Final Exam at the end of his freshman year, he'd figured that he'd never again have to think about chemistry.

Yet now Egbert was in Kanssouri University's Chemistry building, waiting to speak with Dr. Salzmann, KaSU's only biochemistry professor.

Egbert was annoyed. At the moment, the time was fifteen minutes into Doctor Salzmann's posted conference hours, yet Doctor Salzmann's office door was locked, and nobody had answered when Egbert had knocked.

That's when a short man with not enough hair on his scalp, and too much hair on his upper lip, unlocked Salzmann's office door and stepped inside.

Egbert knocked on the door. Then, without waiting for an invitation, he walked in. "Doctor Salzmann, I need—"

The professor was frowning. "Are you in my class? You don't look familiar."

"No, I'm not in any of your classes. But professor—"

"*Don't* call me 'professor'! *Professor* is my job here, but *Doctor* is my title. And guess which one I had to work harder to get?"

"Fine. Doctor Salzmann, I'm here to ask you something important—"

" 'Important,' you say." Salzmann's voice dripped sarcasm.

"*Very* important. I need to know what to do when part of an amino acid gets switched around."

"Switched around," Salzmann repeated. Then he asked, "What amino acid are we talking about, first of all? Guanine, adenine, thymine, cytosine? Glutamic acid, arginine, serine, selenocysteine, tryptophan, or what?"

"Um, none of those. Actually, ahem, you wouldn't know its name."

"I wouldn't know its name," Salzmann repeated coldly. "Why would *I* not know its name?"

"Because it doesn't exist on Earth, so nobody on Earth has named it."

"Oh, I get it now," Salzmann said. "You're writing a *story*, and you want my help. Then let me tell you, first thing, that in real life, intelligent aliens couldn't eat our food and they couldn't get our women pregnant."

Egbert shook his head. "Actually, in this case, the aliens could. I mean, they do. I mean, I'm not writing a story, I've got a real problem that—"

"Young man, I'm busy. Tell me *exactly* what is the problem with your fictional amino acid."

"*It's not fictional!* But okay, it's got the stuff at one end that makes it an amino acid. Then it's got a whole bunch of carbon atoms—"

"The side chain."

"Yeah. Anyway, this amino acid, it isn't from Earth."

"So you've said."

"But there's this virus, that's not from Earth and not from Zlar—Zlar is the planet that this amino acid comes from—"

"Please get to the point."

"This virus goes straight to the amino acid, to the carbon atom that's third from its end. Then the virus, it takes the two carbon atoms after that one carbon atom, and it reverses everything, makes the two atoms downstream be a mirror image of what they were."

"*Impossible!*"

"No, it's not, I'm telling you—"

"You're talking about reversing chirality for even *part* of a molecule? It can't be done. Even in science fiction, it can't be done; nobody would believe it."

"You keep saying that, Dr. Salzmann—it can't be done, it's impossible. But listen to me: Right this minute—"

"Young man, let me explain it in terms you can understand. Imagine a surgeon operating on your left hand. Is it possible for that surgeon to reshape the bones of your left hand, and move the bones of your left hand, likewise the muscles of your left hand, same with the blood vessels of your left hand and its nerve fibers, ditto the skin of your left hand— so that when the surgeon is all done, your left hand looks and works like your right hand? No, it is not possible, no matter how good the surgeon is. But that's what you're talking about, and that's why your story is impossible."

"You keep talking like I'm asking you about a story. No! What I'm talking about is real—"

"Young man, do you know what a benzene ring is?"

"Um, a gang that makes benzene illegally?"

Dr. Salzmann pointed at his office door. "You've wasted enough of my time. Leave now."

****

Monday evening, April 22
Moonlight Motel
Wheat City, Kansas

When Perry found out that Kevin MacDonald had been released, Perry was pissed. He phoned President Buchanan—

—who waffled over the phone, then decided not to override Palmer about releasing MacDonald.

Fuck, thought Perry.

Then Perry wondered: *I wonder if those FBI agents got programmed to let MacDonald out of jail?*

****

Monday evening, April 22
Kevin MacDonald's house
Suburban Wheat City, Kansas

Egbert met with Kevin, Terri, and Lourdes on the front porch of Kevin's house. Egbert gave back to newly-released Kevin his own house keys, then Kevin unlocked the front door and let everyone inside.

Terri was carrying a laptop computer. When she noticed Egbert eyeing it, she explained, "I had Mark ship it to me from Hawaii. It arrived today."

As soon as they all were in the living room, Lourdes grabbed Kevin by the front of his shirt and slammed him against the wall. "I figured out what you did to me, you fuckface codger," Lourdes said.

Kevin looked at Egbert, who shrugged. "You did it to me and Bethany too, but I'm not pissed about it."

"What are you guys talking about?" Terri asked.

Lourdes said, "The *corporal* here used his hypno-talker to reprogram me *and* Egbert *and* Egbert's girlfriend."

Egbert shrugged. "Except Bethany wasn't my girlfriend then. And if Kevin hadn't intervened, she never ever would have become my girlfriend. Not to mention, I would have been a loser all my life."

Meanwhile, Kevin had grabbed Lourdes's wrists and twisted, then had pulled her hands off his shirt. "If not for me 'suggesting' that you resign your commission, Captain Taylor, right now you'd be arriving at the Fort Leavenworth Disciplinary Barracks. In leg-irons. While my neighbors threw a block party. So spare me the fucking outrage."

"Maybe that's true," Lourdes snarled, "but then you went *way beyond—*"

Egbert said, "Lourdes, you deserved what you got. Now shut up, both of you."

They did.

****

Egbert began to tell the others about his misadventure that morning with Dr. Salzmann.

Five minutes later, Kevin said, "Salzmann sounds like a jerk. Of course, you talking like a high-school dropout didn't help any."

Egbert laughed. "Thanks, Kevin, charming as usual."

"Don't worry," Terri said, "I have here on my laptop, contact info for every kind of scientific expert. They'll treat me respectfully if I ask about this stuff and, um—"

Kevin said, "—*you* won't sound like a high-school dropout."

Egbert said, "The problem is, your experts will think the same thing as Salzmann: You want help with a *story*. So they won't push themselves to get you answers, and they won't answer you soon."

Lourdes said, "Yeah, they won't see your request as *urgent*."

Kevin said, "Um, as soon as Terri shares *anything* about the Zlarians, *she'll* be the one headed off to Fort Leavenworth in leg-irons."

"So what do we do?" Terri asked.

Egbert said, "We go talk to your general."

Chapter 19
Meeting With The General

Twenty minutes later

Home of General John "Sand Ghost" Jordan

Fort Carver, Kansas

Terri had needed to flash her (brand-new) military ID card to get Egbert's car onto the post, and it had required Lourdes giving directions to get Egbert's car in front of the general's house.

Just before Egbert rang the doorbell, Kevin said, "This is a big mistake. We'll all wind up in prison. Or Guantanamo. Or a shallow grave."

Egbert had to make himself not roll his eyes. "So you've told us, Kevin, during the entire drive here."

Thirty seconds after Egbert rang the doorbell, the porch light came on and the door opened. An athletic man in his fifties said, "Dr. Rivers. And Captain Taylor?"

Lourdes said, "Please remember, sir, that I resigned my commission." So saying, she gave Kevin a dirty look.

"Ah," said the general, "that would explain the . . ."

"Purple hair," Lourdes said. "Yes, sir."

Terri said, "Sir, is there someplace where we can talk in private?"

"*We* meaning all five of us," Egbert added.

The general, up till now, hadn't given Egbert more than a glance, but now he gave Egbert an appraising look. Then Jordan said, "We can talk in the basement."

****

Terri introduced Egbert and Kevin to General Jordan.

As the five people were walking from the front door to the basement door, Lourdes said loudly, "Gee, corporal, I'll bet you've never been in a general's house before."

Kevin didn't reply, he just glared at Lourdes.

Egbert sighed.

****

General Jordan liked to play video games in his basement. He had a huge, several-thousand-dollar, high-definition television hooked into the game machine. At the moment, the TV was showing a PAUSE'd car race.

At first, the only seating that faced the big-screen TV was a two-person love seat. But then General Jordan broke out five folding chairs and set them in a circle. He took the chair that had his back to the television.

When everyone was seated, Egbert said, "We four are here because we each have a connection to the Zlarian spaceships that came here to Wheat City."

Jordan said, "The public record is that the aliens came here only once. A week and a half ago."

Kevin said, "Want to try again, general? A Zlarian spaceship landed on my street three weeks ago tomorrow. That's how I met the charming Captain Lourdes Taylor."

Jordan said, "Hold on, I thought that when a Zlarian ship landed, it hypnotized everyone so nobody remembered anything afterward."

Kevin smiled. "Sometime plans fail."

Egbert said, "As for that second spaceship, the one that landed here a week and a half ago? I saw it leave, I saw the naked women, Sheila the Australian propositioned me, and I saw the lady alien."

Jordan sighed. "That complicates things."

Lourdes said only, "General Jordan, sir, you know how I'm connected to this."

Egbert decided that either Jordan already knew about Lourdes's connection to the later spaceship, or that Lourdes was keeping this a secret from the general.

Now Jordan looked at Terri. "What do your friends know about your connection to the aliens? Let me remind you: This project is Top Secret."

Lourdes, though still dressed like a hooker, jumped to her feet and came to attention. "Sir, with all due respect, that's bullshit, sir. *You* know, and *I* know, and my neighbor's cat knows, the only reason that any of the stuff related to the Zlarians is Top Secret is because they make our president look like a fool."

"Sit down, Capt—Lourdes," Jordan replied. "Remember, the spaceship of ten days ago hit Fort Carver with an EMP blast. That's a hostile act."

"The spaceship did indeed, sir. But this came after forces of the U.S. Army that originated at Fort Carver"—Lourdes tapped her breastbone with a finger—"killed twelve Zlarians and seized the Zlarian spaceship."

"Correction, Captain Taylor," Kevin said. "*I* killed one of the twelve aliens."

Jordan looked at Terri. "I ask again: What do your friends know about your own connection with the aliens?"

Terri replied, "They know everything I know."

Kevin threw up his hands. "And that's the ball game! Now the Army will 'disappear' us all."

Yet maybe Kevin was wrong, Egbert hoped. Jordan didn't look angry.

Now it was Terri who stood up and came to attention. "General Jordan, my orders are to develop a bioweapon to kill Zlarians. For two reasons, I must disobey this order."

Jordan said nothing; he only looked thoughtfully at the blond woman who was standing at attention.

Seconds passed, in silence.

****

At last General Jordan broke the silence: "Sit down, Dr. Rivers. What are your two reasons for disobeying that order?"

As she took her seat, Terri said, "The first reason is that developing any bioweapon violates my Hippocratic oath."

"I see," Jordan said. Neither Jordan's face nor Jordan's voice gave Egbert a clue to what the general was thinking.

Jordan then asked, "And your second reason?"

Terri said, "Because the Zlarians have a medical problem that they can't solve. *This* is why they are kidnapping and impregnating Earth women."

"Yes, your reports have mentioned all that."

"I don't know that Earth medical science can cure their disease. But we sure as *hell* won't cure it if we keep everything Super Mega Top Secret and we try harder to kill Night Flower than to cure her disease. Sir."

"You've named the alien female?"

Terri said, "The alien female's *parents* named her, sir, not I. Night Flower is a person just like us, sir."

Jordan went silent.

Then he sighed. "Still, I have my orders. And Dr. Rivers, *you* have *your* orders."

Egbert said, "I'm sorry, General Jordan, but if you think 'orders are orders' settles the argument, you're not the strategist that Lourdes was raving about in the car. Fact is, if you deploy a bioweapon against the Zlarians, you will *severely* piss them off—"

"Mr. Whitehall—"

"And since they can hide their mother ship from our detection, who knows what else they can do? You think using a bioweapon might maybe cause some *nasty blowback?*"

General Jordan gave Egbert another appraising look, which lasted an entire minute.

Then Jordan said, "*Touché.* I suspect that if we got the Zlarians angry enough, they would hurt my Army and hurt my country. So I am in agreement with your wishes, Dr. Rivers."

Terri said, "Oh, General Jordan, I'm so—"

"*But* my orders come from President Buchanan himself. I can't be seen as disobeying them."

Kevin said, "See? I *told* you guys he wouldn't help us."

Lourdes backhand-slapped Kevin's stomach. "Listen more closely next time! That is *not* what the general said."

General Jordan didn't reply, he just smiled.

Egbert got hopeful.

Chapter 20
At TV Station KWHT

The next evening, April 23, 7 p.m. (Central time)

" 'Vampire Lawyer' will be seen at its regular time next Tuesday. This is a special presentation by KWHT News Four, with new revelations about Sheila Blackburn and about the *two* spaceships that have landed in Wheat City."

****

The "rescuee" women and the alien couldn't be released from Army confinement, and the Zlarians couldn't be convinced to leave Earth, until the problem of corrupted Zlarian DNA had been solved.

But no scientist on Earth was going to work on the problem till he knew the problem existed.

Which was why Egbert and the others were talking to the news media, in the form of a local television station.

Of course Egbert was nervous now: He'd never been on camera before. *So what? Why should I be nervous? I'm the guy who contacted the TV station and persuaded everyone to come down here.*

It was now a few minutes into the broadcast, and the commercial break was over. KWHT's six o'clock news anchor, Jeff Krankheit, now looked in the camera. "Today, some citizens of Wheat City came forward with an amazing story to tell. Let me introduce you to them. . . ."

Sitting on stage were Egbert, Lourdes, Kevin, and Kevin's neighbor Judy Miller (who had witnessed the spaceship land, three weeks ago, just before the UFO had hypnotized her). Bethany was in the studio, but off-screen; she was there to give Egbert moral support.

Terri Rivers was at the other end of the studio, sitting in front of a gray backdrop. Silhouette lighting, a motorcycle helmet covering her head, and her voice translated into text (which was then translated again, into synthesized speech) all ensured that Terri's real identity could never be uncovered.

". . .and 'X' is the person whose face you can't see," said Krankheit. "Why have you asked us to disguise you, X?"

Terri started speaking, though she was too far away from Egbert for her words to be clear. Then a few seconds later, Egbert heard a robotic voice in his earphone: "Because I work at Fort Carver, performing medical tests on Sheila Blackburn, the other eighteen rescuees, and the alien woman."

Egbert heard the cameraman mutter, "*Fuck.*"

****

Later in the program, Krankheit asked, "How is it, Mr. MacDonald, that Judy Miller, her daughter Karen, and all your other neighbors were affected by the Zlarian hypnosis machines, but you weren't? Are you making up a story now?"

Kevin said, "No. Cap—Lourdes here will tell you I'm telling the truth about that."

Lourdes said, "It's true. Hypnosis machines don't work on him."

Krankheit said, "Do either of you know why?"

Lourdes shrugged.

Kevin said, "I know exactly why they don't work on me, but it would be *dangerous* for me to answer that question."

Krankheit asked, "You're worried about the aliens fixing whatever it is that they're doing wrong?"

"The Zlarians are the least of my worries."

****

Lourdes wasn't dressed up like a hooker, but she still had the purple hair and eyebrows. At the moment, Krankheit was asking, "So you actually had orders to take Judy Miller and the others to Fort Carver, as is alleged to have happened with Sheila Blackburn and the alien female?"

"What do you mean, 'alleged'? I saw First Lt. Parkinson and a squad of soldiers load Sheila Blackburn, the other women, and the blue-blotched alien into a truck and drive away. April 12th. There is no *alleged*—it *happened*."

"But going back to earlier. Three weeks ago, you hypnotized Judy Miller and the other neighborhood women to walk out of the spaceship and climb into the Army trucks. But they never made it to Fort Carver. What happened next?"

Judy Miller said, "I don't know what happened *next*, but I know what happened *later*."

Egbert saw that Judy was giving Lourdes a nasty look.

Lourdes said to the news anchor, "There was a change of plans, but that has nothing to do with the rest of this."

Then Lourdes turned and gave Judy Miller a nasty look back.

****

During the one hour of broadcast, Egbert, Lourdes, and Kevin talked about what they had seen and what they knew.

Terri talked about the Army trying to make a bioweapon against the Zlarians. Not only that, but Terri had brought pictures of the chemical structures of girlzlarine and badgirlzlarine, explained how they were different, and informed the audience how this chemistry lesson related to the Zlarian kidnappings.

Everyone on stage told everything they knew, and it didn't matter whether it was Top Secret or not.

****

Anchorman Krankheit said, "Our time is almost up. Do any of you have any last remarks for our viewers?"

Egbert stood up, and faced the cameras. "President Buchanan, I don't know how much you know, or what you've been told. But I urge you to come here to Wheat City and find out the facts for yourself. Isolation Ward Two won't try to keep *you* out." Egbert sat back down.

Terri said, in her robotized voice, "I want to say to all the physicians and biochemistry experts of Earth: Find a cure for the virus that turns girlzlarine into badgirlzlarine. If you won't do it just because it will end the suffering of alien women, do it because it will stop *our* women from being kidnapped. If you have information that might help, contact KWHT."

****

After the broadcast was over, Egbert was being hugged by a proud and happy Bethany.

Lourdes walked over and looked at Bethany. "You're good for him. You're *beautiful*."

Judy Miller called out, "You stay away from her, Captain Taylor!"

Bethany looked puzzled. "What is that woman talking about, Egbert?"

****

Wednesday morning, April 24, 12:13 a.m. (Central time)

Downtown Wheat City, Kansas

Lourdes was at "work." It was cool out; Lourdes was wearing a baggy sweatshirt as she stood on her patch of curb.

A rental car drove up.

The passenger-side window rolled down.

Lourdes recognized the driver: "Hey, you're that bald cop who helped arrest Kevin MacDonald!"

The bald man said, "I told you, I'm not a cop. I'm with the White House."

"Sure, buddy. So now you're out slumming for pussy?"

"I'm having trouble hearing you. How about you come closer?"

"No way. I don't come closer than five feet from any Fed. It's a rule I have."

Lourdes didn't mention that she absolutely didn't come near anyone who was wearing earplugs, as this guy was doing.

Then Lourdes said, "Listen, I'd love to chat about your exciting life at the White House, but I've got work to do."

"Yeah, about that. I'll pay you a hundred bucks for a blowjob. I'll even wear a rubber."

"No."

"What's your problem? That's better than Wheat City's going rate."

"Not with you. Goodbye. I mean it: Get lost, scram."

"Fine, *bitch*," the bald guy said, and drove away.

In all the time that Lourdes had been focusing her attention on the bald guy in the car, she had not been paying attention to anything else. Like nearby rooftops.

****

As Perry drove away, he noticed in his side mirror that Lourdes Taylor was watching him, just as he still was watching her.

She kept doing that right up to the moment her expression changed, then she dropped to the sidewalk.

Chapter 21
The President Visits Fort Carver

Wednesday morning, April 24, 10 a.m. (Eastern time)

Washington, D.C.

President Barry Buchanan announced that he was leaving Washington within the hour to fly to Wheat City, and "get to the bottom of things. Secrets don't deserve to be secret when they harm the American people!"

The American people rolled their eyes, not believing a word of it.

****

Wednesday morning, 11:15 a.m. (Central Time)

Wheat City Airport

Perry Ringling was part of a crowd of thirty who watched Air Force One land. Perry was the only person in the crowd (other than General Jordan) who was not shivering with excitement. A TV reporter was claiming that the president flying in to town was the biggest thing to happen in Gale County since 1900, when the richest woman in the county had disappeared after a tornado.

No, unlike the reporters and local officials, Perry was not excited to see the president's airplane. But that's not to say that Perry was calm.

Perry had gotten Kevin MacDonald arrested, but then the FBI had *un*arrested him. Would President Buchanan blame Perry for that?

Someone from Fort Carver had gone on local TV last night and blabbed military secrets. Would Buchanan blame Perry for *that?*

Would the president blame Perry for that show about the Zlarians getting broadcast in the first place?

Perry was a wreck from all the worrying.

It didn't help Perry's worrying that during the long minutes of waiting to talk to the president—

—while the presidential limousine was unloaded from Air Force One, and while the president verbally jousted with the local reporters, then posed for grip-and-grin photos with local officials—

—that when Perry *finally* was face to face with President Buchanan, the president's only words to Perry were:

"I need to spend time with General Jordan, so you won't ride in the limo with us. You carry a cel phone, right?"

"In my pocket, fully charged, Mr. President. But let me—"

"Keep your phone on. I'll call you when I finish up at Fort Carver."

"Mister President, I really think"—now Perry lowered his voice—"when you meet the rescuees and the supposed alien, I should be there too."

"You think so?" the president said. "Okay, in that case—"

Then President Buchanan looked at General Jordan, who was standing at attention by the presidential limousine. Buchanan turned back to Perry and said, "No, let's keep to the original plan. The general already thinks I'm a wimp."

****

Twenty minutes later

Terri and Dr. Renfield were briefing the president in General Jordan's conference room. Terri was nervous, but she was able to hide it. All those live speeches that she'd given at all those science-fiction conventions, now came in useful. Now Terri was acting calm and confident, even when she was sure she was about to be slapped in handcuffs!

What puzzled Terri was that *twice*, the general said to the president, "I have utter confidence in Dr. Rivers." Didn't General Jordan at least *suspect* that Terri was the person from Fort Carver who'd spoken on TV last night?

Out of nowhere, the president said, "Before I issued my press statement this morning, three ambassadors asked to speak with me. And all three of them said they were horrified that we were working on a bioweapon, even if it was against aliens. I didn't tell them that yes, we're working on one. What I want to know is: Do we have one that works?"

Renfield said, "I tried, Mr. President, lord knows. I'm sorry."

Terri said, "Mr. President, are you ordering us to stop?"

The Indecider looked indecisive. "I—I'm not sure. If I could order the Zlarians to leave our planet, that would help my approval rating. On the other hand—"

"Mr. President, I think a more important question to ask," General Jordan said, "is whether Zlarian females do indeed have a disease, and whether you will direct our government to find a cure."

"Who cares if the big-eyed bitches are sick as dogs?" Renfield said. "Hippocratic Oath doesn't cover *aliens*."

President Buchanan said, "I'd like to be remembered as kind and generous. On the other hand, the expense—"

Terri said, "The medical problem is that something freaky is going on with a Zlarian amino acid, and they don't know how to treat it. If *we* could treat it, everyone's problems here would be solved."

Renfield said, "We should use American doctors and laboratories to find a cure for an *alien* disease, when cancer still kills millions?"

Jordan said, "I suggest we check out Isolation Ward Two now, and debate this later."

Renfield said, "General Jordan, sir, that would be *not* a good idea. Remember the problem with the *baby-nymphos?*"

Terri smiled. "Not any more. I asked Night Flower how to cure that, she told me, I had the pharmacists make up formula, and it works."

Renfield said, "Really? The alien bitch told *me* that the women couldn't be cured."

Terri said, "Maybe Night Flower remembered something after she talked to you." *Actually, Renfield, Night Flower confided to me that she didn't trust you, so she lied to you.*

"Okay, fine," Buchanan said, "let's go meet the rescuees."

****

All the U.S. Army types had been sent out of the room except for the general and Terri. The nineteen rescuees and Night Flower weren't allowed to leave; the two Secret Service agents who were guarding the doors made sure of that.

Since Buchanan couldn't speak any of the other rescuees' languages, he spoke only with Sheila the Australian.

Sheila was not being respectful to the president. "So you traveled all the way to Woop Woop, just to see if the stories about me were fair dinkum. Took you long enough."

The president replied, "Are they treating you okay? Good food and medical care?"

"Oh, everything's just mickeymouse," fine, "except they won't let me leave here. So now you've met me, can I go home to Brisbane? Will you let the rest of the mob leave too?"

"I'm afraid this is not possible right now. The situation with the Zlarians is delicate—"

Sheila said something loudly, in pidgin, then walked away. Suddenly all the other rescuees were glaring at President Buchanan.

Sheila sat down on her cot, while glaring at President Buchanan. "What a no-hoper wuss whanker."

President Buchanan could have discussed everything from sports to sculpture with Night Flower—her translator-necklace was that good. But Buchanan spoke with Night Flower only briefly.

****

Perry finally got the call he'd been waiting for. The president's voice told him, "I'm at the Wheat City Holiday Inn, bridal suite. Come on over. I need to talk to someone who isn't Army."

President Buchanan sounded depressed.

Feeling dread, Perry asked, "How did things go at Fort Carver?"

Buchanan replied, "Not as I'd hoped."

Which translated to *Things are utterly crapsack.*

"I'm leaving now, Mr. President."

****

Abraham Lincoln was such an admired president, even the office boy in Lincoln's White House could have gotten a great job afterward. But not so for the underlings of Warren Harding—those guys were treated as if they were as stupid and shady as the man himself.

Likewise, Perry could see his whole future swirl down the drain, all because of President Buchanan who never made a decision and stuck with it. Even if Perry pushed the president into seeing some issue his way, the president would be nodding agreement with Perry's opponent five minutes later.

It's not fair! After I came this far, put up with this much shit. . .

Then Perry got an Idea. His briefcase was on the seat next to him, so the Idea was doable.

But *dangerous*. Perry could be dead in ten minutes, if he put his plan into action.

Dare he do what he was thinking of?

He dared. Perry pulled into a car wash, to get his car off the road and motionless. He turned off the car engine, then he unsnapped the latches on his briefcase.

****

Wheat City Holiday Inn, bridal suite

The Secret Service agent in the blue tie, who was going through Perry's briefcase, said, "Mr. President, there's a CIA hypno-talker in here."

The Secret Service agent in the red tie, who had been giving Perry a half-hearted patdown, now started the patdown all over again—this time going by the book.

Soon that agent stuck his hand under Perry's suit jacket, to feel up Perry's breast pocket. Seconds later, that agent called out, "Mr. President, he has earplugs in his pocket."

"Leave that stuff alone," Buchanan said. "I gave Perry the hypno-talker."

"Leave everything alone, are you *sure*, Mr. President?" the blue-tie agent asked. He said *Mr. President* in the tone of voice that anyone else would use to say *you moron*.

Buchanan looked like he might change his mind, and let Perry's hypno-talker be confiscated.

Perry blurted out, "C'mon, you know I'm harmless!"

Buchanan nodded. "Yes, let him keep the thing. In fact, you two clear out; I want to speak with Perry alone."

The two Secret Service agents shared glances, but then they left without a word.

As soon as the doors shut, Buchanan said, "I need a confidant right now. Perry, you're it."

"Wow, Mr. President, I'm honored that you feel highly—"

"Don't feel honored. I'd much rather talk to Melissa, but I'm sure not going to call her when there's a good chance the line would be tapped. Not about *this*."

Perry ignored the putdown, because that was smart. "Do you want to talk about your visit to Fort Carver?"

"Boy, do I. Perry, I fucked up royally, and I don't know how to save myself from catching shit."

Perry had to work to make his voice calm: "How did you fuck up?"

"Keeping a lid on all the alien landings seemed like a good idea when the news media didn't know anything."

"Yeah, it was really the only—"

"But two weeks ago, when that spaceship landed here in Wheat City, I should have *immediately* released those women. Sent 'em home at government expense. Then I should have shared some of what we knew, while I let the press interview the lady alien."

"I don't know that this would be the smart—"

"So tomorrow, I'm going to order the women all released, and I *will* look stupid for holding them so long for no good reason. But if I *don't* release them now, I'm going to look even stupider when I *do* release them."

"If you release the lady alien, that would kill the bioweapon research."

"Oh, that's dead anyway. I'll blame it on 'overenthusiastic subordinates.' So why not release the alien, since she's no longer useful?"

Perry said, "Mr. President, you don't have to throw in the towel! We can still fix this. The old man, Kevin MacDonald, officer-now-hooker Lourdes Taylor, and the Army guy in the goddamn motorcycle helmet, they're all *criminals!* You can discredit the entire motherfucking TV show just by using 'guilt by association.' "

President sighed, walked to the window, and put his hands behind his back.

"Sure, I could discredit Lourdes Taylor. I could say she's now a stripper and whore, so don't listen to her. I could trash-talk the old man, because he gave plans for a hypno-talker to pirate sites. But Judy Miller, wife and mother who saw the goddamn spaceship land? I've checked, and she doesn't even have a shoplifting arrest as a teenager."

Perry said, "So you're going to. . . ?

"Give 'em all pardons. What choice do I have?"

"Mr. President, I have reason to believe that Lourdes Taylor might no longer cause you problems."

Buchanan sighed, as he shrugged.

The president kept standing at the window, staring out.

Perry was depressed too. Come tomorrow, all of Perry's post-White House career hopes would die.

Fuck, no! I won't let this happen!

Very quietly, Perry unsnapped the latches on his briefcase. Then he took the earplugs from his breast pocket and pushed them in his ears.

Seconds later, with his heart pounding, Perry was creeping up on the president, with hypno-talker in hand.

Chapter 22
Good News, Bad News

Wednesday afternoon, April 24
Isolation Ward Two
Fort Carver, Kansas

"Hello, Dr. Rivers? This is KWHT News."

The smartphone had rung in Terri's pocket. When she had checked her phone, Caller ID told her that the call was local, but Terri had not recognized the phone number.

"Oh!" Terri now replied. "Has someone responded to my 'want ad'?"

"Yes," the woman on the phone replied, "a professor from Mexico has written to you. Well, he's written to us, since he didn't know your name. I'm calling because I need an email address from you, so I can forward the email onward."

Terri gave KWHT a seldom-used Hotmail address, which was the name of a character in a Heinlein novel. Terri was sure that there was no way that the Hotmail account could be traced back to her.

****

The woman from the TV station was true to her word. Only a few minutes later, Terri was reading the email that the man had sent to KWHT.

"I am Dr. Manuel Hernandez-Garcia, professor of the biochemistry at the Universidad Autónoma de Yucatán. Please me forgive if my words of English not are correct."

"Biochemistry," huh? Terri thought. *This sounds promising.*

"Here in Yucatán, near where the Chicxulub Meteor hit, grow two strange plants. Each is called 'Holy Mother' because the insects not do the plant eat. The Blue-Leaf Holy Mother Plant"—Dr. Garcia gave its Latin name—"grows where the dirt has much iridium. The Striped-Leaf Holy Mother Plant"— again, a Latin scientific name—"grows near the beach, as far away as the city of Cancún. This plants not needs iridium in the dirt."

Terri thought, *Plants that bugs won't eat? Maybe aliens left them here.* She smiled at her own joke.

"The Holy Mother Plants not are eaten because the plants have the amino acid (madrezine) that the insects not can use. But here is the strange thing: When the plant synthesizes the madrezine as the *l*-isomer, the plant then switches the chirality of the last two carbones in the side chain, just as does the virus with the girlzlarine. But when the Holy Mother Plant needs to use the madrezine for the short-time proteins, the plant 'wags' the two carbones back to the structure they before were."

Doctor Garcia went on to explain that the Blue-Leaf Holy Mother plant used an iridium catalytic reaction and a pair of simple enzymes to "wag" the ethane group at the end of madrezine's side chain. The Striped-Leaf Holy Mother Plant didn't use iridium at all, and its pair of "wag" enzymes were more complex than the enzymes of the first plant.

Dr. Garcia had attached a JPG, which turned out to be madrezine's two chemical structures. At the end of his message, he wrote, "The madrezine-A is not the girlzlarine. But maybe the Holy Mother Plants can help the badgirlzlarine to fix?"

The email closed with citations to articles in Spanish-language scholarly journals. It turned out that Dr. Garcia wasn't merely well-read about how the Holy Mother Plants worked their madrezine, Dr. Garcia had singlehandedly discovered everything.

****

Terri still had her smartphone in her hand, and was intending to call Egbert with the good news, when Sheila grabbed Terri and *dragged* her in front of the television.

President Buchanan was on television. Citing Secret law 2001-23, Buchanan had ordered the arrest of Egbert Whitehall and Kevin MacDonald, for "endangering the United States of America."

Chapter 23
Fleeing

Hearing the president's words, Terri said, "I just remembered, I have something I have to do in my quarters. I don't expect to return today."

By now, Master Sergeant Kelly and other male medics were again working in Isolation Ward Two. Kelly said to Terri, "I understand, ma'am. You go on now, and we'll hold the fort without you."

"I appreciate that, master sergeant. I'm leaving now."

"Bye, ma'am."

As Terri was walking out, other medics said "Goodbye."

As Terri was getting in her car, it occurred to her: Not one person in that whole big room had said *See you tomorrow*.

****

Egbert was in the Student Union, in the midst of a table-top role-playing game with friends, when he got the phone call from Terri.

Seconds later, he was confused. "But the president didn't include Lourdes? That's strange."

"Why?" Terri asked.

"Because she's the biggest criminal of—of the three of us." Egbert had almost said *of all of us*, but then realized, *Someone could be listening in.*

"I'm sure of it, the arrests are for only you and Kevin. But if you'll excuse me, I have things I have to do."

"So do I," Egbert replied.

After Egbert ended the phone call with Terri and was putting his phone back in his pocket, he had a thought. He turned to Jake and said, "Let me borrow your phone."

Jake said, "Huh? Your phone works, right?"

"Yeah, but I can't use it right now. Jake, I don't have time to explain! Just let me use your phone, okay?"

After Jake loaned Egbert his phone, Egbert walked away from the table. When he was sure his friends couldn't hear him, he called Terri. Egbert told her, "Go to the Wal-Mart and wait for me in the McDonald's there."

Then Egbert had another thought. He used Google on Jake's phone to find the phone number he wanted, then made a phone call—

"Hello, Miller residence."

"Judy? Judy Miller? This is Egbert Whitehall, and—"

"Egbert, you're on the news! They're going to arrest you, and that's awful!"

"I know, Judy, I know. Listen, as soon as you hang up, please go knock on Kevin's door. Tell him, 'McDonald's at the Wal-Mart, driving the RV.' Can you remember that? 'McDonald's at the Wal-Mart, driving the RV.' "

"Got it, I'll tell him. Egbert, you need to go!"

"I am, right now. Thanks for your help, bye."

Then Egbert called Kevin, who didn't know about the arrest order. Egbert said, "You need to leave your house now, then meet up with us later."

"But meet up *where?*"

"Listen to me. If you stay in your house for five minutes and think, the answer will come to you. Got me? Stay there five minutes and think."

After ending his call with Kevin, Egbert was sorely tempted to call Bethany. But then he thought, *I better not, for her sake.*

Egbert walked back to the table, gave Jake his phone back, then said, "Guys, sorry, but I have to leave now."

As Egbert hurried out of the Student Union building, he wondered, *Why did the president order Kevin and me arrested, but not Lourdes?*

****

Egbert was walking as fast as he could toward his dormitory building when a woman called out, "Hey, Egbert!"

Egbert glanced at her. She was wearing blue jeans and a "Kanssouri Unicorns" sweatshirt; and had amazingly long, shiny, blond hair.

But Egbert wasn't in the mood for love. Nor did he have time to be told *The president ordered you to be arrested* when Egbert already knew that. And if this girl wanted to copy Egbert's notes for some course—well, she would just have to ask someone else.

So Egbert didn't pause and he didn't talk to the blonde, he kept walking right past her.

"Egbert, *look at me!*" the blonde said, behind his back.

Egbert recognized the voice, if not the girl. He turned and said, "*Lourdes?*"

****

Besides the blond wig, Lourdes was wearing makeup to hide her wrinkles. She looked to be early-twenties.

Egbert said, "Lourdes, I can't guess why you're in disguise, but I don't have time to chat. Buchanan has ordered Kevin and me arrested. But not you, you'll be glad—"

"Because his flunky, Perry the bald guy, thinks I'm dead."

"*What?*"

"Turn around. Back to the dorm. But first"—Lourdes walked up to him, pulled his glasses off his head, and hung them from the throat of her sweatshirt—"your dorm room is on the first floor, on the side away from the parking lot, near the stairs, right?"

"Right. What do you mean, the flunky-guy thinks you're dead?"

"Walk slowly, because my breastbone feels like somebody punched me hard there." Lourdes slipped her arm through Egbert's. "The outside of your dormitory is swarming with FBI. When you get inside your building, take the stairs up to the second floor, walk through the hallway to the stairs by your room, then we'll take the stairs down. Hopefully we'll take the Fibbers by surprise."

Sure enough, just outside the entrance door to Baum Hall was Special Agent Palmer, who was wearing an earpiece and holding a printout. He gave no-glasses Egbert and blond-haired Lourdes only a glance.

Once Egbert and Lourdes were walking along the second-floor hallway, he asked, "So why do Buchanan and Perry think you're dead?"

She whispered back, "Because I got snipered. That bastard Perry distracted me so I wouldn't evade the sniper on the roof."

"*Fuck.*"

"Oh, it gets worse. Perry has a hypno-talker, and he tried to lure me inside his car so he could use it on me."

"I'm still stuck on *you got shot*. Why aren't you dead?"

"I had a feeling that something like this might happen, after our little TV Special. A friend in the Army loaned me a bulletproof vest. I wore it last night. Glad I did."

By now, they were at the end of the second-floor hallway, at the door to the stairwell. Lourdes whispered, "Let me go first, just in case."

Egbert opened his mouth to say *No way, if there's danger, I'll go first.* But Lourdes had already opened the door and had stepped out onto the second-floor landing.

****

As soon as Egbert stepped out onto the second-floor landing, Lourdes said loudly, "*Promise* me, George, you will never *ever* tell my mother what we did. Promise?"

Then Lourdes started down the stairs, without waiting for Egbert.

Halfway down the stairs, she stopped. "Um, George? Ohmigod, there's a *man* at the bottom of the stairs, looking at me. What are you doing at the bottom of the stairs, Mr. Man?"

A voice from the bottom of the stairs said, "We're looking for a dangerous criminal."

Egbert came down the stairs, to where he was standing right behind Lourdes. Now he could see the FBI agent, who likewise could see Egbert. Egbert made himself keep eye contact with the man, and even *smiled*. "Cool! Do you have a gun? Maybe you'll have a firefight, right here in the dorm."

Lourdes said, "Just so nobody shoots *me!* Promise, Mr. FBI man?"

The FBI agent gave bewigged Lourdes a sexy smile. "Not a problem, miss."

By now, all three people were on the first-floor stairway landing. The FBI agent even opened the door for Lourdes.

A door, by the way, that had a little window inset in it. If the FBI agent watched Lourdes and Egbert once they got into the first-floor hallway, Egbert was in big trouble.

Meanwhile, Lourdes was smiling at the FBI man and saying, "You're so brave."

Egbert, keeping in character, said, "What about me? Are you saying *I'm* not brave?"

Lourdes sighed theatrically. "Not like him. Sorry, George."

Lourdes and Egbert started walking down the hallway. Egbert listened for the stairwell door pulling itself shut.

By now Egbert had his dorm key in his hand. Down the hallway they walked—first door on the left, second, third. . .

Egbert jammed the key in the lock, twisted the knob, and yanked Lourdes inside his dorm room.

****

A suitcase would be too obvious. Egbert would have to limit himself to what he could fit in his—admittedly enormous—book bag. Unfortunately, his desktop computer and its goodies would have to stay behind. *I wonder what the FBI will say when they see Bethany's selfie?*

Of course, all this careful planning was assuming that FBI agents didn't shoot Egbert full of lead as soon as he opened his dorm-room door.

Egbert dumped all his books and notebooks out of his book bag and onto the bed. His laptop, he put back into the book bag. Then some underwear and socks, pants, and shirts got dropped into the book bag. He pulled the pillowcase off his pillow and dropped the pillowcase in.

Then Egbert's eyes fell on his "pile of junk": stuff he'd built for class projects, current and past, as well as his camp-light hypno-talker.

Egbert looked at his hypno-talker, and synapses fired. "Lourdes, if that guy Perry has a hypno-talker, I'll bet he used it on the president."

Lourdes said, "That would explain a lot."

Now Egbert was stopped motionless, thinking. Lourdes whispered, "*Move* it, we have to get out of here!"

Egbert had an engineering project due Monday, in his Metal Fatigue class. He had completed the project early. Now

Egbert dropped the Metal Fatigue project-doodad into his book bag, along with his camp-light hypno-talker. "Lourdes," he said with a smile, "if I'm going to be hung for a lamb, why not be hung for a sheep?"

"What does that mean?" she said.

"I'm pissed at President Buchanan, I'm pissed at his sidekick Perry, and I think they deserve some embarrassment, don't you agree? Not to mention what my goal in this project has *always* been."

****

A few seconds later, Egbert had zipped up his book bag. "I'm ready to go."

Lourdes said, "Yeah, about that. Ordinarily I'd suggest climbing out the window and sneaking around the building to the parking lot, making a dash if we have to—but I'm sorry, my chest hurts too much for me to run."

Egbert said, "Then we *don't* run. We walk down the hall and out the building like we have every right to, smiling at the FBI guys till we get to my car."

"*My* car. The Fibbers probably have people watching *your* car."

"Duh." Egbert opened the dorm-room door, was secretly relieved that there were no FBI agents waiting with guns, ushered Lourdes into the hallway, locked his door, donned his book bag, then said to Lourdes, "All ahead impulse."

Soon they were walking outside, with Lourdes's arm now holding Egbert's. Egbert murmured, "What's the one thing the FBI doesn't expect? Let's say hi to Palmer."

Lourdes murmured back, "Ooh, a modern-day Henry the Fifth. I like you."

As soon as they got outside, Egbert said loudly, "No, woman, leave the nice FBI man alone."

Palmer looked at Egbert and bewigged-Lourdes curiously.

Lourdes dragged Egbert straight over to Palmer. Lourdes said to Palmer, "You've got a really cute agent hidden in the stairwell. Will you tell him that Marie says he's hot?"

"Hey!" Egbert said. "Give it a rest, Marie."

Palmer smiled, amused. "I'll be sure to tell him."

Egbert and Lourdes made it to Lourdes's car with no problem. They discovered another FBI agent in the parking lot; but he paid them no attention, because he was too busy—

—watching Egbert's car.

****

While Lourdes was driving herself and Egbert to Wal-Mart, they heard on the radio:

President Buchanan had just ordered the arrest of Army Captain Theresa Rivers.

Chapter 24
Jailbreak 2, Cops, and FBI

3:55 a.m. the next morning, April 25
Inside Kevin MacDonald's RV
Approaching Fort Carver

Terri said, "Egbert, I can't believe it was *you* who cooked up this crazy scheme."

Kevin nodded, while his hands worked the steering wheel. "Yeah, busting everyone out of Isolation Ward Two at four in the morning? I would've figured *Captain Taylor* to be the one pushing this."

Lourdes said, "Is that an insult?"

Kevin said, "Actually, it's not. I don't like you, but you're good at what you do."

"At what I *did*," Lourdes corrected.

"Showtime," Egbert said, as he unfastened his shoulder harness. The RV was rolling up to the guard shack.

****

Kevin rolled down the side window, as the armed sentry stepped forward. "Hi," Kevin said, "I need a visitor's pass."

"At 0400?" the sentry said skeptically. "What's your reason?"

"I've got some post dependents who are too drunk to drive home, and too stupid to carry enough cash—"

"Hold on, buddy," the sentry said. "I recognize you! You're Whatzisface, one of the people the president ordered arrested. You stay right there—"

Egbert was out of his seat, and standing now, leaning over Kevin, his camp-light hypno-talker in his hand. "Kevin, lean back!" Egbert ordered.

The sentry exclaimed, "*Shit!* You're—"

For whatever reason, the sentry's hands started moving. Egbert wondered, *Is he going for his pistol? His radio?*

Egbert didn't wait to find out. He blasted the sentry with his camp-light hypno-talker.

"I will obey Egbert," the sentry started repeating.

Egbert let the sentry chant for fifteen seconds, then turned off the hypno-talker.

Then Egbert said, "I'm Egbert, but not *that* Egbert. We aren't the nerds you're looking for. Skip the visitor's pass but let us enter anyway."

"Yes, *sir!*" the sentry said, coming to attention and saluting Egbert.

"That was easy," Terri said, after the RV began rolling.

"We're not finished yet," Lourdes replied.

****

Five minutes later
Inside Fort Carver Post Hospital

Egbert murmured, "Didn't you say there are supposed to be two sentries on either side of the Isolation Ward Two doors? And two more sentries at the guard station at the entrance to the hallway?"

Terri murmured, "That's how they do it in the daytime. Why? What are they doing?"

"All four women are gathered around the little table. Guns are on the floor, and they're playing cards. Those goof-offs!"

"Hey, at least they're awake," murmured Lourdes. "So what's the problem?"

"I was playing on hypnoing the two sentries at the guard station first, then hypnoing the two on either side of the door. Life just got tricky."

Terri put a hand on his shoulder. "I have an idea. Be ready—when I drop to the floor, you hypno all four of them."

Then Terri walked out of hiding, and headed straight toward the Isolation Ward Two guard table.

"Renee? Kathy?" Terri called out loudly. "You're away from your post. Shame, shame."

One of the four armed women said, "Dr. Rivers, why are you here—hold on, aren't you supposed to be *arrested?*"

Then the four enlisted women looked at each other in horror. Because if Dr. Rivers hadn't been arrested up till now, it fell to *them*—

At that moment, it fell to Terri. Or rather, at that moment, Terri fell to the floor.

The four sentry-women got confused then. They were so focused on looking down at Terri's prone body on the floor—

—that they didn't notice Egbert step out of hiding and point his camp-light hypno-talker at them.

Egbert carefully walked toward the hypnotized, murmuring sentries, with the hypno-talker in his right hand, and his dorm-room pillowcase in his left hand. As Egbert moved toward the guard table, Lourdes and Kevin followed Egbert, each of them carrying a serious-looking pistol.

But all their worries were for nothing. The sentries didn't grab guns or pick up a telephone, and nobody else in the hospital unexpectedly spotted the intruders. Thirty seconds later, Terri was standing up again, and the hospital was quiet except for the snoring of all four sentries.

Kevin said, "Well, *this* was easy."

Lourdes replied, "We're not done yet."

****

Terri looked in through the chicken-wire window. "Poor things are asleep. I'm sorry to wake them." But then she shrugged.

Two steps to the right, and Terri was standing in front of the keypad to the right of the Isolation Ward Two entrance doors. Terri punched in a six-digit number—

—and the indicator light stayed red.

"Guess I'm sleepier than I thought," Terri said.

Terri punched in a six-digit number again. Still no green.

"Are they on to us?" Egbert asked.

"The Army isn't that smart," Kevin replied.

"Speak for yourself, corporal," Lourdes replied. Then she said, "Terri, try again."

No dice.

"It's a good thing I've got a Plan B," Egbert said.

By now, Egbert had already put his camp-light hypno-talker on the floor and had emptied out the pillowcase. Now he picked up the power converter for his laptop computer, and plugged the power converter into a receptacle. Then he booted-up the laptop.

When the laptop had booted up, Egbert picked up a microphone off the floor and plugged it into the computer.

Egbert said, "Please, one of you hold the microphone near the lock."

Kevin did so.

Egbert picked up the hammer (something else from the pillowcase), and hit the lock in several different places with the hammer. *Dink, dank, denk, dink.*

Egbert put down the hammer, picked up the laptop, and worked the trackball. "Okay, frequencies captured. Waiting, waiting . . . frequencies isolated. Now it's party time."

Egbert picked up his senior-project transducer, asking Terri to hold it against the lock while he fixed it in place with duct tape. Finally, Egbert plugged the transducer's USB plug into the laptop, and the transducer's 110-volt AC plug into a receptacle.

Egbert worked the trackball, and clicked a button.

Everyone's ears got blasted by a noise like the world's loudest dental drill. Meanwhile, Egbert was saying (over the noise), "Normally metal fatigue is something you want to minimize, but Dr. Benson assigned us to *cause*—"

Now the lock made sounds like hammer blows, with the *bangs* coming with popcorn-popping swiftness.

Egbert clicked a laptop button, and the sounds stopped. He peeled off the duct tape, put the transducer on the floor, picked up the hammer, and started pounding on the lock.

After ten hard hits with Egbert's hammer, there were little pieces of metal in front of the doors.

Kevin slapped Egbert on the back. "Great engineering there, pardner!"

Egbert pounded the lock one more time—and the doors swung freely.

Also, that's when the head of the hammer broke off.

"Shit, I should've foreseen that," Egbert said, blushing.

****

As soon as the Isolation Ward Two doors could be opened, Terri opened both doors and rushed in.

The rescuees were no longer asleep. Instead, they were all pressed against the far wall, looking terrified. Sheila and Luisa were acting as human shields to protect Night Flower.

Sheila said, "Dr. Rivers, what's—"

The words died in Sheila's throat when Kevin and Lourdes rushed into the room, each carrying a pistol.

Terri said, "We're breaking you out."

"*Really?*" Sheila said. She said something in pidgin, and suddenly every rescuee was smiling.

That's when Egbert walked in, carrying his pillowcase and his camp-light hypno-talker. Terri pointed to him. "That's Egbert, the guy who made everything possible."

"Later," Egbert said. "Ladies, grab only what you can carry, and put on shoes because there are sharp pieces of metal by the doors. Let's go, we need to *move.*"

The women dressed quickly. Since the rescuees currently owned nothing except for what the Army had given them, nobody bothered to pack. Night Flower wore her translator-necklace and carried her cane, and Deniselle and Siyanda carried Night Flower.

Less than two minutes after Egbert had walked into Isolation Ward Two, the room was empty.

****

As the group was rushing past the still-sleeping sentries, Egbert happened to look down at the sentry report. Written big on the current page was:

"Tell President snow-for-brains Buchanan that he needs to find himself a new assassin. I'M STILL HERE!!! Lourdes M. Taylor."

Egbert & Crew were in a hurry, but a brief note of his own wouldn't hurt. Below Lourdes's signature, Egbert wrote, "I busted your lock and saved the women. Egbert Whitehall."

****

Lourdes, Terri, and Egbert were the last to board the RV. Terri and Lourdes had a hard time getting in; behind the driver's and passenger seats, the rescuees were packed tightly into the RV.

Once Egbert had plopped down into the passenger seat, he said, "That was easy."

Terri said, "Except for them nuking my PIN number. Turkeys."

Lourdes said, "There's still time for things to fuck up."

Kevin asked, "Where do we go now?"

Egbert said, "Straight to KWHT. They'll be broadcasting their early-morning news in a few minutes, so they'll have cameramen in the building when we arrive. And I want these ladies *filmed*."

****

Egbert & Crew had herded the rescuees and Night Flower out of the hospital without challenge.

The RV had driven all the way to the main gate, then out the main gate, with nobody on post trying to stop them.

Now, the RV just had to make a simple ten-minute drive to the KWHT studios, and the problems of everyone riding the RV would be over. Once live video footage of the rescuees and the lady alien was put on the air, what could President Buchanan do to them?

Two blocks after the RV rolled past the Fort Carver main gate, the RV passed Dance The Army. The strip club's parking lot was empty, except for a police car in the driveway, facing the street. By the parking lot's argon lights, Egbert got a good look at the cop: a hard-faced man with a gray-haired crew cut.

By then, Egbert was on his smartphone, listening to the phone line ringing. He'd just called KWHT's central switchboard.

Now Kevin was looking at his right-side mirror. "Well, *fuck*," he said.

Egbert was about to ask Kevin what was wrong, but then a voice answered the phone: "Control room."

Egbert said, "Hello, this is Egbert Whitehall, and I've got Kevin, Lourdes, and Terri with me. Can you have a cameraman out in your parking lot in ten minutes? We've got the *nineteen rescuees* with us, and *Night Flower*."

"No shit, you've got *Sheila* with you? And the *lady alien?* Damned straight we'll have a cameraman outside! Hell, I'm gonna wake some guys up!"

"Great, look for us in about ten minutes," Egbert said. He ended the call.

Kevin said, "There's a cop car following us."

Egbert said, "Are its lights on?"

"Not yet. But if he runs the plate, this baby is registered to me."

"Maybe he's just on his way to the donut shop."

"Maybe."

Sheila piped up: "Hey Egbert, Lourdes tells me you're the bloke I wanted to have a baby with, soon as I walked out of the spaceship. That true?"

"Yeah. But don't be embarrassed, you were—"

"The offer's still open, mate. I'm *very* grateful you busted us out. And lots of other women here feel the same way."

"Um. . ."

"Hell, I'll bet even Night Flower would give you a go."

"Um. . ."

Lourdes laughed. "Poor Egbert. I'm sure you mean it, Sheila, but it'll be a while—"

WHOOOO. The sound of a police siren, directly behind the RV, was loud.

Kevin now was looking toward his left-side mirror. "Shit, the cop car has gone disco-lights on me."

****

Kevin's response was to speed up the RV.

"Can you outrun him?" Egbert asked.

"No, but I can make him work for it."

Terri said, "If they catch you, getting charged with 'failure to stop' will be the least of your worries."

Kevin said, "Yeah, they'd just hand me an extra week at Guantanamo."

Egbert chuckled. "Lourdes, maybe it wasn't a good idea for you and I to leave our signatures at the hospital."

Lourdes said, "I dunno, I hope Buchanan reads what I wrote and *shits his pants*."

By now the RV was coming near to an intersection. No cars in front, traffic light green—

The light turned yellow when the RV was still a block away. By the time the RV got to the intersection, the light had just turned red.

A car started to move into the intersection from the left.

"We're going to hit him!" yelled Terri.

Kevin swerved to the right, pressed down the horn, and rolled through.

The police car rolled through as well.

Kevin said, "Fuck. Still got him."

Lourdes said, "And it's only a matter of time before his friends join in."

Now they all heard it: Two more police sirens. They were several blocks away, but getting closer.

Kevin said, "Thank you for the help, Captain Taylor."

****

By now the RV was closer to the edge of town; traffic lights on Marvel Drive had been replaced with flashing red lights. Kevin rolled through those.

Soon they were five blocks away from a 24-hour Shell station that was brightly lit. Behind the RV were three Wheat City PD cars, lights and sirens going.

Egbert was nervous about all those lights and sirens, but there was just enough traffic coming from the other direction that the cop cars couldn't pull any tricks.

But then they did. Way up ahead, two blue sedans pulled into the intersection from the right—and stopped. Their doors opened, and then two Fibbers were pointing guns at Kevin.

"I think they're bluffing," Egbert said.

"We'll find out," Kevin said. "*Here goes!*"

The RV slowed down, as if it were going to stop in front of the blockade. Then the RV swerved around the FBI cars, drove through the Shell station, and began accelerating as soon as it was back on the street.

Two blocks later, the RV was driving through countryside, and Marvel Drive had turned into Kansas State Highway 1900.

Way up ahead, by the road, Egbert could see the "KWHT" sign. They were almost there.

But now the roadway had turned into a divided four-lane roadway; Sheila said, "I hear something to our left."

Kevin said, "Cop car, coming up beside me."

Kevin suddenly wrenched the steering wheel to the left. Egbert felt a jarring impact.

"*Eeeee!*" From the back, Egbert heard squeals of fear.

Kevin yelled, "*Sorry, ladies!*"

Kevin glanced at his left-side mirror. "Drove him off the road," he reported. "But body repair is gonna *cost* me."

The RV started weaving back and forth, using both lanes in their direction. That would have solved the problem with the police cars behind the RV trying to get beside the RV, except that—

Up ahead, Egbert saw a vehicles with lights flashing (Kansas Highway Patrol?) come at them from the other side of the highway. The new cop car turned onto the crossover, and came out on their side of the highway *ahead of them.*

"Pincer movement," Lourdes said. "This is trouble."

The policeman now in front, moved to where he was between the two lanes, straddling the broken white line. Then that policeman jammed on his brakes.

Kevin hit his brakes too, but nowhere as hard as he could. Because of that, he almost hit the police car. But instead of rear-ending the police car, the RV swerved to the right, onto the shoulder.

By now, the RV was on the shoulder, and moving less than 10 miles per hour. It would be easy now for police cars to surround the RV and to force it to stop.

But fortunately for everyone in the RV, they'd reached their destination. Without signaling its intention, the RV turned into the KWHT parking lot, rolled as close to the building as it could get, and stopped.

Headlights revealed three people waiting: one of them had a TV camera; another was holding a microphone.

By the time that Egbert, Lourdes, Terri, and Kevin stepped out of the RV, there were two Wheat City Police Department vehicles and a Kansas Highway Patrol car also in the KWHT parking lot. Seconds later, two unmarked blue sedans drove in, followed by a body-damaged WCPD car.

****

As soon as Kevin shut off the engine, Egbert said, "Kevin and Lourdes, leave all your guns inside."

"Gotcha," they replied.

Then Egbert called out, "Sheila, pass the word: Everyone leaves here, as quickly as you can."

"They're frightened, mate. Afraid the cops will shoot them."

"I understand their fear, but the only chance we have is to let the TV cameras see whom we've got."

Then Egbert looked at his team. "Let's go."

Egbert, Lourdes, Terri, and Kevin stepped out of the RV.

As soon as Kevin stepped out, the crew-cut, gray-haired policeman lifted his face above his open car door and yelled through a bullhorn, "KEVIN MacDONALD AND YOU OTHERS! DOWN ON THE GROUND! *NOW!*"

Egbert took two steps forward (pretending to not know that there were now a lot of guns pointed at him). He said, "No. We will stand."

****

One of the FBI men yelled out, "I am Special Agent Palmer of the FBI, and I say the same thing: *All of you, get down on the ground!*"

Egbert replied, as calmly as he could, "Not gonna happen, Special Agent Palmer of the FBI. Not when Perry Whatzisname from the White House is over there, holding your leash."

Egbert looked at the Wheat City policemen, the KHP cop, the four FBI agents, and Perry from the White House. Behind him, Egbert heard the sound of shoes on the pavement, and women talking to each other in pidgin.

Egbert said, "We have done nothing wrong. We have done only good. Sheila, would you bring up Night Flower?"

Sheila and Lourdes came up beside Egbert, each of them with a hand under one of the alien's armpits, so they could move her quickly.

"*Motherfuck*," said the gray-haired cop. "That's an *alien*."

"*Motherfuck*," a male voice said behind Egbert. "We gotta record this."

A man with a shoulder camera, and a man with a parabolic microphone, hurried along the edge of the parking lot, to get beside the police cars (and in front of Night Flower).

Special Agent Palmer pointed to the KWHT men rushing up. "*You two!* Don't come closer. This is a restricted area."

The cameraman laughed and said, "Fuck you. It's *our* goddamn parking lot, moron."

Sheila said, with Aussie accent cranked up full: "Now, cops, are you going to let us go home—which in my case is Brisbane, Queensland in the crisp autumn air—or are you going to keep waving your guns about, which you Yanks so much love to do?"

The gray-haired cop said, "Shit, President Buchanan *lied* to us all."

The other Wheat City policemen nodded. One of them holstered his pistol.

****

Perry the bald guy yelled, "What are you clowns doing? The president ordered these people arrested, so *arrest them!*"

Special Agent Palmer looked at the Wheat City police. "So what's it going to be, gentlemen? Do we get your help, or do we arrest them ourselves?"

Egbert said, "Really, *the president* ordered us arrested? I thought only judges could do that, hm?"

The gray-crew-cut cop said, "Huh. You're right, no law says he can do that."

"Yes, there is!" Perry said. "Secret Law 2009-3."

The Wheat City policemen muttered. The gray-haired cop said it aloud: "I've never heard of any such law."

Special Agent Palmer said, "Not my problem. The Secret Laws are real, and we're wasting time."

Perry said, "Secret Law 2009-4 says that a suspect can be shot dead for resisting a presidential arrest."

"That's true," Special Agent Palmer said. Now he drew his weapon; he took turns pointing it at Egbert, Lourdes, Terri, and Kevin. "All four of you *will* get down on the ground, and you *will* let yourselves be handcuffed and frisked, or I *will* shoot you down like dogs."

"Fuck you," Lourdes replied. "I'm not on Buchanan's stupid arrest order, because Shinyhead over there thought I'd been killed."

"Secret Law 2009-5," Perry replied, smiling.

Special Agent Palmer nodded. "Evidence suggests you aided Egbert in breaking these women out of the Fort Carver Hospital. That makes you an accessory after the fact. The short version is: Get on the ground, Lourdes Marie Taylor, or I shoot you dead right here."

"And what about me and Night Flower?" Sheila demanded. She nodded down to the female alien.

Palmer replied, "You and the alien will be taken into protective custody. If you refuse to cooperate, you will be charged with Illegal Immigration Due To Suspicious Cause, under Secret Law 2003-15."

By this time, the Wheat City policemen and the one Kansas Highway Patrol officer had gathered together and were whispering.

Now the gray-haired cop pointed his weapon at Special Agent Palmer. "Wheat City does not recognize any Secret Laws. Wheat City does not recognize a president's authority to order these people's arrests. If you kill any of these people, Palmer, Wheat City will arrest you for first-degree homicide. Even if that takes every cop in Wheat City, Gale County, and southeastern Kansas. Drop your weapon, Palmer."

Palmer said, "Greg, Joe, you get ready to take out the local yokels. Robert, pick your targets."

"But sir, the suspects appear unarmed."

"The law's the law, Robert. Do as I say."

Robert sighed. "Yes, sir." He lifted his gun and aimed it at Lourdes.

Terri said loudly, "I will follow Egbert's lead."

Lourdes said, "I'll hit the ground if you tell me to, Egbert. Otherwise, those Fibbers will *have to* shoot me."

Kevin said, "I agree with Captain Taylor."

Egbert said, "Keep calm. Think long-term, people." Then he yelled, "*My team, remain standing!*"

"Oh, bollocks," murmured Sheila.

"Last chance, people!" Palmer yelled. "On the ground."

"*Your* last chance, Palmer," said the cop. "Drop your gun."

Perry yelled, "You talk too much, Palmer. *Shoot them!*"

That's when the spaceship appeared over the parking lot.

Chapter 25
Mother Ship

5:02 a.m., Thursday, April 25
KWHT parking lot
Wheat City, Kansas

Whatever kind of man Special Agent Palmer was, Egbert realized, he hadn't gotten the fancy title by being stupid.

Palmer could outshoot Egbert and his team, who were unarmed. Maybe Palmer really thought that his FBI men could outshoot the Kansas cops. But when he saw the little spaceship appear out of nowhere, twenty feet above the parking-lot pavement, Palmer did the math and said—

"Guys, holster your weapons and get in the cars. We're going back to the hotel."

Perry the White House guy started to bluster.

Palmer replied, "Shut your trap, Ringling, and you can ride with us. Keep yapping, and I leave you here. Where the odds are good that the local boys will arrest you for the attempted murder of Lourdes Taylor."

Perry shut up, got in the car, and the two blue sedans left.

****

It turned out that Night Flower had somehow signaled the mother ship, using her translator-necklace, as soon as she had been carried out of the RV. But just like phoning a taxi, it had taken awhile for her ride to show up.

Now the little spaceship was on the pavement. The spaceship's ramp dropped, and two male aliens walked down the ramp. Sheila and Lourdes carried Night Flower to the male aliens.

The three aliens conferred briefly, then Night Flower gestured for Terri to come over. Terri talked with the aliens for five minutes, then she called Egbert over.

The end result was that Egbert and Terri, and the nineteen rescuees, walked up the ramp and into the spaceship. The rescuees went because, while they didn't trust the male aliens, they trusted Night Flower and Dr. Rivers.

Kevin handed his RV keys to the KWHT news director, saying, "Sorry about the bad parking job. Have your receptionist hold the keys till I come back." Then Kevin and Lourdes walked to the foot of the ramp.

Kevin said, "Lourdes, darling, this is how we met."

Lourdes replied, "Ooh, Kevin, I will always have a unique feeling in my heart for you."

Then Kevin and Lourdes laughed, she linked her arm in his, and they walked up the orange ramp.

****

Several hours later, the bedside phone of biochemistry professor Manuel Hernandez-Garcia rang, waking him out of a sound sleep. Calling was a panicked Campus Security guard.

Soon after dawn came to Mérida, Yucatán, Mexico, a little yellow-orange spaceship had landed on the grounds of Universidad Autónoma de Yucatán.

The ramp had dropped, and the blotchy female alien, the four famous Americans, and an Argentinian woman had come down the ramp. The Argentinian woman had stopped a campus groundskeeper and had asked, very politely, if he would inform Dr. Hernandez-Garcia that he had people waiting to speak to him.

By 8:30 a.m. Mérida time, Dr. Hernandez-Garcia had loaded six potted Blue-Leaf Holy Mother Plants, and six potted Striped-Leaf Holy Mother Plants, into the little spaceship. Dr. Hernandez-Garcia also cancelled all his classes for the indefinite future.

Then the ramp closed, sealing inside the spaceship: nineteen former surrogate mothers of Zlarian babies, four Americans, one Mexican professor, a crew of Zlarians, and twelve potted plants.

The little spaceship flew up and up, and rejoined the mother ship, which was invisibly orbiting Earth.

****

It turned out that the surrogate mothers didn't get the baby-nympho urge when they were pregnant—a condition that they *all* were in, on the mother ship.

So Egbert, Kevin, and Dr. Garcia were *not* sexually attacked *en masse*.

Egbert was relieved to discover this. Kevin expressed disappointment.

****

Once Egbert got to the mother ship, he learned that the Zlarians considered humans to be savages, whose feelings could be disregarded. Yet paradoxically, he, Terri, and Dr. Garcia were considered to be rock stars who would be given anything they asked for.

When Egbert was told this, he demanded that the Zlarians stop hypnotizing and kidnapping Earth women. Terri echoed his demand. The Zlarians quickly agreed.

Egbert also demanded that the Zlarians return the nineteen former surrogate mothers to the places where they had been taken from.

Luisa Ochoa of Argentina passed, saying that Dr. Hernandez-Garcia needed her to help him. But the other eighteen women said in essence, "We ain't left yet?"

Egbert was profusely thanked, in eighteen different languages, for rescuing the women. Then eighteen former surrogate mothers boarded a little spaceship for the last time.

Sheila's final words to Egbert were "If you're ever in Brisbane, mate, the offer still stands." Then she kissed him.

****

The Legend Of The Gold Cubes came about because of five things:

1) The Zlarians had a machine that could replicate gold wire. At Egbert's request, the Zlarians altered the machine so that it could make gold cubes.

2) It made Egbert very uncomfortable to be around the surrogate mothers on the mother ship, all of whom were naked while he himself was clothed.

3) The Zlarians considered Egbert to be a hero, which meant that he could request that a little spaceship and its crew take him to anywhere on Earth, anytime.

4) Egbert could not even slightly help Terri and Dr. Garcia with their research, which meant he had way too much free time on his hands.

5) As soon as Sheila Blackburn had walked out of the spaceship in Brisbane, she had started telling everyone what great people Egbert, Terri, Lourdes, and Kevin were. Sheila's face, and her praises of Egbert, were all over Australian news.

So what started happening was that Egbert and Lourdes would walk into a maternity shop that was somewhere in Australia, and buy the place out. Every color, every size, every style of maternity clothing they had. Then Egbert would pay for his purchases with a gold cube.

A tiny gold cube, measuring only seven-sixteenths of an inch on a side, which was worth about thirteen hundred Australian dollars.

And if a shop's total price came to less than AUD1,300? Egbert would smile and say, "Keep the change."

This got Egbert and Lourdes lots of press attention!

Egbert and Lourdes hit maternity shops all over Australia—Darwin, Sydney, Adelaide, Canberra, Perth, you name it. Then Egbert and Lourdes switched to buying out shoe shops and bakeries. Again, all over Australia.

Australian businesses were taking in thousands of dollars from Egbert, one gold cube at a time—and in the USA, people noticed that American businesses weren't seeing a dime.

****

Within hours of the almost-shootout in the KWHT parking lot, President Buchanan had issued presidential pardons to Perry Ringling and to CIA agent John Bakerson, for the attempted murder of Lourdes Taylor. That meant that the only person now in trouble was Buchanan himself.

The opposition party had started talking up impeachment, saying that the president had abused his office by following Secret Laws that were contrary to the Constitution. But then Buchanan had argued that the Secret Laws were good, and necessary, and so he had not abused his office at all.

Nobody was surprised when prominent politicians in the president's party defended the Secret Laws.

What surprised the Washington press was when politicians in the opposition party switched to defending the Secret Laws. As one opposition-party senator said on "Meet The Press," "The unconstrained Constitutional freedoms that you learned about in school, won't do you one bit of good when terrorists slit your throat in your sleep."

The truth was that the Secret Laws gave a president the powers of a medieval king. Also the truth: Each of the most likely future presidents of both parties wanted to keep the

Secret Laws on the books, so that one day he as president could take advantage of the Secret Laws.

So Ringling and Bakerson had gotten away with trying to whack Lourdes, and for a while it had looked like Buchanan was going to keep his job and the Secret Laws would stay on the books.

****

But all that changed after Helen O'Reilly, a morning-programme radio personality in Sydney, ran into Egbert and Lourdes in a big-barn supermarket in Sydney. Egbert and Lourdes were loading up shopping carts with nothing but ice cream. Helen used her smartphone to interview the two Americans and have her radio station record it—

HELEN: So why are you here? Shopping in Australia, I mean, rather than over in the States?

EGBERT: Because I feel responsible for keeping Lourdes safe. Until Dr. Rivers and Dr. Garcia finish their research, so we leave the mother ship forever and we have to return to the USA, I'm skipping the USA. Are there any limits on what President Buchanan can try to do to Lourdes, so long as the Secret Laws are in place?

LOURDES: Plus we've both gotten hooked on Aussie meat pies.

HELEN: So as long as the Secret Laws are law in the States, you won't be spending any gold cubes there?

EGBERT: Bingo.

It turns out that greed is stronger than fear. Within a week of Americans learning *why* they weren't getting any of

Egbert's gold cubes, a Constitutional amendment that nullified secret laws and secret courts, had passed in the House and Senate—

—and President Buchanan had resigned his office, rather than be impeached.

Newly sworn-in President Bolger pardoned Egbert and his team for all crimes. He also ordered that Captain Theresa Rivers be honorably discharged from the Army when she returned to Earth.

****

Friday, June 21

It took two weeks for legislatures in three-fourths of the states to ratify the Constitutional amendment, so that it became the law of the land.

By coincidence, the day that the Secret Laws were forever nullified in the USA, Terri Rivers and Night Flower stepped out of a little spaceship in KWHT's parking lot and announced that the Zlarians, Dr. Garcia, and Terri had jointly found a cure for the Zlarian disease that corrupted girlzlarine.

Zlar no longer needed women.

On the mother ship, the humans celebrated. Lourdes and Kevin were rewarded by receiving oral sex from their respective surrogate-mother girlfriends. Dr. Garcia and Luisa fucked like bunnies.

Egbert drank a cup of Zlarian fermented tea and voluntarily remained celibate.

Chapter 26
Epilogue

Saturday, June 22

The morning after the celebrations, Lourdes walked up to Egbert as he was gazing at one of the mother ship's viewscreens. "Hey, guy, everything okay with you?"

Egbert smiled. "Are you kidding? My life is better than I've ever dreamed of." Then Egbert looked at her face. "Shit, you actually look worried about me."

"Well, duh. Ever since you broke everyone out of Isolation Ward Two, I know you've gotten offers for sex left and right. But so far you've said no to everybody."

"You got it."

"Do you know how many surrogate moms told me last night that they wanted to give you a thank-you blowjob? So what's the deal? Or do you not want to talk about it?"

"Well, you know that Kevin reprogrammed Bethany."

"*And* me, *and* you. So what does Bethany have to do with you passing up nookie?"

"Kevin told me he reprogrammed her to always be horny for me, and to marry me, and to marry me for life."

"And that's a *problem?*"

"I realized then: I could beat Bethany up, and withhold my paycheck, and belittle her in public, and cheat on her, and she'd never leave me. The programming is that strong."

"So . . . ?"

"I'm a hero now. KWHT says I'm a hero, and everyone in Australia says I'm a hero, and all the surrogate moms here on the ship tell me I'm a hero. But what kind of hero would I be if I did shit to Bethany, just because I could get away with it?"

****

Later that morning
Passageway outside Spaceship Bays 3 and 4, Zlarian mother ship

The Americans hugged Dr. Garcia and Luisa, who were about to enter their own spaceship and be flown back to their part of the world.

As the humans were hugging, a Zlarian male walked by, pulling an antigravity dolly with six boxes on it. Each box was a five-inch cube in size. The Zlarian and the dolly that he was pulling, moved into Spaceship Bay 3. Egbert gave no thought to the cube-shaped boxes.

Seconds later, Dr. Garcia and Luisa stepped into Spaceship Bay 3, even as the Americans stepped into Bay 4.

Night Flower was waiting for the Americans. Egbert wasn't sure, but Night Flower's blotches seemed to be not as brilliant a blue as before. Egbert felt good that he had had a small part in her cure.

Night Flower's translator-necklace said, "I am sorry. You cannot leave yet, until the Gratitude Cargo is loaded."

"Gratitude Cargo?" Kevin said.

Just then the passageway opened. It was the same Zlarian male, with the same antigravity dolly. But this time, instead of six cube-boxes on the dolly, there were ten. The Zlarian and his dolly walked up the orange ramp and disappeared inside the spaceship. A minute later, he walked out, without any boxes on the dolly.

"You board now," Night Flower said.

"What's in the little boxes?" Egbert asked.

"Gold cubes," Night Flower said to Egbert, while everyone gasped. "You get four boxes, Dr. Rivers gets four boxes, and you other two humans each get one box."

****

Thirty minutes later
KWHT parking lot
Wheat City, Kansas

Everyone had unloaded their box(es) of gold cubes from the little spaceship.

Now Lourdes asked Egbert, "Will you hold on to my gold? I'll be back to claim it later."

"Huh? You lost me."

"I'm not getting off here. I've asked the spaceship crew to fly me to Washington, D.C."

"Still lost. What's in Washington, D.C.?"

Lourdes's smile was evil. "Perry Ringling is in Washington, D.C, looking for a new job. Speaking of whom, can I borrow your camp-light hypno-talker? You left it in the RV over there."

Egbert gave Lourdes a long look.

Lourdes kept her evil smile as she replied, "Oh, I won't kill him. I won't even touch him. Otherwise, I'd get prison time! No, I'll just . . . give him a few new bad habits. That he can't control. I predict our friend Perry will soon be the lead story on Fox News."

****

It was a while before Egbert called Bethany. His smartphone hadn't been charged in weeks; and then, after leaving KWHT, everyone thought it wise to head straight to a bank to offload their gold.

When eventually Egbert called Bethany, he said, "There is so much I want to tell you."

"And there is something I want to give you. Can you be at the sorority house in two hours?"

Two hours later, Egbert was cleaned up, dressed up, and climbing out of his car in front of the Alpha Sigma Sigma sorority house. Bethany was waiting for him on the lawn.

She held out a hand. "Lock up your car and come inside."

"I'm not taking you someplace fancy?"

"Nope, the plan is that we spend the rest of the day in the sorority house."

When Egbert got close to Bethany (who smelled good and looked better), he said, "I want you to know that, though I got lots of offers and I was very, very tempted, I didn't cheat on you. You're the last person I've had any kind of sex with."

Bethany kissed him. Then she started to walk toward the front door. "Egbert, I have one thing to say to that."

Bethany opened the front door and beckoned Egbert to come inside. He did.

Bethany continued, "You having sex isn't cheating if I approve of it."

Inside the sorority house, every woman he saw was naked.

Bethany locked the front door. "Now nobody will bother us, my hero. Condoms are in that bowl on the coffee table."

THE END

Read the first few chapters of Doctor MC's previous novels and stories, and read previews of upcoming novels and stories, at:
http://doctormcmadscientist.wordpress.com

If you liked this story: **Please go to its Amazon page and write a five-star review. Thank you.**

www.ingramcontent.com/pod-product-compliance
Lightning Source LLC
Chambersburg PA
CBHW072303020726
47501CB00002B/379